Summer Set

Deni B. Pritchard.
Hydref '93
Torreblanca,
España.

Summer Set

David Evans

Millivres Books
Brighton

First published in 1991 by Millivres Books (Publishers)
33 Bristol Gardens, Brighton BN2 5JR, East Sussex, England

Copyright © David Evans 1991

ISBN 1 873741 02 2

Typeset by Hailsham Typesetting Services, 4-5 Wentworth House,
George Street, Hailsham, East Sussex BN27 1AD

Printed by Billing & Sons Ltd, Worcester

Distributed in the United Kingdom and Western Europe by
Turnaround Distribution Co-Op Ltd, 27 Horsell Road, London N5 1XL

This book is dedicated to the memory of

Colin Higgins

writer and film maker who died in 1988

CAT'S CRADLE

"Have a good day, darling."

"You too."

"She kissed him goodbye in the hall. She had become more romantic with Peter than she had ever been with Oliver. "Doing anything nice, today?"

"Not specially. You must go. You'll be late."

"I'd much prefer to stay here kissing you."

"Well, you can't." Kitty handed him his briefcase. "March."

"He opened the front door. The usual. Grey skies. Clouds scudding in from the South Atlantic. But then it was July, after all.

"You sound as though you want me out of the way."

"I do."

"Expecting a lover?"

"In this dress? You *must* be kidding. I'm a respectable unmarried woman"

"You're not bored with me yet, are you Kitty? You're not suffering from the three year itch?"

"She pretended a yawn and then scratched herself furiously.

"Bored rigid. Anyway it's seven years that makes you itch not three and will you please go to work!"

Peter kissed her again.

"Right." He took the only umbrella left in the hallstand. Kitty wondered who it was at Peter's practice who ate umbrellas. "See you later with the bacon."

"What bacon?"

"Bacon ... As in bringing home the bacon."

"Oh don't buy any bacon, darling. The Ellman's are coming tonight. They're vegetarian."

"I thought they were Jewish. And I was making a joke."

"Peter, *please* go to work!"

1

She shut the door behind him, leant back against it and after heaving a sigh of relief, smiled. "God," she said to no one in particular, "I love him, but ..."

The doorbell rang. Was it the start of one of *those* days? Kitty opened the door. Peter stood there, grinning. He handed her the paper. The school-age delivery girl stood next to him outside on the pavement, non-plussed. Her expression said it all: Grownups?

"Read all about it, read all about it - Islington Love Nest Exposed. Widower Loves Divorcee to Distraction!"

Kitty grabbed the paper and screamed. Peter ran off down the road, laughing. The young newsgirl shook her head, completely mystified.

Behind the closed door, Kitty sat down on the steps and opened the paper. She scanned the front page briefly before a sheaf of mail shuffled through the letterbox and she eyed it suspiciously as the postman worked it through. She assessed it at a glance. Junk. Bills and junk.

She heard the cat miaowing mournfully outside in the garden. Damn! It was obviously going to be one of those days. She folded the paper and went downstairs and unbolted the cat flap. Genius came in and looked at her archly, accusingly and she opened a tin. "There, you horrid feline. Eat. Eat then shit then sleep. I would *quite* like to read my paper in peace."

She spread the *Guardian* out on the table before making herself a coffee. It was Nick who'd converted her from the *Telegraph*. It was a capitulation she still rather resented but it kept the peace.

"I want my mother to be mentally informed," he'd insisted, "not deformed."

"Alright, Nick. Alright. I dread to think what your father would say though."

"I'm not concerned about dad. He's unsalvageable. For you, though, I worry. There's still hope for you."

Kitty smiled as she milked her coffee. Tiresome child, she thought. But I love him. God! How I love him.

Genius was by this time splayed out on the *Guardian*, like a sunbather, under the heat of the anglepoise lamp.

"Oh, Christ!" Kitty swore. "Sod off, will you?" Genius was huge, one of the biggest cats Kitty'd ever seen. And very stubborn. Since moving in with Peter, Kitty was sure that Genius was still testing her, still pushing her to see how far he could go. After all, it was *his* house. He had been there first before this interloper who toyed so with his friend Peter's affections. "Off, I said!" She pushed him and his eyes narrowed and he fixed her with a defiant, challenging appraisal. It was a battle of wills.

The 'phone on the wall rang. Genius seemed to smile as he sensed a pyhrric, though temporary, victory and began to wash himself.

"Yes! Hello!"

"Are you cross?"

"Yes. As a matter of fact, I am cross, Victor."

"Why?"

"Never mind. What can I do for you? And I thought you were supposed to be at Ludo's. Grace is expecting you today."

"I know, I know. I'll get there but I need your help, Kitty."

"I'm certainly not driving you there, Victor. Can't you just get a taxi?"

"What size shoes do you take?"

"Victor? Are you mad? Fives. Why?"

"Oh. I thought you might have had bigger ones."

"Well, I don't. Have you become a foot fetishist?"

"No, but I desperately need some high heels."

"I see. Tired of our motorcycle boots, are we?"

"Kitty, I am many things, I know, but foot fetishist I am not. I'm going to a party."

"As what? A walk on the wild side?"

"No. A French maid." The idea of Victor Burke as a French Maid made Kitty giggle. "And it's tonight. I'm desperate, Kitty."

"You certainly are, dear. But as it happens, I *can* help you. Oliver and I had to go to a fancy dress once. We went as *The Rocky Horror Show'*

"All of it?"

3

"No. Just Frank and Magenta. Anyway, I am an authority on high heels. There's a shop in Upper Street called Cover Girl. I know it intimately."

"What happened to Oliver's shoes? Didn't he keep them?"

"Far too dangerous. I threw them out."

"Ouch!" Victor winced. "Kitty?"

"Now what?"

"Do you have a wig?"

"Goodbye, Victor. And *please* don't be late for your session or I'll have Grace on the 'phone worrying and today I just couldn't stand it. I'll bet she's had those dogs immaculate since last night. 'Bye."

"'Bye. Hope your day gets better."

"So do I. And be careful of Bullshit."

"Why? Dogs love me. I am the Peter Lely of the pet world."

"You're a ridiculous queen, Victor. Goodbye."

Kitty put the 'phone back and sipped at her coffee. She turned slowly, very slowly. Genius had moved from the *Guardian* to the stool. Kitty's stool. Right, she thought and where confrontation had failed she decided to try bribery.

"Who'd like some more brekky, then?" She took down a packet of dried cat food and rattled it. Genius at least had the good manners to prick up his ears. "Listen, you gross lump of uselessness," she crooned syrupily, "lovely, lovely munchie morsels for good pussies." Genius yawned. Kitty gave up and the telephone rang once again.

"Hello again Victor. No you cannot borrow my makeup."

"Kitty?"

"Yes?"

"It's me." It's me, she thought, realising it wasn't Victor and hoping it wasn't anyone important for Peter. Me? Connections flickered and buzzed. God! There were so many me's, which one was it *this* time? Eureka! She got it.

"Ludo?" She guessed right.

"Is it a bad time?"

"No, not at all. Not for me at least. But it's only twenty-

4

past-nine. Are you alright?"

"Course I'm alright."

"It's so early."

"Don't tell me. I've been up all night.

"Kitty sighed.

"Loo, I don't want to be a nag but don't you think you're the tiniest bit too old for gallivanting around nightclubs?"

"I wasn't *at* a nightclub. I was here at what is laughably called my home. And not so much of the old. I'm thirty-nine."

"This is me you're talking to, Ludo. You're not giving an interview. You're forty-three. Same as me."

"You make it sound old, Kit. I can still bop with the best of them. So could you if you'd only let yourself."

"Ah! But I don't *want* to bop, Ludo. I'd rather go to the dentist than set foot in another nightclub.

"She watched helplessly as she saw Genius get up off the stool, jump onto the counter, nuzzle the opened packet of munchie morsels which toppled over spilling hundreds of dry nuggets onto the kitchen floor.

"Oh, no!"

"What's wrong? Are you alright?"

Kitty sighed.

"Yes. I'm alright."

"You don't sound it. You sound really fed up. Are you sure you're happy, Kitty?"

"Why the sudden concern?"

"We were happy, Kit, weren't we? You *were* happy with me, weren't you?"

"Of *course* I was, Loo. You know I was."

"We could be happy again, couldn't we? You've always been the only sort of person I've ever wanted to marry."

"Sort! Thanks a lot, Ludo!"

"No, Kitty, Please. I mean it, hear me out."

Kitty, flustered though she was, for Ludo always managed to fluster her, ran her hands through her hair and decided that attitude was not the attitude required to deal with temperamental singers so early in the morning. Her tone softened. When all was said and done, first loves, she reflected briefly, are first loves.

"I know you mean it, Loo. It's just that you ... Oh, I don't know. You know."

"Don't do a number on me, Kitty Llewellyn. Don't go vague."

"I'm not. Honestly. I'm still not quite sure what you want?" She had to hold the telephone away from her ear.

"For crissakes, Kitty. I've just asked you to marry me!"

The stunned silence was broken only by the sound of Genius racing around the kitchen floor chasing the munchie morsels under the dresser, the fridge, the dish washer ...

"Kitty? Are you still there?"

"Ummmm," she murmured weakly. "But I'm beginning to wish I wasn't."

"So what do you think, Kit?

"Think? She couldn't think. She screwed up her eyes and wished the whole conversation hadn't happened. She bent down and rather aimlessly scooped up four of the spilled nuggets. King Canute had done better with the waves.

"What about The Tits? What does she say?"

"I'm not asking Julie to marry me, for God's sake. I'm asking you! What's that noise? Sounds like marbles.

"Perhaps it's an echo, she observed to herself but thought better of saying it.

"So what do you say, Kitty? I do mean it, you know."

"I know you do, Loo. You meant it twenty years ago and I know I'm a pain in the arse, darling but I'm afraid the answer's still no.

"There was a definite hollowness to the silence which ensued. Even Genius sensed a certain momentousness and arched himself against Kitty's bare legs. Why she suddenly thought of the party, she had no idea but it served as a change of subject.

"I'm so glad you came over the other night. It was such a happy evening, wasn't it?"

She could hear Ludo thinking.

"Umm," he said.

"Did you have a good time, Loo?" He was in no mood to

6

be deflected and Kitty decided to prattle on. "Violetta's really quite a sweetie, isn't she?" Still no reaction. Waves of guilt pulsed down the 'phone line. God, was he good at giving guilt! He always had been. It was Kitty's most tender spot. She had never stopped feeling guilty. His fame hadn't changed Ludo Morgan but it had changed her; she'd said no to him two lifetimes ago and still he made her feel that she'd betrayed him. But he was *so* dear to her.

"Oh, Kitty, Kitty, Kitty. Yes. I had a good time. OK?"

"I was terrified of Violetta before she arrived. I always thought opera singers were all monsters."

"You think *all* singers are monsters."

"No I don't."

"So marry me."

"No. No, no, no. Did *you* like her?"

"Yes! Dammit. I liked her! Satisfied?"

Kitty sensed she had hit some sort of sensitivity. Ludo really was in some degree of twitch.

"Ludo, what's wrong?"

"Nothing."

"Can I help?"

"No. I wish you could. No one can."

"And you're sure nothing's the matter? You're being very mysterious. Is it intentional?"

"Probably." He sighed. "So. You won't marry me. Is that final?"

Was it? She paused. Where was the trap? There was no trap. She knew he wasn't playing games.

"Yes." She paused, expecting to hear... click ... dial tone. He didn't hang up. "Would whatever isn't the matter not matter if I'd said yes."

"Now you mention it, no."

"So you're still not going to tell me what isn't the matter."

"Don't be clever, Kitty. I'm not Nick. I love you, Kit."

"I know you do. And I love you too. Do you want to come over? Peter's at the office. I'm all by myself."

"No thanks. I can't. I have to be somewhere."

"Oh."

7

"Kitty?"

"Yes."

"Thanks, though."

"For what?" .

"For everything. You'll see."

"Promise?"

"Honest injun. Look, I have to go. 'Bye."

"'Bye."

She looked down at Genius who looked up at her as mournfully as she felt. She bent down and picked him up. For once, there was no fight. His paws went round her neck and he nuzzled into her neck. She sat down on her stool, rearranged the heavy cat on her lap and put on her glasses.

"You know, Genius. Life is the most ridiculous thing ever invented."

The anticipated luxury of her own company suddenly palled. One of *those* days indeed. Now she was really worried. Such an inconclusive conversation. What an irritating man! But he was in trouble of some sort; he was upset. If there was one thing Kitty couldn't bear it was that any of her loved ones be unhappy. He usually told her everything. What on earth could be wrong? She reached for her vitamins and swallowed down two Superdrug vitamin C's with the remains of the cold coffee.

"Oh shit!" she said, moving Genius back to the paper. "You know, cat, I think we'd better just forget today."

She picked up the 'phone and dialled.

OF GRACE IN A STATE

On the second floor, at the top of the house, Grace Morgan looked out of the window of the granny flat just as the street doors swung silently open and Wheels drove the big Mercedes away into East Heath Road. She caught sight of Ludo in the back and sighed. She had wanted to talk and she knew that he knew that she wanted to talk. Grace sighed. She could usually wheedle things out of Wheels but he had turned into a clam as well. Now she would have to wait. She went downstairs, all five dogs trailing in her wake in search of Elpidio or Lolli, the Filipino couple who looked after the house and garden.

On the mezzanine she met Julie, coming out of the bedroom.

"Morning," Grace mumbled. She wasn't fond of Julie although, she fondly thought, she tried. Julie, she counted, was the seventeenth and Grace had never been at all sure of any of them. Grace suspected the motives of anyone involved with her only son.

"Hullo," Julie replied morosely. Julie was dressed in Head track clothes, black, the expensive ones with a black towelling bandeau around her heavily streaked blonde hair and the darkest RayBans hiding her eyes. What *does* he see in her, thought Grace? Julie stood to one side, almost deferentially, as Grace swept down the staircase followed by the dogs.

"Where you off, then?" Grace called over her shoulder. Grace was not a small woman and since tumbling down the last few steps earlier in the year she paid particular attention to the stairs.

"Joggin'. Thought I'd get some air on the Heath."

"Stuffy in here, is it?"

"You could say," Julie replied, wishing that the

lumbering bulldog would hurry. Grace made her feel uncomfortable. "Come on Bullshit, for God's sake!"

"His name," Grace said, reaching the bottom of the stairs, "is Edgar."

"I'll see you later," said the girl, walking quickly across the huge sitting room and into the kitchen.

"Be careful on that Heath. You never know who's about." Julie didn't even acknowledge Grace's motherly concern.

"Everything alright?" Grace enquired grudgingly.

"Sure. Why shouldn't it be?" Julie sang out carelessly, though she knew full well that it wasn't. The kitchen door flapped to and fro, fanning the annoyance of both women. Grace frowned and looked down at her five canine friends, assembled in a line. The ribbons she had carefuly tied in the Yorkies' top knots were already awry and Bullshit looked more resentful and down at the mouth than ever, his head bowed with the heavy studded collar Ludo had insisted he wore for his portrait. Grace glanced at him and empathy flowed. She felt like growling too. And where, she wondered crossly, had that damned painter chap got to? She looked at her watch. She softened somewhat as the quizzical looks on the dogs faces touched her. Like her, they could sense that something was going on and, indeed, there was something going on in the house and in her son's life apart from them having their portrait painted by the famous Mr Burke. She wished she could explain it to them but, like her, they didn't know Victor Burke from a hole in the ground.

"You'll just have to be patient, boys. And you too, Harriet. He won't be long and if he is we'll just ring up Aunty Kitty, won't we?" Bullshit spluttered a sigh through his heavy jowls, slobbered and slumped down, the effort of waiting for whatever it was too much to bear. "I know, Edgar. I know. I wish granny knew what the matter was but I don't." Grace could feel the atmosphere in the house and it irritated her that she was being told nothing, reduced to this feeble sleuthing. Ludo had been edgy for at least ten days, more than usually uncommunicative. He hadn't been home for four nights out of the last nine and when she'd asked, he merely mumbled "Studio" to her as if that explanation covered all her worries.

"Lolli!" No answer. Grace went into the kitchen. Spick and span as always and the shopping baskets had gone. Of course. Thursday was Lolli's shopping day. Elpidio would have taken her in the Range Rover. Mutley, the black and white mongrel, put his head round the kitchen door and whined. "Alright, darling. I know you want to go out but you can't. You have to look your best and it's too muddy out there." The 'phone rang. Grace looked at the shrilling instrument. She knew she wasn't supposed to answer it, not that line but, what to do? Everyone was out.

"Hello."

"Grace, it's Kitty."

Relief. Kitty! She would know. Kitty always knew. Kitty had always been the only one, in Grace's eyes. Kitty had class."

Hello, lovey. I was going to call you."

"Darling, is Ludo there?"

"No. He's just gone out."

"You don't know where, do you?"

"No. But if I said studio, would that answer your question?"

"Oh, I see. It's like that, is it?"

"Yes. What's going on, lovey?"

"Beats me. He just asked me to marry him, by the way."

"Oh, Kitty, love. I'm that pleased!" Grace trilled. At last. Kitty wasn't in fecund prime, mind, so maybe grandchildren would be out of the question but at least it was going to be Kitty!

"Hang on to your hat, Grace. Don't get carried away."

"Oh! You didn't say no, lovey, surely?"

"'Fraid so. It wouldn't work, darling. We all know that, don't we? I thought that was all dead and buried years ago. Is he depressed?"

"Very. Sort of shut away, you know?"

"And Julie? Is she alright."

"Sulking if you ask me. She's always been the sulky

type. Maybe she knows her days are numbered."

"I suppose they must be. Oh, how awful. Still, she must have known what she was getting into."

"Her! She's clueless, Kitty. Never known a girl so stupid. What she uses for a brain, I'm sure I don't know."

"Yes, well," said Kitty. She was tempted to say but didn't. It was perfectly obvious what Julie used as a brain and Kitty had always rather envied that facility. Brains do get in the way, she thought. "Darling, can you ask him to call when he gets back or if he calls in?"

"I'll try, lovey, but I'm only supposed to answer my own 'phone. I'll tell Lolli when she gets back from Waitrose."

"Has Victor turned up yet?"

"No, dear. But they all look lovely. Even Harriet looks pretty today." Harriet was a peke, not Grace's favourite. Too aloof, to much of a loner to be as affectionate as Grace liked her proxy grandchildren to be.

"Well, I'm sure he won't be long. He's had to get some ... something."

"What, dear?"

"Er ... props ... things he needs."

"Oh," said Grace, concerned.

"Is this wise, all this painting business? What I say is what's wrong with photos?"

"Since when has wise had anything to do with *our* lives, darling? Look, I have to go. Mrs Haines will be here in a minute and I haven't tidied up."

"Let her tidy up. That's what she's paid for, lovey!" Grace, having been a char herself for many years, could be very grand about what people were paid to do.

"You're probably right, darling, but you know me."

Grace rang off as the bell on the street gate rang. The dogs barked furiously.

Victor waited. He carried his polaroid and his sketch pad in a chic Vuitton holdall in one hand and a plastic carrier from Cover Girl with his new shoes in the other. He smiled into the video camera in the gate unit and Grace's eyes narrowed suspiciously as she checked him for a moment on the monitor.

12

"Yes." She spoke in a snap, always wary of those who came knocking at the door. In the past there had been too many newspapermen and desperate fans for her to have retained any faith in the motives of the human race.

"It's Victor Burke for Ludo Morgan."Grace shook her head and pressed the button.

FATHER FIGURES

Nick Longingly finally abandoned the pretence of subtlety and smiled full face, full on, eyes a blaze of twenty year old come-on and I-dare-you. He immediately knew it was a mistake. The man blinked in astonishment and hurriedly unfolded his paper. Hiding behind it, Nick never saw him again and the train rattled into Old Street Station. Hey ho, he thought. Some you win and some you lose. Shame. The man looked very much his type too.

He swung his Levi jacket over his shoulder and exited the train. He didn't even bother to look back. He sauntered down the platform almost bouncing in the black Doc Martens. At the platform exit, he couldn't help himself and glanced round as the train pulled away. The carriage was still empty, save the man who was still hiding behind the early edition. And up yours, thought Nick who had been cruised by the suited gent all the way from Kings Cross. He hurried up the escalator flashed his travel card and went out into the bright sunshine of City Road.

He was early. Oliver hated unpunctuality and today Nick had no desire to upset his father. It was as much as he had dared to set off for lunch still wearing his ripped at the knees Red Label 501's but what the hell. That much at least Oliver would expect. He had made one gesture and taken out the earring, though now regretted it. He felt naked, like a guardsman without the chin-strap on his busby. He walked slowly down towards Finsbury Square, past Companies House where he had spent several school holidays researching companies for one of his father's friends. Balance sheets, turnover, assets. Two pounds an hour and Nick had counted every hour. Kitty had said she thought it a little unfair and Oliver had paid for the bike in the end anyway but Nick stuck it out, more, he now reflected, to prove something to Oliver than for any satisfaction for himself. Ugh. Loathsome work he now was sure. Nick, much given to 'ists' and 'isms', now defiantly spelled capital with a K yet loved his father all the same.

He arrived at the restored early-Victorian house with the familiar brass plate. Longingly Moorhouse Hole. Nick smiled. The Hole was a recent addition and it still made him laugh especially as the Hole in question was a lady. He was just about to go in when he thought he recognised the long black Mercedes parked ostentatiously outside on double yellow lines. He walked back a few steps and glanced at the number plate. POP 1. He was right. It was Ludo's car although a new model since the one Nick had last ridden in. He rapped on the driver's darkened window.

"Wheels! Are you in there?"

The window descended with an almost inaudible whirring and Wheels grinned.

"Thought you wasn't goin' to recognise me, mate."

Nick leaned against the door and looked in.

"Why on earth would I not recognise you? You berk!"

Wheels laughed. A youngish man with a shock of unruly. straw-coloured thick fair hair, dressed in uniform black 501's. black denim shirt and black cuban-heeled Texan boots. He tucked the book he was reading under the seat.

"Lots don't," he said.

"You'd be surprised."

"Probably not. Most people are prejudiced as well as being conveniently blind."

"Goin' to see yer dad?" Nick nodded and raised his eyes. "Ludo's in with him now. You all having lunch someplace?"

"I don't think so. Mine's a strictly one-to-one, father-to-son lunch. What's happening?"

"Not a lot. His highness is in a mood."

"Oh. Nothing wrong is there? I mean he's alright?"

"Alright?"

"Yes. Health. Come on, Wheels. Nobody's immune these days, you know."

"Oh," said Wheels, clicking into Nick's train of thought.

"No. Not Aids. No, he's fine. Haven't seen your mum lately."

"Oh. She's alright. Young love and all that."

"I heard."

"What's the book?" Ludo peered further into the car. Wheels was always reading.

"Tales of the City. Bloke called Morpin or summat. Read 'im?" Nick shook his head.

"Should I?"

"Yeah. Lovely stuff. San Francisco. Brings back a lotta road memories. When it really was sex, drugs and rock 'n' roll."

"I'll bet. Look, I'll catch you later. Better not be late for the old man. See you."

"'Bye Nick. Oh, an' remember. You can die from a whole bunch of things apart from Aids."

"Point taken."

Wheels pressed a button and the window slid back into place as Nick rounded the front of the gleaming limousine and went up the steps into the inner recesses of Longingly Moorhouse Hole.

Hole herself was standing by the receptionist's desk as he went into to the deeply carpeted room. He smiled openly at her. Hole's eyes narrowed.

"Do I know you or are you a delivery?"

"I am not a delivery and yes, we have met."

Recognition of the curly, dark-haired, well-formed young man dawned.

"It's Nicholas, isn't it?" Hole held out her hand and Nick shook it, wondering if a kiss would be in order. What the hell? He went for it and she stiffened slightly. He felt her relax as he intuitively heard her logic circuits crackling. Nicholas Longingly. Twenty years old. Oliver's son. It's alright to kiss. Kiss. Move back one pace. Smile.

"It is. I'm having lunch with dad."

"Oh. That's nice. You're at UCL now aren't you?"

"I am."

"Reading?"

16

"English."

"Oh."

She sounded unconvinced, even worried. She looked at his shredded denim chic and wondered if there was a chance the brass plate would one day read Longingly Moorhouse Hole Longingly and if so would the two Longinglys be strung together or, option three, if there would be any need to stress the second Longingly at all.

"Your father has a client, I think, or I'd take you in," said Hole.

"I know. My godfather, I believe. Don't worry. I'll wait. I've brought my *Guardian*."

"Really? Is he, honestly? Ludo Morgan? How exciting."

"Don't know about exciting. Don't tell me you're a fan, Ms Hole." Nick made the Ms sound suitably vague, sort of swallowed like it could be anything. Perhaps she was a Virginia, or a Lottie. He hadn't been made privy."

Actually," she blushed and shared a conspiratorial smile with the ice-cold receptionist, "that's the only reason I'm lurking out here. Autograph hunting. Do you think he'd mind? It's for my younger sister, of course."

"It always is," he muttered. Then, brightly, "Course not. Why should he?" Nick took out his *Guardian* and looked round at the newly decorated room as to where to park himself. Hole decided she'd gone too far, revealed too much. She coughed.

"There's a *Financial Times* on the table, if you'd prefer."

"Pink's not my colour, thanks. Much too variable."

"Oh. Right."

Before Nick could sit down, a door opened and Oliver and Ludo came into the reception from one of the inner sancti. Hole removed her spectacles and blossomed, flowering in an instant like a speeded up nature film of a succulent in a desert shower. The receptionist preened and pretended to get on with some urgent task, peeking all the while out of the corner of her eye.

"Ah, Camilla!" exclaimed Oliver heartily. "I must introduce Ludo ..." Ludo had already spotted Nick and was halfway across the reception. The two embraced with a huge hug.

"Jesus! Am I seeing you right? You look like one of the Pet Shop Boys. When did you grow up?"

Oliver looked at Hole and shrugged. He propelled her forward. She realised she was on her own.

"Oh! It's so good to see you. How's Grace?"

"Fine. Just great. Nagging away of course but then that's what mothers do, isn't it?"

Ludo pulled his leather jacket around his shoulders and tipped his Porsche sunglasses onto his forehead. His eyes were red, sleepless and he replaced the glasses quickly ."I've got mine better trained. I must *see* you. Can I come round sometime?"

"Of course. Need a little godfatherly advice?"

Nick grinned at his father standing by the desk.

"Sort of. It would be nice to talk. Thanks for the graduation cheque by the way. You did get my letter, didn't you?"

"No trouble, Nick. Call me, hey. Perhaps next week. I'm a bit tied up at the moment." Ludo hugged Nick again and muttered in his ear. "In fact, I could do with a bit of advice too."

"Anytime. Oh, this is dad's partner, Loo. I think she wants to ask you something." Hole's eyelashes fluttered as Ludo turned round. Her request for an autograph was given with due public flourish. She got a kiss too. Nick noticed her neck redden although he had to give her eight out of ten for cool.

"Thanks, Oliver. As always." Ludo and Oliver shook hands. "And you, Pet Shop Boy. Call me, right? I have to go. I'm going to be late for lunch."

"Right," said Nick and then Ludo was gone. Hole replaced her glasses and disappeared, gracelessly, Nick thought, without thanking him for his intervention.

"Hello, dad."

"Hullo, old chap. I see we dressed up."

"Oh, please, dad."

"OK, OK. Give me five minutes. I have to make a couple of calls."

"Right. I'll be here."

18

NO GO ARIAS

The taxi Gerald had ordered for midday to take them into town was late. It was already ten past twelve when the buzzer sounded.

"Number eighteen? Ground floor? Mr Ward?"

"You're late!"

"Sorry, guv. Traffic."

Gerald swore silently."

Alright. We'll be right down."

He collected his briefcase and a mackintosh from the back of the sofa.

"Violetta! Taxi's here. Aren't you ready yet?"

Violetta appeared in her bedroom doorway, her small but ample person draped in dark green silk, a Liberty shawl draped over her left shoulder. She had already been to her singing teacher that morning and had showered and done her hair on returning.

"Calm down, Gerry, love. There's no train to catch." Her speaking voice was quite high and delicate, unlike the rich, full-throated soprano which sprang like a fine jet of viscose when she sang. Her natural accent was decidedly north country again, most unlike the publicly flattened vowels she produced on radio and television interviews.

"You might not have one but I have to be at The Garden by one. Where are you going, by the way?"

Violetta looked round for her bag. Gerald grabbed it and handed it to her.

"Nowhere special, love. I just fancied a bit of lunch with Millie."

"How come I've never met this Millie," he said as he ushered her out of the front door and out to the waiting taxi.

"You don't know all my friends, Gerry. Millie and I go back a long way and it's not often she gets over from New

York."

He opened the door for her and gave the driver instructions, declining to make the observation that Millie must have been one of the most re-located women in the history of West Yorkshire.

"Will you be back for dinner?"

Violetta looked away from her ex-husband yet still manager. Acting like crazy, she lied like mad. How she hated lying. It pained her.

"Don't know, chuck. Didn't Peter check with you? He and Kitty have asked me to the theatre, don't you remember?"

The black radio cab pulled away from the flat in Broomhouse Road and onto the New Kings Road.

"Oh. Yes. Of course."

"Well don't sound so disappointed, Gerry. You said you had to have dinner with that fella from Belgrade."

"Bucharest."

"Wherever."

"He *is* important, Violetta."

"They *all* are, Gerry."

Gerry drummed his fingers on the door sill as the taxi stop-started in heavy traffic approaching Sloane Square. It was not easy, still living with Violetta. Marriage had been impossible but divorce was proving even more difficult. They sat at opposite sides of the taxi. Together but very far apart, tied by fifteen years of Violetta's burgeoning career and separated by fifteen years of entirely different personal ambitions. Ambition was the problem. Gerald Ward was Violetta's ambition. Alone, she had little. Without him, she would admit privately, she'd have been just as happy in the chippy at Wakefield like her mum, singing every week in the Methodist Choir, giving the 'Hallelujah Chorus' once a year in the town hall.

"Don't fret, Gerry," she said, patting his hand. "You fret too much, chuck."

"Will you take the taxi on?" he mentioned. "To Millie's?"
Gerry believed in Millie as much as he believed in the Holy Ghost but was prepared for the moment to accept the

20

mythical woman's existence.

"Yes," said Violetta, realising that the sinking, churning feeling in her tummy indicated both excitement and nervousness at the charade she had been acting for the past week. It had to stop soon, that she knew. It was beginning to affect her voice and that would never do for Covent Garden the following week.

Gerald told the taxi driver to drop him off at Aldwych.

"Have a good meeting, Gerry."

"Thanks. I'll maybe see you later, then?"

"Of course, chuck. But don't wait up for me if I'm late."

He stood and watched his protegee, ex-wife and only client whisked away into a maze of possibilities. He turned and walked up the lane towards the Opera House. He thought of Rachel Bailey, the only good thing that had appeared in his life lately. And even Rachel was intimately involved with Violetta, now more intricately than she could ever have contemplated two weeks before. Gerald wondered in whom Rachel was most interested; him or his diva.

TABLES D'HOTE

Oliver took Nick to La Gamba in Outwall Street. They walked, it was that close. Oliver didn't use it a lot. He didn't usually do lunch but he hadn't seen Nick for some weeks and he liked sitting with his son and chewing the fat. He needed his son more not less and having him at least in London instead of stuck away at Malvern in school, gave Oliver great pleasure, dress codes notwithstanding. La Gamba was supposed to be Spanish, therefore informal and easy, easy meaning that no one would raise an eyebrow at the young man's wardrobe.

Peter Bailey had lunch with his daughter Rachel. It was she who had requested it, a request prompted by a suggestion from her editor on the *Daily Standard*. They went to Rules in Covent Garden. Peter walked over from Soho Square and got there early. Rachel found herself late. If she had not been so intent on running across the flashing amber light outside Australia House, she would have seen Violetta waving to her from the window of the taxi. Violetta wanted to speak to her urgently.

Ludo slipped unnoticed into the darkened interior of Le Gastrodome. Wheels had booked well. It was his usual table. From the banquette in the booth at the rear of the restaurant, he could see the door. He remained incognito behind the Porsche shades. He saw the door open. Walter, the Maitre d' held it open for a couple of city types and behind them he saw the taxi pull up. He saw her get out and hand over the fare. She turned and walked up the steps. He couldn't believe the butterflies he felt fanning the stress of anticipation. Walter bowed stiffly as the lady acknowledged his welcome. She really was little, Ludo reflected. Had he not noticed before? And she really was no spring chicken, that was plain. And there was no way she could ever be politely described as anything but big.

22

But she was there, she was walking over to the table, she was smiling, her eyes were shining and he felt incredibly proud, happy and content merely to see her

NO FLIES ON BULLSHIT

Victor wondered how much longer he could maintain the interested, involved, fascinated attention he had been paying to Grace's run-down of the origins, habits and characters of all five of Ludo Morgan's kennel. The Filipino maid brought more coffee and surreptitiously Victor looked at his watch. Today he had only wanted to take photographs, a quick ten minutes he'd thought, time enough to make a start and time emough to allow him to get to Queens Park to borrow frilly knickers from a tennis-playing dyke of an acquaintance of long standing.

"Which would your favourite be, Mr Burke?"

The Yorkshire terriers, Stars and Stripes, pricked up their ears and looked cute. Bullshit and Harriet lay side by side, chins on paws, very bored and Mutley panted, tail wagging.

"Please call me Victor, Mrs Morgan." He looked round for the inspiration to commit himself to an honest appraisal. How Victor loathed sentiment which was probably, he often told himself, why he earned his not inconsiderable living from this selfsame sentimentality he was now enduring. "I think probably the mongrel has the greatest character."

"Oh! Mutley's not a mongrel!" Grace sprang to Mutley's defence. "He's a collie. The working sort. He's Welsh."

That, thought Victor, I have heard a million times before and he raised his eyes, reflecting that Mutley was about as Welsh as Shirley Bassey.

He stretched out and lugged the holdall to his side."I really have to get going, Mrs Morgan." He took out the polaroid. Grace looked confused as Victor checked the film stock and jammed in a cartridge.

"But where are your paints, Mr Burke?" Grace was really confused. "I was just about to ask if you'd like some

24

water for your brushes. Kitty, Miss Llewellyn that is, told me you did water colours."

"I do," said Victor aiming the camera at Stars and Stripes who blinked stupidly as the flash went off four feet from their faces. "But I have to have these to remind me."

"So you don't actually do it here, then?"

"Do what, Mrs Morgan?" murmured Victor grimly.

"Paint."

"Not actually here, no."

"Then where do you do it?"

"In my studio, Mrs Morgan."

"Oh," said Grace rather sadly. "That's where my son does it too."

"Really," said Victor setting off a flash in the vague direction of Mutley who was cowering behind the Chinese silk sofa, terrified at the goings on. "How fascinating." Victor pursued Mutley relentlessly and Mutley seemed to be winning.

The kitchen door opened and Julie returned from her run. Her track suit was immaculate. It had been too muddy to jog. She hadn't wanted to get it dirty.

"Oh," she said, removing the RayBans. "Didn't know the vet was comin'."

"Hello," said Victor as Mutley raced away through the swing-door to hide under the kitchen table. "I'm Victor Burke."

"It's not the vet," said Grace sharply. "Mr Burke is a famous painter."

"You're Julie Burge, aren't you?"

"Yeah," she said, brightening a little at Victor's recognition. She assumed the position that had made her famous by unzipping the front of the tight track suit top and forcing her shoulders so far back that they almost met at some point in the middle of her lower back. Mountains of voluptuousness resulted, straining at the man-made fabric. Poor Julie. Victor, handsome though he was, was not about to be impressed except in the strictly anatomical sense. He smiled, though. He had heard her nickname and now saw how very appropriate it was. The Tits was how Julie Burge was known in the trade. "You're the bloke that's paintin' our little doggies, eh?"

"Right, Miss Burge. If I can ever get them to stay still long enough to get a decent mug shot."

"S'what one photographer always says to me," sang out Julie. "I model, you know."

"Model!" muttered Grace not sufficiently to herself. "More like expose!"

"Sorry? Didn't quite catch that Mrs Morgan," barked Julie as yappily as Stars and Stripes, the famous tits wobbling indignantly.

Oh, Lord, thought Victor. Spare me. The life styles of the rich and famous. No one would believe him. They never did. Most of Victor's famous stories about his famous clients were thought grossly apocryphal.

Grace struggled out of the armchair and bent to pick Harriet up and set her on the glass coffee table, fluffing up her long minky coat

."You'll get a better picture of Harriet up here, Mr Burke," she said. Victor crouched down in front of the coffee table, shuffled back and somehow his heel came to rest on Bullshit's forepaw. Bullshit snarled savagely and the pincer jaws went for Victor's bum in a lungeing nip. He missed.

"Christ!" exclaimed Victor as Bullshit stood up determinedly, growling like Cerebus defending the gates of the Underworld.

"Watch 'im," cried Julie. "'E'll 'ave the arse out your trousers an' no mistake."

"Edgar!" warned Grace. "Manners, darling. Mustn't bite nice Mr Burke, must we? What will daddy say?"

Victor backed away as Bullshit retreated behind the sofa, only to emerge on the other side carrying the Cover Girl carrier bag clamped firmly in his jaws. Slobber dribbled down the plastic.

"Oh, really!" said Victor and flashed off a final polaroid at the defiant British bulldog. "Now put down that bag you....you nice dog!"

Julie laughed. The famous tits wobbled in giggles, two vast jellies wandering tipsily across a cobbled street."You'll never get your bag back now. He never lets go does Bullshit. 'Ad the postman pinned outside the front door all mornin' last month."

"Only 'cos the postman was teasin' 'im. But, Edgar! You're a naughty boy," said Grace fearlessly. "Put nice Mr Burke's bag down." She grabbed one side of the carrier bag and tugged. True to form, Bullshit refused to let go and the struggle for the bag became a tug of war between two small mountains and although both teams were equally short, both were equally determined.

Victor wanted to die. As the bag ripped asunder under the unbearable strain, Grace landed on her backside against the sofa, Bullshit shot across the parquet and the size nine black stilettos were tossed into the air as though from a blanket.

"Oh no!" moaned Victor wishing the earth would open and swallow him up. Julie rescued the shoes from the floor and handed them back to Victor.

"I'll get Lolli to fetch you another bag," she giggled. "They yours, then?"

"Er ..." stammered Victor, hastily stuffing the shoes into the holdall. "No, actually. I borrowed them. From a friend. His name's Oliver. He's a ... I'm a ... I'm ... "

"S'oright," grinned Julie. "I shan't tell. You alright, Mrs Morgan? Came a nasty cropper there, didn't we?"

Bullshit, still crumpled against the base of a bookcase, glared hungrily at Victor as he made a hasty retreat. The heavy jowls spluttered once more and following Victor's scent, he staggered after the fleeing painter, seeing him off the premises.

"Oh, dear," said Grace ruefully, untying the bows in the Yorkies' hairdo's, "I was so looking forward to a bit of company, boys. He seemed such a *nice* man, too." She let Mutley out into the garden, Harriet stayed asleep as she had throughout, the Yorkies followed Grace upstairs to her flat where food was more plentiful.

Only Bullshit remained in any purposeful fashion. He lay slumped by the street door on the path, watching and waiting.

CAREER MOVES

Rachel ordered sole. Peter chose a salad and suggested a Chablis. Rules was filling up and the conversations around them loudened.

"Chablis alright with you?"

"Fine, dad. Anything."

The wine waiter arrived promptly with the cooled Chablis and Peter approved it. They didn't speak until he had poured two glasses.

"Cheers, darling."

"Cheers."

"You seem a little preoccupied. Anything wrong?"

Rachel sighed.

"No. Nothing's wrong. I mean it, too. In fact nothing could be righter."

"Interview with Violetta all set?"

"Umm. Tomorrow. Gerald suggested it should be at the Ritz. What do you think?"

Peter frowned as he pondered the suggestion.

"Why the Ritz? It's not where the real Violet Hargreaves would ever be found. But then," he added, "the real Violet Hargreaves wouldn't make the best copy. Right?"

"True. So I do what Macdonald tells me and Macdonald thinks the pictures would look good, too. He would. That and probably some frightful caption like Ritzi Abizzi."

"Very good for your career, though. On the paper, I mean."

"So I'm well aware, dad."

"You get on well with Gerald, don't you. I noticed the other night."

"Quite. No better than with most managers on that level."

"There are others?"

Rachel seemed, to Peter, to blush. He was close to his

daughter but he had always given her space, always kept one step further from the palisades of her world than he would have liked. In that area he envied Kitty her almost sisterly relationship with Nick. Rachel was very much like her mother; contained, seemingly impregnable. Kitty on the other hand was the opposite, all simmer and flare, boil and burst and very, very vulnerable.

"He's made a few moves, yes," Rachel admitted. "If that's what you're after."

"Oh, I'm not after anything, darling. I just want you to be happy."

"Dad. I'm twenty-eight. There's tons of time for happiness. Whatever happiness is."

Peter laughed.

"Funny, that's just how Nick talks."

"How sweet."

"What? What is this I detect? Don't tell me you're jealous. You've got no reason to be, you know that."

"Sorry, dad. I was being cynical, not jealous." She paused. "Do you think he's gay, by the way?"

"Gerald Ward? I shouldn't think so."

She laughed. He smiled. It was good to see his serious daughter laugh. It seemed that she hadn't done enough of it.

"No, silly. I meant Nick."

"I don't think so. At least, Kitty's never *said* anything."

"Kitty would be the last to know," observed Rachel. Her asparagus arrived. Peter had waived a starter. She added dollops of butter to the hot vegetable and allowed one spear to slip into her up-tilted mouth. "It's something she just wouldn't think of."

"Why on earth not? It's not as though she doesn't have gay friends. Look at Victor for heaven's sake."

"Well, I know *he's* gay. Mark my words. And don't get me wrong. I like him. A lot."

"So do I." "Anyway, Kitty wouldn't give a hoot. As long as he was happy. She's such a darling, you know, Rache. All she wants is for us all to be happy. You do like her, don't you? She gets very worried that you might not."

"Course I like her, silly. She's great. Just what you need too, after mummy."

"I loved your mother, Rachel. Very, very much."

"I know you did. Honestly. But you've changed and it's good that you've found someone who complements the new you. Are you going to get married?"

"She won't. Believe me, I've asked often enough. She just laughs and says we'll get married when we've stopped being in love."

"And you *are* still in love?"

"Ridiculously."

Rachel smiled, her expression was encouraging and, Peter fancied, a little rueful.

"I think I envy you."

"Think?"

"Yes. Think."

"Oh."

The waiter removed Rachel's plate and Peter poured her more wine.

"What are you doing at the weekend?"

"Ah," he said rubbing his hands togther in obvious anticipation. "Simple. Nothing. We're having the weekend to ourselves and indulging. Long lie-in, lunch, videos, champagne. That's Saturday. Then papers, late breakfast, more videos and more champagne. That's Sunday."

"No Littlecombe?"

"No. Kitty says she wants to feel like a mistress this weekend and at Littlecombe she never stops being a divorcee."

"You are so sweet, the pair of you. And you're right. Kitty is a darling. It was her idea to invite me the other night to meet Violetta, wasn't it?"

Peter nodded as the sole was ushered on with great ceremony and his magnificent pink roast beef salad appeared in front of him.

"How do you think she'll go down next week at the Garden? I got a wonderful deal for her, by the way. If she's alright on the night, she'll be made."

Rachel was enjoying her sole.

"Well, my fellow scribblers seem to be thinking as one. The production we know about. It's been seen before and most think it's rubbish. But I think she'll come out of it with raves. I adore her. She's badly needed. England is very short of new generation divas."

"Agreed," remarked Peter vehemently. "Although I thought the fashion for divas was a bit old hat now?"

"Until a new one comes along," Rachel observed wisely. "But she must remain credible," she added. "None of the Kiri stuff. No albums of pop songs and garbage like that. I've told Gerald and he agrees entirely."

"What does Miss Abizzi formerly Hargreaves think?"

"That," said Rachel, "I shall find out tomorrow, shan't I?"

SINS OF OMISSION

"Hole's pretty cool, isn't she?"

"Cool?" queried Oliver."As in calm and collected."

"Oh, yes. Camilla the Cool. But cool as in fridge, I'd say."

"Ah," said Nick."That sounded disapproving."

"So you're not, then?"

"No. Definitely not. Never dip the pen in the office ink. Are you sure you don't want wine?"

Nick shook his head.

"Can't. I have a lecture this afternoon. I'd nod off in a minute."

Nick had chosen paella, no chicken. Oliver had liver.

"So, you still insist on living in that pokey little room. Where is it? Gower Street?"

"Just behind. And yes. I like it."

"And Chelsea Square wouldn't go with the image, would it? Though I must tell you, we had punks in the Kings Road before they filtered up to Gower Street."

"Dad! I am *not* a punk and this isn't an image. It's me. Just like that terrible suit is you."

"The way of the world," observed Oliver, immaculately. "Terrible suits paying for terrible jeans. How's your mother?"

"Fine. I'm supposed to be going to dinner tonight. The Ellmans are going."

"So what are you going as? The light relief? Tom Ellman is *such* heavy going and she's such a timid little thing. Can't see what Kitty sees in them. No more de rigeur dinner parties! That's one of the great reliefs about being a bachelor gay!" Oliver laughed and forked in another mouthful of bloody liver. Nick swallowed hard.

"Dad ..." The paella had lost it's temptation."Yes."

"What would you ...?"

32

"Yes. Go on. What would I what?"

So many times had Nick been on the point of telling his father and on every occasion that tiniest final doubt had crept in and he'd backed off.

"You would use a condom, wouldn't you?" he blurted out.

"Christ, Nick, you sound like Marie Stopes. I already have one child, I hardly need any more at my age. I'm just beginning to enjoy myself."

"That's what I mean. Being careful."

Oliver's mastications stopped as he looked across the table at his messianic son. There'd always been something - You won't use chemical fertilisers, will you, dad; you will change to unleaded petrol when it comes in, won't you, dad; you won't be chauvinistic about the divorce, will you, dad. And now, birth control!

"Look, Nick, I know you think I'm a dirty old man but I'm not that rampant."

"I mean Aids, dad. Safer sex. Ever heard about it?"

"Of course I have. I should be asking you the same question."

Ask me, thought Nick. Oh, *please* ask me and save me having to tell you!

"I'm sure you're very sensible, Nick and that's all I need to know. You've always been sensible. In fact, both your mother and I have often thought you were too sensible. There are times I don't understand you at all. Paella OK? The liver is superb."

Oliver looked round to catch the waiter's eye. Nick had already caught it, the moment they had come into the restaurant.

"You haven't been down to Littlecombe lately?"

Nick wondered if this was an admonishment or mere curiousity."

No. I haven't."

"You should do. Mrs Tarpitt misses you."

"I was thinking of going down this weekend, actually."

"Good idea. Is your mother going too?"

"No. Definitely not. She's off limits this weekend.

33

They're staying in town. Listen, dad, why don't *we* go? It would be a chance to talk and stuff."

Oliver stopped chewing for a moment and thought.

"No," he said ultimately. "I was there the weekend before last and to tell you the truth, I fancy a weekend on my own. But you go - why not? Take a friend."

Nick chased a pink shrimp round his plate with his fork.

"Haven't really got anyone to go with," he said.

"Then *find* someone!" was his father's only piece of concerned advice forthcoming that lunchtime.

The waiter smiled again at Nick from behind the espresso machine. No, thought Nick, on second thoughts not really me at all.

KNICKERS

Kitty made sure that Mrs Haines left early. The woman's incessant prattle always involved long eulogies to the memory of Mary Bailey and, often, tears over coffee. Today, Kitty was too preoccupied with thoughts of Ludo and Peter and Oliver and the stability of life in general to be bothered with Mrs Haines' attempts to breathe life into a corpse. Mrs Haines had a bad case of unrequited bereavement.

Kitty felt like a gin and tonic and so she poured one. Dammit. Why shouldn't she be a secret drinker?

The doorbell rang. Genius was lying in the hall in a patch of sunlight which had appeared from somewhere in the otherwise lowering sky.

"Hedonist!"Genius stayed right where he was. Kitty opened the door, fearing the worthy Mrs Haines had forgotten something.

Victor looked hot and far from debonair.

"You must have heard the ice cubes, darling."

"Can I come in, Kitty. I've had the *most* ghastly morning."

Kitty opened the door fully and Victor came in. One look at Victor and Genius bolted. The memory of his being held down by Kitty for his portrait shots still smarted. His dignity had been, as far as he was concerned, forever compromised. Victor followed Kitty downstairs.

"Gin, dear?"

"Why not. You were right about that demented bulldog, darling. How that breed ever came to symbolise our beloved Motherland I shall never know."

"How was Grace? I haven't heard from her, so everything must have gone reasonably alright." Victor sat down in one corner of the old leather chesterfield in the kitchen.

"At least she got a submission out of the beast. Personally, I'd hate to go more than one round with her in any ring. Now *she* should be the symbol of England."

"She is," Kitty replied handing Victor his drink. "Cheers. Her and millions like her. Like Naomi Jacobs said: It's the shit of the little women of England that makes this country great."

"Cheers!" said Victor, raising his glass. "I shan't argue. But what about that Miss Julie? Where was she when they handed out the grey matter?"

"Oh, she's alright. I'm sure she gives as good as she gets. I can't say I envy her, though. Grace thinks she's on the way out and I know she is. I take it Ludo wasn't there."

"No. Rather a shame actually. He is hugely tasty, isn't he. But then I'm telling you. Ha!"

Kitty grinned.

"Let's say he'd certainly put a smile on your face, dear."

"Oh, Like that, eh? Still, prowess never worried me. For me they have to be merely cute and perfectly formed."

"And twenty-three."

"Far too old, my dear. Past twenty and they begin to think. Then they talk and before you know where you are they start answering you back."

"Just what you need, Victor. The love of a good man."

"But how many good men does it take?"

"I pass. Have you been for your shoes yet?"

"Don't speak to me about the shoes. The whole things's a ghastly mistake, I know it. And Adrienne's knickers were far too butch. Waste of time schlepping over to Queens Park."

"You've been there? How are they?"

"Brawling, as usual. I'm afraid it takes a braver man than me to separate two scrapping lesbians. Terrifying."

"So you've come for my knickers, right?"

"Only if you have frilly ones."

"I don't. Do you want a sandwich?"

"Thank you, no. The gin is easing the pain quite well enough." Victor's eyes came to rest on his portrait of Genius above the dining table. "That really is quite superb, you know. One of my best. Have you paid me yet?"

Kitty coughed into her drink.

36

"It was supposed to be a present, Victor!"

"Oh, yes. I forgot. But why should I give you a present?"

"In return for twenty years worth of free dinners, you cheapskate."

"Oh, right. Come with me, Kitty. Please. I just *have* to have these knickers and I can't bring myself to buy any."

"There! You are cheap!"

"No. I mean I couldn't bring myself to *ask* for them. I'll pay."

Kitty groaned.

"Do I have to? I have dinner to cook tonight. A vegetarian dinner. For the Ellmans. There! I knew there was a good reason why I couldn't come."

The 'phone rang. Kitty answered it and after what seemed to Victor to be a pause and a lots of "Oh, I'm so sorry's" from Kitty and a "Yes, of course I understand" with a final "I'll call you next week to see how Tom is. We'll re-fix another time", she rang off.

"I heard. They're not coming. So now you can come. let's go to Oxford Street and I'll buy you lunch in John Lewis."

"Oh!" said Kitty crossly. "No. Sorry."

"But why not?"

"Well, I persuaded Nick to come tonight and he was so good about it. Tom and Lily are a *little* dull. I'm not sure I can get hold of him to cancel."

"So, you'll have him all to yourself, won't you? Come on, Kit. Please come with me!"

"But, there's Peter," sighed Kitty. "He has to eat too, you know."

"Then get something from the deli counter. *Please* Kitty. My costume!"

POP GOES THE DIVA

Several people had recognised them even in the dimly lit corner of Le Gastrodome but no one had disturbed them.

"Don't look now," said Ludo, "but the woman in the pink hat by the pudding trolley is very puzzled. What she'll be thinking going home on the train to Bromley I'd be very interested to hear."

"D'you know something, chuck? I don't give a tinker's damn what she thinks."

"You're right, I s'pose. Nor do I really."

Ludo smiled and covered her hand with his. Hers: a little hand, basically, the old wedding ring still on her finger, good nails, short, strong fingers. His: huge, spatulate, an enormous solitaire diamond as well as a Cartier three gold band, chewed nails but similar, strong fingers.

"That feels nice," said Violetta.

"Umm," he said, smiling broadly. He looked up at her. She was the funniest thing; dumply, dimply, all smiles and laugh lines. He liked the hope in her eyes best, the way she looked full and honest straight into his own with no fear.

"But I don't mind telling you, love, you look dog rough this morning."

"It's afternoon, Vee."

"Precisely. Now. Out with it. What have you been up to? And if you say Studio to me, I'll clobber you."

"I was thinking."

"All night?"

"All night. First I bathed the dogs. I'm having Victor Burke do their portrait. Remember? The bloke who did that picture of Kitty's cat?"

"How many dogs have you got?"

"Five."

"Five?"

"Umm," he admitted. "You do like dogs, don't you?"

"Love 'em. Never been able to have one, though. Comes of always being on the move. Worse for me than for you, chuck. I think that was some of the reason why Gerald and I didn't work. But go on."

"Then I brushed them. Well, all except Bullshit."

"Bullshit? What sort of a name is that for a dog?"

"He's a bulldog. I love him best, I think. Never demands, always there. Dependable."

"Hark at John Bull 'ere," she laughed. Walter arrived with the bill. They were almost the last to leave. Violetta opened her bag and reached for the bill. Ludo slipped it off the plate and palmed it first.

"Uh uh," he said shaking his head. "I'm *very* old fashioned."

"Good. I like that. But only occasionally, mind," she said with a dimpled grin. Ludo passed the bill, his plastic and the plate back to Walter who bowed and made off.

"Where was I?"

"Canine cosmetics, I believe."

"Oh yes. Well. That's it. Seemed to take all night, anyway."

"And all this thinking? What was that about, if I might be so bold?"

"Taking stock, I suppose. Sorting out some things I should have done long ago that I've been too busy or too lazy to get round to."

"Satisfactory?"

"Very." Ludo sighed. Walter returned the bill.

"Will there be anything else, Mr Morgan? Madam?"

"No thank you, Walter. Not for me. I don't know about Miss Abizzi. Anything for you, love? A brandy?"

"I'd murder another cup of coffee, lad?" Violetta said to Walter who was old enough to be her father. "If there's any in the pot, that is. Don't go to any trouble." He beamed.

"My dear Miss Abizzi, nothing would ever be too much trouble for you. You have given me so much pleasure." He bowed and scurried off, hands waving, in the direction of the kitchen.

Ludo laughed.

"You and me," he said, shaking his head. "Together we cover just about everyone, don't we?. You get the *Times*, *The Telegraph* and the *Guardian* and I get the *Sun*, the *Star* and the *Mirror*."

"What about the *Mail* and the *Express*?"

"Fuck 'em. They don't buy *either* of our records, love."

She laughed and held onto his hand. Then they fell silent.

"What are we going to do, Ludo? I'm afraid I'm acting like a schoolgirl. Y'see ..." She hesitated. "I've not felt like this since I *was* a schoolgirl."

"I know the feeling. It's a bit odd. Bit sad when you think about it. All those wasted years."

"When were you last ... I mean, what was she like? There must have been someone. You're the type."

"Surely, you know?" Violetta shook her head. "You must know!"

"I don't, love. I'm afraid we're both a bit ignorant about what either of us has been up to for the last twenty years."

"It was Kitty," he said simply

."Kitty? Peter's Kitty?"

"My Kitty, Oliver's Kitty, Peter's Kitty."

"Well! I'll be blowed. You don't ... mean, you're not still ...?"

"No! Not since we split up. She was twenty-three. I was twenty-three. But she's still the only person I've ever asked to marry me."

"And she said no?"

Ludo nodded his head. He wondered if he ought to tell her now. He also wondered if he'd already put her off.

"Come on, chuck? What is it? Something's the matter. Please tell me. We have to be honest with each other."

"I've lived with it for so long, see. Kitty. It's always been Kitty. 'Til now, that is. Oh, I know, I've had a zillion birds but I've been very selfish. Very cruel, really. But there's always been Kitty."

"And that's why you were up all night? I know the feeling, love. Like going through old photos or old address

40

books. You just can't bring yourself to throw them away."

"But I have," he insisted. "You must believe me, love. Not thrown her away but ... placed her, you know? She is a very important part of my life."

Walter brought a tray of coffee. He obviously wanted to pour it but Violetta smiled and indicated she would take over.

"I owe everything to Kitty. And Oliver's marvellous too. He's never let me down and always played straight. Lots haven't. And Nick, their son. He's my godson. Apart from mum of course, whenever I've needed family it's always been them who've been there for me."

He looked at her, the look of a little boy, she fancied. Struggling to grow up very quickly.

"I buggered it up once and I'm not going to do it again, Vee. I've been a very lucky man but I daren't fuck up on this score a second time. Excuse my French."

"I know, love. I use French too."

"I have to tell you that I asked her to marry me again, this morning." Violetta started back, not in anger but in pain. His pain. "I knew she'd say no. But I had to ask. Now I'm free, Violetta. I'm a free man.

"She sipped at her coffee."And I'm a free woman, Ludo."

"So," he said. Over them hung a conclusion they had both acknowledged for some days. "What do we do with all this freedom?"

"I'm waiting," she said, her lips poised at the rim of her cup, her eyes shining and encouraging.

"Your place or mine?"

"Neither. Yet."

"We're a bit old for necking in the car, love!"

"Quite agree. Much too uncomfortable."

"Any suggestions?"

Violetta put down her cup and grinned.

"Would it shock you terribly if I said that I've always wondered what it would be like to be very, very naughty in a very posh hotel?"

Ludo pushed his chair back and stood up. He pulled

down the Porsche sunglasses and felt fourteen.

"Is the Ritz posh enough for you, milady?"

Violetta too stood up and leaned across the table towards him. He bent down and brushed his lips against hers. The restaurant was empty, except for Walter who was far too polite to notice.

"Now *that*," she said, sweeping her bag from the table, "is talking, lad!"

MIRROR, MIRROR

That afternoon was on the whole predictably uneventful. On the whole in the centre of the metropolis, at least.

At University College, Nick went to his four o'clock lecture which was suitably obscure and all about two Beaumont and Fletcher plays he hadn't read. He was being led not so much by his intellect that day but by a certain instinct. He could feel that feeling; nervousness, excitement, a fluttering in his belly. Something was going to happen to him. But what?

Oliver returned to the office and made quite a few thousand pounds on a deal he'd been tipped off about but he spent a lot of the afternoon pondering the reasons why Ludo had come to see him. Ludo was the dream client and had never showed any particular interest in exactly how much money he had or where it was. Not that Oliver had ever given him any cause to think of interfering. But it seemed strange to Oliver that Ludo should have asked about his wealth and then asked Oliver to fix up a meeting with his solicitor next week. Ludo said no more than he wanted to arrange his will and some settlements.

After his meeting at the Opera House, Gerald wandered round Covent Garden, tried calling Rachel at the Fleet Street number but was told she'd be out for the rest of the day. The last thing he wanted to do was return to the empty flat in Fulham. He tried Rachel at home without success. What he would have said to her should he have got through, he wasn't sure. He walked round Foyles, bought a pair of socks in the Sock Shop and then went to see *The Last Emperor* in St Martins Lane where he fell asleep.

Victor finally got his knickers and also two pairs of tights. Kitty suggested he buy two because if there was a prize for the fancy dress, one pair wouldn't conceal his extremely hairy and very muscular legs. They kissed goodbye at Oxford Circus and Kitty went into Liberty's lugging a carrier packed with the cold collation she'd bought at the deli in Selfridge's food hall. Where Victor went is not known.

As to what Violetta and Ludo got up to, nothing need be added to conjecture.

So much for the goings on down below.

On the other hand, high above the seething city, in what should have been a leafy, contemplative and peaceful surrounding, the afternoon was taking an entirely more decisive turn.

Grace Morgan was more than a little unhappy. For years she had resisted Ludo's attempts to get her to move into the Gothic house he had bought himself, suitably grand, suitably imposing, suitably private, overlooking the eastern part of Hampstead Heath leading in the direction of Parliament Hill Fields. Grace had been characteristically stubborn although for years she had come on the bus from Holloway to enjoy his garden and his dogs. The garden was now a mini-Wisley. Grace was a natural gardener and had worked tirelessly with Elpidio, Lolli's silent husband, in creating a truly magnificent garden of borders, terraces, shrubberies, ponds set around a gently sloping lawn. She longed for a greenhouse.

For a sixty-two year old widow from a council flat with only a balcony at the back of Jones Brothers, many would be forgiven for thinking that Grace Morgan hadn't half done well.

But there were days, many days, when she questioned the wisdom of leaving Holloway and moving in to the granny flat. True, she wasn't getting any younger. True, Ludo was her only son and closest family. She had an elder sister who'd moved after the war to Bristol but Stella was now in a home. Grace shivered. Homes. She loathed the idea.

But Grace loathed the idea of dependence on anyone. Now, not only was she dependent on Ludo for her home, she was also dependent on him for her peace of mind. Living alone and away from him, she hadn't worried so

44

much. Now all she did was worry. She had only recently got used to being able to go to sleep before he came home. Coming home for Ludo was never before two in the morning.

Grace arrived in Hampstead almost at the same time as Julie Burge moved in. Ludo had always brought his girlfriends to see her and she wondered about each one. Was so-and-so going to be *the* one? There'd been Carolines and Cathies, Ingrids and Kellies. None of them had cut any ice with Grace at all. All very pretty of course in a very obvious way; all undoubtedly after the main chance, she suspected and she had been proved, in the main, right. Julie Burge came in on the crest of a wave of champagne after some awards ceremony when Ludo had collected yet another statuette. Grace had lain in bed and heard the giggling downstairs; she heard the giggling coming up the stairs and then she heard nothing as the door to Ludo's master suite slammed shut. She heard nothing else until the following evening when Ludo called upstairs and asked her to come and have a drink with them.

Grace and Julie got off to a bad start.

Grace decided from the beginning that Julie wasn't right and Julie knew it. Ludo knew it but then Ludo Morgan was not a man to revert to being the obedient son just because his mother had come to live with him. Ludo Morgan had become used to always having his own, unquestioned way. On the whole, Grace was very good about the situation although she regretted being unable to talk to Ludo. She tried, occasionally, but if anything uncomfortable was broached, he would clam up and simply disappear from the room.

Grace would have moved. She wanted to move but she knew she couldn't. Apart from Kitty and her family, she was her son's only connection with everyday reality. The dogs and the garden were the only positive reason she had stayed. And Wheels, of course. She had grown fond of the boy. Boy! She smiled. The man was thirty-five but Grace saw him as a boy. First adopted, not knowing where he came from, then brought up in a Barnardo's home, Wheels loved Grace looking after him. For him she could cook and wash and she could talk to him. He would talk to her. And yet she felt sad. Sad and empty because he wasn't, after all, her son.

Grace thought Julie treated Wheels very badly, like a servant and Grace didn't think it was right. But then, she reminded herself, it wasn't right that she didn't think it was right. It was none of her business but she couldn't help it being her business.

That afternoon, when the first real crack appeared in the previously stable fabric of all their lives, Julie was furious that Wheels wasn't around to take her into town. What was more, Elpidio had used the Range Rover to take some hi-fi equipment back to Tottenham Court Road without telling her! Grace could hear the twenty-three year old effing and blinding in the kitchen to Lolli that she wasn't being treated with respect. Ha! thought Grace. It's respect now, is it? Right or wrong, Grace couldn't help herself and she went downstairs. Yes, she was cross. Yes, she was frustrated but she descended the stairs not in a spirit of anger but in one of determined appeasement. Something had to be sorted out.

"Everything alright?"

Julie was standing by the huge north facing window. The house had been built for a painter and the drawing room had once been his studio. Studio! That word again!

"Oh! You made me jump. Didn't hear you come down." Julie was eating an apple and was dressed, it seemed to Grace, to go out.

"It's none of my business, I know, but you shouldn't take it out on Lolli."

"Take what out?" Julie snapped back.

"Whatever it is, Julie. I know. I've felt it too."

Julie tossed her head, the mane of streaked, half permed hair cascading over her shoulders.

"Don't know what you're talkin' about, Mrs Morgan." She had never been able to bring herself to say Grace. Julie's unreceptiveness got to Grace.

She'd come down to bury the hatchet but it was

46

patently obvious that the only place Julie Burge wanted to bury a hatchet was between Grace's shoulder blades.

"An' anyway, I don't want to talk about it."

Grace looked at that pouty, sulky expression and wanted to smack it off the girl's face.

"Then you're a fool, my girl!"

"That's what you all think!" Julie shouted, flinging down the half-eaten apple in temper. "Well, I'm not. You'll see I'm not. I'll show you!"

"Show us what, dear?" said Grace in perfect calmness,. She was clever enough to realise when she had the upper hand."You're upset because Ludo's ignoring you. And don't tell me I'm wrong because it's exactly what's upsetting me. I don't like it either."

"How do *you* know? He's not ignoring me. He's just ... he's ..."

"He's what?"

"He's got things on 'is mind, that's all."

"That's for sure," observed Grace and bent to pick up the apple core. "Have you asked him what's wrong?"

Julie shook her head.

"'E'll tell me when 'e's ready."

"But you already know, don't you, dear?" Grace spoke slowly. "Don't you, Julie?" Julie turned away and looked out into the garden. July. Grey skies. Where was the sunshine? "I've seen it before, love. Believe me. The writing's on the wall."

Julie's famous shoulders began to shake. Julie's famous everythings began to shake as she sobbed.

"'S'not fair," she managed to say.

"Who is it?" Grace asked gently. "Do you know?"

Julie shook her head and from her bag ferreted out a tissue.

"It's all that Kitty's fault. 'E 'asn't bin the same since 'e went over to 'er 'ouse when I was away on that night shoot." She emptied her sinuses into the tissue and then pulled herself together. "I knew I shouldn't 'ave taken that poxy job! There! Satisfied?"

"Far from it," Grace replied. "And nor should you be,

47

young lady. Don't be the loser in all this. I've seen it time and time again. You're a pretty girl, I'll give you that and you've got a career which is more than some of them 'ave had. Don't mess up your life. Take control."

"What d'you mean?"

"Get out, love. While the going's good. Get out with a bit of dignity." Dignity had always been very important to Grace.

Lolli came in to the sitting-room to tell Julie her taxi had arrived. Without another word to Grace, Julie picked up her bag and left. Lolli looked at Grace and shook her head.

Harriet, the shambling, snuffling mink pekinese, shuffled over and put her head on Grace's shoe. She gave an enormous sigh.

"I know, lovey. Granny knows." She picked the little dog up. Oh dear, thought Grace as she turned to return up those lonely stairs to her flat, I hope I haven't said too much.

A STRINGENT MISS JULIE

After Liberty's, Kitty walked down Regent Street, through the West End, past the queues of coaches disgorging their hordes of tourists and over into Covent Garden. The sun had finally come out and she felt like walking. She saw no one she knew or recognised and, obviously, no one saw or recognised her. It was a good feeling, being able to stroll with no apparent aim, free as air and unconstrained. She smiled as she looked into the faces of some of those passing by and she took a rather perverse pleasure in wondering how they would react to her if they knew she had, not a few hours before, turned down the chance of becoming Mrs Ludo Morgan.

Of course, she'd been thinking of nothing else since he'd called. She turned the situation over and over but from whichever way, the perspective always had been fundamentally flawed. But, she thought ultimately, it was nice to have been asked. She wondered what Peter's reaction would be when he came home and she told him as she knew she would. She had to talk about it. She had to tell someone. Kitty was that sort of person; she found it impossible noy to tell everyone everything.

At the junction of Long Acre and St Martins Lane, she bumped into Gerald Ward, still bleary eyed from having woken only as the lengthy credits rolled at the end of *The Last Emperor.*

"Hello, Gerald."

At first he didn't recognise her, having only met her once, albeit at her dinner table.

"Oh. Kitty. Hello."

"Thank you for your card."

"Thank you for the lovely evening. We did enjoy it."

"It was fun wasn't it. And I'm so thrilled you were able to fix up an interview for Rachel. She works so hard and she admires Violetta so much. It was sweet of you to be so helpful."

"It was nothing. I must say all I'd heard about her was amply justified. You must be very proud of her."

"Me? Well, yes. Of course. Although she isn't *my* daughter, you know." From Gerald's expression she knew he had assumed that she and Peter were married. "She's Peter's daughter. From his first marriage."

"Oh. I hadn't realised. I'm so sorry. Of course, now I think about it, you are more like sisters. Do forgive me."

Clever, thought Kitty but she pretended he had flattered her. And it amused her to observe that just because the first flush of youth had passed, everyone assumed that she and Peter were married. It both curried and appeased the rebel in her.

"That's very sweet of you, Gerald. I'm afraid I should be so lucky. Rachel's far more erudite than I will ever be."

"She certainly has a tremendous knowledge. And very definite ideas. I must say, I've rarely met a woman ... I mean anyone with such committment to contemporary opera. Don't you think?"

Kitty laughed. "I'm afraid I really wouldn't know, Gerald. My knowledge of the higher arts only started when I met Peter. I'm a total ignoramus, I'm afraid. But tell me, there is something that's fascinated me since meeting you both. Where does the Abizzi come from?"

It was Gerald's turn to laugh.

"I can't tell you how many times I've been asked that. It's Violetta's maternal grandfather's name. He was Italian. She *is* a quarter Italian."

"How fascinating," said Kitty. "Well, I must be going. I'm expecting my son for dinner tonight."

"Right. Oh. One thing, Kitty. Rachel isn't married, is she? Or anything?"

"Not even anything," Kitty replied. "She's far too independent. I imagine she's the sort who devours men for breakfast." Kitty stopped. The look on Gerald's face was enough to tell her she had put her foot in it. "But," she said, frantically but lamely backtracking, "there's always a first time, of course." She looked at her watch. "Heavens. I must fly. Goodbye, Gerald. My love to Violetta."

Kitty hurried off, leaving a very deflated Gerald Ward to make his way to Leicester Square tube station.

Well, well, well, Kitty thought, walking quickly through Covent Garden. What next? If she'd served cans of worms at that innocuous little dinner party she couldn't have done worse.

She was just approaching the entrance to The Sanctuary when a black cab pulled up. Though Kitty wasn't an afficionado of Page Three in any newspaper, Julie Burge was very recognisable.

"Julie!" she called as the taxi driver made some waggish remark along the lines of a Bruce Forsyth innuendo: Nice to see them, to see them, nice! Julie was used to it. No, Julie *loved* it, the attention and the foxy cracks. Julie turned and tilted her head to peer over the rims of her RayBans.

"Oh, shit!" she murmured to herself. The taxi pulled away as Kitty ran up.

"Hello!" said Kitty effusively. "How nice to see you.

"Julie was unmoved and stood as still as a bottle of sulphuric acid on a laboratory shelf waiting to be spilled. Ominously still.

"I was so sorry you couldn't come the other night. Ludo said you were working out of town? How did it go?"

Kitty was, as always, being absolutely genuine. She did know how it felt to be excluded for whatever reason from a social gathering based as most social gatherings usually were in London, on couples. Julie was, as far as Kitty was concerned, part of a couple.

Julie slowly removed the ubiquitous sunglasses.

"You bitch!" she said. "You scheming, lying bitch!" She picked up her clothes bag and tottered into The Sanctuary .Kitty was truly aghast and was left speechless on the busy pavement. Heads turned. People stopped.

"But, Julie ...," she called out after the retreating sex symbol. "What do you mean? What have I done?"

Julie turned and fairly spat her reply."You've screwed up my life, you cow! I *hate* you, Kitty Llewellyn! You're so ... so ... Laura Ashley!" It was the worst insult The Tits could think up and the door of The Sanctuary swung closed.

"What a mouth on that!" was one remark Kitty overheard from a passing scaffolder.

"And I thought she was just another dumb blonde," joked the scaffolder's friend.

Their laughter receded down the street as Kitty felt like crying. It wasn't the humiliation she minded. It was not knowing what had brought about the outburst. Surely, *surely* Ludo hadn't told Julie about their conversation that morning? He couldn't have! Not even Ludo could be so insensitive. At first, Kitty wanted to go into The Sanctuary and have it out with Julie but she thought better of it and, clutching her cold collation, hurried away to catch the number 19 back home. Back to sanity.

Had she followed Miss Julie, she would have later overheard a conversation between Julie and the masseuse that went something like this.

"Oh! You're real tense today, Julie. What have you been up to? Swinging on the chandeliers again?"

Julie didn't feel like laughing.

"Summat like that, you could say?"

"Tension's a terrible thing. So common now. Course, I get a lot of public figures in here. Actresses, models like yourself. D'you know, I even had an opera singer in here yesterday. Said she needed loosening up and did she need it! That tense. But then, it goes with the job, I s'pose."

"I s'pose it does," grunted Julie as the girl probed a particularly knotted lower neck. "Oooh. There. *Just* there."

"'Course, I 'ad to confess to 'er," babbled the masseuse. "I told her straight. No disrespect, I said, but wild horses wouldn't drag me to an op'ra. She took it in good part, though. Big woman, mind you. She took a lot of pummelling. D'you like op'ra, Julie?"

Julie moaned, a negative sort of grunt which obviously conveyed her feelings.

"I know what you mean. Leaves me cold, op'ra. I did like that big French chap, you know. Wossisname. P'raps 'e's Spanish now I come to think of it. Did that lovely song with John Denver. Now that's what I *do* call singin'."

52

After a final rub down, Julie went and sat in the steam, clearing her pores and her mind at the same time.

"Dammit," she swore to herself, "I *will* show 'em. I *do* 'ave a brain!"

Kitty sat on the top of a number 19 caught in the inevitable homeward rush hour traffic in Bloomsbury Square. She was still shocked. She now felt cross too, cross with Ludo and she was determined the first thing she did when she got home was to tell the son of a bitch that he was just exactly that.

POST-FEMINIST VACUUM

Rachel Bailey got home just after six. Home was a very attractive maisonette over a hairdresser in Waterloo, not far from The Old Vic. Both her parents had helped her with the deposit when she moved up from Bristol after her NUJ card had finally come through. Her flat had been the badge of her independence and she wore it with pride, on her sleeve, keeping her heart, for the time being, firmly where it had been put by nature.

Her behaviour that night was nothing unusual. She bought her paper from Mr Georgiou in the kiosk on The Cut, double- locked the street entrance behind her and climbed the spiral staircase which led into the immaculate kitchen/dining room. Her two cats, Benjamin and Peter, met her, tails erect and standing expectantly by the cupboard where the tins of food lived. She looked down at them and couldn't help smiling. Cats were so direct. They had no need for deception or phoney emotions. Even affection. Yes, the occasional scratch around the ears but never that nagging, urgent need for a hug. To cats, humans were only really necessary because of two particular and seemingly uncanny abilities: conjuring and manual dexterity. Where *did* those tins magically appear from and *how* did they *ever* work those strange machines called tin-openers?

Rachel kicked off her shoes, turned on *Radio 4* for the news and stretched out on the sofa with the *Standard*.

.She couldn't concentrate. She'd spent the afternoon researching the history of an opera last performed a hundred years ago of which she was very fond and wanted to resurrect. But the research had been pretty fruitless and she hadn't been able to concentrate in the library. Was she nervous and if so about what? Had the lunchtime wine with her father upset her? She analysed herself regularly but tonight, she came up with no answers. Was she restless? Yes. Why? Was she bored? No. Irritated, perhaps, that there were no performances that night she could attend, but not bored.

Reluctantly, she had to admit that it was Gerald. He was on her mind and wouldn't get off. Why Gerald Ward? Not specially attractive, not specially powerful, not specially anything that she could turn to her advantage in her work. True, she had always admired Violetta, always promoted her although, as far as she was aware and Rachel Bailey was nothing if not scrupulous, she had never done so uncritically. She thought forward to the next day and the interview. She thought and she thought. All the obvious questions she had already written down. All the research into the curriculum vitae had been done and logged. Perhaps, she conceeded, she *was* a little nervous. After all, Violetta had been married to Gerald for years. She *was* his only client.

What Rachel did not admit was that she had been confused by the signals she'd been getting from Gerald. At first she'd banished their overtones from her mind. Gerald Ward was, to a greater or lesser extent, Violetta Abizzi. But now, after their several conversations on the 'phone, the lunch they'd had two days after Kitty's party, Rachel wondered just how much of a hold Violetta still maintained over the other Gerald Ward, the man as opposed to the manager.

Rachel's mother, Mary Bailey, had been the driving force in her life. Mary had not been a mumsy sort of mother at all. She was fiercely intellectual, determined that her daughter would not have to suffer the uphill struggle she herself had had to endure in being the first woman in her family to pursue a university career. Rachel had always admired Mary, so much so that she had wanted nothing more than to be like her. Mary had always worked, lecturing at Bedford College until her cancer became so advanced that she'd had to give up. Mary encouraged Rachel's career, was only too pleased for her daughter to move immediately into her own flat rather than returning home to live.

Lying on the sofa, that Thursday night, Rachel realised for the first time how easy it had been for her mother to back her as a single woman in a man's world. She also realised what it was that was making her, currently, so uneasy, the lacking ingredient it was that she now missed so keenly. For the first time in her life, Rachel realised how necessary her father had been to her mother. Call it ... love?

Rachel suddenly crumpled up the paper and wanted more than anything to be hugged. She picked up the 'phone.

"Kitty? It's me."

Me? Which ...?"Um ... Ah! Rachel. Hello darling."

"Is dad home yet?"

"Not yet, darling. About seven. Everything alright?"

"Oh. Yes. Of course. Everything's fine."

"Come over if you like. Nick's coming too. It's only the four of us. Cold supper. Nothing special."

"Thanks. That's sweet but I'm doing something tonight."

"I'll get Peter to call you as soon as he comes in."

"Oh, don't bother, Kitty. There's no need."

"I'll still tell him you called. 'Bye, darling. See you soon?"

"Of course. Soon. 'Bye."

Rachel felt such a chump. What a pathetically limp cop-out. She replaced the now inert 'phone and the empty evening stretched out in front of her.

She was in the loo when the 'phone rang.

"Hello."

Rachel was expecting her father. Kitty would have been bound to have told him. Kitty was like radar, Rachel had decided, and would have noticed that something wasn't right.

"Hello, Rachel. It's Gerald."

"Oh," she said, as she sank slowly down onto the sofa. "Gerald. What a surprise."

"A nice one, I hope?"

"Well ... Yes. Yes."

"You aren't by any chance free tonight are you?"

"As a matter of fact I am. I'll tell you what, I'd *love* to go to a film. Have you seen *The Last Emperor*?"

HIS MASTER'S VOICE

Violetta woke up. Ludo was lying, propped up on one elbow, grinning.

"Oooh," she said. She'd only dozed off for a moment. "Y'look that good, chuck. I could eat you."

"Again?"

Violetta laughed. Her laugh was deep, full-throated, the sort of billowing chuckle that threatens to explode at any moment into huge mirth.

"You're a bad, bad boy and you're everything I've ever wanted."

"D'you love me, then?"

She pulled herself slightly further up in the bed and smoothed her long, thick, black hair from her face. Good, Italian hair. Italian, via Yorkshire.

"That," she said with a Mona Lisa of a smile, "depends."

"On what?"

"On whether or not you love me."

He manoeuvred slightly to be next to her. He threw his arm over what had to be the only chest that could obliterate Julie Burge from any Page Three.

"So, if I said I did ...?" he murmured softly and with urgent intensity. Ludo, when roused, was insatiably and seriously passionate.

Her face suddenly became equally as serious as her lover's desire. She even frowned. She looked intently and deeply into his eyes as though searching for something, tilting her head very slightly first left, then right, as though peering into a microscope.

"By gum," she murmured. "You really *do* love me, don't you?"

"I even want to have your babies, lady."

Violetta knew that she was going to cry. Although the curtains were drawn and there was that wonderfully naughty afternoon sort of darkness in the room, she didn't want him to see. She reached up, threw her arms around his neck and pulled him on top of her again, enclosing his head and shoulders in her caresses. Ludo made wonderful love.

In the end she couldn't help herself. She cried from a happiness she had only ever imagined.

"I never knew ...," she kept saying. "I never knew ..."

Afterwards, almost stuck together, they both drifted into a short sleep.

When they awoke, they lay in each others arms, Ludo's head between her magnificent breasts.

"What have you done wi' the lad in the car?" she suddenly asked, remembering Wheels.

"What lad?" he murmured.

"Your driver chap."

"Oh, Wheels, you mean. Don't worry. He's still down there."

"Shouldn't you send him home?" she asked. "It's past six."

"Why? He's happy waiting. He gets paid for it."

"Oh, Ludo, love. That's mean."

Ludo laughed.

"It's not mean. Honestly, Vee. That's what I pay him to do. Drive and wait."

"But when does the lad sleep? When does he get any time off?"

"When I do."

Violetta raised an eyebrow.

"But when does he get to do what you're doing now? Don't tell me 'e does *that* when you do?"

"It's a very big car."

"You mean?"

"It has been known, love." Ludo raised his head and looked at her. "If it makes you feel uncomfortable, Vee, I'll send him home. On one condition."

"And what might that be?" she said with a knowing smile.

"That we have dinner up here, room service, and then go *straight* back to bed."

58

"'Til morning?"

"'Til morning. Deal?"

"Deal."

Ludo rolled over on the huge, king size bed and picked up the telephone and dialled a longer than usual series of numbers.

Parked in Bennet Street, off Piccadilly, Wheels had just finished a Big Mac. He was sipping at the straw stuck into the strawberry milk shake and reading his third newspaper of the day. The *Guardian*. It was his favourite though he always devoured the gutter press before he heaved himself up to the giddy heights of the *Guardian*. Old habits died hard but reading was one of the reasons he'd decided to take the driving job Ludo had offered. Fifteen years of loading and unloading pantechnicons of flight cases and speakers, lighting rigs and stage sections had finally palled. He decided his brain was atrophying with the monotonous banality of the other roadies' banter. Sex, drugs and rock 'n' roll were still very much alive and well. But, to Wheels, mindless, brain-numbing now he'd got to be thirty five. Half way there, he reminded himself. Now he was able to read, un-ribbed by the coke-dazed, speed-raddled mates of years of touring the world with Ludo's circus. And, he'd set himself an ambition, three in fact. He wanted to take a university course, he wanted to write a book and he wanted more than ever to find his real parents.

He'd just settled into an article about how water particles seem to have a memory of other water particles. His mind had no sooner transferred that premise to the possibility that therefore air particles could also have a memory which could explain ghosts and all the other psychic phenomenon which fascinated him, than the car 'phone buzzed.

"Yeah. Wheels 'ere."

"You can go home."

"What?" Wheels jerked upright in his seat and the strawberry shake slid off his lap. Thank God for the hermetic top.

59

"I said you can go home, you deaf prat."

"But ..."

"But what?"

"But how will *you* get home?"

"I'm not coming home. Not tonight anyway. I'll call you in the morning."

"But your mum?"

"What about her?"

"She'll grill me."

"Then pretend you've lost your voice. Goodbye Wheels."

Ludo rang off and Wheels was left not only holding the 'phone but also, and at this point only metaphorically speaking, the baby.

"There," said Ludo, returning his attention to Violetta who looked not a little unlike the *Naked Maja*. He reached up and touched her hair. "Better?"

"Much. Thanks, love. I felt a bit like I was in a taxi with the lad waiting out there. Like the meter was still running."

"Let it run," he said and kissed her. "Oh, dear God, let it run and run and run ..."

WHEN DID YOU LAST SEE YOUR FATHER?

Kitty had just finished setting the table when she heard Peter's key in the door. She ran upstairs to the hall. She'd already put the ice in the bucket. They both enjoyed a hefty cocktail and the sun was way below the yard-arm.

"You're late! You must have been to see your mistress!"

He grinned. It was a favourite routine. "She wasn't in."

"How disgraceful What *is* the world coming to?"

They embraced in the hall. Kitty nuzzled into his shoulder. She loved the smell of his business suits, slightly smoky, a bit dusty, that faint odour of man. He kissed her again.

"Two kisses? I must have done something right."

"You always do it right," he said.

They broke their embrace and she made the drinks. He took off his jacket and stretched.

"So, how was your day? And what time are the Ellmans coming?"

"You're off the hook," she said, handing him a whisky and soda. "Lily cancelled. Tom's got summer flu or something."

He smiled over the top of his glass as he toasted her words with a naughty grin.

"Dare I say - whoopee?"

"You're as bad as Oliver," Kitty replied, taking her seat on the sofa and tucking her legs under her. "No one understands how I feel about Tom and Lily. They were *very* good to me when daddy died and they are my oldest friends in London. I owe them." Kitty had lived with Tom and Lily Ellman in between Ludo and Oliver.

"I drink to your loyalty, Kitty." Peter took another sip at the very full glass. "Oh, how glorious. Just the two of us."

"Er ... Not quite. Sorry. I couldn't get hold of Nick to

cancel him. And Rachel rang, by the way. I think she wanted you to call her back although of course she said she didn't."

"Nick's coming? Oh good. It's family, anyway. No dressing up at least. And when did Rachel ring?"

"About six."

Peter frowned.

"Strange."

"Why?"

"I had lunch with her today. I didn't think she was herself then."

"Do you think she misses Mary a lot?"

"I honestly wouldn't know, darling. Of course, she must do but she's always played things so close to the chest. I do have one idea, though."

"And what's that?"

"Gerald Ward."

"Him? Now, *funny* you should say that. I bumped into the said Mr Ward this afternoon in Covent Garden. In fact I've had a day and a half all in all but I'll tell you about that in a minute. Re Gerald, he actually asked me if Rachel was involved?"

"You mean ... *involved*?"

Kitty nodded.

"Do you think they're ...?" Kitty made a little gesture with her hand to emphasise the possibility.

"I don't think it's quite got that far," Peter replied. "But I have a feeling it's close."

"Well, well, well," said Kitty. "Here's to them, anyway." She raised her glass and they drank again.

"So what about this day and a half of yours. Tell me all."

"Are you sitting comfortably?"

"Oh Lord! I have a nasty feeling it's not going to be very nice."

"Well, I think it's *very* nice," said Kitty. "For you. It's very complimentary, actually."

"Then I can't wait. Tell me all."

"Ludo asked me to marry him."

Peter looked dumbfounded."I shan't ask you to repeat

62

that but would you please say it again?"

"At nine-fifteen, just after you'd gone. He asked me to marry him."

"Seriously? I mean, he ..." Kitty shook her head and Peter nodded his. "Right. He's not exactly known for his jokes, is he?"

"And, as you might have gathered, I said no."

"I love you, Kitty. I love you *so* much."

He put down his drink and crossed the room to kneel in front of her. He folded her in his arms and kissed her.

"I know you do. And I love you too. But it does rather catapult me at a stroke into a very exclusive elite. I felt quite special today."

"You're always special."

"Thanks. But you know what I mean. Not many women in England have actually turned down proposals like that."

Peter got up and returned to his chair.

"Yes. Very exclusive. And you're right. I *am* flattered."

"Then," said Kitty and she told Peter about meeting Julie outside The Sanctuary and finished up by saying, "So you see I'm sort of a bit cross and yet I'm also worried about him. What *is* he up to?"

The doorbell rang.

"That's Nick." Kitty jumped up and opened the door to her son who was padlocking his trail bike to the lamp post outside on the pavement. He had changed his denims and was wearing knee-length black Lycra cycling trousers, baseball boots and white hiking socks, topped off with a white T-shirt and leather motor cycle jacket.

"Darling," Peter heard her say. "You look like a messenger!"

"Thanks, ma! That's the second time today someone's accused me of that."

Nick came in and dropped his black nylon rucksack in the hall. He kissed his mother and came into the body of the room.

"Hello, Peter." Nick walked across the room and shook hands. They hadn't yet worked out any other way of greeting each other. It is the often the way with step-relationships.

63

Peter got up.

"Drink, Nick? Or is cycling the same as driving?"

"Legally no, I suppose, and so I'll have a glass of wine. Only if there's some open. Where are the Ellmans?"

"You'll be relieved to hear they're not coming," said Kitty, resuming her seat on the sofa.

"Red or white, Nick?"

"Red, please, Peter."

Peter took a bottle of drinkable red from the sofa table and pulled the cork. Nick sat on the other sofa. He still felt a little awkward about demonstrative shows of affection to his mother in front of her lover. Why? He didn't know but it was hardly a problem. Step-protocol would work out.

"I'm sorry, darling. There was no way I could contact you to let you know. You were an angel to say you'd come in the first place."

Peter handed Nick his glass and they all toasted each other.

"I am, aren't I? Actually, I rather like them. Old fashioned Fabians. Not a lot of those left." Kitty looked puzzled. "Fabians, ma. Like Shaw? The playwright? Nineteen twenties. Early socialists? Never mind."

"I've only just got to grips with Militant," said Kitty defensively. "Don't rush me, darling."

"So, Nick. How's things?" Peter asked.

"Oh, you know. Fine."

"And daddy," Kitty enquired. "How is he?"

"Saw him for lunch today. He's fine. I saw Ludo too."

"Really?" said Peter and Kitty in unison.

"Where, darling."

"At dad's office." Peter and Kitty exchanged conspiratorial looks, the sort that children aren't supposed to see or remark upon. Nick was twenty.

"Er, did daddy say if he was going to the country this weekend?"

"He did say and he's not. And don't try to change the subject, mum. What's going on?" he asked. "Something up with Ludo?"

"No," said Kitty quickly.

64

Nick glanced reproachfully at her.

"She means yes," Peter elucidated.

"So, what's wrong?" Nick asked, with some urgency

."I don't know," Kitty replied. "Look, you might as well hear this, Nick. He rang up this morning, out of the blue, cool as a cucumber and asked me to marry him."

"Ludo did! But why? Why on earth should he do that?"

Perhaps, o child of mine, because he considers me to be an attractive and interesting woman!"

"But you're much ... you're more like ... I mean you're so ..."

"So what?" said Kitty. "Go on. Say old and I'll commit belated infanticide."

"No. I was going to say you're more like brother and sister."

"Not at one time, they weren't," Peter interrupted. "Ludo's always carried a torch for your mother, you know that."

"It's a mystery," said Kitty. "A total mystery. And what was he doing at your Father's office. I doubt he's ever been there more than once in his life. Oliver usually goes to him."

"Money obviously not only talks," remarked Peter, "it fairly commands."

"Yes," said Kitty. "It's about the only thing I miss about being married to Oliver. I got to go along for the rides. New York, Switzerland, Australia. I saw the world."

"Now I come to think about it," Nick interjected, "he whispered something in my ear about wanting some advice."

"That settles it," Kitty said, jumping up off the sofa. "I'm going to call him. Right now. He's in trouble. I can just smell it!"

DICING WITH DACQUIRIS

After expending not a little excess nervous energy by pumping some delicate, though undoubtedly therapeutic, iron, Julie had a shower and called home.

Elpidio never touched the 'phone, it was always Lolli who answered in that sing-song voice whose timbre and pitch always remained the same. Whether in turmoil or tranquillity, Lolli always sounded happy. Ludo liked it. It drove Julie insane.

"Herro?" The inflexion squeaked querulously upwards like a bow drawn over a taut string.

"Lolli. It's Julie. Is Ludo there?"

"No. Mr Morgan he no home." Lolli never said Ludo because it came out like Rudo and Grace had told her about it.

"Has he called?"

"No. You want Mrs Morgan?"

"No. Hasn't he even been back today?"

"No. Mr Wheers comin' soon though. You want him to ca' you?"

"Wheels is coming home? Without Ludo?"

"Yes, Miss Jurie. He ca' ten minute ago. Asked for Mrs Morgan. He havin' river and bacon tonight."

"OK. Thanks, Lolli."

"You want I reave message?"

"No, Lolli. No message. 'Bye."

Julie replaced the receiver. River and bacon indeed. Ha! She returned to the changing room and put on the black cotton jersey mini-dress she'd bought that afternoon from Ebony in South Moulton Street, pinned her hair up in a wild, untidy pile on her head and finished the outfit off with a string of dice, each face a six, she'd bought from a street stall on Oxford Street. She felt far from lucky, however. More angry than anything.

Satisfied with her outfit, she checked her face in the

mirror.

"OK, girl," she spoke to her reflection. "You're not the only one who can go absent without leave." She stashed her shoulder bag with the sweaty leotard in a locker, picked up her bag and left The Sanctuary.

She walked from Floral Street to Zanzibar in Great Queen Street. Covent Garden on that Thursday evening seemed busier than it had been during the day. People meeting each other after work, people going home, people enjoying late shopping. She liked the atmosphere.

Oliver parked his Jaguar in an NCP at the top of Drury Lane. In his pocket, two tickets for *Follies* at The Shaftesbury. The plan had been to meet Angela in Zanzibar, have a drink and then go on to the theatre, all very walkable. Angela was a stalwart. Not a stalwart prospect but a stalwart mate and shared his passion for musicals. Angela Carbury, widowed, well-heeled but sloanily mumsy, was the sort of woman who put the gravy into Belgravia - Lumpy, thick, smooth and aaaahh! Oliver had seen *Follies* in Los Angeles when it had first been resurrected and loved it, with Yvonne de Carlo and a host of other faded Hollywood star ladies and was looking forward to seeing Eartha Kitt who'd just replaced Dolores Gray.

No sooner had he walked into Zanzibar than the barman called his name. There was a 'phone call. Angela couldn't come.

Oliver was not a little pissed off. What to do with a twenty-five pound seat for a show that started in three-quarters of an hour?

He resumed his seat at the bar. He felt summery and ordered a banana dacquiri. It came with the customary accoutrements, sheltering under a yellow umbrella. Two stools away, a blonde girl removed the red umbrella in her strawberry dacquiri and twirled it in one hand between one immaculate forefinger and one immaculate thumb as she drained the pippy dregs. Oliver caught the barman's eye. He was drying a series of tall glasses and winked at Oliver, nodding his head in the direction of the tall blonde with the big dacquiris to Oliver's left.

As Julie finished her drink, she turned and, in turn, caught Oliver's eye. Oliver smiled and raised his glass.

"Cheers!" said Miss Julie. "Oh! Snap! Both drinkin' dacquiris, eh?"

Oliver smiled again and nodded. He straightened his tie. In his business suit, striped Hilditch and Key shirt with the prominent gold and enamel Asprey's cufflinks, he cut no mean figure. He looked exactly what he was: rich.

Zanzibar was not at all full. The pain of the unusable ticket burned a little less strongly in Oliver's breast pocket.

"Is that a banana?" Julie asked, still twirling the paper umbrella and looking for all the world like one of those leggy girls who displays the prizes on tv game shows, having no better prize to show off than her own good self.

"Yes. Just the job for a long summer evening, don't you think." Oliver was gone.

"I love 'em. Can I buy you another? One sip and that one'll be finished."

"I wouldn't dream of it," Oliver replied with utmost courtesy. His upbringing had not equipped him to deflect such now usual feminine directness. "But I'd love to buy you one. Strawberry, is it?"

Julie nodded and squirmed a little on his seat so that the skirt of the black mini-dress rode just that little bit higher over her undeniably delectable thighs. Oliver delivered the order to the barman who swept away the old glasses with a flourish and yet another lascivious wink.

"Well, as we're drinking together, we may as well sit together." He moved off his stool and threw his leg over the stool next to Miss Julie. "Should we know each other?" he asked, there being something familiar about the blonde.

"Nope. Don't think so?" Julie replied with a little girl pout. Oh, Julie was now on her third dacquiri, the first two having been demolished in no tardy manner. Julie Burge in her present mood was not a respecter of cocktails.

"My name's Ollie," said Oliver. He found the diminutive won more instant appeal in such circumstances.

"Mine's Julie. Pleased to meet you."

They shook hands before quaffing the next dacquiri. Oliver made a complimentary remark about the string of dice and immediately asked her what she was doing later. They ended up going to *Follies* where they ate ice cream in the warm summer evening on the pavement outside during the interval. She confessed it was the first time she'd ever been to a *real* theatre. Oliver purred. Oliver was having a lovely time introducing her.

THE MARQUEE DE SADIE

On the first floor of the house in Dawson Place, Victor fidgeted in front of the bathroom mirror as Courtney applied the finishing touches to his make-up. The knickers were too tight, the tights were itchy and the boned top to the outfit dug into him. The hairs on his chest scratched under the muslin vest Courtney had run up that afternoon and the hairs on his legs kept sticking through the first pair of sheer tights and then through the second layer of black fish net mesh. His thighs, Courtney cruelly remarked, looked more like two butterball turkeys at the bottom of a string bag.

"Say one more nasty thing and I shan't go," said Victor before Courtney made him make a moue and painted on another coat of lip gloss. "This is purgatory and the bloody shoes are hell. I shall never understand what possessed me to agree to this madness in the first place."

"It's only a bit of dressing up," said Courtney standing back to admire his handiwork. "And it's in a very good cause." It was, indeed, for the birthday party was also an opportunity to collect large donations from the sympathetically oriented guests for the Terrence Higgins Trust. There would be no one there that night who had not been in some way touched by the scythe. "Now the wig."

Courtney attached a huge white organdie bow to the back of the teased wig and eased it over Victor's short, shorn coiffure. The effect was both startling and scary. Victor was transformed instantly into a particularly ravishing woman. Both his masculinity and his forty nine years fell away like the peel from an old orange and he looked like a saucy young French maid in a Feydeau farce, exactly the object of the exercise.

"Christ!"

"Magic, eh?" said Courtney proudly. "Hooray for slap."

"Makes you think, doesn't it?" Victor replied, feeling

much less apprehensive as he appraised the miracle of Courtney's creation in his bathroom mirror. Courtney worked at the BBC. He did costumes, hence the short black bombazine skirt with the yards of tutu petticoats underneath. Gratis wardrobe. Courtney had no conscience. After all, he insisted, he payed his television licence like anyone else.

"We *mus*t go!" said Courtney applying a twirled, ready cut moustache to his upper lip, popping the monocle in his eye and reviewing the finished situation. It must be emphasised that the whole point of the charade was, after all, Sadie's birthday, Sadie being Sam Fielding. Sam was being fifty that night. His lover, Jack, had taken it upon himself to organise the party which was to be held at their home in Hampstead, in the walled garden. Jack had plumped to hire a firm of caterers together with a marquee and had absolutely insisted that everyone came in fancy dress. Courtney and Victor, after a drunken dinner, had decided to go as the Marquis de Sade and a French maid.

"I shall wear my long Barbour," Victor said. "Now I've seen what I look like, I don't mind driving up there with my face like this but I'm *not* risking being seen in the dress. There I draw the line."

"Well, hurry. We have to be there by seven-thirty. Sadie's coming back at eight and the whole thing's a giant surprise."

"It can't be."

"It is. It's unbelieveable. They've done *everything* since she went off to the office this morning. She thinks it's just one or two friends for dinner." Courtney picked up his top hat and his whacky, Jimmy Edwards cane. "Ready."

"Courtney, I can't!" Victor suddenly wailed. "I have a *terrible* premonition! Why can't I just send a cheque!"

"Rubbish. I'm driving you there. I shall be bringing you back and in between we'll have a perfectly divine time, dear."

"If anything, it should be *me* going as the Marquis de Sade, not *you!*"

"But that's the art of surprise, dear. You as the Marquis

71

de Sade and it would go down like a lead balloon. *Very* predictable. In fact, you needn't even have bothered to get a costume. Just throw on those terrible old leathers again. *What* a bore!"

"But I look such a frightful queen!"

"Victor, you *are*."

"I'm taking a change of clothes."

"Oh, you can't!" Courtney protested, throwing up his hands."Well, I'm going to. They can all have their ration of screams and giggles and then I shall go and change."

"Oh," Courtney sighed. "Please yourself but for heaven's sake, hurry!"

"And if you say anything about getting my knickers in a twist," Victor threatened, "I swear I'll bop you, Courtney.

"Into the Louis Vuitton hold-all went the motorcycle boots, the leather jeans and jacket and a few other little props which usually accompanied Victor Burke after dark.

"I promised Kitty you'd take a photograph," he said checking that the polaroid was indeed still in the holdall.

"Is that wise?" Courtney remarked. "I know several vicious faggots who'd positively *kill* for pictures of you in drag, dear."

"Oh, come on," said Victor, wrapping the riding Barbour closely round him. "You go first. I am *not* coming out if there is anyone to see me. And I mean *anyone*. I have a reputation in this street."

"Oh spare me the righteous citizen act, Victor, really. And it *is* only a bit of dressing up, dear," Courtney repeated. "Don't worry. You haven't changed into a pervert just by putting on some perfectly harmless lipstick."

A DOG'S LIFE

Wheels loved the hill from Hampstead Heath station up to the top of East Heath Road. The home stretch. He relished the power in the Mercedes as an effortless surge of energy took it and him home.

That night, however, Wheels was also in two minds. He was looking forward to Grace's liver and bacon yet he wondered if he could hold up under the gentle but insistent questions she would ask as she sat at her kitchen table watching him eat. Like many mothers, Grace would have been an easy recruit into the Spanish Inquisition.

It was not the first time Wheels had found his loyalties torn between Ludo and Grace. Since she had moved into the granny flat, those loyalties had been strained more and more often. Wheels never judged. He wanted no one to judge him and, being a man of integrity, felt he could not expect what he did not reciprocate. However, he and Kitty Llewellyn were probably the only two people who could see that now they lived under the same roof, Grace had maternal rights in the same way that Ludo had filial ones. Although in theory there was, in practice there was no Freedom of Information Act chez Morgan. Not even the merest sniff of a White Paper on the subject. Ludo ruled in his own domain as omnipotently as any czar.

Wheels swung off the main road and decelerated as he manoeuvred the big car into position outside the garage doors. He aimed the radio-controlled ray unit at the door and it swung upwards. Wheels drove in next to the gold Range Rover and switched off.

As he opened the garage door onto the garden, he saw Bullshit lying in front of the street door. Bullshit raised his head and attempted to wag what remained of his tail. His whole rear end swayed on the paving stones although he didn't get up.

"Hey, old boy? What's up?"

Wheels walked over to the dog who opened his mouth and panted. Wheels bent his head low, next to the dog's face and got a very wet, slobbery lick for his pains.

"You OK then, old bruiser? What's up?" Wheels stood up and slapped his thigh. "Come on. Come on, boy. Supper time. Come on!"

Bullshit made no move to follow and turned away, resting his huge head on his equally huge feet. Wheels looked up as he heard the sound of a sash window being raised.

"It's no good!" Grace called out as she stuck her head through her kitchen window. "He won't budge. He's been there since the accident."

"What accident?"

"With the painting man. Mr Burke. Edgar went for him. Can't understand it. I've tried everything. Even a bit of your liver but he won't budge."

"Oh," said Wheels, glancing back at the dog whom no one in the household could make do what the dog didn't want to do. Except Ludo. They adored each other. Ludo could roll him over, tickle him, slap him about and the old dog would merely pant, a radiant contentment smiling out of his toothsome jaws.But Ludo wasn't there.

"Come on up, lovey," Grace called down. "Or it'll spoil."

Wheels went into the kitchen. Lolli and Elpidio were watching television. He could hear the strains of *Wogan* floating through from the flat at the rear of the house. He ran up the stairs and came out on the landing where Grace met him, wiping her hands on her pinny.

"Traffic bad, dear?"

"Awful."

That was his first lie. The traffic for a Thursday evening had been remarkably light despite late night shopping in Oxford Street. Wheels had driven home a roundabout way, trying to work out a suitably defensive strategy for the interrogation he knew was to come.

"Oh, well. Never mind. You're in now. Makes a difference, doesn't it. An early night occasionally."

"Certainly does." He took a deep breath. "Ummm. That

74

smells great, Mrs M."

"It's all dished up. Come on, dear. Eat it while it's hot."

Wheels sat down at the kitchen table. Grace took off her pinny, poured a cup of tea for him and then one for her and sat down as he started to eat.

"Ludo must be enjoying himself?"

By now, Wheels had his mouthful. Blessed relief. He managed a vague "Mmmm". Would Grace be deterred? Never.

"Is he going anywhere nice tonight? Or is it studio again?" Grace folded her arms, leant back in her chair and merely waited. She knew she was behaving badly. She knew she was turning poor Wheels into easy prey but Grace wanted to know.

"Please, Mrs M. It's not fair." Wheels had plumped for sympathy.

Grace changed tack.

"Oh, don't get me wrong, lovey. I'm not prying. As if I would?" She chuckled. Wheels wasn't convinced. "But when you're a mother, you notice things. You know."

"'Fraid I don't, Mrs M. I never 'ad one."

"Well, take my word for it. Miss Llewellyn too. She's worried sick, just like me. And that Julie. *Very* off colour, if you ask me." Grace sighed. "In fact, Miss Llewellyn rang, just before you came back. I felt so silly, not bein' able to tell 'er where he was. And me his mother too."

Wheels chewed, his mind divided equally in two, a scales of justice, weighing the two sides of the argument. Oh, he thought, what the hell.

"He's actually 'avin' dinner with a lady."

"Early or late?" she pounced."Er ... er ..."

"Early?"

Wheels stopped chewing and sat staring at the river, sorry, liver, his knife and fork raised in a sort of pathetic gesture of surrender. He shook his head.

"Late."

"And a lady. Do you *mean* a 'lady'?"

"Definitely. Not just any old bird."

"Do I know her?"

Wheels shook his head.

"But I got a feelin' you will." He scraped up the last few peas in gravy onto his fork. Wheels was a fast eater, a habit he'd picked up since driving Ludo. He never knew when the call would come. "I can't say no more, Mrs M. I'd like to, but you can understand, can't you?"

"Of course, dear," she said and patted his hand before removing his plate. "A lady you say?" she observed from the sink. "Well, well. I knew the writing was on the wall for that Julie. Can't help feelin' a bit sorry for the girl, though. I mean to say, what'll she do?"

Wheels burped and excused himself.

"Oh, she'll be alright," he said. "She can look after herself, that one, believe me. Got 'er 'ead more than screwed on right."

"I hope that doesn't mean another thing in the papers," said Grace. "They'd lap up a story like 'ers."

From down below in the garden, there came a frenzied barking. Grace peered out of the window and opened it. Wheels joined her and as they looked out they saw Bullshit in a state of extreme agitation. The scent of something or someone only too familiar drifted down the hill on the faint evening breeze. The enemy. He barked and barked, jumping, as far as he was able, up and down in the height of excitement.

"Wos wrong with the old boy?" Wheels remarked. "D'you think 'e's OK?"

"Think we'd better go down and see," Grace replied as Bullshit's barking was taken up by every dog between Hampstead Pond and the Royal Free Hospital. The baying of the pack, the scent of a prospective kill, all the primitive instincts unassuaged by a simple can of *Chum* were howling through the leafy gardens.

Wheels and Grace hurried downstairs and out into the garden.

"P'raps it's something outside?" Wheels volunteered. "I'll take a look."

Bullshit had run back from the gate for a moment and was standing, as though on guard, outside the kitchen

76

door. As Wheels, with Grace a few paces behind him, opened the street door, neither saw the heavy bulldog gather his musculature and hurl himself from the doormat in the direction of the chink of hope which Wheels created by opening the street gate.

Like a giant bowling ball, for the second time that day, Bullshit swept Grace's legs from under her and she went down on the grass by the path like a felled oak. By the time she'd yelled, Bullshit was past Wheels and out into the road.

"Hey! Bullshit!" Wheels roared at the top of his voice. The dog took not a blind bit of notice and careered down the lane, out into East Heath Road and round the corner.

Grace picked herself up, no damage done except to her pride and hurried out to the gate.

Wheels ran down the lane but by the time he got to the end, Bullshit was nowhere in sight. He could have crossed the now quiet road and vanished onto the unmown Heath on the opposite side. Gone.

Wheels hurried back to Grace.

"You alright?" he asked as she rubbed her left hip which had taken the force of her heavy fall.

"Oooh," she said. "I think so." She hobbled a few steps.

Wheels sighed.

"I'd better go and look for 'im. I'll take the lead." He hurried back into the kitchen and retrieved the thick studded leather lead from the hook behind the laundry room door and set off in pursuit.

"Shall I call the police, d'you reckon?" Grace called after him.

"Not yet, Mrs M. 'E can't have got far. He usually comes back. Takes 'is time, though."

Oh dear, Grace thought, worried what Ludo would have to say. She often thought to herself that Ludo loved that dog, a present from Kitty when he moved into the Hampstead house, more than anyone in his life.

77

ON YER BIKE

Kitty cleared away the yoghurts and the cheese, rearranged the fruit bowl and offered coffee.

"Yes, please. Black for me, mum."

Peter waived the coffee but offered Nick a brandy.

"Or we have Benedictine, Grand Marnier, Creme de Menthe or something very suspicious from Denmark."

"Oh don't have that," Kitty volunteered. "It's like petrol."

"I'll try it," said Nick as Genius jumped onto his lap, threatening the cycling shorts with instant ladders. Genius had been waiting patiently for this moment ever since they'd sat down to dinner. "Ouch. Careful, cat."

"Watch the crown jewels, Nick."

"Really, darling," said Kitty. "How gross."

"Would you prefer the anatomical?" Peter winked at Nick who mouthed "Balls". The men smirked.

As the coffee finally filtered through, the 'phone rang and Grace explained to Kitty the latest disaster, the bolting of Bullshit.

"But what can I do, darling?" Kitty said, holding the 'phone away from her ear so that the others could hear. Peter was almost giggling after a bottle of rather good Bulgarian Merlot from the cellar. Well, from the cupboard under the stairs.

Grace carried on.

"Hold on a moment, Grace. I need to talk to Peter. No, darling, I'll ask him."

Kitty covered the mouthpiece.

"It's that damn bulldog. He's done a bunk and Wheels can't find him and Ludo's not there. Grace wonders whether she should call the police."

"But he always comes back, surely?" Nick offered.

"Grace doesn't think he's got a licence, darling."

"Oh," said Nick.

78

"Peter? You're the lawyer. What d'you think?"

Peter rolled his eyes halfway through a swig of Remy Martin. He coughed.

"Christ! I don't know. I'm sure it's not *that* serious a crime."

"But it is a crime, though, isn't it?" Kitty persisted.

"I suppose. But hardly a transportable offence."

"Of that, dearest, we are all aware, but you know how Grace worries."

Grace, impatient at the other end, started talking again.

"Then if she's that worried," Peter suggested, "tell her to call the police."

Kitty uncovered the mouthpiece.

"After due consideration," she said, "the only lawyer we have in the family suggests you do call the police ... No, I don't ... With a lady? What lady? ... Well, darling, he's a big boy ... Yes, I know it's worrying but what can we do? Where's Wheels? ... Oh, I see."

Nick turned round and gestured to Kitty to hand the 'phone over.

"Grace? It's Nick. Look, I'm just about to leave here. I'll come up and help Wheels look for him ... No, of course it's alright. Be glad to. Yes ... Yes ... In about twenty minutes. Right. 'Bye."

Kitty replaced the receiver.

"That's awfully nice of you, darling. You are a brick."

"Rather you than me," Peter observed. "It's a big place, Hampstead Heath. He could be anywhere."

"Oh," said Nick carelessly. "It's nothing. I could do with a walk anyway."

He got up and kissed Kitty, bade goodnight to Peter, collected his rucksack from the hall and left.

"What a sweetheart he is," said Kitty as she closed the door.

"Yes," said Peter, suddenly more sober than he'd felt a few moments ago and remembering Rachel's observation from that lunchtime.

"I mean," she continued, "not many boys of his age would go tearing off on a bicycle up to Hampstead late at night to look for a lost dog, would they?"

"No."

"Of course he's very fond of Grace. She used to come to Chelsea and babysit. Stay the night, you know."

"Of course."

Kitty frowned."You're right," she said. "It is odd."

"Odder and odder," Peter replied. "Shall we go to bed?"

Kitty sighed."Yes. I suppose so."

"That doesn't sound very encouraging."

"I'm sorry, darling. But you said it. Children are so *very* odd, aren't they? I mean, I can't think of our family ever having had one solitary socialist in five hundred years."

Peter had to laugh.

"He's twenty years old, Kitty. And whatever his ... well, his political persuasions, he's not a child."

Peter turned out the lights in the drawing room. Genius miaowed. He was already half way up the stairs and looked round to see if they were following him. Genius didn't need a watch. He knew it was way past their bedtime.

"Come on, old girl," he said, putting his arm round her waist and firmly propelling her to the foot of the stairs. "I've got something to show you."

Kitty giggled."You *are* naughty, Peter!"

ROOM SERVICE

To be very circumspect, Ludo had booked two rooms at the Ritz, interconnecting of course.

For dinner, they dressed and went into the room booked under his name. To be extra-circumspect, Violetta left her room and walked down the landing to Ludo's room and knocked. The door was slightly ajar and when Ludo opened it she saw the room service waiter making the finishing touches to a superbly presented champagne supper for two. Even a single, long-stemmed rose in a crystal vase. Aaah!

She took a deep breath and shook her head in disbelief. As she'd originally suggested, she'd often wondered but this was beyond her wildest dreams.

Ludo tipped the waiter generously who left, bowing deferentially as Violetta sailed into the room.

He was yet another fan.

"Ah! Miss Abizzi. My friends and I are coming to see you next week."

"'ow nice, love. Hope you enjoy it."

The dear boy was speechless, gazed in wonder and awe as though a latter-day Bernadette before the grotto. Only reluctantly and very, very slowly did he leave the room. Once outside, he scampered to the nearest pay phone to tell his friends. Courtney Hart especially would be *so* jealous!

Violetta indicated with her thumb in a gesture over her shoulder in the direction of the departed acolyte.

"You don't mind, do you, love?"

"Mind?"

"That. 'Im. I just want to be sure you're not jealous or 'owt."

Ludo laughed and held out his arms to her.

"You must be out of your mind! Not in the least bit jealous. I *love* it. It's such a bloody relief!"

81

They kissed and Ludo fell naturally into the role of courtier. Violetta's chair was ceremoniously pulled out. He waited on her with both a sense of fun and schoolboy gauche.

"Good. I'm glad. We don't want any of that, do we and it's nice to get all the silly stuff cleared up at the start."

"Mind you," Ludo said, sitting down opposite her, "if you were Freddie Mercury it would be a different story."

"But I'm not, lovey and you're not Madame Montserrat either, are you?"

"I'm glad you've noticed!"

They began their melon; Ogen stuffed with the thinnest parings of Parma ham and brusella, a few green peppercorns and mint.

"Have you rung your mother?" Violetta asked.

Ludo shook his head.

"Nope. Have you rung Gerald?"

Violetta shook hers and giggled.

"Awful, aren't we?"

"Let 'em stew," Ludo replied. "For as long as possible. Where are you supposed to be, by the way? Tonight?"

"With Millie."

"Who's Millie?"

Violetta finished her mouthful before replying. Ludo poured champagne.

"Millie is ..." She laughed as he toasted her and they drank. "D'you remember, when you were a kid? Did you ever have an imaginary friend?"

Ludo looked surprised.

"Can't say I remember."

"Ask your mother. I bet you did. Well, Millie was my friend. No one could see her, no one even believed she was there, but I did."

"Obviously I'm having it away with a very imaginative lady?"

Violetta grinned.

"And you ain't seen nothin' yet, lad!" He poured her more champagne. "Well, Millie's still with me and I must say she never lets me down."

"Here's to Millie!" Ludo proposed, raising his glass.

"Here's to us," responded Violetta.

"This Millie," Ludo asked, suddenly serious, "what sort of a bridesmaid d'you think she'd make?"

THE BLASTED HEATH

Sam's face was a picture. Several of the party guests were peeping out from undergrowth which topped the garden wall and saw him slow his pace from a brisk walk to a dawdle as he took in the sight of the white marquee covering his front garden. Jack had arranged it so that the garden door led directly into the tent, decorated with purple streamers, purple balloons, huge cutout purple 50 signs hanging and rotating from the ridge of the marquee. Purple tablecloths, purple napkins, even the waiters wore purple shirts and mauve bow ties.

"What's this with purple?" Victor hissed out of the corner of his mouth. Courtney was oohing and aahing with delight.

"Well, it's ... it's stately, don't you think. And fifty, may I remind you, dear, is a very stately age."

"I wouldn't know," Victor replied with a superior sniff. "Hasn't happened to me yet."

"You," said Courtney, "will perversely be the exception which proves the rule!"

A hundred assorted guests, garbed in outfits ranging from Nero to Jacqueline Kennedy Onassis, broke out into a pretty fair chorus of Happy Birthday dear Sadie, Happy Birthday to you. Sam cried and hugged both Zoe, his majestic mama, and Jack together while the guests clapped.

Then the disco started up and everyone fell to dancing with a will, most of them being pretty sozzled even by eight o'clock. Cleopatra was seen boogying with Sid Vicious, several Dusty Springfield clones partied with at least two Dolly Parton lookalikes, the third supposed Parton being discounted by one and all as looking more like Mae West. And as for Romans, it seemed that most of the white linen sheets in the airing cupboards of the upper echelons of gay London society had been pillaged for the occasion, never to be clean again judging by the amount of red wine that they were soaking up.

After the initial parade, during which Victor lost count of the number of times he had to bend down while Courtney took several mis-aimed whacks at his frilly bottom, wearing the costume palled quickly. Victor also got very tired of no one being able to recognise him. He also felt thwarted. Dressed as a French tart, the likelihood of his striking up anything more than silly, camp repartie with the decidedly gorgeous selection of waiters and fund-gatherers was precisely nil. Donations were large and generous and by ten o'clock, after they'd had a fork buffet and champagne, Jack jumped up on the disco stage to propose the toast. Being ardently traditional and more patrician than *Burke's peerage*, they had the loyal toast - surprisingly few giggles - and then the toast to Sam. Sam took a bow, muttered a few words of thanks and then burst into tears again. As Zoe comforted him and he was led away by two attentive waiters, Jack announced the winner of the fancy dress. Mutters and murmurs skittled through the assembly; queens in drag can be very competitive. Lots were angry and maintained that if they'd *known* there was a prize ... well, really!

Victor's was a popular win, popular, that is, with every-one except Victor. Courtney had virtually to manhandle him through the throng and up onto the disco stage. Victor was apoplectic with embarrassment and rage and, all-in-all Courtney thought, took it in rather bad part. Of course Courtney accompanied the winner and as Jack presented the prize, a rather lovely crystal rose bowl, it was Courtney who got his hands on it first.

"It *was* my idea," he whispered through smiling, clenched teeth.

"You bitch!" hissed Victor and immediately snatched it back. The guests clamoured for a speech.

"Go on," said Jack, "*Say* something."

Victor leered at Courtney who was still eyeing the rose bowl.

"I'd like to donate this superb rose bowl to an auction," he announced. "I understand we've raised a lot of money this evening but a bit more still won't be enough. So, what am I bid?"

Victor turned to Courtney with a wicked grin smeared over his beginning-to-be-lopsided lipsticked lips.

"Courtney? Can I start with yours for twenty pounds?"

Courtney scowled but realised he couldn't get out of it.

"Yes. Twenty pounds!"

There was a cry of twenty-five, then thirty and the bids went up in leaps and bounds until Zoe, the widow Fielding, and well into the clutches of Bacchus, almost screamed out her bid.

"One hundred pounds!" She rose to her feet as the applause rang out. As no one looked as though they would go higher and not wanting to rob Zoe of her moment of triumph, Victor proclaimed her the new owner of the rose bowl. The moment was too much as she found herself totally incapable of walking across the room. She had come as Queen Mary and, like both her namesakes, was now firmly rooted to the earth. Courtney obliged and took the rose bowl. More applause and Victor bowed, feeling rather pleased with himself.

The obeisance was too much for both the dress, the knickers and the tights which all rent with a mighty farting sound which thankfully only Victor heard as the disco had started up over the applause.

Covering his dignity as best he could and with his Cover Girl shoes in his hands behind him, Victor ran for cover to change his clothes.

On went the tried and trusted leather trousers and jacket over what remained of the tights and the knickers.

Victor emerged from the cloakroom and met Sam.

"Happy Birthday, Sam!"

"Thanks, Victor. You're not leaving are you?"

"Not a bit, dear. It's a wonderful party but I *am* thankful to be out of the drag. It's never been my scene."

"Well, you made a marvellous tart."

"Thanks. *Now* for that cute little waiter whom I now have to convince of my carnal intentions."

"Good Luck!"

Sam was mingling. Not one for parties usually, he had been very touched by Jack's efforts and the fund-raising. Senior civil servants are not usually able to demonstrate their true emotions in the hallowed halls of the Home Office.

"One more glass and you won't be able to stand!" said Courtney half an hour later after Victor had unsuccessfully pursued his suit. The waiter had been proved straight. Fun, but straight. Victor always knew when the unlikely became the impossible.

"So what?" Victor slurred. "You're driving, aren't you?"

"I do not *need* alcohol to get high," Courtney quoted loftily.

"Sshpoilssshport."

"You're pissed!" said Courtney.

They were standing by the garden door.

"So I am!" said Victor as the gate buzzer sounded.

Glass in hand, he opened the gate.

"Good evening! Welcome!" He swayed dangerously. "Oh, I say. Jolly good. Look, Courtney! Late arrivals. And *very* good costumes, aren't they?"

The two police officers outside on the pavement looked at each other oddly.

"Come in, come in!" said Victor, flinging wide the door. "You've missed the best bit. I won, you know. Tell them, Courtney! I won, didn't I?"

Courtney was sober. Even over the decibels of the disco, he could hear the crackle of the radio sets on the policemens' lapels.

"Victor," he said slowly, his hand restraining Victor from making, God forbid, a pass at either of the gentlemen who were plainly not in fancy dress. "Let me handle this."

"Are you the owner of this house, sir?"

"No. The owner is ... well, he's somewhere. This is a birthday party, you see, officer."

"Really, sir?" said the first policeman laconically.

"You don't say, sir," added the second.

"I'll just go and get him," said Courtney and disappeared through the dancers in search of Sam.

87

"I say," said Victor, through whose drink-befuddled brain reality was at last seeping. "You're real, aren't you?"

"Quite real, sir."

"Ye Gods! What's up then?"

"We're looking for a dog, sir. A rather important dog."

Victor lurched a little and peered blearily at the policeman.

"A dog?"

"Yes, sir. A dog."

Victor giggled. Then he laughed. Then he guffawed.

"Anything amusing, sir?"

"Dogs! Ha! Plenty of dogs in here, ossifer."

Sam arrived at that point with Jack and took over.

Victor put down his glass and tottered away, not in the direction of the dance floor or the house but through the street door and out into the lane leading to East Heath Road. He crossed the road and wandered, still laughing, into the warm night and further and further onto the Heath.

"Come on doggie ... Come on, *good* doggie. They're after you, doggie, doggie! You won't get away!"

Nick and Wheels had decided to split up. Wheels was combing the area over to the swimming ponds and Parliament Hill and Nick was cruising, sorry, covering the area up to Jack Straws Castle.

And beyond ...

THE GOOD SAMARITAN

On the wooded and overhung path behind the car park at Jack Straws Castle, the famous pub at the top of London, Nick suddenly realised that even if he found Bullshit, there would be no way he could persuade, cajole or drag the dog back home. He further realised that, even on this dark and relatively secluded section of the Heath, the thought of calling out either Bullshit or, worse, Edgar would fall on not a few attentive ears. Nick rather feared who or what might come running in his direction. On hearing rustling in the undergrowth under a stand of hawthorns, he did venture a hoarse, whispered, "Bullshit!" and thanked whatever God there might have been that night that Ludo hadn't called the dog Dick!

He still had that driving, visceral feeling in his guts. He'd had it all day, couldn't understand it yet otherwise felt on top of the world. Two figures appeared out of the dark and turned to look at him as they passed by on the other side of the track.

"Interested?" said one.

"Me. Nah, mate. Too pissed, me!"

"Then what you bloody come for?" hissed the first waspishly. "If you think I'm bloody takin' you home you got another think comin'! Quite cute if you ask me."

"Leave it out!" was the parting riposte.

Nick flinched at the banter. How he hated being gay at times like that. Just an object and an object not even given the courtesy of a silent appraisal.

He was just about to turn and head back for the lights of Hampstead, when he heard the sound of a man's voice approaching down the path. There were mutterings, ravings even but not shouted or yelled. Mutterings. Nick thought he made out something like : "Doggie! Nice doggie!"

Oh Christ, thought Nick. He knew it couldn't be Wheels.

He stepped back off the path to allow who or whatever lunatic being this was to pass by. It was obviously a drunk. Must be. Nick ducked under some overhanging holly. The silhouette drew nearer, quite tall, slim and, between the muttered calls about doggies, there were a few good-humoured chuckles.

Nick tried to draw back further into the holly but couldn't. Brambles grazed his bare calves and he felt the tell-tale prickles imparted by a clump of stinging nettles.

"Ow!" escaped involuntarily, just at the worst moment and the passing figure stopped. The moon came out from behind a cloud and from his thorny hiding place, Nick thought he recognised the face of the butch gay in the leather jacket, jeans and the short, short hair standing not five yards away from him. The face was definitely familiar. The body, however, swayed slightly, pitching and yawing like a rudderless boat in a gentle swell, the man's instinctive posing attitude attempting to overcome the effects of too much strong drink. Their eyes met. It was a good-looking face too, thought Nick. The man's eyes narrowed as he silently calculated the intereaction and assessed his chances.

Nick was just about to step forward into the moonlight when, from undergrowth behind him a tremendous growling preceded the headlong onrush of one very large and very cross bulldog. As he had done to Grace, so Bullshit now did to Nick, bowling his legs from under him, landing Nick inevitably on his arse in the middle of what turned out to be a very extensive patch of nettles. Not satisfied, Bullshit charged onwards, ever onwards. It was all too quick and the man in leather was too stunned by the surprise to recognise what was happening.

"Ouch!" and "My God!" were two of the less blasphemous expletives uttered as Bullshit finally found his prey and wreaked the thwarted vengeance he had been patiently awaiting all day on the lower half of Victor Burke's left calf.

One nip was all Bullshit seemed to want and, as quickly as he had appeared, he vanished. All that Nick saw of the disappearing dog was a wobbling white rear end blundering away through the brambles.

"Oh shit!" Victor wailed. "The bloody thing's bitten me!"

Sobriety returned to Victor's happily blurred senses painfully quickly.

"Oh no!" said Nick and immediately ran to the man's side. Victor was sitting on the edge of the path, swearing volubly. Suddenly, from all around, there were crashing sounds, sounds of breaking twigs, thrashing leaves and branches as well as heavy oaths and curses as the undergrowth in their vicinity emptied smartly. "Hey! Are you alright?" In the moonlight, Nick thought the victim looked ready to faint.

"The blasted thing's sunk its teeth into my leg!"

"Where?"

"This leg. In the calf!"

"Sit still. Just relax. God! I wish there was more light," said Nick who had fallen to his knees in the grass. "D'you think you can walk? We need to see. We need to roll up your trouser leg."

"Oh, *no!*" Victor suddenly yelled.

"What?" Nick urged anxiously. "What's wrong? Does it hurt badly?"

Victor could have wept. He remembered as soon as Nick mentioned rolling up his trouser leg that, underneath, he was still wearing the two pairs of tights and what remained of those ridiculous knickers.

"Damn you Courtney Hart. You and your silly ideas. I'll *kill* you tomorrow!"

"Who's Courtney? Is he your friend? Is he here with you?"

"Friend! Ha!"

"Look, we have to get you back to some light and then to a hospital," Nick persisted. "Can you stand?"

Nick helped Victor to his feet. With one arm round Nick's shoulder, half hopping, half stepping, he made his way back up the path to the pond. Nick helped Victor to sit down on a wooden seat in the better light of the street

91

lamps. The leather trousers were still wet with Bullshit's slobber and Nick could easily see the teeth marks."

Now, let me take a look. I did some first aid at school. Lets hope I can remember it. I might be able to do something."

Victor stayed Nick's hands as they began to shimmy the leg of the leather jeans over the boots which Victor was wearing.

"No!" said Victor quickly.

"But we have to."

For the first time, Victor took a good look at the face of his rescuer. Oh God! He *would* have to be a dish, thought Victor ruefully

."Look ... er ..."

"Nick. My name's Nick."

"Look, Nick. Promise me you won't be shocked?"

"At what? Have you got a wooden leg or something? Please don't be embarrassed."

Even in pain, Victor had to smile. The boy was so sweet and sincere.

"No. I'm not an amputee. It's just that I've ... well, I've been to this fancy dress party tonight and I got a bit pissed and ... and ..."

"And what? Go on."

"And I went as a French tart and ... and ... I've still got the bloody tights and knickers on."

Nick laughed.

"Is that all? What a relief. Well, I'm very broad-minded and it doesn't worry me even if you were a ... a whatever they're called ..."

"But I'm *not*," Victor begged. "I *promise* I'm not."

"Come on. Lets take a look at that leg."

"It seemed that the top of Victor's be-chained motorcycle boot had saved him worse injury. Certain of Bullshit's haphazardly spaced incisors had found flesh but the real damage had been taken by the boot.

"Tell me," Victor pleaded. "Just tell me the worst. I can't bear to look. I *hate* blood."

"There isn't any blood," Nick diagnosed. "But his teeth

92

have broken the skin. I have a feeling there'll be a heck of a bruise there tomorrow. In any case, we have to get you to a hospital."

"Not like this! I'm wearing ladies' underwear!"

"Do you want to die of embarrassment or rabies?" Nick asked.

"Are you serious?"

"Very. You can never be too safe in this world, er ... I don't know your name, by the way."

"Oh," Victor replied, switching into cruise control mode, a state in which he never gave his real name. "John."

"Pleased to meet you." Nick held out his hand and Victor shook it. "Now, come on. Up you get. We'll go and stand over there by the pond and get a cab down to the Royal Free."

"But I don't have any money."

"I do. We can settle up after. The priority is getting that leg seen to."

Victor struggled to his feet, winced with pain as his foot touched the ground. The bruise was beginning to come out. With Nick supporting him, he hobbled over to the main road. They hailed a cab and in three minutes they were at the Royal Free Hospital in Pond Street.

After Nick had explained what had happened to the duty staff, he excused himself and made a 'phone call.

"Grace? It's Nick."

"Oh, Nick. Dear. Thank heaven you called. We can all stop worrying. He's back."

"Who? The dog or Ludo?"

"Edgar, dear. It's such a relief, I can tell you. What an old fusspot I am. Wheels said he'd come in his own time and, sure enough, he did. The dear."

"Not so dear, I'm afraid. He's bitten somone."

"Bitten! Did you say *bitten*?" Grace was aghast.

"I found him just as it happened. I've brought the chap down to the Royal Free. That's where I'm calling from."

"Oh, heavens. I can't understand it. He *never* bites ... Well, almost never."

"He has now. Is Wheels there?"

93

"No, dear. He's still out lookin'. D'you want him to come down and fetch you?"

"No. No that's not a good idea. That big car and there'd be questions asked and then God knows. All hell could break loose."

"What d'you mean, dear?"

"Grace, Ludo's dog has just bitten a perfectly innocent man. What sort of a field day would some lawyers have with *that*?"

"Oh! I see what you mean, lovey. Oh!"

"What?"

"And he hasn't got his new licence neither."

"Well, that can't be helped. Perhaps it'll just all blow over. I'm going to stay here anyway and take the chap back to where he lives. Notting Hill, I think he said. Can you look after my bike 'til tomorrow?"

"Of course, dear. Shall I ring your mother and tell her everything's alright?"

"Not a good idea. Just stay cool and I'll talk to you tomorrow. OK?"

"Alright, dear. 'Bye."

Nick went back to the reception. A nurse pointed to a curtained cubicle from which came ooohs and aaghs as whatever was being done to Victor seemed to be hitting the spot.

Nick sat down and waited. He smiled. That funny feeling in his stomach had gone. He composed himself and settled in for what was going to be a long night.

WHAT BECOMES OF THE BROKEN-HEARTED?

After *Follies*, Oliver suggested dinner. Why, he couldn't particularly understand and didn't really care to delve, but he had had a very enjoyable evening. He didn't want it to end. On the other hand, he didn't want to risk steam-rollering the course of this new acquaintance in the direction of either bedrom, his or, assuming she had one, her's. Oliver was actually quite intrigued.

Far from being broken-hearted, Julie was having a lovely time too and Ollie's suggestion of dinner was more than acceptable.

"Would La Famiglia be alright? It's just off the Kings Road."

"Sounds lovely."

"And not too far out of your way?"

Julie shook her head and grinned. They were still on first name terms. Julie and Ollie. Ollie had found out she was a photographic model and Julie had found out Ollie worked in the City. Everything was going swimmingly. They'd talked about holidays, Barbados, Florida and Spain. Nice safe subjects. They'd talked about films. They both enjoyed films. Oliver knew something about their financing and Julie wanted to be in them.

They walked back to the NCP and collected Oliver's Jaguar, one of the new ones with the computer screen that all but tells how to drive it. Julie was impressed. Although everything about hew new friend impressed her, she was touched especially by one thing. He was *very* attentive, *extremely* courteous and *listened* to what she had to say. And Julie, when allowed, discovered she had rather a lot to say.

The Jaguar purred down Kingsway, round Aldwych, fairly zipped down a reasonably quiet Strand, through

Trafalgar Square and down the Mall in the direction of Chelsea. It was a lovely warm evening. Buckingham Palace flew the flag and strolling couples mingled with the odd late night jogger as they chatted about how lovely London was at this time of the year, about how they'd never live anywhere else.

Oliver, to the best of his knowledge, had never looked at *The Sun* in his life and so was somewhat surprised when the waiter at La Famiglia who brought their drinks greeted his new friend.

"Buona Sera, Miss Burge."

"'Ello," chirruped Julie.

"Do you know him?" Oliver enquired as the young man who could have been no more than twenty, went about his business.

"No. Never seen him before in my life."

"Then ...?"

Julie sighed. This was blow it time. And Ollie was *such* a gent.

"What's wrong?" Oliver asked.

"I got to tell you summat," Julie began, marshalling her confession. "Ready?"

"Of course."

"I'm a Page Three Girl."

"Really?" said Oliver, whose only interest in newsprint was the *FT*. Julie could see he hadn't clicked.

"I go topless."

"Do you?"

"In *The Sun*. Y'know? The newspaper?"

The penny dropped and Oliver felt very silly.

"Oh! That kind of modelling. I see."

"Sorry."

Julie picked up her rum and Coke and swirled the ice cubes nervously, waiting for the axe to fall.

"Why should you be? I'm sure it's a very good living."

Julie looked up, eyes wide.

"You mean, you don't mind? You're not shocked?"

"Not at all. Now. What are you going to eat?"

You, thought Julie to herself as she smiled in grateful

96

anticipation across the table. To be on the safe side, she crossed her fingers under the table. The restaurant was full and noisy but she felt very comfortable, very safe as though on an island in the middle of what had been earlier that day, a very threatening sea.

"I'd love a bit of liver," she said. "With rosemary. An' sautee spuds. With spinach. Do they do that 'ere?"

"They do. And very well too. I shan't have liver. I had some at lunchtime with my ... my ... a client." Oliver caught himself before introducing his son. First things first, he reminded himself in the nick, as it were, of time.

Oliver chose a simple carbonara and green salad.

"Where do you live?" he asked as the waiter hurried away with their order.

"Me? Oh ... Well, I'm stayin' with a friend at the moment. It's just ... well, temporary. But I got a flat ... I got three actually."

"Three?"

Julie nodded her head.

"Yeh. The one I'm gonna live in's still bein' done up and the other two's for investment. I'm a great saver, me. I let 'em out through my agency. To other models, y'know. Very convenient. Most of them's from overseas an' I get a good rent wivvout 'em becomin' a bovver."

"Good thinking," said Oliver, impressed with the coolness of her good sense. "You've obviously got your head screwed on."

"Yeh," Julie said, flattered at his congratulation. "Yeah. I 'ave, 'aven't I? Where d'you live then, Ollie?"

"Oh. I ... er ... Just round the corner, actually. Chelsea Square. Do you know it?"

"No," she said, although something told her that she might be getting to know it pretty soon.

"And I have a country place too. Well, it's not actually mine. I share it with my ex-wife."

"Oh. Nice. Sounds very civilised."

"We are, thank God. Very civilised. You'd like her."

"I'm sure."

"You're not ... not ...?"

"No," she said, shaking that beautiful head on that wonderful neck so that the oh-so-strokable mane of hair shimmered in the candlelight. "No. I'm not married. Nuffin' like that."

"Oh," said Oliver as though he'd just approved a particularly profitable balance sheet. "Oh. I see."

Gerald could not think of any occasion in his life when he had seen the same film twice in one day. But he had enjoyed it. He felt as though he was out on a Saturday date, one of those summer holiday romances when he'd been home from Giggleswick and had met a girl at the local youth club and asked her out. The serious Gerald Ward was feeling strangely giddy.

The, usually, equally serious Rachel Bailey was also beginning to think that her life could be measured in terms other than column inches. Memories of her first year at Cambridge crept into her mind. The May Balls, punting on the Cam; that first, carefree student year and all the earnest young men in the Music Society who would take her to inexpensive suppers in one of the many undergraduate restaurants in the town. It was why tonight she had suggested the Stock Pot in Panton Street. She used to come here with friends after performances in those not-so-far-off halcyon days.

They'd finished their one course and had ordered black coffees.

"So you think she won't mistake me for an hors d'oeuvre tomorrow?"

Gerald laughed.

"Her bark's much worse than her bite, believe me. And it's not as though you haven't already met. She liked you."

"She did?"

"Honestly. She'd be a fool not to, in my humble opinion."

"Don't be so self-deprecating, Gerald. Your opinion is very valued."

"Thanks for the vote of confidence."

"Anytime."

They finished their coffees. Gerald suggested walking and they paid their bill; Rachel insisted on it being her treat. They walked down Haymarket, then through Trafalgar Square. The West End was quietening down. The coach parties had already been collected from the theatres in the Strand, the last stragglers were hurrying to Charing Cross and the illuminated globe burned brightly above the Coliseum.

"Look. It's like a lighthouse," Rachel remarked as they turned into Northumberland Avenue, walking down to the river.

"I'd love to have a theatre," said Gerald.

"Would you? Would you really?"

"Yes. Why not? Everyone's entitled to one dream."

"That's very interesting."

"Why?"

"Well, it answers one of my questions."

"Which is?"

"What you really want out of your life in opera. What you've done for Violetta's marvellous but ..."

"But what?"

"Is it really enough?"

They reached the river. The Embankment, with its beautifully wrought street lamps, was almost deserted. The lights shimmered over the Thames. The tide was full, almost on the turn. The river was at that point where all life on its banks was similarly poised on the pivot of a single moment - Whither, whither? Upstream or down.

Rachel rather regretted her last question. It was more than impertinent, given their brief acquaintance.

"No. It's not enough. It was, when we were married. But not anymore."

"Would you like to come back for a drink?" Rachel heard herself asking. "It's such a lovely night and we can walk across the footbridge and along the South Bank."

"I'm so glad you asked. I'd love to."

They climbed the steps into the station and crossed over the river as the last trains clattered beside them on the iron bridge, hauling the last commuters back to the southern suburbs. Couples and singles sat in the trains, looking out at the panorama of London which Rachel felt she was seeing for the first time. Halfway across the bridge he took her arm. She didn't resist.

"There's no reason why you shouldn't, you know," Rachel said.

"Shouldn't what?"

"Have your own theatre. Well, a company, at least. You're one of the very few people I know who has all the right qualifications. You understand performers, you're used to dealing with the powers that be and you have a wonderful knowledge of the art."

Gerald squeezed her arm.

"That's not the critic in you talking."

"Sometimes I don't like the critic in me," she replied. "It's only the way I earn my living. Just like you earn your's through Violetta. But how we start isn't necessarily how we finish.

"They reached the end of the bridge and passed through a patch of darkness. Rachel stopped and looked over the railing to the river below. Gerald put his arm round her waist and as she turned towards him, he kissed her.

"No," he said afterwards. "It's not, is it?."

MEANWHILE,
BACK AT THE RANCH ...

Both Jenks and Mrs Tarpitt lived in the converted coach house at Littlecombe Park and there was nothing improper in the arrangement. Two separate dwellings had been created out of the disused building after the Major died. Oliver and Kitty never garaged their cars while at Littlecombe and it seemed the perfect solution to a lodgings problem which would have otherwise meant that Jenks might have to go even as far as Bath for a council flat and Mrs Tarpitt to her sister's in Littlecombe.

Living in the coach-house had meant that Jenks could keep his beloved dogs and Mrs Tarpitt did not have to face them nosey parkers as she referred to the village of Littlecombe in general. And it meant that Oliver and Kitty would be able to manage Littlecombe on a trustworthy and productive basis.

Littlecombe Park was an odd house. Odd in the way that clashing bits of architectural style had seemed to grow on the original Victorian Gothic villa, some of these bits being not unlike undesirable warts. But, being benign, they had been left.

Built out of the glowing, honey-coloured local stone, the house stood just a little back from the main road surrounded by a small park of outstanding botanical relevance and possessed of a magnificent view over the combe to Salisbury Plain. In summer, the gardens and park were heavy with blossom and foliage, the days lazy with bees and the hot smell of the pollen of wildflowers. A place for lovers and lying in the grass and listening to the hum of wild things. At night, the dusk was thick and long-lived. Fireflies flew in mysterious arcs through the tulip trees and the viburnums, the wygelia, broom and syringa.

Jenks stood at his door, watching Queenie intently. It

was by now thoroughly dark although the moon was full and he could see the dog perfectly. Queenie, his last remaining labrador, watched Jenks, knowing she would never make it even if she tried to breakaway. She was on heat and the call of the village dogs from beyond the vicarage was almost too much to bear.

"Come on, Queenie," Jenks growled.

Mrs Tarpitt heard him and smiled. Poor Queenie, she thought although she turned out her light immediately and closed her eyes. A soft breeze rustled her curtains and as she turned in her single bed, under her pillow she felt the hardness of the photograph frame containing the photograph of the infant boy. She heard the claws in Queenie's paws making scratching noises on the paved path which led up the Jenks' door through the herb garden.

"That's a good girl!" she heard as the door slammed.

Jenks knocked his pipe against the hearth in his small sitting room and turned off the light. Queenie followed him into his bedroom where he removed his gardener's overalls and his strong-smelling work shirt, put on his pyjamas and too got into his small, single bed. As the dog settled at the foot of the bed, he took up a copy of *Gardener's Monthly* and turned to a section on propagation.

Across the paddocks and stables hard by Littlecombe Priory, the lights in the vicarage were turned out one by one.

"Still up?" Adam asked as he came into the kitchen. Ernest looked up from his seat at the long, pine table covered with jottings, notes and photographs and stretched.

"Almost done," he said. "I'll be up presently. You go on."

"What d'you think about Jerusalem on Sunday?"

"Don't know," Ernest replied absently. "When did you last have it?"

"Exactly," Adam replied. "It wasn't that long ago. But I do love it so."

"Then have it again," Ernest replied, framing a photograph of a pear and banana crumble roughly with his hands. "You're the vicar for God's sake. Who's to argue?"

Adam stood behind his friend's chair and looked at the collation of the latest book, this one entitled English Puddings.

"Oh! I like that. Looks good enough to eat!"

"You did eat it," Ernest remarked. "Last Saturday."

"Is that the pear and banana?"

"Umm," said Ernest. "Though in the book, I'm going to pretend it was made with creme patissiere."

"Very good, dear boy. Very, very good." Adam Ridley sighed. "I do wish my work could see as many results as yours but then human beings are such an imperfect medium."

"I thought your God was supposed to have made them in his own image?"

"Well, yes," said Adam. "But perhaps, just perhaps mind you, he could have been suffering from overwork that day and left out some vital ingredients."

"Without wishing to compete, I can truthfully say that I know the feeling. Tell you what," said Ernest detecting a downbeat note in Adam's usually cheerful disposition, "if you have 'Jerusalem' on Sunday, even I will come and sing. How about that?"

"You're a dear boy," Adam replied. "And I do appreciate it."

"I might be an atheist," Ernest replied, "but I'm not a philistine."

TO BED, TO BED,
SAID SLEEPYHEAD ...

The taxi zipped down Marylebone Road and under the
M40 at Paddington. It was after twelve and there was little
traffic about.

"I promise I'll pay you back just as soon as I get home,"
said Victor more than contritely as for the twentieth
delicious time, the swaying of the speeding cab forced him
to lean against Nick for support.

"Don't worry about it, John. The main thing is you're
alright and you've had all the relevant shots. At least
you're not going to wake up in the morning foaming at the
mouth"

You wanna bet, thought Victor to himself. The injured
and injected Mr Burke was now feeling extremely
uncomfortable from a cause other than the red and blue
bruise on the fleshy muscle of his calf. To Nick, he was still
John, that silly made up name he had given so
thoughtlessly to someone who had not only gone out of his
way to help him but who had also forked out money for
the privilege. Victor wondered just how he was going to
redress the balance.

"Just here, driver," said Victor sliding the window
between the rear and the front of the black cab. "By this
lamp post."

Nick paid the driver and helped Victor to hobble across
the pavement and up the steps of the cream-painted
Regency villa which was his home.

"I shall have to get the spare keys, Nick. I keep a set
buried, just in case."

"Good thinking, Batman," replied Nick with a grin. "I
shan't ask where they are, don't worry. I'll turn round."

"But I've got to tell you. I can't reach them like this."

"Oh, right. Change the hiding place tomorrow, if you're

worried."

"Strangely enough, I'm not," Victor replied. "See that holly tree? By the wall? In the cleft of the branches there's a hole. In the hole there's a plastic bag. Would you mind?"

Nick reached up, had to jump up and hold on to a bough with one arm whilst raking in a fetid, waterlogged tree trunk for the bag.

"I see your point. Here." Nick handed over the soggy plastic package.

"Could you? Sorry to be such a wimp, Nick."

Nick unlocked the front door and helped Victor in. The hallway was perfect neo-Georgian, all black and white marble tiles and minimalist furniture, so was the drawing room as he saw when Victor switched on the lights. Victor slumped down on the Empire sofa and unzipped his leather jacket.

"Drink, Nick?"

"I thought you'd never ask. Scotch if you have one." He looked at Victor and laughed. "Alright. I'll do it. What for you?"

"I think I'll pass," said Victor. "Drink's done enough to me for one night. Help yourself. It's over there. Ice in the kitchen if you want it."

Nick waived the ice and poured himself a Scotch. Before he took a seat, he wandered around the room whose walls were covered in ... What else? Victor Burkes.

"These look just like a chap my mum knows," he said. Oh, the perspicacity of youth! "Well, dad, too. Chap called Victor Burke. Do you know him? You've certainly got a lot of them."

Victor's jaw positively dropped. He looked, and was, gob smacked.

"Er ..."

"Really lovely work," Nick continued. "He did my mother's lover's cat. Sounds complicated, I know but it's a wonderful painting. It has the soul of the cat. In the eyes, I think."

Two and two tumbled through Victor's mind and, whichever way up, the answer kept coming out four. One

106

question would of course do the trick.

"What's your other name, Nick?" Victor heard himself ask, a dreadful trepidation haunting the words.

"Longingly," Nick said with a matter-of-factness which had Victor finally floored.

"Oh, shit."

Nick walked over to the opposite sofa and sat down quickly.

"What's the matter, John?"

"John's my middle name."

"Oh. Mine's Owen. But lots of people often end up by being called by their middle name."

"Nick?"

"Yes."

"I'm afraid I won't be able to pay you back 'til tomorrow. I left my money with my bag at the party."

"That's alright. I'm not in a hurry."

Victor, his injured leg lying out on the sofa, his arm stretched across the carved wooden back, looked intently at his salvation. His heart pounded not only with the enormity of his deceit but with the prospect of losing his two oldest friends if the evening continued in the way that Nick's smiling eyes obviously implied.

"But it means you'll have to stay the night," Victor said in a low voice. "Unless of course you feel compromised. I promise I'd understand if you wanted to go home but it's a long way to ..."

"Gower Street."

"Yes, Gower Street."

Nick felt the butterflies return and the reason for their presence was now clear. Wheels would have a word for it - ESP or something. His mouth felt dry. His heart pounded too. He took a long drink of whisky which burned his throat.

Other thoughts tumbled into Victor's mind. Memories of school days and school holidays, one especially when Oliver had come to stay in Norfolk. Days of first cigarettes, first beers, firsts of every description. Oliver had been able to do it for two months. Victor tried and tried 'til he made

107

himself sore. Then that first time. With Oliver, behind a hayrick, nothing more ever to be said again about it between them, nothing to spoil a friendship which had so far endured almost forty years. And Kitty. He'd been their best man. The wedding, the wedding night. Christ! Victor had been all but present at this child's conception! Incredible. Mind boggling. But then what did Kitty always say: "You know, darling, life is the most ridiculous thing ever invented."

Nick suddenly got up. He put his glass down carefully on top of a pile of magazines and came over to stand in front of Victor. And Victor didn't know what to do as the boy stretched out his hand.

"If it freaks you that much, I do understand," said Nick gently.

Victor cleared his throat. He tried to speak but the words jammed.

"Freaked? Me?"

"Yes, Victor."

Victor started forwards, tried to stand and couldn't.

"How did you know?"

"Oh, you know. This and that."

"The paintings?"

"In the end, yes."

"And in the beginning? I haven't seen you since you were ..."

"In short trousers? I still am."

Victor looked abashed."But not quite as tight. Go on, when did you know I was a liar as well as a drunk and an unholy idiot?"

"When you told me about the tights and things. Mum told us all about the shopping expedition tonight over dinner. But what I really want to know is, what happened to the shoes?"

Victor threw his head back and laughed. Nick stood there, grinning until the contagion of Victor's laughter got to him too.

It was a lovely way to start.

READY, STEADY, GO!

And so Friday dawned and the weekend started.

For some it started on cloud nine, for others it started at a slightly less Olympian level. One of these less blessed mortals was Courtney Hart who, being an early riser and also intensely curious, drove over from Shepherds Bush where he lived in a delightful, although somewhat over-flounced little house off the Uxbridge Road, to Dawson Place.

Courtney was also rather cross.

Victor groaned as he glimpsed Courtney parking the car as he came downstairs to refill the coffee mugs. Victor limped. Like many victims, his initial thought that morning, apart from boundless joy, was the nagging worry that he might just limp for the rest of his life. He also, in the clear light of day, was also putting two and two together about the possible identity of the previous evening's canine aggressor. Victor forgot little and forgave less.

In his dressing-gown, he opened the door to Courtney.

Courtney began by playing the scene from a particularly wounded motivation and merely turned away as he thrust Victor's holdall in the general direction of the open front door.

"Yours, I believe."

"Why, thank you, Courtney! How kind."

"Too kind, if you ask me."

"Possibly."

Courtney sniffed and turned round.

"At least you could have telephoned."

"I tried."

"Liar."

"Again, dear. Too kind."

"Well, honestly, Victor! I was *worried*. We were all worried. Where did you get to?"

Courtney's eyes, even the lazy one, were like a hawk's

and at that moment, through the opened door, he spotted the tray with the two coffee mugs.

"Well, really! As if I needed to ask. You've got *trade*!"

Victor folded his arms and rebalanced on his good leg. He looked extremely beadily at his waspish friend.

"I have *not* got trade! You're so ... so ... Fifties, Courtney."

"So what's in a word? And *don't* wriggle out of it by pretending to be so groovy. Doubtless one of those trollopy little waiters! I told Sadie that's where you'd got to. And if you think I'm naff, take a look at yourself, behaving like a dirty old man. I take it you won't be asking me in?"

"Courtney, my house is your house - usually. But, I'm afraid, not today."

Courtney sighed. It was a long time since he'd had an overnight guest of any age."

And what is *that*, may I ask?" Courtney pointed to the dressing on Victor's leg.

"It's a bite."

"A *love* bite? There?"

"No. A dog bite. It's a long story."

"Too Mills and Boon to be true, I'm sure," quipped Courtney.

"Roxy, dear, will you please bugger off."

"Alright. I get the message."

He turned and waddled down the wide steps.

"And thanks for the bag. Honestly."

"Don't mention it. You can buy me something *really* nice after I've spent the day sewing up the damage in the dress. On reflection, perhaps a size sixteen was a little ambitious!"

The front gate slammed and Victor closed the front door. In the garden, the birds were singing and there was all the promise of not only a wonderful day but ... Shut up you silly old fart, thought Victor as he reminded himself to take things one wonderful day at a time.

Nick was leaning over the bannister rail on the landing, stark naked.

"Can't say I think much of the service in this hotel," he said with a grin. "Trouble with the domestics is it?"

"Nothing I can't handle."

"I heard. He didn't sound that cross."

"He wasn't. Coffee's coming. By the way, you can have a dressing-gown if you want?"

"I don't want."

"Oh, good!" said Victor and limped down the steps into the kitchen. Nick went to the bathroom, feeling wonderful.

The coffee had only just percolated through the machine when the doorbell rang again.

Victor hobbled to the door. On the doorstep were two uniformed constables. Victor blinked. Wasn't this where he'd come in?

"Er ... Yes?"The first policeman glanced down at Victor's bare, hairy left leg which still sported the adhesive dressing the hospital had attached the night before. It hung a little loosely after such an eventful and inventive night. The useless leg had rather got in the way.

"Mr Burke?"

"Yes," replied Victor, his heart sinking like a stone to his stomach and his mind whirring trying to work out if the boy wonder upstairs was the reason for the visit. But no one knew? Did they?

"We were informed of your little accident last night, sir. On Hampstead Heath. In the dark.

"The policeman was obviously enjoying scoring these little points. Victor decided to be grand.

He could be. Very grand.

"Oh. By whom?"

"By the hospital, sir. Procedure."

"I see."

"We think we might have a lead as to the owner of what bit you, sir. Can you tell us something about the size and colour of what attacked you?"

Victor heard the bathroom door open and prayed that Nick wouldn't come downstairs. He hovered on the doorstep, terrified that the policemen might ask to come in.

"Well, it was big."

"Big, sir? How big?"

"Big big. Heavy big and short."

111

"Umm," said the policeman glancing at his companion who seemed to be suppressing a snigger. Victor's eyes narrowed.

"As short as, say, a bulldog, sir?"

"Very probably," Victor replied.

Nick listened from the landing. Through the bathroom window he had seen the police car arrive and the constables walk up to the house.

"Of course it was very dark," said the second officer. "On Hampstead Heath."

"Indeed it was. But I know the dog was mainly white."

"Well, that's a comfort," replied the first officer.

"I beg your pardon?" Victor said.

"Because the dog we were informed was loose last night was mainly white, sir," replied the officer, almost abandoning the pretence of gravity.

"So what now?" asked Victor cursorily. He knew in his heart of hearts that he had been bitten by Bullshit but at that moment couldn't marshall his thoughts sufficiently as to what course to take.

"We shall be in touch, sir. Thank you for your assistance." He nodded. The second officer nodded and they hurried down the path back to their car.

"Officer!" Victor called after them. "Would I be within my rights to press charges?"

"Very possibly, sir."

Victor shut the door and went back to the kitchen for the coffee.

Upstairs, Nick hurried back to the bedroom. Poor old Bullshit, he thought as he heard Victor's irregular progress up the stairs. Poor old Grace. Poor old Ludo.

However, for the moment, he put such thoughts to the back of his mind.

A SON'S A SON
'TIL HE GETS HIM A WIFE

Ludo 'phoned early for Wheels to collect him from the
Ritz. Grace, in her dressing gown, watched from her top
floor kitchen window as he left then dressed hurriedly. She
was determined to be downstairs when Ludo arrived.
Perhaps in the garden, casually wielding her secateurs or
maybe helping Lolli polish some silver in the kitchen. Lolli
had compounded the impending drama by announcing
when she took the dogs downstairs that Miss Julie hadn't
come home either.

Ludo and Violetta came out of the side door of the Ritz
after Wheels had telephoned his arrival and slipped
quickly into the back of the Mercedes. The commuting
crowds on Piccadilly took absolutely no notice of such a
commonplace departure from the hotel.

Plans had already been laid. Ludo had had a feeling
Julie would not be home and her abscence that morning
accelerated his intention to proceed quickly.

"Where to, boss? Home?" Wheels asked without turning
round. He felt a little awkward that morning, somewhat
intrusive. Togetherness wafted in an overpowering wave
of shared cologne from the back seat.

"Er, no. We're going to Fulham first, then home."

"Parsons Green, love. Broomhouse Road," said Violetta.
"Just get us down the Kings Road and I'll show you where
to turn off."

"On our way," Wheels replied, wondering that if what
he suspected had blossomed in the back seat developed
further, whether he would have to wear a grey uniform
and a peaked cap. Change was definitely in the air. He
could sense it as surely as he could tell when it was going
to rain. It was definitely something cosmic.

They drove against the morning traffic and were soon at

Parsons Green. Outside the flat in Broomhouse Road, Ludo waited in the car whilst Violetta ran upstairs to pack a case and explain to Gerald that as she was not needed for rehearsal until Monday, she and Millie were going to pop out to the country for the day. In her enthusiasm, Violetta had completely forgotten about the interview with Rachel and, as Gerald was not at home when she entered the flat, her memory was not to be prompted.

Outside, in the car, Ludo took the 'phone from Wheels and dialled Kitty's number.

Kitty had just taken in a delivery from the wine merchants - Champagne and orange juice and two cases of the Bulgarian Merlot which Peter had become fond of. She signed the note and was tipping the delivery man at the door as the 'phone rang by a sleeping Genius. Kitty looked at the cat oddly. She had often wondered if he was deaf or just pretended to be.

"Yes. 0071."

"Kitty? It's me."

Kitty pulled the stool up to the counter and settled on it.

"And *where* have you been, may I ask?"

"Kitty! Please! Don't. I've got to face mum soon. Not you as well!"

"OK. Shoot. I suppose you heard about Bullshit?"

"Yeah. Wheels told me. But he always comes back. I don't know what all the fuss was about. Mum panicking again."

"Don't blame her, Loo. She does get worried about you. You know how she feels. Be a little sensitive, darling."

"Point taken. Look, I'm calling to ask your help."

"So you are in trouble!"

"No trouble, Kit. I promise."

"Grace thinks you've got a new girlfriend."

"I have."

"So what's going to happen to Julie. I can't begin to tell you about yesterday. She nearly bit my head off in Covent Garden. Honestly!"

"Well, I'm sorry about that. I've got to talk to her, I know but no one knows where she is."

114

"Don't tell me she's gone AWOL too."

"Apparently. Listen, girl, what are you doing this weekend?"

"Not getting married, that's for certain. To you or anyone else for that matter."

"Ouch!"

"Well, really! What do you expect? And to answer your question, Peter and I are staying here, at home, with the telephone off the hook and having the weekend to ourselves for a change?"

"So you're not going to Littlecombe?"

"No. Why?"

"Could I go? I'd be no bother."

"With your new ladyfriend, I presume."

"And Wheels."

Kitty sighed."OK. Three. I'll call Mrs Tarpitt and warn her."

"So it's alright?"

"Of course, darling. But on one condition."

"Which is?"

"First thing Monday morning and I *mean* first thing, you get your arse round here and tell me what is going on."

"Absolutely. Promise. But will you promise me something too?"

"What?"

"That you won't tell anyone where I am? Please? Just to let us have some space for a bit?"

Kitty frowned. Ludo sounded almost bubbling. And at nine o'clock. Two mornings in a row. Something wasn't wrong, but something was definitely up. A veil was whisked away in Kitty's mind as the unlikely was revealed as the obvious.

"Ludo Morgan, you're in love!"

"Clever girl!" Ludo replied with glee. "I wanted to tell you yesterday but ... well, I couldn't be sure. I wasn't sure of anything yesterday."

"Well, good luck. I shan't ask who it is but I cannot deny being intensely curious. I'll ring Mrs Tarpitt now. Have a good time and don't frighten the horses."

"You haven't got any horses."

"Even so. 'Bye!"

Peter came downstairs at that moment, looking for his jacket. Kitty handed it to him automatically.

"Who was that?"

"Loo."

"Again! Is my tie straight?"

Kitty checked, straightened the knot and kissed him.

"Again indeed."

"Mystery solved?"

"Almost. I'll tell you about it tonight. Try not to be late, darling."

As usual, she saw him to the door and she was left with her own, warm thoughts until Mrs Haines arrived.

Violetta was soon back in the car. She had changed quickly upstairs into a loose shirt and trousers and packed a few things in a hand case. Years of travelling had ensured she was a quick packer. She'd left a note for Gerald: "Millie and I have gone to Bath. Will call later. V."

As Wheels closed the car door behind her and she kissed Ludo in the darkened interior, a yuppie mummy marching purposefully past with her baby in a pushchair thought she recognised the man inside the car. She stopped and turned, then she reversed, bending low to peer into the car.

"Wheels! Scoot!"

"Home?"

"Hans Place first, by Harrods."

The Mercedes drew effortlessly and majestically away from the kerb side taking Violetta to her singing teacher whilst Ludo drove home for a caseful of clothes and an earful from Grace.

ALL LINES FROM LONDON ARE ENGAGED. PLEASE TRY LATER.

Kitty started ringing the Littlecombe number as soon as she'd seen Peter off to work. Each time she dialled, she heard a familiar recorded message: yes, she decided after the third try, I shall try later.

In Waterloo, Rachel put the finishing touches to her make up and changed her suit for the second time. It didn't feel right. Too aggressive, she felt and finally plumped for a brightly coloured floral print with full skirt. And flat shoes. She had tried heels with the first suit. Heels were right for the suit but not right for the occasion. They would have made her taller than Violetta. Not a good idea, she decided. And yes, she was nervous.

Gerald came out of the bedroom rather sheepishly, his hair still wet from the shower. He had just telephoned the Fulham flat for the third time. The answer 'phone already bore two of his messages and he had felt it unnecessary to leave a third. It was patently obvious that Violetta and Millie were having an inseparable time.

"More coffee? Toast?" Rachel offered. He grinned and shook his head. A little sadly, Rachel thought.

"No. I'm fine. Fine." He kissed her lightly on the cheek, understanding the make up. Rachel needed the hug and brushed her lips across his cheek and onto his lips.

"So am I." She knew he had been trying to call Violetta and she had decided to enquire no further. It would be her business; after their night together, she was certain of that. But for the moment, it was only Gerald's affair. "And I've had an idea."

"What? Tell me."

"About the weekend. What are you doing?"

"Me?" he said, pointing at himself. "Not a lot."

"Fancy a weekend in the country?"

117

"Which country?"

"England, silly. Kitty's house. I know they're not going down and I'm *sure* she wouldn't mind. She's always telling me to treat it as my home too."

"Kitty has a house in the country?"

"Kitty's a country girl," replied Rachel. "Can't you tell? Major's daughter and all that. Pony Club and Guides. Dib dib dib." She made a mock salute.

"I vaguely remember I was a Scout for a while but I don't think Guides say that?"

"Who cares. Are you game? Long walks, swims in the river if it's hot? It really is a lovely place. In Somerset."

"But shouldn't you ring her? First?"

"Of course. I'll do it after the interview. But there's really no need. They have staff there and everything."

"I'm sold. Done." They shook hands. "Do you want me to come with you, to the Ritz?"

Rachel shook her head.

"Definitely not. I'm a big girl. So is she. And I have to go to Fleet Street first to collect the photographer.

"Benjamin and Peter began to miaow piteously. What cats hear, none can tell but they seemed somehow to sense a weekend of being abandoned. After all, they had been shut out of the bedroom the previous night and, by now, anything was possible.

"Alright, alright. You'll be fed, don't worry."

"So where shall I meet you?" Gerald asked. "I don't think it's a very good idea for you to come to the flat. Not just at the moment."

"No," she agreed. "That would be a very bad idea. How about if I pick you up at four, on the corner of New King's Road.?"

"Sounds fine. What do I bring?"

"Just your toothbrush," she grinned. "And, just to be on the safe side ..."

"Dib dib dib," he said, patting his wallet.

Rachel turned back to the mirror and adjusted an earring, thinking how very sweet it was that men never really stop being little boys. He even still kept them in his wallet!

By eleven o'clock, Kitty still hadn't been able to get a call through to Littlecombe. She'd called directory enquiries. She tried the operator. As Mrs Haines made a terrible noise in the saucepan cupboard and all the lids came clattering out onto the floor, Kitty clamped her spare hand to her spare ear and was told that there were problems on the Littlecombe exchange and, no, they couldn't promise when the line would be cleared.

By midday, there was still no line!

"No!" Kitty yelled into the infuriating mouthpiece. "I shall *not* try again later!"

HIS CHELSEA BUNS

Daylight filtered in both through the gap in the curtains and from the arched doorway into the en suite bathroom in Oliver's bedroom. Ludo's bathroom was en suite as well but this arrangement had a different feeling. Ludo's bathroom was so masculine, almost like a hotel's, which was indeed the intended effect. Ludo loved hotels.

Julie luxuriated in the queen size bed, in the king size bedroom, with its soft, white, Chinese cotton sheets. Somewhere, she pondered idly, there were womens' hands in the decoration of this room. But as to whose, Julie at that moment wasn't too fussed to discover.

Oliver had gone down for coffee. She had offered but he gallantly declined. It was the sort of house where there should have been servants but any sign of any, Julie had not detected.

She liked the house, what she'd seen of it. She liked it very much. Oliver had cracked a bottle of Bollinger in the drawing room on coming in from the restaurant prior to the seduction. That was the best bit, she reminded herself as she re-ran the reel of the previous night's romancings. She felt very womanly, she felt very pampered and she felt very appreciated. She did not delve into which of the many available levels it was on which Oliver appreciated her and she didn't care. ·

He appeared in the doorway, clad in the Turnbull and Asser dressing gown. She looked up and smiled, covering herself instinctively with the sheet. God, was he cute. Bit on the old side maybe, but very cute and that was how she liked her men. Moreover, Oliver was possessed of one of the masculine world's most enticing attributes. He had a really nice bum. And, as Julie added to herself, the rest of him wasn't bad either.

"Hello, again," he said with a wide grin.

"'Ello, squire!" she joked.

He put the coffee tray down on the edge of the bed. Mugs be blowed. He'd brought the works. Silver pot. Silver milk jug, silver sugar bowl and pretty porcelain *cups*!

"So," she asked, "don't tell me you got all this ready?"

"Who else?"

"I dunno. Just thought you might have 'ad people livin' in."

"Sorry. No. Just you and me. We did have someone once, when I was married. A Spaniard. He was supposed to be the houseboy."

"What 'appened?"

"Sad story, I'm afraid. We always knew that when we went out he'd dress up in my wife's clothes. We didn't mind that. My wife was very broad-minded. But one day, he put on her mink coat, mink hat and all her jewellery and off he went."

"Jesus!" whistled Julie.

"Did you know him?" asked Oliver suddenly.

"No, why?"

"That was his name. Jesus. Except it's pronounced Haysoos." Oliver giggled. "Frightful story, don't you think?"

"I've 'eard worse," said Julie. "What happened to him?"

"Oh, we caught up with him. A painter friend of mine, gay chap y'know, located him in a pub somewhere. We got it all back."

"An' 'e got 'iself locked up?"

"No," said Oliver shaking his head. "He went on to have that strange operation and he works in Paris now. On the stage. Covered in feathers and sequins and having a ball. So to speak."

"Blimey," said Julie. "Still, takes all sorts, dunnit?"

"Oh," he said, "let me get you a dressing gown. You might want to ... you know."

"As a matter of fact, I do want to ... you know. Funny, in'it? After all that last night, I feel a bit embarrassed."

"Why is it funny?"

"Well, y'know. Put me in front of a camera starkers an' it don't bother me at all. But, with a fella ... 'S'different."

121

And indeed it was. That inscrutible lens was just that - inscrutible. It had no emotions, it didn't even pry. It only saw what she wanted it to see. A man was a different matter. Especially Oliver. Discernment, appreciation, desire, attentiveness - It was all there, in his eyes. Julie didn't quite know yet how much she wanted to show him of herself; not her body; that he'd seen. Her self .

He handed her a silk robe he'd brought back from Raffles in Singapore. She put it on and slid out of bed.

"Shan't be a mo'," she called as she went through into the bathroom.

"Black or white?"

"Black, please. No sugar, love."

Oliver poured the coffee and then made a quick 'phone call. Kitty's number was engaged. He shrugged. Nick had told him she wasn't going to Littlecombe anyway. It was just a courtesy call. A scheme for the weekend had already hatched in Oliver's mind. All he had to do was ask her.

In the bathroom, Julie finished her toilette, ran her fingers through her tousled hair and started back to the bedroom.

Between the bathroom and the bedroom there was a dressing room; closets along one wall and a beautiful eighteenth century walnut chest of drawers against the other. There were photographs on top of the chest and no dust. So, Julie thought, there must be at least *one* servant if only a cleaning lady. She glanced at the photographs. One especially caught her eye. It was a wedding photograph, groom in top hat and tails, bride in a pre-Raphaelite sort of dress carrying white lilies. And someone else too. Julie moved closer and picked it up. She almost dropped it. It was unmistakeable. An old photograph, certainly; probably late Sixties, she thought but there was Oliver, looking hardly any different and on either side of him, as large as life, stood Kitty Llewellyn and Ludo Morgan! Shitty Kitty Llewellyn!

"Well I'll be a monkey's uncle!"

"Sorry?" Oliver called. "What was that?"

Julie put the photograph down and, both amused and

intrigued, stood with her arms folded in the bedroom doorway.

"Anything the matter? Did you find everything you wanted?"

She grinned.

"I'll say. Y'know something, Ollie? You know my surname but I just remembered. I don't know who the bleedin' 'ell you are?"

"Oh, I'm sorry," he said from the bed, putting his cup and saucer down. "How awfully rude. It's Longingly. Oliver Longingly."

"Aaah," she said with a mischievous grin.

"It's a bit of a mouthful, I know."

"Oh no," she said, almost bounding with renewed enthusiasm back to the bed. "No, I think it's a lovely name!"

She took her cup and knelt beside him, her long legs tucked up under her and held the cup in two hands, fixing him with an intent and ravishing smile.

"God, you're lovely," he said.

"Not so bad yourself, mate."

"Would you think it very forward of me if I asked what you were doing this weekend?"

"Just you try me, Ollie."

"Oh," he said as they both put down their polite cups of coffee in a surge of mutual intentions.

"Oh. Golly."

"Oh, Ollie!"

DEPENDENT RELATIONS

All five dogs were in the garden. At the sight of Ludo coming out of the garage, hysteria ensued immediately. Yapping Yorkies, Mutley chasing his tail, Harriet standing slightly to one side but grinning hugely but mainly Bullshit. His delight at seeing his master was almost too much for him to bear.

Grace heard the barking. She had decided to help Lolli with polishing the silver even though the silver had only been cleaned the week before. Lolli had other things to do. Grace appeared in the kitchen door with her white gloves and brandishing a Georg Jensen fish-slice which had never seen a sardine let alone a poached salmon.

"Hello, mum."

Ludo extricated himself from the dogs, brushing hairs and slobber from his leather trousers and walked down the path.

"Hello, dear. Had a nice time?" Grace managed to begin softly, caringly as though nothing had happened, as though he'd just popped out to the pub. Wheels appeared from the garage, took one look at Grace and scurried back again.

"Yeah. OK I suppose. What's that bike doing here?"

"Oh. That's Nick's. He came up last night to help me and Wheels look for Edgar."

She stood aside to let Ludo in and followed him.

"Can I make you some coffee, dear? Or perhaps you'd like some breakfast?"

"No thanks, love. I've done all that."

"Will you be staying for lunch?"

"Mum! Please."

"What, dear?"

"Questions, questions ..."

He slung his jacket onto the sofa and sat down, stretching his long legs under the coffee table and resting his head on folded arms behind it. He looked out through the huge picture window. He wondered if Violetta would like the view. He couldn't wait to bring her to the house. He wanted her to love it as much as he did. But mainly he remembered what Kitty had told him ... Be a bit sensitive ...

"I hear Julie's out."

Grace, standing in front of the swing-door to the kitchen, didn't answer at first and polished furiously with the Goddards.

"Mum? Did you hear me? I asked you if Julie was out."

Grace had decided that he'd been sufficiently snappish with her to afford her the indulgence of feeling hurt.

"I don't hear questions like that," she replied woundedly. "Gets me in all sorts of trouble."

"Mother! Put that wretched thing down and come here."

He couldn't help smiling as she spread the silver cloth on the table, reverently topped it with the fish-slice and then peeled off the white cotton gloves with all the superiority of a ancient stripper.

"Where do you want me?"

"Here. On this sofa. Next to me."

She sniffed.

"Where you belong, you silly old bat!"

Grace patted her neat, salt 'n' pepper perm and obeyed. She limped slightly, the result of last night's spill on the lawn. She sat down.

"Well. I'm here," she said stiffly.

Ludo leaned slightly away from her and looked at her, grinning.

"Now what sort of face is that on my best girl?"

"It's the face God gave me. It was good enough for your father may I remind you."

"Ah!" he said. "Not that one. He liked the smiling version. Not the pouty one." He put his arm round her and drew her to him. Grace knew she was going to cry. She was not the sort of woman to bear grudges or to extend domestic dramas. She felt the tears flow down her cheeks and she searched in the pocket of her housecoat for a tissue.

"It's no good," she sobbed. "It's awful. But I just can't help it. I worry. I'm a worrier. I'm the *last* person you need."

"Hey, hey. Now dry those eyes. Come on." She withdrew slightly from him, blew her nose and wiped her eyes. "Now a smile." She smiled, as best she could and then saw the funny side.

"Oh, go on with you. You *always* get round me in the end, don't you?"

"Always. And that's just the way it's going to be. Friends again?"

She nodded her head.

"Of course we are. But it's true what I said. I shouldn't be here, lovey. It's not right. For me. For either of us. You know that. We always 'ad lovely times when you came to visit. Now all we do is quarrel."

Ludo sighed.

"Why do we quarrel, mum?"

"Because we're too alike, that's why. Both stubborn, both selfish and we've *both* been spoiled rotten. We're two very lucky people, Ludo. We have so much that we find we haven't got enough to do."

"And that's the bottom line?"

"The way I see it, anyhow. You don't need me, lovey. You need a wife. Yes. There! Never thought you'd hear your old mother say it, did you? Apart from Kitty of course but she's special. Always has been, always will be."

"God, it's a funny old thing, isn't it?"

"What is?"

"Love. Love is *odd*. D'you know, mum, I've written so many songs about it, sung so many songs about and yet I don't think I've really ever known just how complicated it all is. I mean, there's so many different sorts. I love you, I love Kitty, I love Wheels, I love Bullshit ... there's four. All different, each one doing a different job."

"And Julie?" Grace encouraged.

"Oh, mum! That's not love. I know it, you know it, she knows it. She's a great girl, don't get me wrong but it's not ... not ... well, is it?"

126

"No, dear. It's not." Ludo got up and strode across the room to the piano and sat down. He started playing a Bach prelude.

"I remember that!" Grace said. She felt happy again, glad that they'd had their cuddle. She knew she didn't have to ask any more questions. She could see by the look on his face, his famous smile, that the lady in question was going to be more than a bit special.

"My grade six piece," Ludo said. "Funny the things you remember. Haven't thought about it in ages."

"Is she ...?" Grace started to say. She stopped herself although Ludo had heard. He grinned at her and stopped playing. He put his finger to his lips.

"Not yet, mum. Soon, I promise. But not yet. I can't risk tempting providence. Trust me?"

"Course I do, love. Hope she can!"

"Ah!" he said jumping up from the piano stool. "I can see I'm not going to be able to get away with anything."

He came across the room to her as she stood up. He hugged her.

"I love you, mum."

"It would have been a wicked waste of two lives if you didn't."

Wheels came into the drawing room.

"Want a hand, boss?"

"Yeah. In a minute. Better go and get your things together."

"Right. Usual for you, boss?"

"Wheels?" Grace called after him as he sprang up the stairs. "Where are you off to?"

Wheels fled.

"We're going for a little drive in the country, mum."

"Where?" Grace asked anxiously, loathing the prospect of any extension of the mystery. "What country?"

"The country country. England's green and pleasant land? Coupla days at the most. Then on Monday, you'll know everything."

"Oh dear! It's so ... so vague!"

"Mum! Don't worry! Honestly. I have my reasons. *We*

127

have our reasons. You'll understand, I promise."

"P'raps I'll just go and help Wheels," said Grace with grim determination as she made for the foot of the stairs.

"Mother! Leave Wheels alone. None of your gentle Gestapo tactics if you please. Be patient."

"Mothers aren't," she protested. "It's not in their nature."

Ludo firmly moved her aside as he started up the stairs.

"Stay!" he commanded. "Sit!" he said in Barbara Woodhouse tones. Grace tutted but obeyed. She would call Kitty, that's what she'd do. After they'd gone.

BLANK TAPE

Rachel was flustered. She was already flustered when Craig Macdonald, her editor, told her the photographer had just called in to say he'd meet her at the Ritz. That hiccup in the logistics threw her from fluster to panic and she raced through the late morning traffic in a taxi.

She arrived at the Ritz promptly at half-past-twelve and went into the bar, the pre-arranged rendezvous with Violetta. No Violetta, no photographer. She sat down at a table and was asked by a waiter what her pleasure was? She ordered a Perrier, safe. She checked her shoulder bag for the umpteenth time - Wirebound reporter's pad, yes; tape recorder, yes; spare batteries just in case, yes. She looked at her watch. Two minutes gone half- past. The waiter brought her Perrier.

The Ritz bar was a haven, an insulated pocket of calm amidst the writhing of London's traffic, tourists and townsfolk all about. Well, it should have been a haven. Rachel sipped again at her Perrier and checked her watch.

At twenty-five-to-one, the photographer, John Rogers, arrived. He was a freelance, good but uncontrollable. If he thought a photo of a royal could get him more money, his commissioned work was elbowed to one side - never abandoned, merely delayed. But he was good.

"Not here then?" he said jauntily as he pulled up a chair. "Twelve-thirty I was booked for." He too looked at his watch.

"As you can see," said Rachel edgily. "Probably the traffic."

"Oh well. What's that?" he asked, pointing to her glass.

"Perrier."

"Fancy anything stronger? G and T?"

She shook her head.

"Spritzer?" He ordered himself a lager from the bar and rejoined her.

"So who have you been hounding this morning?"

"Me?" he said, pretending to be shocked. "As if I would. Fergie, actually. Shopping in Beauchamp Place. Rumour had it Di was going with her."

"What a scoop," Rachel remarked acidly.

"Yeah. That would have paid the mortgage for a few weeks," he remarked. "Still, a bird in the hand, as they say."

"Or in the lens," Rachel offered. She checked the time again. "Where the hell is she?"

"You're a bit tetchy?" Rogers observed, not unkindly. "They say she's pretty much OK, this Violetta. Not at all the valkyrie."

"Oh, very good, John. Nice cultural analogy there."

"Yeah," he said with a grin. "Not bad." He eyed Rachel's legs. Is she a dyke, he wondered in passing? Several serpent scribblers had hissed at the possibility. He wiped it out. He'd always fancied her but today time was pressing. A pass would have to wait. This should have been a five minute job.

Ten-to-one. No show.

"This is not like her," Rachel insisted, by now terrified that if Violetta had decided to abort the interview, perhaps it was because she had found out about herself and Gerald. But how? Rachel rummaged through all the likely ways but there were none. No one knew. Except Gerald and he wouldn't have said anything. He wouldn't! But what if he had? What would she tell Craig Macdonald who had saved space for her? What would she do if it ever got out that the Bailey/Abizzi interview was spiked unwritten because of bonking Bailey herself?

"She's not going to show," opined Rogers, draining his lager. "I can tell."

"How? How on earth can you tell?" said Rachel viciously.

"A feeling. You develop it. Waiting around for people. You know when they're not going to show. Sorry, love, but I have another shoot. Will you call Mac or shall I?"

Rachel sighed. Now she was angry as well as frightened.

130

"I will. We'll just have to use a library shot."

"Yuk! Gross," he said, standing up, his shoulders and chest draped with photographic apparatus. "Shame, too. I'd've liked a few shots myself. Hear she's gonna be a biggie."

"She *is* a biggie already," muttered Rachel defensively."

Well, cheers then, Rach. See you around." He bid his farewell and was gone.

Rachel checked her purse for change and then went to make some calls. Gerald wasn't in at the Fulham flat. Only the answer machine. She didn't leave a message.

Then she tried her father. He was also out. Lunch and then a meeting at the Arts Council so his secretary said. She left a message. Peter's secretary, Jessa, took good message and she could be trusted. Rachel told her she'd call back.

She went back into the bar to check once more but it sported no divas of any size, shape or lateness.

She rang Craig Macdonald. He was not pleased. Surely, he snarled, opera singers don't just disappear. Of course not, she parried, and assured him she would track Violetta down. By Monday, he ultimated, Monday, had she got that? Monday at the latest or he'd give the space to something more zappy. Yes, she agreed, Monday.

She went to the reception and asked if they would cancel her reservation in the dining room. It had been made by Gerald in the name of Abizzi.

"Ah," said the desk clerk who was a friend of the room service waiter on the first floor, "Yes. Miss Abizzi. You must have missed her. She checked out earlier."

"Checked out!" said Rachel, her teeth deeply bedded in his casual remark.

"Yes, Madam. Very much earlier this morning."

Rachel glared at him. His training reminded him that he had been more than indiscreet. Rachel could be anyone, a reporter even.

"What time was this?" she demanded.

"Er ... I'm afraid I can't say, madam."

"But you just said earlier. How *much* earlier? Five

131

minutes? Five hours? How long!"

He blanked her and shrugged, turning away to fulfill her request on the telephone to cancel the table.

"Thank *you*!" Rachel said and stormed across the reception foyer.

She collared the doorman, smiling sweetly.

"Excuse me, I'm Rachel Bailey. I was supposed to be meeting my friend Violetta Abizzi here? I've just had a message that she had to rush off. It's all very odd, you see, I've travelled down from York to meet her and it's, well, most mysterious?"

The doorman appraised her and, finding it quite likely this flower printed young woman could be bona fide, spilled a few beans.

"Oh, I am sorry, madam. Yes. Miss Abizzi left at about nine-thirty this morning. Big limo was waiting for them."

"Them?" said Rachel, but a little too quickly, arching an eyebrow.

It was too much, too insidious and the doorman spotted it immediately."Yes, madam." He turned away as a Rolls pulled up at the pavement. He hurried across to open the door.

"So her husband was with her?" Rachel called after him.

"That's right, madam," was all the doorman would say.

Really, thought Rachel. Then I wonder who it was in my bed last night?

LONG LUNCH HOURS

At ten-to-one, Kitty was almost beside herself. The line to Somerset was still out of order and so she decided to ring Ludo.

Lolli and Elpidio had the afternoon off and had gone to visit Lolli's sister in Kings Cross. Grace answered the 'phone, not content with the answer machine. She was on guard and she was taking it seriously.

"Oh, it's you, lovey! ... What? ... You sound in a right state."

"I am," said Kitty. "I *have* to speak to Ludo."

"You just missed him, dear. Well, not just. He left about an hour ago. Going off somewhere for the weekend, he said. Told me not to worry and I'm not. In fact, I'm quite pleased ... " Grace drew breath. "I suppose you've heard, lovey?"

"Heard what?" replied Kitty diplomatically.

"About the new lady friend. Sounds ever so serious to me."

"Oh, yes. He did mention something about it."

"So he 'as spoken to you, then. I am pleased. Course, I'm sorry too 'cos I honestly thought that one day, well ... things never work out like you plan, do they?"

"They certainly don't," said Kitty grimly. "Darling, can you give me the number of the car 'phone, then. You see it's about the weekend, I need to talk to him."

Grace sighed.

"Can't 'elp you there, love. That's one number he never gives me. Wheels neither. Says it's more than 'is job's worth."

"So we can't contact him at all?"

"Not until he rings in, love. Then I'll tell him to call you, shall I?"

It was Kitty's turn to sigh. Grace was right. The best laid plans et cetera, et cetera. She could see her peaceful weekend getting off to a bumpy beginning.

"No. It'll be too late. Darling, I have to go. Talk to you later. 'Bye."

"Righty-o Kitty. 'Bye, dear!"

Kitty put the 'phone down and immediately picked it up to dial Peter. She had to let him know that she had no alternative under the circumstances but to jump in the car and drive down to Littlecombe to warn Mrs Tarpitt.

Mrs Haines called down the stairs from the bathroom.

"Got any razor-blades, Mrs Llewellyn?"

"Why?" shouted Kitty her fingers flying over the buttons and wondering if Mrs Haines needed a shave.

"This furring on the taps. An' on the sink. 'S'dreadful! Mrs Bailey wouldn't have liked it at all. I get rid of it in a jiffy with a nice sharp razor blade."

Peter's office number was engaged too. Kitty jabbed her finger down on the re-dial button.

"Try in Mr Bailey's wash bag," she called. "You might be lucky." Still engaged. Re-dial. "Where did Mrs Bailey keep them?" she called again, archly

."Same place," was the reply.

Then perhaps the old regime was still alive after all, thought Kitty as she got her call through.

"Hello. This is Mrs ... Mrs ... Llewellyn," she said. She usually said Bailey but with the bat-eared Mrs Haines upstairs she decided she oughtn't to risk it. "Mr Bailey, please."

"Sorry. Out to lunch. Can I take a message?" asked the temporary switchboard operator who didn't recognise Kitty's voice.

"No. Can I speak to Jessa, please. His secretary."

"Hold the line," instructed the operator.

Kitty waited. And waited.

"Kitty?"

"Yes. Jessa. Where is he?"

"Lunch and then the Arts Council. I was just going to call you. I'm afraid he has to go to a meeting at six-thirty and won't be with you 'til seven-fifteen. He did say make sure and say sorry. There. I've said it."

"Oh, poop!"

"Anything the matter?"

"Oh, Jessa. Don't ask. Even if I told you, you wouldn't believe me."

"Try me."

"You'd be better off listening to the speaking clock. Listen, tell him that I've had a little emergency. Nothing serious but I've had to drive down to Littlecombe. Tell him I'll be back ... No, on second thoughts, if the traffic's alright, I should be back before him."

"Message ends?"

"Over and out."

"OK 'Bye. Have a nice weekend."

"Thanks, Jessa. Believe me, I intend to, whatever the odds!"

Kitty finished off the last of a mug of coffee and hurried upstairs. She took her bag and her keys and an anorak and called up to Mrs Haines.

"I have to go out, Mrs Haines."

The cleaning lady came to the top of the stairs.

"Oh, right. Will you be long?"

"I have to drive down to Littlecombe so can you make sure you lock up properly and make sure Genius is back in the house? He's sitting in the sun on the lawn. Yes?"

"Right you are. See you Monday, Mrs Llewellyn."

Kitty flew out of the door, for once wishing that she was Mrs Bailey so people wouldn't *keep* calling her Mrs Llewellyn. She felt like her own mother.

Grace settled back on the sofa and went back to reading *The People's Friend*. It always had lovely stories and Grace did like a good story. She had a bag of Clarnico chocolate mint creams by her, Stars and Stripes at her feet and her other vicarious children arranged in various shapes of sleeping forms around the room.

The buzzer in the kitchen heralded the prescence of someone at the street door.

"Oh, bother!" she sighed, struggling up as she had to from the feathery depths of the sofa. "If it's fans again, they'll get a piece of my mind. Invading our privacy. What

135

do you say, boys?" Mutley was the only one to have got up. he followed her to the kitchen, tail wagging and whining. Bullshit opened one eye, didn't think the interruption was serious enough to warrant actually barking and went back to sleep. Harriet didn't even react. She didn't want to spoil her hair.

"Who is it?" sparked Grace into the receiver. She switched on the video which surveyed anyone who stood in the street outside the house. She didn't need a verbal response to have her question answered.

Two policemen stood in the road, their patrol car, parked on the pavement.

"Police, madam. Can we come in?"

"There's nobody here," said Grace.

"You're here, madam. Are you Mrs Grace Morgan?"

"I might be," Grace replied. "What do you want?"

"We've come about your missing dog." The officer pulled out his warrant card and flashed it to the camera. "Remember? You called us last night. I spoke to you then."

"Oh," said Grace. "Yes. But 'e came back, officer. Edgar's here. He's not lost anymore."

"We need to talk to you about what he was doing when he was lo‹t," replied the policeman. "I take it he is your dog, Mrs Morgan."

"Oh, no. Edgar's my son's."

"That would be Mr Ludo Morgan?"

"Yes. But he's out."

"Look, can I come in, madam? It would be easier face to face."

Grace frowned; she wasn't sure what to do. True he had flashed a warrant card but without her glasses, it could have been a Marks and Spencer credit card.

"Well, alright. But I have a very fierce dog, you know!"

"We're well aware of that, madam."

She saw the policemen exchange looks but she couldn't see them raising their eyebrows and nor did she see the second officer, who remained outside, screwing his finger into the side of his head.

Grace pressed the entry button and after she saw the

136

policeman come in she hurried to the kitchen door. By now, all the dogs, even Harriet, had become curious and crowded round her legs as she looked out through the crack.

The officer looked through and over her shoulder to where Bullshit stood squarely, scowling and snuffling as he tried to identify the newcomer as friend or foe.

"I am sorry about this, Mrs Morgan, but we have reason to believe that your bulldog there attacked a man last night."

"Nonsense," said Grace defiantly. "He doesn't bite. Ever."

"That may be so, madam but the victim has given us to believe that he was attacked by a bulldog. And I thought you just said the dog was fierce."

"He's like this country!" Grace cracked. "Very quiet if he's left alone but 'e's got teeth if he needs to defend what's right."

"Quite, madam."

"Anyway, there must be dozens of bulldogs round 'ere. Who says it was our Edgar? Who's this victim you keep goin' on about?"

"The victim's name is Burke," replied the officer as patiently as he could. "Victor Burke."

"Never ..." Grace was about to say she'd never heard of him but of course, she had. She also had the presence of mind to say no more. "Oh," was all she replied eventually but couldn't help adding in the dog's defence, "An' 'e was probably taunting the dog in any case."

"That's as maybe, Mrs Morgan but I'm afraid dogs' rights isn't the same as human beings'."

"The law's an ass," she replied stoutly. "Everyone knows that."

The officer glared at her, gimlet-eyed.

"So what's to happen?" she persisted."Nothing as yet, madam. We're merely verifying a few facts. Perhaps nothing will happen if the gentlemen decides not to press charges."

"And if he does?"

"Then the dog may have to be destroyed," said the policeman flatly. "Depends on what the magistrate says. Can't have this 'appening again. Could be a little child next time."

Grace couldn't believe her ears. Destroyed? Impossible! Never. Not if she had anything to do with it. But where was everyone? Why did it *have* to be today when she was alone in the house?

"I'll be in touch, Mrs Morgan. Good afternoon."

"Good ... afternoon," Grace whispered as the policeman walked away and back to his car. The street door slammed.

"Oh! Oh dear!"

Grace closed the kitchen door and tried to think. She'd 'phone Kitty. that's what. She hurried to the wall phone and dialled. She waited, it seemed, a millenium before there was an answer.

"Yaaays." It was Mrs Haines. Not good on the telephone was Mrs Haines.

"Kitty?"

"No. Out."

"Who's that?"

"This is Patricia Haines."

"Who are you?"

"I work for Mr Bailey. Who are you?"

"Where's Kitty?"

"I jus' said. Out. Gorn to Littlecombe she said."

"Do you have the number?" Grace asked. Mrs Haines looked at the pad hanging by the telephone. There was a list of numbers - Nick's, Rachel's, Peter's office, Littlecombe. Mrs Haines read the number and the code to Grace.

"'Course," she said, "I shouldn't be doin' this, you know. An' it won't do you no good, neither."

"Why?"

"Mrs Llewellyn's been tryin' it 'erself all mornin'. Something about a toilet."

"A toilet?"

"Yeah. Kept sayin "O Loo, O Loo" as she dialled. Very worried she was."

138

"Thank you," said Grace and put the receiver down. So, that's where he'd gone. Him, Wheels, Kitty *and* the new lady friend. It was incomprehensible. Nothing was making sense today. Grace shook her head and looked down at the row of faces who sensed her anxiety. Mutley whined and came and lay at her feet. Bullshit blinked. Even Stars and Stripes and Harriet seemed to stand as one. And that's just as it should be with family, Grace thought to herself; all for one and one for all.

"No one's going to touch a hair of your head, my darlin'," she said to Bullshit who snuffled and sighed. "You jus' wait there and granny'll go and get her coat and a few things and we'll get you away from 'ere. They'll never take you, my darlin'. Never! 'Cept over my dead body!"

She quickly scribbled a note to Lolli and Elpidio which she put on the floor inside the Filipinos' flat. Lolli would be sure to find it.

"Gone to Mrs Llewellyn's in Littlecombe. Here's the number. Will call you later. Tell no one. Signed G Morgan."

Half-an-hour later, with Bullshit sitting on the floor of the taxi because he was too heavy to climb on the seat, Grace, in flowered dress and coat and a hat to rival any of the Queen Mother's, was off to Paddington to catch a train to Bath.

139

INTO THE SUNSET

There came that time, in their case it was about half- past-twelve, when a move from the bedroom had to be made. Victor had showered and changed into jeans, Reeboks and a favourite, faded chambray shirt he'd bought in San Francisco. As he made the bed, Nick came back from the bathroom, dressed in the clothes he'd come in.

Victor finished off the bed and threw on the huge assortment of cushions. The bedroom was not in the style of the ground floor of the house. Nothing Georgian in sight. High-tech, all white, basic and extremely functional with built in mirrored closets and a huge Bang and Olufsen thin television standing on a video unit.

The last cushion found it's way to the head end.

"A horrible thing is a made bed," said Nick.

"Why?"

"It looks so final. So cleared up. Like wiping the memory on a computer."

Victor walked over and put his arms round his boy. Nick reciprocated and they stood hugging each other, the smell of shampoo and Eau Sauvage still fresh and wet.

"That sounded very sad," Victor said tenderly. "You don't feel sad, do you?"

Nick smiled in the soft folds of the shirt at Victor's shoulder. He felt far from sad; apprehensive, perhaps and just a little bewildered but certainly not sad.

But it was that time to talk. Victor broke the embrace and released the white blind at the window. The intimacy they had created the previous night fled with the anonymous daylight which streamed in.

"Come on. I'll make you some brunch."

"Great. I'm starving."

"No lectures today or whatever it is you do?" said Victor on the way downstairs. The bruise that Bullshit had inflicted on his calf had now come out although there was

140

no festering of the puncture marks on the skin. Victor had abandoned the dressing.

"They can wait. I have a very assiduous friend who takes copious notes. I won't miss anything and, anyway, there are more important things to do in this world sometimes."

"I don't want to get you into bad habits."

"You won't. I had them long before last night."

"Here. Take the papers," said Victor. "I'll call you when brunch is ready."

"Don't spoil me."

"Oh," said Victor with a grin. "I think you're worth it. Just this once."

"Only once?"

Victor once again engulfed his precious cargo in his arms and felt very, very good about everything. Everything except his leg. He winced a little.

"Are you alright, Victor? I should be making brunch for you."

"I'm fine. Honestly."

"Think you'll live?"

"I think I shall."

"Good. Best forgotten, I think. Out of adversity and all that?"

"Umm," Victor replied, a little uncertainly, Nick thought.

He sat in the drawing room and began to thumb through the *Times*. Not his favourite paper by any means. He gave up after page one and sat looking out into Victor's garden. So, this was IT? It, in capital letters and all that. He smiled. He'd slept so well, had woken up without that irritating full feeling nagging in his crutch. He felt replete in another way, brimming with the total contentment which comes only after sleeping wrapped up, enveloped and locked in the sleep of another body without which his own, he realised, would seem incomplete. Nick wanted whatever IT was to go on forever. IT wouldn't, he reminded himself. IT couldn't, IT never did. But, for as long as possible ... Wasn't that a fair enough dream?

Victor made toast, grilled bacon and scrambled eggs and

141

thought similar thoughts. On another level, he was
worried. What possible sort of future was there? Passion,
yes. But didn't passion pale and pall? Ultimately? What
came after? Something had to, obviously. Other people did
it. Others managed it, after all. He thought of Sam and
Jack. How long was it for them? Seventeen years? He
thought of ... There were few other such couples. How did
those who were still couples do it? Did they still fancy each
other? Did they even still *do* it?

He set places at his round kitchen table, poured orange
juice. Two places. It looked right, somehow. There had
been two places at this table many times, usually on
Sunday mornings. For a while, the second place had been
occupied by a regular visitor. For a while, Darren had been
one. Darren used to come on Saturday afternoon, on his
motorbike from Chelmsford and had left promptly at one
on Sunday in time to catch the last hour at the Coleherne.
But Darren had found other places to spend Saturday
nights. One Saturday, he never showed up. That was that.
Victor still saw him, cruising here, cruising there and they
would nod to each other, formally, almost coldly, their
meetings reviving no vestige of the passion they had
shared so often. Memories like that were bleak and many
and Victor shook them from his mind, once again swept
along by that limitless, unfettered surge of enthusiasm,
hope and magic he had often thought he would never feel
again.

"Come and get it!" he called.

Nick appeared in the kitchen doorway and Victor
recalled with instant regret what he had said to Kitty about
how after twenty they started to talk then to argue ... Had
he *really* uttered such crap?

"Sit. Eat," he said. "And before I forget. There's the
money I owe you for the taxi."

Nick looked at the three notes on his plate. He didn't
want them. Somehow, it was like payment, not repayment.

"How about it being on me?"

"I wouldn't hear of it," Victor said.

"But I insist. Think of it as my investment. A fifteen quid

142

stake in the motherlode."

Victor smiled. He kissed the boy on the top of the head.

"You're sweet."

"Not always. Ask mum."

"Don't try and frighten me off. I don't scare easily."

"Victor?"

"Yes."

Victor put the plates on the table where Nick was already sitting.

"I have to tell mum. At least mum."

"You do what you have to do, Nick. And Oliver?"

"Umm," said Nick. "I take your point. It is time, though."

"Is it?"

"In our family. You know what they're like." Nick set to the scrambled eggs with a will.

"Just take it easy, Nick. One step at a time. Believe me, I know."

"But I'd like to get it over with. I've been meaning to for ages but ... something pulls me back. Not like me at all. And I honestly think they'd be alright about it."

"About you, perhaps," Victor remarked. "But what about me? I love your father. He's my oldest friend. And Kitty too. They're my family, Nick. I've got no one else. A couple of trouty aunts in the country are hardly shoulders to cry on when you need one."

"So ... so what do you mean?"

"I mean, if you would, for my sake, take it easy. Like I said."

Nick ate. He finished his mouthful.

"OK. Hey," he said, lightening the tone, "what are you doing this weekend?"

"Nothing. Well, the usual. I should start on a commission I've got but I can't truthfully say my heart's in this particular one. Why?"

"Dad said I should go down to Littlecombe. Will you come? No one else is going."

"Well, I ... I ..."

"Oh, please! You've been before, haven't you? You must

have."

"I have, indeed. But ... Are you *sure* no one else is going?"

"Positive."

"But I haven't got a car. I don't drive."

"I'll hire one."

"Then I'll pay," said Victor swept away helplessly on the exuberant tide of youth. It's mad, said a little voice in his ear. It's absolutely *barking* mad but ... so what!

"It was my idea," Nick countered.

"If you're investing, let me too. Partners?"

Nick nodded and wolfed down the remainder of the brunch.

After Nick had left to collect the car he'd booked by telephone from Hertz at Marble Arch and to change clothes at Gower Street, Victor fell to thinking. He tried to turn his attention to work, thumbing through the polaroids of Ludo's dogs, trying to think constructively. The photo of Bullshit with the Cover Girl carrier clamped in his jaws haunted him. Victor knew that it had been Bullshit who'd bitten him and it rankled. Not only was his leg hurt, his pride had been hurt too. He'd been looking forward to talking to Ludo about the commissions and felt piqued that the man hadn't even bothered about showing up for the initial discussions. Just another whim of an overly and undeservedly rich man, Victor felt. He didn't like cavalier behaviour. He regretted his own. Last night's being not the least to cause him guilt.

In the middle of wondering, Courtney called.

"Have you got rid of him yet?" Courtney enquired.

"Said with true feeling, Roxy."

"Don't tell me you've fallen in love, Victor. Not at your age!"

Victor was silent.

"Victor? Are you alright?"

"Ummm," Victor sighed. "Yes, of course I'm alright."

"Oh God."

"Oh God what?"

"You have, haven't you?"

144

"Have what?"

"Fallen in love."Victor mused; he hardly heard Courtney babbling. His mind was way away.

"Oh, Victor." Courtney's tone was laden with gloomy implications.

"Aren't you happy for me, Roxy? I thought you would be? I'd be happy for you."

"But no one'd fall in love with me," moaned Courtney.

"It can happen to anyone, even you, dear."

"And what about that dog bite?" said Courtney, reverting to his role of nag. "How on earth did you get bitten? And by what?"

"Oh, that. By a client's dog, would you believe?"

"Today I'd believe anything. Which client?"

"Remember I told you I was doing that pop star's five dogs?"

"Yes. Ludo something or the other."

"Him. Well, it was his bulldog that the police came looking for last night at Sadie's. Ludo lives just down the hill. When I wandered away onto the Heath, the damn thing bit me. It was Nick who took me to the hospital."

"Ah! So it's Nick, is it? A name at last."

"Oh, come on, Courtney. Leave off."

"So what are you going to do about the dog? You can't just let it go. You should sue."

"It's not as easy as that."

"Course it is. Just pick up the 'phone and tell the police you want to press charges. You'll get a fortune."

"I can't."

"Course you can. In America they do it all the time without a second thought. It's all settled by insurance companies anyway."

"But ..."

"But nothing. Get on the 'phone *now* Don't do yourself down. You should get something out of it."

Victor picked up the polaroid again. Perhaps Courtney was right. Insurance would settle it.

"I'll see."

"Do it!" Courtney shrieked and rang off.

Victor paused for a moment before the moment of decision arrived. Then he looked up the number of the police station in Hampstead and spoke to a Sergeant Griffiths.

It was not long after making his formal complaint that Nick returned with the car. In the excitement, Victor soon forgot his unease.

AN ECONOMY OF TRUTH

It was with similarly mixed emotions that Julie sat in the cab taking her back to Hampstead to collect some clothes for the weekend. Not that she'd need many but Oliver had indicated maybe a little black dress if they went out for dinner one evening and perhaps a bathing costume if the weather stayed hot and they swam in the river. Umm, she thought, as she planned her wardrobe. Funny old life, she thought, as the taxi took her past places en route which jogged memories. Everything was chance. Her career, Ludo now this meeting with Oliver. In a way she had begun to wish that he wasn't Kitty's ex-husband. She liked him. She knew she could like him a lot. But as well as being more than pleased with herself, she was also still smarting from the way Ludo had treated her, she still bridled as she remembered Grace's advice to her about getting out with dignity

Julie paid the cab and fumbled in her bag for her keys. There was no one in the garden which was odd. Not like Grace to miss a sunny afternoon. She saw a row of faces looking at her through the drawing room window. Stars and Stripes ran along the top of the cushions on the window seat, wagging their tails and yapping. She looked in the garage. No Range Rover either. Funny, it was as though the place had been deserted. Still, she thought more brightly, no recriminations at least. No tongue lashings from Grace and at least a postponement of the showdown with Ludo.She unlocked the kitchen door, switched off the alarm and, in the quiet of the empty house, knew that Grace was right. Get out, girl. Pack and git. She fully intended to do just that, however things turned out with Oliver. In fact, even if they turned out alright, Julie decided that her future operations would be run on her own territory. Her flat was almost ready. She could live with builders' dust if need be, for a few weeks. Yeah, she thought, dignity. That's about right. She swore that from that moment on, no one would look at her and think bimbo ever again.

Oliver had taken the day off. One thought rather nagged in the back of his mind and that was whether or not Nick would take his advice of the previous day and go down to Littlecombe. But then, he thought, what the heck? Nick wasn't a child and he was surely realistic enought to have worked out that his father hadn't taken any vows of celibacy. Oliver laughed as he packed his case. Of course Nick knew. Why otherwise the remark yesterday about the condoms? Oh. Yes. Oliver checked his wash bag.

Littlecombe. As he pulled out a couple of polo shirts from his closet, Oliver caught sight of a photograph on the dresser. Nick's christening at Littlecombe. Ludo with long hair, Adam Ridley in his dog-collar looking saint-like and holy even at forty. Dear Adam. Oliver had many fond memories of Littlecombe. Even though it was really Kitty's, he felt very proprietorial about the place. But it was essentially a family home, a place of perpetuity and stability where the nucleus could be added to with the coming of new family members. Nick would marry, yes. Of course. But where did that leave Oliver? Divorced from Kitty. All very well to be liberal and civilised but the years had passed and they were passing more and more quickly. Three years now since the divorce and he was still paying the bills. Not that he minded but ... well, perhaps Littlecombe *had* had its day. Perhaps he should at last let go? But letting go was not easy, it was alien to Oliver's nature.

He put the photograph down and continued his packing. He checked himself as he reflected that Julie Burge didn't look to be a natural recruit to the green wellies and long walks brigade. How could he be so arrogant to presume that? He hardly knew her. He closed the case and snapped the brass locks shut. But what he knew, he liked. She was fun. Carefree. She wasn't pushy, had not one pretension about her and she liked him. At least, he felt she liked him. What would they say? Cecil

148

Moorhouse, Camilla Hole, Kitty? Stop it, he said to himself, don't run before you've walked. Take it easy.

As he carried his case downstairs, Oliver felt good. What a nice change it made to have someone with whom you'd spent a wonderful night actually coming back to set off, together, for a wonderfully promising weekend. Yes, he thought, it feels good.

Having packed a bag, perhaps a mite over-packed for what was only a weekend away, Julie called a cab. She locked the house up, petted the dogs for the last time and left. She had arrived this selfsame way, in a cab and with just one bag four months before. She regretted not one moment of those four months but Julie Burge was a practical woman and had never been known to waste a moment. What she perhaps lacked in academic qualifications, she surely made up for in the lessons of life.

She waited outside the house and never looked back. She had only a fleeting moment of doubt. She knew she ought to have told Oliver about her relationship with Ludo. It had been naughty and silly of her not to do so. But, at the time, it had seemed counter-productive to break such delicate ground quite so soon.

The cab arrived. She gave directions and climbed in. The rush hour hadn't started and the taxi made good time. She wondered when the best time might be to tell Oliver. She gave up thinking. Some might dub what she had done as a lie. But she didn't see it like that. After all, what had that cabinet bloke told the court in Australia? No different. What had they called it? Being economical with the truth. That was it. And he'd been made a lord. No, she concluded, let what happens happen. It had always been her way and such a philosophy hadn't done her too badly either.

Lolli and Elpidio in the Range Rover passed the taxi taking Julie back to Chelsea on the hill. Unlike Julie, however, they were not surprised to find the house empty. Nothing surprised either of them any more and if it ever did, neither showed it.

Lolli duly found Grace's note and put it on the main

kitchen table. It was not long left there. A buzzing on the street door heralded the arrival of Sergeant Griffiths from Hampstead police station. Lolli saw him on the video unit and, unlike Grace, had no second thoughts about letting him in. Police were police and where the Filipinos came from, one didn't argue with anyone in any sort of uniform like that.

Thus it was that Sergeant Griffiths discovered that not only had the unlicensed bulldog been removed from the Morgan premises but that its owners had conspired to thwart the course of justice by so doing. And a pop star to boot.

And Sergeant Griffiths had the telephone number.

By the following morning, a fulsome report would land on the desk of a very thorough and not unambitious detective inspector in the county of Somerset by the name of Yates. Detective Inspector Yates, being a country sort of chap, was not the sort of officer to display the sort of tolerance which could have been the case at a more sophisticated police station such as Hampstead. Pop stars? Unlicensed killer dogs? What next?

CRITICAL FACULTIES

Rachel, in le car, drove up and down Broomhouse Road a couple of times before parking at the end opposite a telephone box. She had seen movement in the flat but without stopping and peering in, she couldn't be sure whether she had seen Violetta or Gerald or both.

After the non-interview, she'd returned to Waterloo, fed Benjamin and Peter and filled their automatic cat feeder and telephoned her father at least three times. By three-thirty, he still wasn't back from his meeting and Rachel set off to collect Gerald.

She was in no mood for the planned bucolic interlude. At last, she found her father in his office.

"Dad! Oh! At last!"

"Rachel? What's wrong?"

"The bitch didn't show up!"

"Violetta?"

"Yes."

"Why?"

"No explanation, no message. Nothing. Who *knows* why? It's so embarrassing, dad. Have you any ideas?"

"Certainly. Call Gerald."

"I can't. Not 'til four. He's ... we're having a meeting at four."

"It's five-to now. Hope it's not a crisis."

No, thought Rachel, it's not a crisis, yet.

"Dad, you don't happen to know if Violetta is seeing anyone else, do you?"

"How do you mean?"

"I mean seeing, dad. Seeing as in having it off with ... Bonking."

"I have absolutely no idea, darling. If I knew anything like that, you'd be sure you would too. It would be common knowledge, surely?"

It was hot in the telephone box and Rachel was getting

151

nowhere. She checked her watch.

"Dad. I have to go. Oh. One thing. Kitty wouldn't mind if I went down to Littlecombe, would she? She's always telling me to but I can't get hold of her to check."

"Course not. But you'll miss her. Jessa gave me a message that she had had to drive down this afternoon for some reason. She'll be on her way back to London by now. Don't be too late, though. Mrs Tarpitt goes to bed pretty early."

"We won't. Promise."

"We?"

"Er ... yes. We."

"Nice we?"

"We'll see. I'll talk to you later, dad and if you hear anything about Violetta, will you call me at Littlecombe?"

"I will. 'Bye. Have fun with ... with we!"Rachel smiled. She wished she could tell him. But not just yet.

"'Bye."

By the time she returned to the car, Gerald was walking up Broomhouse Road. He was wearing short-sleeved shirt and jeans and carrying a sports bag. She stood by le car and watched him, her sunglasses pushed back over her loose dark hair. But she wasn't smiling.

"Hi!" he said from a few yards off. "How's this for timing?"

"Better than your client's?"

He stopped, assessing what he correctly perceived as her accumulated frustration.

"How late was she?"

"Late I wouldn't have minded. Not turning up at all is what I call the height of bloody rudeness! Let's talk." She flung her door open, got in and leant across to unlock the passenger door. Gerald threw his bag on the back seat and sat down. He looked worried, on two levels.

"I can't believe it."

"Believe it. It happened. I was there."

"She didn't call. No message?"

"Zilch." Rachel banged her fists on the steering wheel. "How *could* she? The photograper's time wasted, my

152

editor screaming down the 'phone at me and that's nothing as to how furious I feel!"

"Something's happened."

"You're damn right something's happened. And I can tell you something else too!"

"What? I am sorry, Rachel. I wouldn't have had this happen for the world, you know that."

His words registered but Rachel was in full spate, too pent up to do anything but overflow.

"Let me finish ... It seems that Miss Abizzi actually *spent* last night at the Ritz. With a man! Is this news or is this news?"

Gerald rubbed his face with his hands, He didn't answer.

"Well? I think it's news and I'm the journalist round here!"

He spoke but one word.

"Millie."

"Millie? Who the hell's Millie?"

"Millie is ... Millie doesn't exist. Millie is Violetta's cover-up."

"But you said she doesn't exist."

"I know she doesn't but Violetta uses the fiction of this old, old friend who lives in New York or Paris or Cornwall or wherever happens to be convenient when she needs an excuse." Gerald leant back in his seat, fished in the back pocket of his jeans and passed over Violetta's crumpled note. Rachel unfolded it and read it.

"To Bath ...? Why Bath? And when did you get this?"

"When I got back to the flat this morning."

"She didn't come back?"

"She'd been back, yes. But very early. She won't be back until tomorrow at the earliest. She's taken an overnight bag and all her things from the bathroom. Make up, that sort of stuff."

Rachel felt calmer. Gerald wasn't leading her on, she was sure. She could tell he was just as perplexed as she was. And hurt. Hurt that Violetta couldn't trust him, hurt that Millie was being paraded and dragged along to lay false trails. It was not only had Rachel who had been made to look a fool.

"Macdonald's given me 'til Monday," Rachel said. "To come up with the interview."

"Otherwise?"

"He'll use something else, some crass, turgid interview with a visiting pop star. Someone like Prince or Michael Jackson."

"He'll be lucky," Gerald remarked.

"Knowing Macdonald, he probably will be."

As they sat silently in the car, Gerald examined his fingernails whilst Rachel ran through the possibilities of her own situation.

"There's nothing we can do 'til tomorrow," Gerald said.

"So where does that leave us?"

"Well," said Gerald speaking carefully, "we are all dressed up and we do have somewhere to go."

"But *who* was the man at the Ritz? You must have some idea."

"I swear to you, Rachel. I haven't. She has been acting strangely, lately. I thought it was all to do with the Garden next week and believe me, I'm as pissed off as you are. I knew she'd been lying to me yesterday afternoon. She said she was going to the theatre with your father and Kitty last night. I know that wasn't true because Kitty told me what she and Peter were doing; staying at home and not in the company of Violetta.

"Rachel was already placated. What use was there in prolonging her irritation? Gerald was right. And they did have somewhere to go.

"Rachel, we will get to the bottom of it. It *is* the first time she's ever forgotten an interview but then ..."

"But what?"

"But it's the first time she hasn't had me to remind her. I know it's not an excuse but try to understand."

After a moment's hesitation caused by a brief struggle between the journalist and the woman, Rachel laughed. She reached up and opened le car's sun-roof and then started the engine. She put on her sun-glasses.

"I can't very well object, can I? And don't forget your seat-belt."

He smiled, a quizzical smile as he sensed her change of mood.

"Why?"

"Because I'm the reason you weren't there to remind her."

TAKE ME HOME, COUNTRY ROADS

The Wiltshire countryside between Chippenham and Littlecombe is littered with the memories and the memorials of thousands of years of English history. Barrows, long and round, white horses carved into the chalky slopes of the downs, hilltop fastnesses long abandoned to nature and the grazing sheep, stone circles and innumerable standing stones all serve as signposts to a rich past.

As she drove, Kitty recalled not a little of her own. More recent, perhaps, but nonetheless absorbing.

Between London and Chippenham, listening to the Massanet music from MacMillan's *Manon*, her mind dwelt on the generalities. The big issues. Life and death, things like that. She was forty-three and there were still no answers. There'd been good moves, bad moves. Moments of decision, years of a dearth of decision.

In her younger days, death had been the most alarming of the preoccupying bigger issues. The enormity of the moment of passing never left her mind for long. She spent some thinking time, most days, dwelling on its implications. It was the finality of it that bugged her most and the snide inference that waiting for it was all such a silly waste of time.

However, she admitted to consolations, the latest being a thought which had flown in through the car window one day with a wasp. Kitty hated killing anything but wasps were the exception. Mercifully she was alone in the car and alone on the otherwise empty road as the car, a Y reg Golf, careered and veered across the carriageway.

Having successfully whacked the last vestige of life out of the hapless insect with a rolled up copy of the *Islington Chronicle*, she had reflected as to where she had despatched the extinguished life.

Of course. It came like a flash. We are born, she thought and then we die. Hardly original. But then she deduced that to be born she had had to come from somewhere just as when she died, she had to go somewhere. She pulled off the road that afternoon in a lay-by where there was a tea stand and bought a scalding hot cup of rather poor tea. Her mind, having grasped the coming and going, then told her that if she was due to go to oblivion, then it stood to her reason that she came from oblivion for, had she not, indeed, been oblivious for centuries and millenia before she had popped out on the day of her birth in the big bedroom at Littlecombe? She then felt terribly guilty at such a flight of perception as she thought of dear old Adam Ridley, the church at Littlecombe and all those vows. Wedding, baptism and, inevitably, the muttered prayers at the funerals.

Nevertheless, as though in wonder, she reckoned in the privacy of her own belief that when you die, you just return to being unborn and if you can't remember anything scary from before you were born, then what was there to be afraid of if you died? Simple. The tea suddenly tasted metallic and she walked back to the tea stand to jettison the remains in a black bin bag. The young man in the converted ice-cream van eyed her suspiciously. She threw him a dazzling smile upon which his eyes promptly returned to his paper.

She drove on, not a little pleased with herself and feeling more comfortable about something which usually pained her, that being her own end, her beginning and all that came between.

However, approaching the turn off which took her down to Littlecombe village, it was more with life that Kitty was currently preoccupied. Life, her life, and its complexities. It seemed to Kitty as she passed the church and then the vicarage, waving to Adam and his cousin Ernest who were sitting in the garden, that her life inevitably came full circle back to this simple, sleepy village where she had been born.

157

She decided as she drove through the pillars flanking the curving drive that in all her wanderings, after all the detours, dead ends, short cuts and reverses, life hadn't taught her very much. Kitty had tripped over her life, fallen into it by accident; it was the first life she had found after escaping from Littlecombe twenty-five years before and she had swum with it as helplessly as a de-masted yacht is swept along on a following sea. Now she realised that she had done so because there had always been Littlecombe, where living and dying had been going on for thousands of years, from the time of the people who had first erected their palisade on Went Hill, through the Romans, the Dark Age tribes, the Saxons and the Normans, where, for the greatest portion of that chunk of time, there had always been more to fear in being born than in dying.

Such maudlin flirtations with the greater why's and wherefore's were shortlived. Kitty was only a casual depressive. Her bouts of melancholy were brief and she was drawn into them only occasionally when in her own company. She indulged herself in them more as a hippo wallows in mud rather than a potential suicide teetering on the clifftop at Beachy Head. In a strange yet functional way, the giddiness of the rush of sadness these moods generated helped her to get on with it as her father used to advise her to do.

"You're a big girl now, get on with it."

"What do you expect me to do about it? Get on with it?"

"You're a married woman. Get on with it."

"You're a mother. Just get on with it."

The notion of getting on with it seemed to Kitty that afternoon to be the perennial philosophy of the centuries of England's history from which she had herself been sprung. As she left the lane and changed down through the gears, Kitty accepted comfortably that getting on with it was still what she did best.

She saw Jenks first. He was scything the longer grass in that part of the park nearest the gate, between the flowering cherry trees. Kitty pulled up as Queenie strained at a very long leash which was tied to one of the trunks.

The older man, still wearing his thick work shirt and vest even on such a gloriously hot day, leaned on the long scythe and grinned as she walked through the long, seeded grass.

"Hi," she said.

The yellow labrador jumped up and Kitty scratched her head, between her ears the way she liked it.

"'Ello, my dear. What you doin' down? Thought you was givin' up on us this weekend. Down, Queenie."

"The 'phone's out of order. I've been trying to get through all day to let you know some friends of mine will be coming down."

"'Phone you say? That be what all them vans be doin' up at the exchange. Vicar says they bin there sin' early mornin'."

"Well, they're not there now."

"So 'phones mus' be workin'," said Jenks. "You know what they says about Sod's Law."

"But why am I always the sod?" Kitty laughed. "And always guilty!"

"Aaah, I knows," Jenks smiled. "I knows 'ow you must feel a' times. Things is always 'appenin' to you and that's for sure."

"You can say that again. Is everything alright? Why is Queenie tied up?"

The dog panted and whined at her tether.

"On heat, my dear. She's fair itchin' to go off with anything on four legs."

"It's in the air, Jenks. Believe me."

"You may be right, miss. This is fair old place for that sort of thing. Always 'as been."

Kitty smiled.

"It's certainly seen its share of courting. How did you escape, Jenks?"

"Mebbe one day," he said, taking up the scythe again and in a graceful, almost balletic swing, cutting a swathe through the grass, vetch and dog daisies. "I'm only waitin' for a good woman to come along. The right 'un, mind. Don't give up on me, Miss Kitty. I might surprise you yet."

159

"Oh, I shan't, don't worry. Look, I'd better get up to see Mrs Tarpitt. I don't know how long my friends will be here for but take care of them won't you?"

"Anyone I knows?"

"Remember Ludo?"

"Oh, 'im. The singin' chap. Likes 'im a lot, I does. So does Mrs T. Remembers 'im from your weddin', miss."

"Well, it's him and a young lady. And his driver."

"Driver, is it? Very posh."

"Oh, nothing like that. He's nice. You'll like him too."

Kitty returned to her car through the meadow grass. The dog whined after her, paw raised in anticipation of a possible release.

Kitty drove round to the rear of the house where there was a courtyard, open to the view over the downs on one side but having the house, the old stables and the coach house where lived both Jenks and Mrs Tarpitt on the other three. She drove the car into one of the open stables and switched off.

Mrs Tarpitt had seen her through the kitchen window and came hurrying out of the back door.

"Why, Miss Kitty. What brings you?"

"I had to. The wretched 'phone was out. Jenks says they've been there all day."

"So they 'ave. 'Cept they be workin' now. Vicar told me when 'e come to ask if you'd be down. 'Course, I told 'im, no, I didn't think you would."

"Well I've just waved to him so he knows now."

"He'll be that pleased. He came to say he'd put 'Jerusalem' on again Sunday an' he knew it was your favourite. Shall you be stoppin' now? Promises to be grand weather. And where's Mr Peter?"

"Working."

"And Mr Longingly? Working too?"

Kitty nodded. She was still rather impressed at the way both Mrs Tarpitt and Jenks had assimilated the whirligig nature of her life and loves. For two people she thought would disapprove heartily of the civilised way her ex-husband and, so they believed, new husband co-existed,

160

they had proved her entirely wrong. Love? Definitely. The only answer. Mrs Tarpitt and Jenks had been her family more than ever had her mother, whom she'd never really known, or The Major. Especially The Major. He was, as younger generations often refer to the older, difficult. But the memory of him still made Kitty smile. Difficult was too mild a description of the crusty, barking state of childlike selfishness into which he had escaped after her mother's death. Impossible was a better word. And Mrs Tarpitt had borne the full brunt. The thought of that made Kitty both very guilty and, ergo, extremely grateful.

The two women went into the house, through the now disused scullery which still sported the old copper and the laundry sinks.

Kitty picked up the 'phone on the wall in the kitchen. Dial tone. Sod's Law indeed!

"Any chance of a cuppa, Mrs T? I'm parched."

Mrs Tarpitt hurried to plug the kettle in. In summer, the Aga was turned off and she used either electricity or the back-up gas cooker.

"Don't tell me you've come all this way to tell me about Mr Ludo comin'."

"How in the world did you know that?"

Mrs Tarpitt laughed.

"Don't worry. Wasn't one of my feelin's, Miss Kitty. 'Aven't 'ad one of them in a long time. No, 'e called. Rather some young chap what's drivin' him phoned not five minutes back."

"Oh bother!" said Kitty. "After two hours on the road that's all I needed to hear. And now two hours back. At least two in this Friday traffic."

"Well, why not stay, now you're here? Call Mr Peter and tell 'im. Surely he likes it down 'ere? 'E's always sayin' he do. 'E won't mind."

"How he puts up with me at all is a constant amazement, Mrs T."

Mrs Tarpitt warmed the pot. Kitty frowned. Dear Peter and he *was* so dear. Would he mind? She sighed as the kettle boiled.

161

"Do you know, Mrs T, I might do just that."

Mrs Tarpitt made their tea and they sat down at the kitchen table.

"Now," Kitty began. "Let me tell you about Ludo ..."

And so she explained, to the best of her scant knowledge, what Mrs Tarpitt must expect. Mrs T's eyes were wide. Part of a secret. Well! Mrs Tarpitt knew all about secrets. She had kept one of her own for many years but she'd become too used to that. This new secret made her feel part of a wider world than she usually inhabited. Being made party to the goings on of the famous imparted not a little ready glamour. Glamour, in Littlecombe, was not exactly thick on the ground.

LEGAL MANOEUVRES

It was to his eternal credit that Peter Bailey was an equable man. Placid was not a word which came near to encompassing his inherent equability. Neither was diffident, nor deferential. And he certainly didn't feel manipulable or dissuadable. Peter liked being equable. He was famous for it and he made a rather good living from it and as legal adviser to a list of clients whose fiery temperaments could collectively supply the national grid, equability was a handy stock in trade.

In summing up, Peter Bailey was a wonderful listener. After listening, of course, he made up his mind and spoke it, handing out the most carefully considered opinion or decision he could elicit, but only after listening.

With the telephone tucked between his ear and his shoulder, he listened to Kitty. He even signed some letters while he was listening and read through the sheaf of telephone messages which Jessa thrust onto his blotter.

"Oh, Peter darling, I wish I could see your face just to be sure that you're not saying yes because I'm playing all helpless and wet."

"But you can't, can you?"

"I know. It's agonizing."

There was a pause as he passed only two of the messages back to Jessa for return calls.

"Kitty."

"Yes."

"It's alright, darling. I'm smiling. I honestly don't mind."

"But you'll be exhausted. Jessa told me you had a late meeting and you're always so pooped at the end of the week ..."

He tried to interrupt.

"It's just been cancelled."

"... and I feel *so* guilty but we can go swimming and I promise you won't have to lift even a finger ... It's been

163

what?"

"Cancelled. And what's more I'm going to leave now."

"Have you ...?"

"Yes. I've rung Mrs Haines and she'll feed Genius."

"Oh."

"Oh what?"

"I'm such an idiot. I got myself so worked up thinking you'd be cross."

"When am I ever cross?"

"Well. Quiet. You know."

"And am I being quiet?"

"No."

"Then see you in a couple of hours. In fact, I'll meet you in the George and you can beat me at darts."

"Oh, yes! Have you had a good day by the way, darling."

"I have," he said, emphasising the I.

"Who hasn't?"

"Rachel. Violetta didn't turn up for the interview. It seems she's vanished."

"Violetta? How?"

"I hardly think in a puff of smoke."

Kitty giggled.

"It would have to be a pretty big puff."

"Don't be unkind."

"Sorry. Seriously though, how awful for Rachel. What's she going to do?"

"Are you sitting comfortably?"

"Ohh, no! Today it's my turn. What now?"

"She's coming down to Littlecombe."

"Oh, that's nice. What's so terrible about that?"

"With Gerald Ward."

"Oh. Gosh!"

Kitty was doing bedroom calculations. Littlecombe had six. She was also calculating whether or not to tell Peter about Ludo now or leave it as a surprise. No. Peter was equable but there was a limit to equable. It was already stretched.

"That's fine. I'll tell Mrs T. She will be pleased." Kitty

paused. "Darling ..."

"Yes."

"You know my little emergency."

"I was meaning to ask. What was all that about?"

"Well ..."

And she explained.

"Full house almost," he said afterwards. "Actually, it might be quite jolly. Who did you say the new girlfriend is?"

"I didn't. 'Cos I don't know."

Jessa buzzed through on Peter's other 'phone with a returned call.

"Kitty, I must go. I'll be at the George between seven-thirty and eight. I must say, this weekend's a bit like a bran tub. What will we pull out next?"

Yes, thought Kitty. What indeed?

"Mrs Tarpitt ...," she called.

BIRD'S EYE VIEW

If the hawk that Victor pointed out to Nick hovering a hundred feet above the verge of the M4 could have 'phoned home, he or she would have told mother that Grace Morgan could be seen in a very crowded 125 train with the bewildered Bullshit sitting cramped under her legs; Oliver's Jaguar was clearly visible some three miles behind Nick and Victor's Escort, fairly eating up the miles; Gerald and Rachel in le car were taking a more relaxed route along the A30 and finally a large, bottle green Mercedes limousine could be observed parked in a field entrance in a lane just off the road at Box.

"I love hawks," said Victor, turning round to see if the bird would swoop. "They're so predatory. You just know they have no emotions whatsoever."

"Do you admire that?" Nick asked.

"In them. Same with lions or cheetahs or spiders. Anything that hunts."

"And in humans?"

"Ah!" Victor replied. "We're a funny mixture, aren't we?"

"I suppose."

"The hunting instinct is still there, even though we don't need to."

"We obviously do," Nick observed and turned to Victor with a wide grin. "Some by day and some by night and some all the time."

"But not to devour."

"Depends on the meat, I would think," said Nick, depressing the indicator stick to pull off into the service stop. He rubbed Victor's leg with his left hand and squeezed his knee.

"I can see you're a bad, bad boy," Victor said, returning the tactile compliment. "And why are we stopping?"

"I need to pee."

"Oh. Right. Be alright on your own? Don't go off with any strange men. I'd be stranded.

"Nick pulled the car into a space close to the service buildings and unbelted.

"Not for long, Victor," he said as he got out of the car. "I might be young but I'm not that naieve!"

Victor watched the boy run across the tarmac. One of the rips in the faded 501's was strategically placed just under the right buttock. Victor smiled. Nick climbed the steps and turned to wave before disappearing to answer the call of nature, leaving Victor with a carful of conflicting thoughts.

Running the current programme though the intellectual channel of his mind, he knew it was crazy. It couldn't possibly last. He would have to put a stop to it before it ran too far, before either he or Nick became involved too deeply. Oliver and Kitty's friendship was too precious to put at risk. This weekend was a folly, a folie d'amour and he was prepared to allow it to happen. But afterwards ... He banished all thoughts of the following week, thoughts which would have wrecked the weekend before it had properly begun.

Emotionally chanelled, however, the situation assumed an entirely different scenario. Very rarely had Victor experienced the complete contentment he had found in the last twenty-four hours. Physically, temperamentally, psychologically, his tall, lean constitution was perfectly complemented by the slighter, stockier, yet nonetheless urgent nature of his young companion. And, worst of all, Victor liked him. Even in the two minutes it took for Nick to have a pee, Victor began to miss him. It was almost alien for Victor to feel such a pang.

During that same two minutes, Oliver's Jaguar zipped past the entrance to the services. The hawk could have been forgiven for thinking that the two cars were deliberately avoiding each other.

Until last night, Victor had been rather happy with his life, not smugly or blindly happy, but happy in the way that he neither sought nor anticipated any change in it. His

167

life had changed little in the preceeding quarter century. Times had changed, certainly. Gay life had expanded in some ways, contracted in others. Aids had come, granted, but then Victor was not one to be panicked, not like some he knew. Poor Courtney. Thought he could catch it from a fumbled grope. But then Courtney was Courtney. Victor had merely adapted. Rationally and determinedly, he had stopped doing those things which were now acknowledged high risk. But stop? For Victor to stop hunting would have been tantamount to taking the wild out of the roadside hawk. It wasn't possible.

That thought frightened him too. It was enough to deter his feelings towards this boy. He would never be able to do it, he would never be able to match up to the idealistic demands of one so young and so untried by living gay and dangerous. And even if he tried. It would be an effort, a phoney charade which when disclosed would hurt the boy even more.

He glanced through the open window out of which his arm hung alongside the sun-warmed car door. He looked across at the next vehicle. A Volkswagen camper. In the driver's seat, a man in his late thirties, short cropped hair, wearing a T-shirt and leather waistcoat. Looking at Victor. Looking straight at him and grinning, uninvited. Oh no, thought Victor, his heart almost missing a beat. I do not need to be cruised at this particular moment!

He averted his eyes only to see Nick smiling at him not five yards away as he ran towards the car. He got in.

"God," he said, "you can't get away from it anywhere, can you?"

He started the engine and reversed out of the space.

"Get away from what?" Victor said innocently as the car manoeuvred out of the crowded car park.

"Sex."

"Where?"

"Victor! That guy was cruising you."

"What guy?"

Nick pulled out into the middle lane of the motorway and laughed.

"You haven't become a nun, Victor just by coming away for the weekend with me."

"I don't understand."

"The guy cruised you! Great! Don't hide it. There's nothing to be ashamed of. In fact," he said, overtaking a slow-moving maintenance truck, "it's very flattering."

Victor blinked. This, from a twenty year old?

"I think you're a great looking guy," Nick went on. "So, stands to reason other people think so too. You don't think I'd run off with someone I wasn't proud of, do you?"

"But ..."

"But nothing. Lets enjoy this, Victor. Let's enjoy it before it gets heavy. There's plenty of time for that."

Nick drove on and Victor slung his arm over the back of the driver's seat. After Nick's profoundly sensible remark, he asked himself no more questions for many miles although he found himself pondering that as well as being able to hurt, he was also able to *be* hurt.

THE BIMBOS FIGHT BACK

Oliver too had spotted the hawk.

"See him? Up there? Just hovering, almost as though he were weightless."

Julie followed the line of his finger.

"Sort of scary, I reckon," she said. "I'd hate to be the little mouse or whatever it is he's after."

"Kill or be killed, I'm afraid."

"Just like us," Julie replied. "Like business, really."

"Oh, I don't know. I don't think business is that gory."

"It must be. Stands to reason, dunnit? If you gain, someone else 'as to lose."

"Not necessarily. Take farmers. They plant a crop, they harvest it, they keep some of the seeds and plant them again the next year. No one loses. Everyone gains."

"Yeah, 'cept if you look it from another way, what happened to all those other little plants that couldn't grow because the farmer had cleared them away, seeds an' all, to plant 'is spuds or 'is corn or whatever. Someone or something *always* loses. Same everywhere. For me to get a job, there's thirty or forty others girls who lose out on the chance. For you to make a few grand, it means that someone else has missed the opportunity. Believe me, Ollie. I bin at the other end too."

He smiled at her. She looked suddenly serious. She'd lost the vulnerability and carefully applied faux naivete which was her mask. The girl he had picked up in Zanzibar the previous evening had metamorphosed into the woman with whom he was going to spend a weekend.

"You may be right," he said.

"I know I'm bloody right."

The Jaguar sped on, only overtaking, never overtaken."There's 'aves and there's 'ave-nots," she said, continuing her thought. "Like there's black and white, givers and takers."

"How do you vote?" Oliver asked suddenly.Julie giggled."S'private that!" she exclaimed, feigning outrage. "Votin's secret."

"Of course. Forgive me."

"Only teasin'," she replied and squeezed his hand where it lay on the gear selector. "Last but one time, I voted for Maggie. That was when I was eighteen and I'd just started earnin' a bit, puttin' a bit by an' that. I thought it made sense. Still does in many ways."

"And last time?"

"Last time," she said slowly. "Tell the truth, I was goin' to vote for 'er again but then I said to myself, Jool, 'ang on, gel. P'raps you're alright but what about them other people. I'd just bought my third place, the one I'm gonna live in. I thought, Jool, you've taken 'omes from three lots of people, think about them a bit. My mum, she lived in a council flat. Widowed most of 'er life, she was an' now she's gorn. Never 'ad nothing 'cept me and she poured everything she ever 'ad into me just so's I could be a success. Well, I thought, now I'm a success but what about all them like my mum." "Don't tell me you voted for Kinnock."She shook her head."I joined the Liberals. I went and got fully paid up. Even shoved leaflets through peoples' boxes."

"But they haven't an earthly," Oliver opined. "Not a snowflake in hell's chance."

"Mebbe. But they're gentler, somehow. Not so much them and us like all the other lot. An' I mean Labour as well as Tories. I know my vote meant sod all but it made me feel better. 'Ere," she giggled, "'ark at us. Bashin' on about politics an stuff. We 'ardly even know each other."Good Lord, thought Oliver. He was amused and yet, at the same time, humbled as he reflected along the lines of books and their covers. It was his turn to find her hand and squeeze it."Isn't this fun," he said."Dunno about you, love but I'm 'avin' a lovely time. Can't wait to see this 'ouse of yours."

"I wish I wish," Oliver replied."Wish what?"

"Oh, nothing. Nothing in particular."

"Come on. Tell me. Is it that it's not really yours?"

"Something like that."

"You could 'ave your own, surely? Shouldn't think an old Tory like you is strapped for a mortgage?"He laughed."Mortgages are for homes. You should know that. That's why they only let you have the tax relief on one and I've got mine."

"No you 'aven't."

"I have! You've seen it," he protested."That's not a home, Ollie. It's a house." Julie smiled a wry smile. "You're so like ..." She felt so easy, so relaxed. He almost caught her off guard. She stopped herself from saying the wrong thing just in time."Who?"

"No one. Just someone I know."

"But like me."

"Like lots of you. Believe me, you're not an endangered species. You might be divorced on paper, mister, but you still haven't let go, have you?" She straightened up in the leather seat and glanced kindly in his direction. She spoke softly, kindly. "Am I right or am I right?"

WHEELS WITHIN WHEELS

Earlier in the afternoon, Wheels had pulled the Mercedes off the road in Hungerford and stopped in front of a grocery shop.

"This do, boss?"

"OK with you Violetta?"

"Oh, I think so, love. It's only Spar, not Fortnum's but I'm sure we'll find something."

"Do you want me to go in for you?" Wheels asked.

"No love, you stay here and have a break. Ludo and I will do the shopping. Any preferences?"

Violetta had suggested on the strength of the beautiful day that they have a picnic dinner.

"He eats anything," Ludo said. "Come on, mother."

She laughed and smacked his arm playfully.

Wheels watched in amazement as they hurried in to the shop. He had never known Ludo show the slightest desire to go into a grocer's. It was getting stranger and stranger. He wound down his window and waited.

Perhaps it was the heat of the day, perhaps the uncertainty as to what the future held. He had overheard Ludo's whispered proposal to Violetta in the back seat and he had quickly corrected the jolted steering wheel as he heard her breathy acceptance.

Well, well, he thought, the end of an era. And maybe, he reminded himself, the end of him? What if she didn't like him? It had happened before to his certain knowledge. He could number many amongst his acquaintances who had been summarily sacked for a reason no stronger than that their faces didn't fit in the opinion of a new band member or, worse, a new wife or girlfriend. Too many good jobs had been lost that way and Wheels had no security, no contract, nothing but the fact that Ludo liked him, trusted him and confided in him. Perhaps Mrs Morgan-to-be wouldn't like that? Ludo wouldn't need his ear any more, wouldn't talk to him late into the night as the Hine bottle became emptier and emptier and the dawn rose over Hampstead as they staggered to bed, their world righted of all wrong.

Tough in many respects and used to the worst of life's hard knocks and disappointments, Wheels was very emotional. He not only liked stability, he craved it. He felt himself flush as the thoughts flashed into his mind. Where would he live if he was no longer needed? Ludo's house was his home. Yes, he had savings; he'd even been wise enough to start a pension but not nearly enough to buy a place of his own. Drinking in the places that rock 'n' roll royalty frequented didn't come cheap, especially if you got there at ten anddidn't leave 'til closing time. Five hours drinking at that level was most people's weekly salary.

But she seemed so nice, this Violetta. Vee, as Ludo called her. What should *he* call her? What *should* he call her? Miss? Miss Abizzi? Perhaps she would like him after all? His stomach knotted and the reflux indigestion twinged. Bile began to flood his mouth and he scrabbled in the glove compartment for another tube of Setlers. He crammed two into his mouth and chomped them up quickly. The relief came more slowly these days and he always had to take two at once. Grace said it was because he ate too fast. Wheels knew it wasn't that but was too scared to go to a doctor. He thought he knew what it was and he didn't want his fears confirmed. It was why he wanted to know, for the first time in his life, from whom and from where he came.

As he waited for the pain in his stomach to clear, his vision seemed to blur. A grey mist seeped across his eyes. He blinked. The sunny street outside was still sunny but far away, isolated behind a veil. Wheels wasn't concerned. It was a sensation he had noticed several times before. He's wondered about it at first yet after the third time, he realised that it always presaged an event of some drastic importance. A death. A great change. He'd felt it on tour in

174

France when his mate Andy had been killed by the tailgate of a truck. Without warning, incorrectly fastened, a fatigued spring had snapped and the heavy tailgate executed Andy as surely as any sentence of death. And Wheels had sensed it. In a way it wasn't a surprise. Wheels had smelt something on the wind of change, but both then and now, he was unable to know exactly what.

Slowly his vision returned to normal. It left him with an apprehension he knew would not leave him until whatever was going to happen, happened.

Some little distance before Box, they stopped. Ludo directed Wheels down a lane and the car was parked in the entrance of a recently harvested field. Violetta and Ludo carried the bags of provisions they'd bought and Wheels spread the carriage rugs out on to the stubble behind the car. As Ludo passed her ingredients, Violetta stuffed bread rolls with cheese and ham and tomato, stacked up peaches and nectarines. Ludo poured out cider into plastic mugs and knelt down next to her while she worked.

Wheels didn't know what to do. He felt useless and excluded. He wasn't asked to do anything and he felt volunteering would be unwelcome. He leant against the side of the car and chewed a long stem of grass. His stomach felt easier but there was still some discomfort. Against the hedge, the combine harvester had missed a stand of barley. It was now heavy with grain, the ears bent over almost double. Poppies flashed amongst the stalks as the slight wind rustled through the ears. Birds sang. Somewhere near a cow lowed and there was the sound of a tractor as it drove up and down or back and forth a few fields distant.

"Come on lad!" Violetta called cheerily. "Your tea's ready." Wheels threw down the grass stem and looked over the car's boot to where the picnic had been spread out. She smiled broadly at him. "Wheels? Don't be shy. You've done more than your fair share today, it's our turn to do a bit for you."

Ludo looked up and grinned.

"You're spoiling him," he joked with her and winked at

Wheels. "He's not used to it."

"Well, from now on he'll get used to it," Violetta said definitely. Wheels took his hands out of his jeans pockets and squatted down at one corner of the rug. "These are ham and cheese and these are chicken. Go on. Tuck in. As usual there's enough for an army."

"Great," said Wheels and after first looking at Ludo who was already well into a sausage roll, picked up one of Violetta's filled rolls and ate. Maybe, he thought to himself as he watched them laughing and tucking stray bits of tomato into their mouths, maybe he'd been wrong. Maybe there weren't any cataclysmic changes about to be sprung upon them.

They stayed in the field for at least an hour-and-a-half. Ludo and Violetta went off for a walk and Wheels stayed with the car, snatching a few minutes kip as he lay in the sun, still warm at seven o'clock.

When he woke, the swallows were soaring and dipping in the evening sky, hunting their insect supper. Out of the same sky, from behind the huge foliage of an oak growing in the hedge, a hawk flew into view. Wheels shaded his eyes against the sun as he watched the inimical shape assume sovereignty over the swallows. It wasn't a bird, it was a shape. A flock of wood pigeons, pecking at the grain left behind by the harvester, sensed its prescence immediately and in a great flapping of grey wings they were gone.

Wheels had cleared the picnic away by the time love, hand in hand, returned. Violetta's hair was down. Lovely, thought Wheels. She's really lovely when you think about it. Well Ludo, me old mucker, he mused, you've really gone and done it this time.

RUFFLED FEATHERS

Gerald and Rachel had decided to stop for something to eat in a pub in Corsham. They sat outside beneath a Skol umbrella, Gerald with chicken and chips, Rachel with lasagne. They had driven slowly, stopping in Marlborough to look at the school and had detoured to see the temple at Avebury, the late afternoon light casting elongated shadows around and between the ancient standing stones.

"I wonder where she really went?" Rachel queried for the tenth time since leaving London.

Gerald offered her some chips. She refused and patted her tummy.

"You know," he said, "at this particular moment, I honestly don't care. I just hope she's feeling as good as I am."

"But who is *he*? That's the key to it all. If only we could find that out, the mystery would be solved."

"I just hope he's nice."

"Nice!" Rachel exclaimed. "Nice be blowed. All we know is that he's rich. Poor people poke in a rented room in Pimlico."

"Don't get so worked up about it," he said, tearing a strip of meat off the leg.

"Dammit, Gerald! I am worked up. And what makes me even more worked up is that I can't for the life of me understand how you can be so cool about it!"

Rachel still smarted. Violetta's rebuff had stung. Violetta wasn't sitting under a pub umbrella beside the A4. Gerald was.

He seemed cowed by her blazing dark eyes; wary of her temper as she tossed her long hair back over her shoulders. She seemed to be challenging him, taunting him to rouse his own anger to heights which would match and then defuse her own. Either that, or, he thought, she was begging to be smacked down, inviting confrontation. Testing him. He wasn't ready.

"If I say anything," he observed gingerly, "I'd be afraid you'd bite my head off."

He glanced across at her; she sat poised with her fork over the half-eaten lasagne; she somehow made the fork in her grasp look more passionate than it was designed, more like a dagger. He knew he couldn't smile, worse laugh. But she was magnificent in her anger. So righteous and imperious. Rachel, rather than Violetta, looked the epitome of the thwarted prima donna.

"I shan't," she snapped.

I know you won't, he thought.

"Just answer me one question. Did I tell you that it would sort itself out?"

"You did, but ..."

"Then," he interrupted, "did you believe me?"

"Of course."

"Then trust me? Just a little?"

Rachel closed her eyes and gradually the tautness in her straightened shoulders lessened. She sighed and when she opened her eyes again she was smiling. He looked at her squarely, the warm blue eyes firm and patient. She dropped the fork and reached her hand across the tabletop.

"I do apologise, Gerald. I was ... taking it out on you. I am so sorry."

"No need."

"Oh, there is. I get too angry. It's not good."

"We all get angry, Rachel. It's only natural."

"But I've been angry for years. Even more so since my mother died."

"It's one way of coping."

"I haven't placed it, that's the trouble," she replied. "Daddy says it's because I haven't placed myself yet."

"Is he right?"

"He usually is. He's one of the wisest men who ever got off a camel."

He laughed. She did too.

178

"I suppose I get angry when I'm frightened."

"So do I. Lots of people do. But what frightens you so much? I hope it's not me. Or being with me."

Rachel sipped at her white wine and looked away before she answered him. A foursome, two boys and two girls, were laughing and joking at a table three away. The girls were being girls, the boys boys, loving being played up to by the girls, revelling in the giggles and attention, each sharing the adulation. The girls seemed to sense their expected roles, almost instinctively. They flirted, simpered and smirked at the jokes the boys made, felt utterly confident in handing over their glasses with that expectant, little-girl-wants, take-me-show-me-buy-me pouting smile.

"Being on my own," she replied. "Being me, maintaining my own image of myself. It's such an overwhelming anti-climax when you know you *can't* be you all the time. I feel so useless at times. So incomplete."

"I think you do just fine."

"But I need help," she said soberly. "And that *is* an admission."

"I'd like to volunteer," he said. "In my own small way." He leant across the table and kissed her.

A motorcycle pulled up and two very tall, very big be-leathered men got off, removing their helmets with almost sinister authority as they walked up to the pub entrance. They stopped, by the table with the youthful foursome and stood, looking at the girls and then with sneering, bullish disdain at the boys. The bikers were unkempt and dirty, purposely dirty. The local foursome were each well-scrubbed, deodorised and neatly coiffed.

The table went instantly quiet in the prescence of such omen. Then, after standing just long enough to establish their superiority through their attitude of threat, the rider of the motorcycle beckoned his friend on with a nod of his head and they went into the pub. The table was very quiet for a moment before one of the boys, safely out of earshot of the new arrivals, made a joke about the two bikers. The girls trilled and giggled but their request for another drink was not granted. The boys finished their pints, muttered an

179

alternative destination and the foursome split up, one couple into an over-manicured Ford Capri and the other into a wide-wheeled, souped-up Cortina.

"Wow," said Rachel as the two cars roared away in a scorch of burning rubber. "That wasn't very nice."

"Just a lot of strutting and fretting. Are you ready?"

Rachel nodded and collected her bag and sun-glasses and the car keys and they walked, arm in arm back to le car.

Some miles further on, as they were approaching Box, Rachel pulled in to a lay-by.

"The windscreen's like a cemetery," she said. "I can hardly see through it." She unrolled two lengths of kitchen roll, passed one to Gerald and then squirted the windscreen. As they cleaned off the squashed corpses, there was a terrific bang from somewhere to their left amongst the mown fields. It surprised them, made them jump. It sounded liked a massive blow-out of a car tyre. They both ran to where the hedge was thinner and looked through.

In the middle of the harvested field, a man stood with a shotgun. He was breaking the breach and ejecting the spent cartridges. Rachel and Gerald watched him walk a few yards across the field and bend down.

When he stood up, he held a feathered shape by its legs. The wings fell open, their dark colour silhouetting a familiar outline against the golden stubble of the crop.

"Looks like a hawk," said Gerald.

Rachel shivered.

"How cruel!" she whispered. "I thought they were protected. Surely there are laws about it?"

"Absolutely senseless," he agreed. "I loathe that kind of wanton destruction, taking cheap pot-shots at something so magnificent."

"It could even have had a nest. Babies too."

He put his arm round her and steered her away from the scene.

SUM EGO IN ARCADIA

Kitty and Mrs Tarpitt finished the rooms about a quarter-past-seven. Kitty had asked Jenks to bring in some roses which she'd put in Ludo's Miss X's room. She'd given them the big one, at the front. It had its own bathroom as did all the three main bedrooms at Littlecombe and a view which American bankers and at least two Saudi princes had tried to buy. There had been moments when Kitty had been only too tempted to sell.

The bed was what was called a half tester; draped curtains hanging from brass rails at the head and brass rails at the end hung with Victorian quilts. There were sofas and armchairs and two magnificent wardrobes which looked more like castles than pieces of furniture, so profuse were the crenellated and castellated embellishments on the cornice and doors. Little Gothic hall chairs served as side tables for drinks, telephones and magazines and there was a television standing next to the gothicised fireplace on an oak blanket chest, inscribed and dated amongst the linenfold decoration with the name of a distant, seventeenth century Llewellyn.

It had been her parents' room. She had been born in it and both her mother and father had died there. On being bequeathed the house, Kitty and Oliver, married for only three months, had decided to permanently occupy the room next door, which was smaller, cosier and with windows which were set into the angle of the roof. Now she shared the bed in that room with Peter. Oliver always used the other master suite, next door to the big bedroom. The whole of the front of Littlecombe Park, both the Regency villa and the Victorian extensions, were festooned with wistaria, even in July yet sporting a few lilac chandeliers of blossom. Jasmine intermingled with the wistaria and a sweet, almost overpowering scent imbued the room.

"Looks lovely, Miss Kitty," said Mrs Tarpitt proudly as they surveyed their preparations. "'S'right romantic."

"Oh, Mrs T! What a sweet thought!"

Kitty hugged the older woman and Mrs T wiped away a tear.

"Well!" she said, chiding herself and drying away the evidence with a man's hanky, "we're all only young once, aren't we? Best make the most of it."

Kitty smiled at her and squeezed her hand. Mrs Tarpitt, she knew well, had certainly been young once but the experience had been brief. Brief and achingly sad but not without its consequences. Kitty's mother had told her about it many years ago when Kitty had naively asked rather loudly where Mr Tarpitt was. Mrs T had hurried away, out of earshot, hoping that Mrs Llewellyn would give a suitably vague and unquestionable explanation. She hadn't and that was how Kitty had come to learn that there was no Mr Tarpitt, nor had there been nor, in all likelihood, would there be other than Mrs T's own father, even then very much brown bread in the churchyard and the infant Mr Tarpitt, currently squalling in the uncomfortable swaddling of a Doctor Barnardo's home somewhere in the south of England.

Mrs was merely a courtesy title. Had the young man survived Korea, the Mrs would have been the legitimate prefix to the surname of Hinton. But Ena Tarpitt and Arthur Hinton hadn't even got to the point of getting engaged.

"We are, my dear," Kitty agreed. "Well, some of us. Don't forget Ludo's the same age as me. That's hardly young, now, is it?"

"Ah," replied Mrs T. "But the young lady. That's as to 'oo I was referrin', Miss."

"Yes," said Kitty thoughtfully as they turned and left the room, wondering for the first time who and what Ludo had become involved with this time. She must be special, Kitty decided. None of the other seventeen had ever been

182

within spitting distance of Littlecombe. She thought as they went downstairs to the kitchen about Julie Burge and hoped more than anything that the girl had been able to muster a little more equanimity than she had displayed the previous afternoon. But, Kitty reminded herself, most people always need someone else to blame for their own misfortunes and if Julie needed to think that Kitty was at the root of her misfortunes, so be it. It was, after all, most unlikely that their paths would ever cross again.

"I'm just off to change," Mrs T announced. "Shan't be a moment. Just get myself smartened up a bit in case they might want something."

"Don't let them bamboozle you into waiting on them hand and foot," Kitty called after her.

"Oh, I don't mind," Mrs T called back. "S'not everyday we get a real life pop star to stay, is it? Might not 'appen again."

Kitty shook her head and smiled as she watched Mrs Tarpitt hurry across the yard. Mrs Tarpitt's excitement was almost as enjoyable as Kitty's own warm feelings of being home. Safe and stable and snug. A feeling too of satisfaction in knowing that her nearest and dearest also felt the same way about the house and what it meant to her.

The kitchen wall clock chimed the half hour. Kitty scribbled a quick note to Ludo and left it on the hall table. She grabbed her keys and her purse and hurried out to the car. Not the weekend she'd planned, but nevertheless, she thought as she accelerated down towards the gates, to even think about complaining in such a fortunate position would be niggardly in the extreme.

Kitty emerged from the lane, crossed the main road, and drove past the Priory to Littlecombe village. She and Peter parked in front of the George almost simultaneously.

"And that's the Priory," Oliver explained as the Jaguar turned into the lane. "Very, very old. See the dovecote. Sixteenth century, they say. Perhaps older." Oliver had been playing tour guide ever since they passed Claverton Manor.

"So where's your place then?" asked Julie eagerly.

"Right here, my dear."

Oliver swung the car into the drive and drove very slowly up through the park. The house stood at the far end, surrounded by Jenks' immaculately striped lawns, looking like a perfectly cooked Madeira cake, glowing golden and warm in the evening sun as though some divine chef had just taken it from the oven and set it to cool.

Julie immediately knew why Oliver felt so strongly about the place. The place was obviously loved. The trees were majestic and permanent, the edges of the drive so carefully trimmed, the meadow grass at just the right length to allow the wildflowers to be able to thrive and bloom. Just seeing it struck a chord deep within her and she swallowed.

It was so beautiful, she wanted to cry. And because it was so beautiful, the ugliness of her deceit and the baser reasons for wanting to desecrate the place that Kitty Llewellyn loved so much tasted bitter. Revenge didn't lie easily in such a timelessly perfect setting. In truth, revenge didn't lie easily in the breast of Julie Burge either.

Oliver drove quickly round the house and parked in one of the open stables.

Mrs Tarpitt didn't see the car. She was freshening up in the privacy of her windowless bathroom. Jenks saw the car. And Jenks also saw the bubbling, blonde stranger whose arm Mr Longingly took as he steered her towards the back door

."Well, well, Queenie," Jenks muttered to his dog, who had started to whine as soon as she heard the car doors slam. "What 'ave we 'ere, I wonder?" He pressed down the last of the tobacco he'd filled into his pipe and casually lit a match. The sweet smell of Old Holborn floated through the open window and drifted away. "Mind you, bit young for the likes of me, wouldn't you say?" Queenie barked. Twice. "And perhaps a bit on the young side for 'im 'an all come to think of it." But he chuckled nevertheless.

Oliver shepherded Julie through the kitchen and into the oak floored entrance hall at the front of the house where

184

the wide staircase descended in two flights from the balustraded landing above.

"Oh, it's lovely. Really ... well, cosy."

"It is, isn't it?"

"Shouldn't be, mind. It's pretty big but you don't get the impression it's not lived in. Know what I mean?"

"Oh, I do. I do. Come with me, Julie. I want to show you the bedroom. It's got a superb view."

"Lead on, Ollie."

She followed him up the staircase and rounded the corner of the landing. There were pieces of furniture from both families, Llewellyns and Longinglys as well as china, paintings and rugs. Collections of a lifetime added to by successive generations of two country dynasties.

Oliver opened the door of the room he had made his own since the divorce. A big room, decorated in browns and creams with heavy tapestry curtains. It had a masculinity about it but one which was not exclusive or overpowering. Just, comfortable. Oliver had installed a fridge and another television as well as a video recorder. He had his own telephone too, separate from the 'phones downstairs and in the kitchen. Kitty had suggested it as Oliver's long distance calls were long, frequent and expensive. The bed was huge and firm. Oliver liked posture-controlling matresses and he loved pillows. There were eight on the bed as well as two big round bolsters covered in the same material as the bedspread and the curtains.

"What do you think?" he asked with a hint of pride.

"Oh! It's lovely, Ollie." Julie dropped her handbag on the bed and hurried to the window and threw it open. The smell of the jasmine floated in as the bees went buzzing away, frightened off by the sudden opening of the window. "It's so peaceful. You can 'ardly 'ear anything. So quiet!"

"You can hear the cars on the main road alright, but not a lot else." He laughed. "Tell the truth, there's not a lot else to hear." He walked over and stood behind her. Julie reached back and found his hands which she drew around her. Oliver pressed himself closer against her magnificent body. But, despite the intimacy, Oliver was merely very happy that she liked the Park and although the one-eyed trouser snake had stirred, it was not yet ready to strike.

"'Ere, who's that?" she hissed, pointing to the figure of a man and a dog walking down the drive, the dog straining at a leash made of baling twine. Smoke puffed from his pipe.

"That's Jenks. Our gardener. You'll like him. He's lived here all his life."

Julie giggled.

"Thought it might 'ave been a relation or something."

"No. Nothing like that. Neither Kitty or I have anyone left now. Not close ones."

"Sad."

"Umm," Oliver agreed. "It is. My family lived about five miles away. That direction." He pointed from the window in the direction of Frome. "It was a lovely house. Not a bit like this one. Much, much grander."

"What 'appened to it?"

"Her Majesty's government.

"Julie looked puzzled.

"Death duties, my dear. We had to sell it."

"I am sorry, Oliver. Honestly."

"Thanks. But it's all in the past. Come on! Let's not get gloomy."

Julie regained her previous enthusiasm. She exclaimed and pointed to the end of the park, to the corner of the property formed by the lane and the main road.

"Oh! An' you got a tennis court, too. D'you play, Ollie?"

"I do," he said enthusiastically. "Don't tell me ..."

"I'll take you on anyday, mate, and beat you blind."

"Tomorrow," he said. "And then if it's hot, we'll go down to the old mill and swim."

"Great!" said Julie. She turned from the window and threw her arms round his neck. She kissed him. A long and very urgent kiss. "But first things first, old chap!"

"Oh," he said, "golly!"

"I meant a drink!"

"Oh. Yes. Of course. How rude."

186

He let her go and went over to the fridge. He took out a bottle of Lanson and held it up.

"Not so good as the Bolly last night but will it do?"

"It will do nicely, sir," she said, sinking a mock curtsey. "Glasses?"

"Over there. On that desk."

He popped the cork and poured drinks. They raised their glasses.

"To a wonderful weekend," he said.

"To us," she replied. The toasts were duly drunk.

"I'd better go down and see Mrs Tarpitt. Let her know I'm here."

"Who's Mrs Tarpitt?"

"The housekeeper. She looks after the place. Hope she's got something in the fridge. There usually is. Are you hungry?"

Julie sat down on the edge of the bed and pulled herself up to lean on the mass of pillows. She licked the rim of the fluted glass with the tip of her tongue and smiled.

"You bet," she said.

"Can you wait?"

"Not for ever. Don't be too long with Mrs Whatsit. I can get very jealous."

Oliver put down his glass. "The bathroom's just through here if you want anything. I won't be a tick."

As he left the room, he heard the thud thud as she kicked off her shoes onto the floor.

Mrs Tarpitt in her second best skirt and blouse was on her way into the hall when Oliver came bounding down the staircase.

"Hello, Mrs T!"

"Mr Oliver! What are you doing here? I thought you were s'posed to be workin'!"

"All work and no play, Mrs T. You know what that makes Jack?"

"Who's Jack?" said the housekeeper, wondering who else was going to turn up unexpectedly.

"Tried to call you earlier to let you know but couldn't get through."

"Some trouble in the exchange, sir. All fixed now, though."

"Good. Look, there's ... er ... there's no need for you to wait up. I'm just having a drink upstairs and I've got some ... er, some calls to make. I'll see to supper. Any eggs?"

"Yes, Mr Oliver."

"Bread?"

"Now when isn't there bread, Mr Oliver?"

"Sorry. So, I'll see you in the morning, Mrs T, yes?"

Oliver bounded back up the stairs leaving Mrs Tarpitt open-mouthed. What was wrong with the man, she thought. Like he's got ants in 'is pants.

"Mr Oliver," she called after him. "What'll I tell Miss Kitty?"

"That's alright, Mrs T. I'll have a word with her."

He vanished and Mrs Tarpitt heard the door of his room slam shut. She shook her head and returned to her vigil in the kitchen. The clock chimed the hour as she heard the sound of wheels on the gravel outside the front of the house. She hurried back into the hall, pulled back the heavy door curtain and brushed off several imaginary specks from her skirt before opening the door. She didn't recognise the red Ford Escort at all.

Of course, it wasn't Ludo she saw but Nick. Nick and a friend. Mrs Tarpitt was sure she recognised the face of the gentleman who got out of the car with some difficulty and limped after Nick up to the front door.

Nick ran up to her and threw his arms round her and gave her the biggest kiss.

"Hello, Mrs T. Surprise, surprise. Bet you weren't expecting anyone this weekend were you? You remember Victor Burke, don't you. Friend of dad's and mum's."

Victor smiled and extended his hand.

"Of course. Well, this is a surprise. I thought you were someone else completely."

"Someone else?" Nick enquired.

"Er ... yes ... Mr ... er ... yes." Poor Mrs Tarpitt was flustered. Sworn to secrecy by Kitty about Ludo's visit, she wasn't sure whether the secret had to encompass the whole family as well as the rest of the listening world.

"Anyway, it's lovely to see you. You look wonderful, doesn't she Victor?"

Victor nodded and smiled.

"And Jenks?" Nick called as he ran back to the car for the two bags. "He OK?"

"Fine. 'E's fine. Master Nick, where are we going to put Mr Burke?"

"Oh, don't worry about that. We can share my room, Mrs T. I'll take the studio couch." Mrs Tarpitt missed the broad wink that Nick flashed at Victor. Victor had forgotten about Mrs Tarpitt. He felt slightly uneasy. He was used to anonymity and the prospect of doing the business under the sharp eye of this formidable country woman made him now distinctly uncomfortable.

"Oh," was all Mrs Tarpitt could find to say as Nick steered first her and then Victor indoors.

"Victor's had a bit of an accident," he explained. "Probably better if I show him upstairs. He has to have a dressing changed."

"Nothing serious, I trust, Mr Burke?"

"Dog bite," said Victor graciously. "But as you say, nothing a bit of rest won't help along."

"Well, up you go, then. You'll let me know if there's anything you want, Master Nick. You know where everything is in any case. I shall be in the kitchen listenin' to *Any Questions*

"Are you sure this isn't a bit risky?" Victor whispered as Mrs Tarpitt disappeared into the kitchen.

"Of course not! What's risky? Mrs Tarpitt is the last of our worries. Come on. Lean on me."

Leaving the bags in the hall, Nick helped Victor up the stairs. Nick's room was at the back of the house and shared a bathroom with its neighbour. The view was not of the park but over the gentle valley and down to the village. The room was very much as it had always been throughout Nick's life. School prizes and trophies, books, a sound system. Boys' things.

"Where did you stay when you came before?" Nick

asked.

"Oh. In the front, I think. Big room. But I was a guest then."

"What are you now?" Nick asked."I believe the word is trick?"

"Then come here, you poor old trick."

Victor limped across the room. They embraced although Nick felt a reticence about Victor's response and he reminded himself that Victor had every right not to feel too comfortable too quickly.

"I'll just nip down and park the car, then get the bags and have a word with Mrs Tarpitt," he said. "Then we'll go down and have a drink. Bit of telly maybe? I don't think you're quite ready for a walk."

"Unless there's a Bath chair in the attic," Victor replied.

"Bathroom's one door along the hall. Shan't be long."

Nick fairly ran down the stairs. His happiness knew no bounds. For the first time he had come to what was his home not having to face his only-ness. During the two years since he'd been living permanently in London, he hadn't met anyone who had been special enough to him to want to bring them to Littlecombe. Sharing the place was like sharing himself. He wanted to, badly; he needed to but there had never been anyone right enough to do it with. It was why he had forsaken the place of late. It's what his father had reminded him of; "Mrs Tarpitt misses you ... Take a friend down ... *Find* a friend ..."

Not that Nick had ever been lonely at Littlecombe; there had always been friends in the village with whom he had explored the countryside and made camps and forts when little, rode horses when older and played mad, ruleless tennis during the summer holidays. But he'd always felt an only, at best resigned to his own company and his own thoughts rather than happy with them.

What he felt now was a wondrous completeness, as though he really had come home for the first time. He was no longer an only but part of a much larger whole, larger in implication as well as number. But he knew he mustn't rush this new condition. Too fast and Victor might easily be

190

frightened off.

He jumped into the car, reversed from the front of the house and drove around to the back.

He realised as soon as he rounded the corner. It was where he had been going to park.

E509 EJT. The number plate on his father's dark blue car gleamed in the shadowy interior of the open stable. Nick pulled up sharply. Damn! he swore to himself. Damn and damn! He couldn't think. He couldn't remember although he was certain his father had said that he wouldn't be coming down. Why? Why this weekend?

Nick parked the car next to the Jaguar and got out. he closed the door as quietly as he could.

Victor watching from the bedroom window, couldn't see Oliver's car. He knocked loudly on the window. Nick looked up, almost leaping in the air with fright. Then Victor opened the sash and leaned out.

"Sorry! Did I scare you?"

Nick smiled, the most pained and excruciating smile of his life. He knew not what to think, what to do, how to react. He knew they would have to go home. Victor would insist on it. It was probably best. But then, why? Why should Victor feel he should have to return to London? Littlecombe was Nick's home, the only home he had. And Victor was not only his friend but his father's friend too. OK Perhaps they couldn't share a bedroom but they could still be together. Why should his father think anything odd? They could bluff it out, surely? But, bluff ... Bluff was only another word for a lie. Another lie; was life always to be that way? Lie on lie on lie? No, it was time. Oliver should know. But what about Victor? What would he do? Nick felt in his gut that Victor would just leave.

Nick hurried into the house and found Mrs Tarpitt in the kitchen soaking a ham.

"Didn't know you'd got yourself a car, Nick?" she said, pouring water away into the sink.

"Er ... it's not mine."

"Mr Burke's, I suppose."

"Er ... yes. Dad's here I see."

191

"Now wasn't that a nice surprise? I dunno," she went on. "it's a weekend of surprises if you ask me. Your mother thought that no one was comin'. Still, she'll be that pleased when she gets back?"

"Mum? Back? From where? She's in London. She *told* me she was staying in London!"

Mrs Tarpitt filled the huge pan with another scald of hot water and lifted the two handled vessel from the sink to the stove. She laughed at what she thought was Nick's delight.

"She's not! She's gone to the George to meet Mr Peter."

Oh shit! thought Nick. They're all here!

"You hungry, Nick? Or shall you wait for your father? He's makin' some calls upstairs. Seemed very edgy to me. Works too hard, that man. Always 'as done. Needs to ease up. You should 'ave a word with 'im."

"Yes ... Right ... Look, I've just got to take the bags upstairs. And ..."

"Yes," replied the housekeeper absently, turning up the gas under the ham.

"I was going to say that perhaps another room for Mr Burke would be a good idea," he stammered. "His leg ... I'd hate to keep him awake or anything."

"Indeed. Dog bites can be nasty things. He's 'ad it seen to, I hope."

"Oh, yes. I'll see you in a minute, then."

Nick hurried out and collected the bags and, listening to make sure of no parental footfalls on the landing, raced up the stairs and back to his room. His face was ashen as he closed the door behind him.

"You look as though you've seen the ghost of Littlecombe Park," said Victor cheerfully. "I've always thought Kitty's father would be back one day to haunt you all. Heaven wouldn't have been quite his cup of tea somehow."

Nick shut his eyes and took a very deep breath.

"Forget my grandfather," he sighed. "Try ... *my* father !"

Victor blinked and swayed. He sat down on the edge of the bed.

"Dad's here. *Here!*"

"You're joking!"

"If I am it's certainly a very sick joke."

"Oh, Jesus!"

"And," said Nick, steeling himself to deliver the double blow.

"Oh, no!" groaned Victor. "Let's have it. The worst is yet to come, right?"

"Mum's here too." Victor pounded the bed with a clenched fist.

"I knew it! Oh, dear Lord. I *knew* something like this was going to happen!" Nick joined his friend on the edge of the bed.

"Please don't blame me, Victor. I beg you. I swear to you they both told me they weren't coming down this weekend. I would never have brought you here. I *do* respect what you said about your friendship with them. I ... I ..." Nick felt frightened now. He could feel Victor withdrawing from him. Nick held on and he held on tight.

"We'll go. Leave immediately. You were quite right to be apprehensive and I'm so, so sorry. I'll go down and tell Mrs Tarpitt your leg was bad and we had to take you back to London."

"You can't do that Nick. She's seen me for heaven's sake. She'll tell your mother anyway! We'll have to bluff it out. For now. It may work out. Who knows."

Victor whistled and shook his head, clearing his mind. Nick wanted to cry. It was babyish, he knew, but he hurt. He doubled up on the edge of the bed, wishing the hurt would go away, wishing they were anywhere but in that bedroom in that house with them! A couple of minutes passed in silence.

"Hey, hey," said Victor gently. He put his arm round Nick. "This isn't the knight in shining armour who saved me from a fate worse than death. I want my knight back. Please. Come back to me."

"Oh, Vic! Could we? I mean, would you? For me? It's not as though we don't have a story. It's weird, sure. But it is true."

193

"How will you explain how you came to be on the Heath last night? Your mother's not simple, you know!"

"Easy. No problem. Mum knew all about that. I was helping Grace and Wheels look for Ludo's dog. His old bulldog."

"You were what?" exclaimed Victor. "So it *was* Ludo's dog that bit me?"

"'Fraid so," Nick admitted. "But that's all over now. What happened to us is what happened, no more, no less. Just a massive coincidence.

"Victor groaned again and covered his face with his hands. He groaned again.

"Now I do feel awful," he said.

"Why?"

"Because I've just filed an official complaint with the police. I knew that was wrong too. God! What *have* we got ourselves into? Your mother will go spare!"

At that moment, they heard three toots on a car horn. It was too close to have come from the main road. Nick jumped up.

"Who's that? It's not mum's car. She'd never sound the horn like that."

Nick opened the bedroom door and crossed the landing. He went into the bedroom overlooking the crescent-shaped turning space in front of the house and saw Ludo's green Mercedes pull up. He knew he wasn't mistaken. There was the number plate. POP 1.

Wheels got out slowly. He wasn't smiling. He looked up fearfully at the house and Nick ducked down behind the sill. When he peeked again, Wheels was holding open the back door. Ludo was already standing on the gravel drive and a woman was getting out of the back door of the limo. It wasn't anyone Nick knew. He hurried back into his room and closed the door.

"It's Ludo!"

Victor froze. What *was* happening?

"I don't believe it."

"Believe it. He's with some strange woman and Wheels."

194

"Who or what the hell is Wheels?"

"His driver. Look, I'd better go down. Stay here."

"God, I need a drink!" exclaimed Victor.

"Don't worry," said Nick halfway out of the door, "I'll bring one up when I come back."

Ludo had already pressed the front door bell. Mrs Tarpitt hurried from the kitchen just as Nick reached the foot of the stairs.

"Oh, please, let me, Nick," begged Mrs Tarpitt whose face was a glorious blend of excitement and nervousness. "Let me open the door to them?" She threw back the door curtain and fairly wrenched the heavy oak door from its casement.

Ludo was now in performance gear. Charm seeped from every pore.

"And here's Mrs Tarpitt!" he exclaimed, holding out his arms as though greeting a woman who'd saved his life. "Well, well. You haven't changed a bit in, what is it, twenty years? You look so young!"

If there was an eighth heaven, Mrs Tarpitt was in it. As Ludo let her out of his embrace, she was radiant, happier than a sunbeam. The man whose voice she listened to on the radio for years was standing in *her* hall and had just hugged her! Ha! she thought, if only the whole village were here to see it. They'd never believe her but she didn't care.

"Oh welcome, welcome, Mr Ludo. It's so lovely to 'ave you back at Littlecombe."

Mrs Tarpitt was so overcome, she hadn't noticed Violetta, standing behind Ludo. Violetta was enjoying Ludo's performance enormously. She'd been known to put on pretty decent ones herself in her time.

"Can I introduce Violetta Abizzi? Violetta, this is Kitty's famous Mrs Tarpitt!"

Violetta came forward and shook Mrs T's hand.

"'Ello, Mrs Tarpitt. I'm very pleased to meet you at last."

"Likewise Miss ... er, Miss," replied Mrs Tarpitt knowing very well that her country tongue would never get itself round Abizzi in a month of Friday evenings. "Come in, come in, do." Mrs Tarpitt opened the door wider and Ludo and Violetta came in. Then Ludo saw Nick.

"Hey! It's my Pet Shop Boy again. Kitty didn't say you were going to be here!" Ludo hugged his godson and Nick hugged him back. Very, very tightly.

"What the hell are you doing here?" Nick said in welcome, grinning from ear to ear."

Kitty said we could use the place for the weekend. She thought it was going to be empty."

"Hey, man! We all thought it was going to be empty."

"All?" exclaimed Ludo. "Oh, this is terrible of me." He took Violetta's arm and gently led her forward. "Nick, I'd like you to meet Violetta Abizzi. Vee, this is Nick Longingly, my godson. Kitty and Oliver's boy."

Violetta smiled. Nick smiled. It was like at first sight. No hesitation about whether it was alright to kiss or not by either party. Kisses were forthcoming all round.

"It's good to meet you, Nick," she said warmly. "'E's told us so much about you all. I almost feel you're family."

"Well," said Nick, scratching his head. "I suppose we are ... I mean ..." He threw up his hands and shrugged and pointed to Ludo and then to Violetta and smiled an impish smile. Ludo was bubbling. Nick hadn't seen him look so genuinely happy for years. He took Violetta's hand.

"Shall we tell him, Vee?"

She blushed. She looked at the floor. Then at Mrs Tarpitt and nodded.

"Go on, then."

"You're the first to know. We're going to be married," Ludo announced proudly. He spoke the line to her, to his Violetta and they kissed in the hallway of Littlecombe Park. Now it was public and they both knew it was true.

"Oh!" said Mrs Tarpitt and promptly burst into tears.

"That's marvellous!" Nick shouted and hugged the happy couple. "Wait 'til mum hears. And dad. Hey, dad! Dad!"

"You mean, they're here?" said Ludo in amazement. "Both of them?"

"Dad is. Mum's gone to the pub to met Peter. They'll be

196

back in a minute. Hey, dad!"

The car horns, the noise in the hall and the subsequent peals of joy, brought Oliver from his room, leaving a terrified Julie wondering what kind of madhouse she'd arrived at. Oliver appeared in his dressing gown at the top of the stairs.

"What on earth ... My God!" Oliver saw only Ludo and Nick. He knew nothing of opera and didn't recognise Violetta. He ran down the stairs, not knowing who to welcome first.

"They're getting married, dad. Ludo and Vee!"

Oliver shook hands with Violetta, tightening the cord of his dressing gown beforehand.

"Sorry about the attire," he apologised. "I'm Oliver. I was ... er ... in the bath. I'm so pleased to meet you, Miss ...?"

"Abizzi, Oliver. Violetta Abizzi," said Ludo proudly.

"Hello, Oliver!" Violetta kissed him on both cheeks. "Like I just said to Nick, Ludo's bin goin' on about you all so much, I feel I know you already. Of course, you're not a bit like how he described but then people never are, are they?"

There was general laughter.

"Mrs T? Bring a bottle of champagne, will you? Into the drawing room? Nick! Show them in and give me a moment to change. I'll be down instantly. Welcome to Littlecombe, by the way."

"Thanks, Oliver," said Ludo, clapping his friend on the back. "It's good to be here."

Oliver raced off upstairs. He was happy but somewhat taken aback. His weekend hadn't exactly turned out the way he planned it and he just hoped Julie would understand. On his way back to the bedroom, he'd almost made up his mind to bring her down. Why not, he reasoned? Nick would understand, surely? And Julie Burge was no slouch, in anyone's book.

Nick was showing Ludo and Violetta through to the drawing room. Mrs Tarpitt was hovering, beaming when Wheels appeared in the front door with the bags. Nick

197

turned and saw him.

"Wheels! Great to see you, man!"

Wheels looked pale. He smiled sheepishly.

Mrs Tarpitt turned at the mention of this newest arrival. She felt queer, decidedly queer. It must be the excitement, she told herself. She steadied herself on the edge of the hall table. The sensation of faintness passed but it was immediately replaced by something she instantly recognised. One of her feelings. Unmistakable.

As Wheels stood in the doorway, being scrutinised and surveyed in such strange circumstances, he felt his stomach spasm as it had never done before. Slowly he felt the handles of the suitcases slipping from his hands. The smile slid from his face and he felt himself helplessly overtaken by a warm, thick, velvety blackness.

They watched in disbelief as he slumped to the floor.

"Oh my God!" Nick murmured, taken completely by surprise.

"Wheels!" cried Ludo and ran across the oak floor. They both knelt down beside the crumpled Wheels. Nick straightened him out. Mrs Tarpitt came across and knelt at his head. Nick put Wheels' head onto her lap and Ludo straightened his legs.

"Wheels! Wheels!" Nick called, and felt the man's damp brow.

Violetta hurried over, concern and compassion furrowing her face.

"I'll get some cushions," she said. "And cover 'im up wi' this." She tossed her Liberty shawl down and Ludo covered his friend's chest.

"Best loose 'is shirt," commanded Mrs Tarpitt. "And run for a glass of water, Nick. An' let 'im 'ave some air!"

Ludo unbuttoned the collar of Wheels' denim shirt and unloosed the leather thongs of the Texan tie which ran through the large piece of Indian turquoise.

Mrs Tarpitt raised the man's head higher in her lap and as she did so, the denim shirt fell open more, revealing Wheels' chest. Ludo moved the position of the turquoise clip. Mrs Tarpitt gasped. She gave a little moan, almost as though she were in pain.

What she had seen was the birthmark. Wheels always called it his psychic wound. It was most distinctive, shaped like a butterfly and about the size of a fifty pence piece. It was a birthmark so unique, that once seen it was never to be forgotten.

Nick returned with the water as Wheels eyes fluttered open. He looked up; he didn't appear to be frightened but his eyes were wide open, more in wonder than panic.

"'Ello old lad," murmured Ludo kindly. "It's only us."

"Just relax," said Nick. Violetta returned with cushions from the drawing room. They weren't needed. She stood by, clasping them to her bosom.

Wheels tried to struggle up on his elbow. He caught sight of Mrs Tarpitt. Now it was her turn to be wide-eyed as Wheels looked straight into her eyes.

"'Ello, 'ello" he said and managed a grin. "Sorry about this. Dunno what come over me? All over your nice clean floor too."

"Let's get him to bed," said Nick. "Where can we put him, Mrs T?"

"I'll look after 'im," she heard herself saying. "We'll take 'im through to the flat. 'E can 'ave my spare room."

"Not upstairs?" Nick asked.

"No," she said emphatically. "No. I'll see to 'im. I can look out for 'im better in my own place." Involuntarily, without meaning to be so familiar, she stroked Wheels' hair away from his forehead. "The dear boy. An' 'e'll need to see the doctor."

"No!" said Wheels quickly, becoming agitated and flustered. "No doctor! Please! Ludo! Promise me you won't call a doctor!"

Violetta knelt down too and she took Wheels' hand.

"Now don't fret, lad. No one's calling a doctor if you don't want one. Let's get you into bed, though, eh?"

Wheels nodded and smiled.

"Do you think you can get up?" Nick asked.

"Yeah. Think so." Ludo and Nick helped the man to his feet. Mrs Tarpitt then took over.

199

"You lean on me, young man. Nick'll take the other side. There. Now, off we go."

Violetta picked up the cushions and slipped her arm through Ludo's.

"I'll be back in a jiffy with something to drink for you, Mister Ludo. Just pop through into the drawing room and make yourselves comfortable."

"There's no hurry, Mrs Tarpitt. Let us know if there's anything we can do."

"Sorry, Loo," Wheels called weakly as they led him away.

Ludo and Violetta went into the drawing room.

"Well, there's one good thing about all that," said Violetta. "We'll never forget the day we got engaged!"

"You can say that again," Ludo replied. "What do you think's the matter? He's never fainted before."

A BOW OF BURNING GOLD

When Peter and Kitty entered the bar of the George, Littlecombe's only pub, there were few people drinking. Both John and Stephanie Gilroy were behind the bar and greeted their neighbours.

"Thought you two were staying in the smoke this weekend?" said the jovial Scottish landlord as Peter feigned exhaustion and asked for his usual.

"That was the original intention," commented Kitty wryly.

"Cider, Kitty?" asked Stephanie.

"Umm, lovely. I could do with it too."

"Sounds like it," said Stephanie as she filled a half pint mug with locally brewed cider. "But by the sound of it, I'd better not ask any more."

"Very wise, Stephanie," said Peter. He took up the foaming pint John had pulled and quaffed the head and the first inch with great satisfaction. "Haven't had time to gauge the lie of the lady's feelings yet."

"The lady," said Kitty with a laugh, "is quite calm. But you know what it is, Stephanie. Why is it that we always seem to be at everyone's beck and call?"

"Here we go," John interjected. "Peter, I think we're just about to be got at."

"As if I would," Kitty replied. The baby alarm screwed to the wall of the bar called mummy! and Stephanie raised an eyebrow.

"So will you get that, then?" she said, hands on hips, to her husband.

"I'd love to, darlin', but she asked for you!"

"There," said Stephanie, "I think you've been proved right, Kitty."

As Stephanie turned to leave the bar, the door opened

and Ernest Sanders came in. In his mid-fifties, a jolly man, dressed in shorts, a T-shirt which had seen better days and trainers which had forgotten that there ever had been better days.

"'Evening, Ernest," said John. "Usual?"

"Please," replied the newcomer. Hello Kitty, dear. Peter. Adam said you were down after all."

"John!" called Stephanie from the foot of the stairs. "Would you pay Ernest for the two pies, please!"

"Starting a little outside catering?" Peter enquired as the gin and tonic appeared on the bar.

"Never! That's a mug's game, my dear chap."

"So, tell us, darling. What's with the pies?" Kitty asked.

"Experiments, my dear. John and Stephanie very kindly take my try outs. Adam and I couldn't possibly eat them all."

"So what's the latest?" Peter enquired. "I sense a deadline in the air."

Ernest took a good swig at the gin.

"How right you are, sir. They've asked me to do a book on English puddings. And the deadline's the end of August."

"And the best puddings you'll ever taste," interjected the landlord. "English or no."

"Spoken like a true Scot, Jack," Ernest replied.

"Where's Adam?" Kitty enquired.

"Choir practice, my dear." Ernest shook his head sadly. "If you can call it a choir."

"Poor Adam," Kitty reflected. "It has been a bit thin of late. Mrs T tells me he's putting 'Jerusalem' in again on Sunday and that really needs a lot of singing. Such a shame for him."

"How many turn up to practice now?" Peter asked.

"About ten, I think," said Ernest. The Rivers family make up five of those. Then Miss Norman, Mrs Creese and that huge Hollingshurst woman."

"Any men, apart from Mr Rivers? And I thought Jenks was a singer."

"Was is the word. Of course, there's Adam, Len Curtis

202

and Mr Hollingshurst. But that's it. Hardly basso profundo, is it? They lost Jenks after he fell out with Mrs Hollingshurst."

"I didn't know about that," said Kitty. "What happened?"

"Sperm," Ernest replied flatly and finished off the gin.

Kitty and Peter looked at each other and suppressed a giggle. John Gilroy rumbled with laughter and handed Ernest his money for the pies.

"Did you say what I thought you said?" Peter gasped.

"Oh, the nitty gritty of country life," laughed Ernest. "You see, they'd made an agreement. Mrs H's Beau was to be put to Mr Jenkin's Queenie. Nothing happened after a week and Jenks passed the comment that perhaps Mrs Hollingshurst's Beau Boy of Bankside was sterile if not worse."

"Oh, Lord," said Peter. "Not in Littlecombe, surely!"

"Peter! Then what happened?" asked Kitty, almost convulsed with laughter.

"Oh nothing. Only World War Three. There's nothing as senstitive as virility impugned." Ernest looked at his watch. "I've got to go. Devil makes work and all that."

"Come for a drink tomorrow lunchtime," called Kitty as he waved and made to go. "Tell Adam, will you?"

"Will do, my dears. Back to the grindstone. Farewell. Oh, and by the way, I think it would be much appreciated if you'd come to church on Sunday as it's 'Jerusalem'. Even I'm going, enough said?"

"Enough said," Peter and Kitty replied together. "'Bye."

Ernest left as two tourist couples came into the bar. John welcomed them. Peter finished his pint and Kitty downed her cider. They looked at each other and each blew a silent kiss to the other at the bar. Kitty slipped her arm through his.

"Mind if we skip darts, Peter? Ludo should have arrived by now."

"Agreed," Peter replied. "Tell you the truth, I'm pooped. It's been such a hot day. I could do with a shower. Lets go."

They bade their farewells to their host and went to their

cars. Swallows were fluttering at the low eaves of the old coaching stop amongst the hanging baskets of dark blue lobelia, trailing scarlet and pink geraniums and nasturtiums. Kitty and Peter walked arm in arm to the car park. Sounds of laughter came from the beer garden at the rear of the pub. From across the road, they could hear the organ playing the introduction to 'Jerusalem' as Margaret Clark fought what seemed an uneven battle with the black notes and the pedals.

Kitty winced and Peter nodded sympathetically.

"I must say, darling, life with you is never dull," he said.

She sighed deeply and nodded her head.

"I know. What have we done to deserve it? But there must be a quieter life somewhere. Surely?"

"But would you be as happy?" he asked.

"I don't think it honestly matters what I am," she replied. "As long as everyone else is alright, it's enough. It's all a bit of a melting pot at the moment. Makes me wish I was an alchemist. So I could turn everything into gold."

"Well, I love living with you, my darling. And," he added, "I must admit that at this moment, even I am consumed with curiousity as to what your ex-lover is up to."

"Not half as much as I am."

"We must keep out of the way, though, Kitty. It's only fair. Give them a chance."

Kitty reached her car. She kissed her man before getting in.

"Well, it's only us and them," she said. "At least we can keep ourselves to ourselves." He nodded and shut her door after her. She wound down the window. "And you honestly and really don't mind about this weekend?"

"Not in the slightest," he assured her. "It's a sort of watershed, isn't it? In your life, at least. I wouldn't not be here for anything. Who knows? If you can get each other cleared out of your systems, maybe ...?"

She laughed and started the engine.

"Maybe," she said. "Then perhaps I can start coming to grips with all the rest."

One after the other, they reversed out onto the main road and set off back to the park.

O CLOUDS, UNFOLD!

Although the atmosphere in Oliver's bedroom contained something of the interruptus, the mood was far from acrimonious. Neither Oliver nor Julie were very much put out by the temporary cessation of frivolities. Julie was in too good a mood and Oliver was not the sort of man to allow his inamorata to suffer for too long. And anyway, they both knew that there was more of the same to come; much more.

"And you really don't mind meeting them?" Oliver asked for the second time. "You know you don't have to if you don't want to. I shan't be long. Just to have a drink with them. It's sort of business too. The chap's a client as well as a friend."

"'Course I don't, silly. Just 'ope I won't let you down,'" said Julie, pulling on her panties and rummaging in her bag for a skirt she remembered packing which was of a more modest length than the one in which she had arrived. Oliver put on chinos and a Ralph Lauren shirt and slipped his feet, sockless, into his New York penny loafers. As he did up the last of the buttons on the fly, he took a deep breath and decided to make a clean breast of the other thing.

"There is one other thing, though," he said as the beginning of his admission.

Julie misinterpreted his cautious opening.

"Ollie, I promise! I won't say a thing. An' if I do I promise not to drop a single 'aitch'. I can, you know. If I 'ave to. Took elocution last year."

He laughed.

"No, it's not that, darling."

Julie's ears pricked up but she didn't betray herself. However, inwardly she preened. It was the first time he had called her darling and Oliver wasn't the theatrical type.

"What, then?"

"I ... I have a son," he blurted out. "He's downstairs too. I didn't know he'd be here you see and ..."

"So," she said with a broad grin. "You got a son. I'm not prejudiced. I quite like sons. Some of them grow up to be men."

"But you don't mind meeting him? He's not a brattish infant or anything. He's twenty."

"Why should I?"

"Thanks, Julie. He's awfully nice. I do hope you'll like him."

Oliver looked at his odd, youthful companion. God, he thought, you're a far cry from Angela Carbury. He sighed as his mind fluttered through the files of the women with whom he would ordinarily dally. Julie Burge was certainly surprisingly different.

"It's just that he's never met any ... you know. He's never actually *seen* me with anyone else but his mother."

"Then it's about time 'e did," said Julie positively.

"'E's goin' to 'ave to sometime, best get it over with. Then you'll know, won't you? Silly to 'ave secrets like that in families. Starts all sorts of ructions, dunnit?"

He held out his arms and she came to him, burying her face in the soft linen of the shirt. He put his hand on the back of her head and pulled her in.

"You are so uncomplicated," he whispered appreciatively, kissing the top of her head. "That's what I like about you. Straight to the heart of things."

"And no messin'," she added. "Only way to be, Ollie. Believe me." She withdrew and kissed him. "But I better put a bit of face on, love. Gimme five minutes."

"OK. Let me pop down and get things going and I'll be back for you. Five minutes, alright?"

Julie went through to the bathroom and waved her mascara stick over her shoulder as Oliver quietly closed the bedroom door.

As he rounded the corner of the landing he saw

someone carrying a bag into the room next to Nick's. The room swap had been a swift rearrangement. Nick had hurried upstairs between settling Wheels on Mrs Tarpitt's spare bed and seeing to the champagne.

Oliver had no reason to think that the figure in the jeans and denim shirt wasn't Nick.

"Has Mrs T taken in the champagne, Nick?"

Victor whipped round; he had the glass of whisky in his hand which Nick had brought up for him. He'd hardly taken a sip and the whole lot slopped over the front of his shirt.

"Victor!"

"Oliver!" Victor looked terror-stricken. "Dear."

"What ...? No one told me you were here? When did you arrive?"

"Er ... er ... earlier. I thought Kitty would have told you."

"Kitty's in London."

"No! She's not. She ... er ... decided to come down. I think she's at the pub, meeting Peter."

It was Oliver's turn to be surprised. Ambushed. Alarm bells not only rang, they clanged deafeningly. Nick, yes. That was sensible. But one step at a time. Kitty too? Could she stand it? Could Julie? Could *he*? His expression betrayed his panic, although Victor interpreted his friend's surprise as something quite else.

"Are you alright, Ollie?" Victor was the only person in the world who ever called Oliver by his childhood diminutive. "Speak to me, old son?"

"Well, well," Oliver gulped, wondering how much time he had to whip downstairs, knock back a quick glass of champagne and then get out. "Full house, eh?"

"So it seems. You don't seem too happy about it?" said Victor, arming himself with all the right explanations if Oliver should decide to go for an immediate showdown.

"Er ... no ... I mean, yes! Of course. It's ... great. Mrs Tarpitt's put you in there, I see?" Oliver was obviously on edge, Victor thought. There was an awkwardness about their meeting which wasn't usual. Victor was convinced that Oliver knew.

"Er ... Yes. I was just taking in my bag. You gave me quite a fright."

"What's life without a fright occasionally? Sorry. Here, let me take that glass and I'll refill it. In fact, why not come down stairs and have a drink with the others. You've obviously seen Nick." Victor thought the obviously was delivered too deliberately. Victor was now ultra-sensitive. "Ludo's here too. With his fiancee! How about that for a surprise?"

Oliver took Victor's glass and started off down the stairs.

"Quite a revelation," Victor replied nervously, steeling himself to attempt to get through the upcoming bluff. "What next, you might say?"

"Indeed. Tonight I could expect anything. See you in the drawing room. It's great to have you here, by the way!" Oliver called as he disappeared into the hall.

But will you love me tomorrow, thought Victor as he limped miserably into his newly allocated accomodation, sensing that Oliver's reaction to his being at Littlecombe so coincidentally with only Longingly son and heir had come a little sooner than he had anticipated.

In the drawing room, Ludo and Violetta were admiring the view of the garden and the park through the bay window as Oliver came in. Nick was popping a cork which ejected with a bang into the air.

"That's the stuff," exclaimed Oliver, holding two glasses over the tray as Nick poured. He carried them over and handed one each to Ludo and Violetta. Nick poured another two.

"Pour another one, Nick. Victor's here too."

Nick looked blank and stared at his father.

"Victor?" he murmured.

"Yes. You remember Victor Burke. My oldest friend. Apparently your mother asked him down."

Nick continued to stare at his father strangely.

"You did know your mother was here too, didn't you? Don't you young people *ever* communicate?"

"We didn't know about Kitty either," said Ludo. "But I can't tell you how glad you're all here. We're very pleased, aren't we Vee?"

"Very," smiled Violetta.

"Yes," added Oliver grimly. "Very."

"Nick, don't stand there like a lemon, go upstairs and fetch Victor and we can have our toast. I have a call coming in soon on the upstairs line. I can't miss it."

"Oh, er ... sure, dad," Nick replied and did as he'd been told.

"Where's Mrs T?" said Oliver. "She should have a glass of bubbly as well."

"She's taking care of Ludo's young lad," Violetta explained. "The driver. Had a bit of a turn. Passed right out. Like a light."

"Is he alright?" Oliver asked with concern, more in the hope that such a convenient faint might also momentarily overcome him to get him out of the probability of bumping into Kitty.

"Hope so. Not like him at all," said Ludo. "I thought he had the constitution of an ox. I'll go and see him in a minute."

"Well, if Mrs T's looking after him, he's in the best hands."

Nick and Victor appeared in the doorway. Nick coughed nervously.

No one heard the sound on the gravel outside made by the return of Kitty's Golf and Peter's Rover. No one in the drawing room heard Kitty's key in the lock of the old oak front door.

And, unnoticed by anyone in front or behind him, Victor squeezed Nick's hand before somehow mustering all his reserves and, assuming all his usual poise and outrageous aplomb, entered the room.

"Ah! Ludo. We meet again."

He shook hands with Ludo and inclined his head politely to Violetta.

"Good to see you, Victor. Sorry about the other day at the house. I'm sorry you had to do battle with my mum alone. Hope it went alright?"

"Oh, swimmingly!" Victor said, accepting the glass of

champagne Nick handed to him.

"By the way, Victor, this is Violetta Abizzi."

The painter and the opera singer shook hands.

"A toast, then!" Oliver called just as Kitty appeared in the doorway, Peter standing just behind her.

And then, not two minutes behind him, Julie Burge, freshly made up and raring to go, snapped a couple of colourful hair clips into her top knot and decided to go downstairs without waiting for Oliver to excuse himself from his guests to collect her.

"Oliver!" Kitty exclaimed.

"Oh! Kitty! You're back! So ... so soon!"

Kitty came into the room and saw Ludo, whom she was expecting. She hurried across the big room to embrace him. But on the way over the red turkey rug she spotted not only Nick, but also Victor and ... who else? Her pace slowed as her head revolved from one to the other, slowly, disbelievingly until her eyes, on stalks though they were, came to rest on the small, plump figure of the woman whom Ludo led forward by the hand ... *Violetta*?

Peter was hard on her heels.

"Violetta?" he whispered in amazement. "How in heaven's name ...?"

Kitty merely stood dumbly and aped him, mouthing Violetta silently, with a look of open-mouthed amazement on her face.

"Hello, Peter. And Kitty, love. Thank you so much for letting us come!"

Violetta hurried across the room and kissed her lawyer and then her lawyer's catatonic lady.

"And Victor?" murmured Kitty as she neared the surface of her bemused state of shock. "Oliver didn't tell me you were coming?"

Victor too kissed Kitty and then finally Ludo gave her a huge hug, twirling her round and round in his arms.

"Kitty, Kitty! At last! This is *so* fantastic! You're *here*!"

Ludo at last let her go. Kitty steadied herself on the back of one of the over-stuffed sofas.

"And you, darling?" she said to Nick who finally got to

210

kiss his mother. "Last heard of you were hunting dogs on Hampstead Heath. What on earth brings you here too?"

Nick blushed, returned to his butler's station and filled two more glasses which he hurriedly thrust into Kitty's and Peter's hands.

"So what was this toast?" Kitty asked Oliver. "What are we drinking to, apart from us, that is?"

"To Ludo and Violetta!" proposed Oliver hastily. "Long life and happiness."

Glasses were raised and echoed "Long lifes and happinesses" sounded. Nick went and stood next to Victor and pinched his bottom. No one else saw. Victor nearly choked.

"Now," said Kitty, "would someone *please* tell me what is going on?"

Oliver, Nick and Ludo all started to talk at once.

"One at a time will do nicely," said Kitty.

Ludo grinned, like a little boy with a secret.

"Loo?" Kitty asked.

"We're getting married, Kitty."

Kitty paused, initially finding the announcement indigestible.

"You," she said slowly, pointing to Ludo, "are going to marry ..." She pointed at Violetta and Peter finished off her conclusion.

"Vi-o-letta," he murmured almost inaudibly as though struck mute by an invisible, paralysing ray.

"I must sit down," said Kitty quickly and sank onto the edge of a Gainsborough chair. She could not take her eyes off the singers, who, now re-entwined, beamed happily.

"Sorry, love," said Violetta sympathetically. "I suppose it is a bit of a shock. But you're the first to know."

"Well, I think it's marvellous news," said Oliver.

"So do I!" Nick agreed and raised his glass again.

"Hear, hear," said Victor. "To Ludo and Violetta. And to all the other happy couples in the world tonight." He winked at Nick, clicked glasses and then raised his own towards Ludo and Violetta.

"Oh, my God!" exclaimed Peter suddenly just as Julie

211

Burge swept into the room. The only person facing the door was Ludo, standing in the window with the evening light behind him. His raised glass didn't get as far as his lips. It slipped from his hand onto the floor as he froze to the spot at the sight of number seventeen. Their eyes met instantly. Julie stifled a scream and spun on her flat, black, noiseless pumps and dashed from the room.

Everyone turned to Peter, thinking his ejaculation had been the cause of the crashed glass.

"What, darling?" Kitty asked.

Peter too sat down.

"We're two short, my darling. Remember?"

Kitty frowned before the realisation dawned.

"Oh, good grief," she murmured. "Rachel and Gerald!"

Violetta, Nick and Victor were busy on their knees collecting the pieces of the shattered glass and didn't notice Ludo loosening the collar of his shirt.

"Of course, they do something like this in Russia," said Violetta as she stood up. "Y'know. Chuckin' the glasses into the back of the fire." Then she noticed. "You alright, Ludo? You look a bit wobbly."

"I ... I think so ...," he stammered. "Perhaps I'm tired."

"What's up Loo?" asked Kitty.

He paused for a moment and then laughed the thought away.

"No. It's nothing." He had already begun to persuade himself that what he had seen, who he had seen, was a figment of his imagination.

"Go on," urged Kitty."Well, I could have sworn I saw a girl standing in that doorway."

"A girl?" Violetta echoed.

"Oh, her," said Oliver dismissively. "Lots of blonde hair? Carrying a notebook?"

"I didn't see the notebook but, yes. Who is she?"

All eyes in the room turned to Oliver. Nick went round with the wastepaper basket in which the broken glass was collected.

"My new secretary," he said quickly, airily. "I didn't think anyone would be down this weekend and so I took

212

the opportunity of ... "

Kitty raised her eyes to Nick who winked at her.

"Oliver, darling. You sly old fox!"

"What do you mean, Kitty?"

"Come on, dad."

"Come on, what?" blustered Oliver defensively."

Is she a new girlfriend?" Kitty asked outright. "Don't be so shy!"

"Yes, Ollie. It's not against the law," said Victor precipitously. Nick nudged him.

Oliver looked fearfully embarrassed and shifted from one foot to the other.

"Oliver, love, you can't leave the poor thing locked in the bedroom, can she Ludo?" said Violetta spiritedly.

Ludo looked strangely at Oliver and didn't answer.

"Yes," Nick persisted, "go and get her, dad. We're not going to eat her, for God's sake. Or you for that matter."

Peter came to Oliver's rescue.

"Don't worry, Oliver. I'm with you. It is a bit overpowering, I agree."

"Thanks, Peter." Oliver grinned at the assembly of amused faces. "Perhaps later, yes?"

"Unless she intends to spend the whole weekend in your bedroom, I would say undoubtedly later," said Kitty.

"Would you ... er ... excuse me, then?" Oliver said. "I ought to pop up and explain."

"Yes, go on with you," said Kitty.

"Oliver!" Ludo called. "Could I just have a quick word with you?"

"And I'll show Violetta to your room while you're having this little word," added Kitty. She held out her hand to Violetta and the party began to break up.

As Kitty led the way up the stairs, chattering to Violetta, Oliver and Ludo went into the study.

"What can I do for you, old chap?" Oliver asked.

"It's that girl."

"Who? You mean Julie?"

Ludo nodded.

"I don't know how you managed it, old son, but you've

213

just met up with my last old lady."

"Your *what*?"

"Julie Burge. That's her name isn't it?"

"Well ... yes ... but I don't understand."

"She's been living with me, Oliver. For the past four months."

"But you and ... and Violetta?"

"Very recent, old son. She was at Kitty and Peter's one night at dinner. We met. We met again. The rest you know. Only trouble is ..." He pointed upwards, in the direction of the storey above.

"I *thought* there was something strange," said Oliver.

"So she didn't tell you?"

"Ludo, I swear! If I'd known, there'd have been no question of ... well, you know. I'm most terribly sorry, old chap!"

Ludo grinned.

"Don't be. Not on my account, mate. In fact, I couldn't be more pleased for you." Ludo looked over his shoulder, ensuring privacy. "It's just that I don't fancy Vee knowing." He winked at Oliver. "Get my drift?"

Oliver whistled through his teeth.

"I can't understand," he reflected sadly. "She seemed to be fond of me?"

"Oliver, I'm sure she is. She's a great girl. But it wasn't for me ... Any chance I could have a word with her?"

"And Kitty? Did she know her too? You'll have to talk to Kitty as well."

Kitty called down into the hall from the balcony.

"Ludo! That's a very long little word you're having. You can talk about business later. Come upstairs. Violetta's taking a shower."

"OK, Ludo. I'll fix it," Oliver assured. "Knock on my door. In half-an-hour."

"You're a pal, Oliver," Ludo said. "I owe you one."

"You owe me several," Oliver replied laconically as Ludo left the study.

Oliver too started upstairs. He too had some talking to do. Was he being used? Had he been cleverly caught like a fly in the jaws of a Venus Fly-Trap? He couldn't believe it so. There had been too many other pointers. But why? Why hadn't she told him?

"Who's for a proper drink?" Peter asked both Nick and Victor in the drawing room. "Scotch anyone?"

"Thanks, Peter. Never did a single word sound as sweet."

"Nick?"

"Why not, indeed."

Peter went over to the sofa table and began collating glasses, ice and whisky at the drinks tray.

"Perhaps you'd each like to help yourselves to your mix. I take it neat."

"Me too," said Victor who sank gratefully into an armchair. His leg was throbbing. But then so was his conscience. He had already made up his mind to cancel the charges he'd filed with the police about Bullshit but the current circumstances made it all the more urgent he do so at the first opportunity. He was also beginning to think that they just might escape from this weekend unscathed.

Nick took Victor his drink and then returned to mix his with Coke. Peter joined Victor in the opposite armchair and they raised their glasses.

"So did you come down with Oliver and his ... friend?"

"Er ... no."

Victor flashed a mayday glance to Nick. Nick shrugged helplessly.

"Don't tell me you took the train to Bath?" Peter persisted. "That's a killer on Friday evenings. Packed with Sloanes. Accents like broken glass. Lot of twittering starlings in pearls." Both Peter's question and his analogy went unanswered. He looked puzzled.

Nick came over and sat on the floor in front of the coffee table which separated the men.

"Victor came with me, Peter."

Victor took a big swallow at the well-filled tumbler of whisky.

"That was good of you, Nick. So it's your little red Escort out there? Did Oliver spring for it?"

215

"It's Hertz," said Nick.

"Whose?"

"It belongs to Hertz. We hired it."

"Oh. Well, probably cheaper than two train tickets and you can use it to ... to ... to get ... to ... to wherever you want to ... to get to."

Peter's ramblings slowed as the penny began to drop. It could not have failed to drop. Nick was sitting, cross-legged, looking at him appealingly. Victor looked at Nick and braced himself.

"Oh," said Peter simply. "Oh."

"Sorry, Peter," Nick said. "Better out than in."

Peter blinked and sighed.

"As the actress said to the bishop," he said, attempting the feeblest of feeble jokes. So, he thought, Rachel had been spot on. He looked at Victor.

"How long ... when did you meet?" Peter asked limply, groping in the dark for what he felt was a constructive direction.

"Last night, believe it or not," Victor replied. "And perfectly innocently, too, I might add."

"I was looking for Bullshit on the Heath," explained Nick. "And I found Victor. But only after Bullshit had taken a chew on his leg." Nick pulled up the leg of Victor's jeans and displayed the bruise and the teeth marks. "What d'you think mum'll say?"

"I should imagine," said Peter, "she'll want to know if Victor's had that bite looked at."

"I think Nick was meaning about ... about me being here. With him. Her son?"

Peter downed the remainder of his scotch and slumped back in his chair. He was considering. He wished he was considering a fine legal point. He wished, just as Kitty had wished earlier, that he was an alchemist instead of a simple lawyer.

"Well?" Nick urged. "And what do you think, too?"

"What do I think ...? What *do* I think?" said Peter, as though prompting himself. "I think nothing. I honestly, truly think nothing. I'm very fond of you, Nick. And you,

Victor. You're both good, sound people. That's what I think."

"And it doesn't worry you?" Victor asked, hoping that they might have found an ally.

"Being gay? No. It honestly doesn't worry me." He smiled. "Feel better?"

They both nodded and Victor held Nick's shoulder for a brief, affectionate moment.

"How do you suggest I handle mum?" Nick pressed. "Straight out? Or a bit of beating in the bush?"

They heard Kitty calling as she came down the stairs.

"Can we sleep on it?" Peter said quickly. "Save it 'til tomorrow, eh?"

"Thanks, Peter. You're a friend," said Nick and Victor nodded as Kitty came into the room.

"Well, that's the lovers settled," she said happily. "Mystery solved. Who would have thought it would turn out to be Violetta? What *did* I do when I asked Ludo to that dinner?"

The three male faces turned towards her.

"I think you made two people very happy, darling," said Peter. "It's your gift."

"I wish, I wish," said Kitty pouring a gin and tonic. "But you're right. It's enough to see them happy. Everyone should be happy." She sat down on the sofa. "So what's this chauvinistic little huddle all about?" she asked. "And I hope you haven't forgotten our troubles are only just beginning."

"Sorry?" said Nick.

"Hasn't Peter told you? Well, my little dears, it seems that Rachel is on her way down."

"Our Rachel?" Nick asked.

"The very same. With Gerald Ward."

"Who's Gerald Ward?" Victor wondered aloud."

Victor! Your memory, darling. Gerald Ward you met at our house with Ludo and Violetta."

"Gerald," Peter explained, "was once married to Violetta and is her manager."

"This is getting seriously ridiculous," Victor opined.

217

"Hush, dear," said Kitty. "There's more. Wait."

"Rachel was supposed to interview Violetta today and Violetta didn't show up," Peter went on.

"Why should Rach want to interview Violetta?" Nick questioned. "Is she somebody I should know?"

"Violetta Abizzi is an opera singer, Nick," Victor interposed. "Courtney says she's the only English singer worth listening to."

"Dear Courtney," said Kitty. "How is he?"

"May I finish?" Peter said. "As the bombshell is about to burst any minute, we might all like to be clear as to why we are being annihilated."

"Sorry, darling."

"Violetta didn't turn up for the interview. Rachel is hopping mad. Rachel is also a journalist. Rachel works for the *Daily Standard*." He paused. "Anyone getting the drift?"

"I don't understand where Gerald Ward fits in," said Nick.

"Bless the boy!" exclaimed Kitty. "He fits, darling, the way two perfectly matched teaspoons sit in the cutlery drawer."

"Oh," said Nick. "Sorry."

Victor giggled.

"And that's enough from you, Victor," Kitty jokingly reprimanded. "And why on earth Oliver needed you here this weekend when he's got a much more flexible alternative upstairs is quite beyond me."

Victor blushed. Kitty was blithely unaware. Peter came to the rescue.

"How about a potter round the park, darling?" he suggested. "Just the two of us."

"Lovely. And we might catch Rachel and Gerald before they stumble across the evidence."

"They'll have to sometime," Peter replied, draining his glass.

"Agreed," said Kitty, getting up. "But there are ways of breaking things to people, don't you think? Kinder ways?"

"Oh, I do," Peter replied, taking her arm and winking at

the boys. "I do indeed."

"Shan't be long," called Kitty over her shoulder. "Then I'll make something to eat for whoever's hungry. And Victor, may I remind you my son is only twenty and certainly doesn't need corrupting by you. I suggest you sit on your hands."

And with that, Nick and Victor were left to their own devices.

"I tell you," said Victor, after he had slid to the floor and after Nick had joined him on the carpet. "She will just *die*."

He didn't say anything else. He couldn't. Nick was kissing him hungrily.

REFUGEES

As Kitty and Peter set off for their evening perambulation, they had no idea why Mrs Tarpitt should be so upset. Having been at the pub, they had missed the drama of Wheels passing out in the hall.

As they crossed the yard to walk down through the vegetable garden, Mrs T emerged from her flat in the coach house with tears streaming down her face but with a contradictory facial expression of perfect joy, not dissimilar to icons of beatified saints.

"Oh!" she said as Kitty ran towards her, "he's sleeping now! I can't believe it! I just *can't* believe it, Miss Kitty."

"I'm sure you can't, darling," said Kitty. "Who is sleeping?"

"The dear boy. That dear, dear boy!"

"How nice," said Kitty. "Are you sure you're alright?"

Another bout of joyous sobbing brought Peter across the yard.

"Hey, hey," he said comfortingly. "What's upset you, Mrs Tarpitt?" He put his arm around her shoulder whilst Kitty held her hands and massaged them comfortingly.

She sniffed an enormous, slurping sniff and smiled a huge smile.

"Oh, I'm not upset, Mr Peter! Quite the contrary. I'm so, so happy. I never thought I'd be this happy again!"

Mrs Tarpitt suddenly lunged with her broad chin at Kitty and kissed her quite unexpectedly. Then she did the same to Peter and made to go into the main house.

"Where are you going?" Peter called out. "You should be lying down."

"No, no. I'm fine Mr Peter. I'm going to see to some supper for you all."

"But I can do that, Mrs T," said Kitty. "Honestly. You

rest."

"Wouldn't hear of it, my dear. What shall I put out? Some salads? I've got cold meat and cheeses and some lovely home made bread. An' a big pot of pea soup for them that wants something warmin'."

"Er ... fine ... yes," said Kitty uncertainly as she glanced at Peter.

Mrs Tarpitt waved her hand, then stood for a moment, her arms crossed over her ample bosom staring with adoration at her spare room window. She hurried into the house.

"Well," said Kitty. "What was all that about?"

"Perhaps it's Ludo," Peter suggested as they started their walk. "Celebrities do have that effect on people."

"People, yes," said Kitty as they passed Jenks' immaculately kept greenhouses, cornucopias of bulging tomatoes and long, thick cucumbers, hanging from the carefully tied vines like giant green saucissons. "But not Mrs Tarpitt. She's far too sensible."

"I often think it's a dreadful virtue," Peter murmured. "Being sensible. There are times when I fairly ache with regret about having always been sensible."

"Well I came to it rather later in life than you. I did all the mad things when I was young."

"I envy you."

They stopped at an iron gate set in a frame of beech hedge. The gap allowed them an uninterrupted view down to the village. Two of their neighbour's horses nuzzled by the water trough as cows milled around for their turn to drink. The horses seemed oblivious of the cows and vice versa. The light was beginning to fade. The high-pitched calls of bats had replaced the incessant summer birdsong. They walked on, outside the perimeter of the walled garden and into the head of the park where the drive curved round for the approach to the gates.

"What do I do with this place, Peter?"

Peter's thoughts were several million miles away. He was trying to work out the best way of breaking to Kitty as gently as possible the circumstances of Nick and Victor. He

221

was also wondering whether it was his responsibility to do so and whether it should not be Oliver taking this walk in the twilight.

"What do you mean?"

"It's so ... so impractical now."

"How so?"

"I don't think I can hold it together, the way things are going."

"You don't have to, darling. For once, the burden doesn't fall on your shoulders."

"You're not understanding me. It's a family house. That's what I mean. Now everyone's breaking off and going their own separate ways. It's more like a hotel. Take tonight. Do you realise that every single room in the place is taken? If this new girl of Oliver's becomes permanent, we'll have to start making bookings."

"But why? And why am I so different from Oliver's girlfriend? It's the same principle."

"But what if Oliver hadn't liked you? What if I don't like Oliver's girlfriend?"

"That's families, Kitty. What and if have never got the world anywhere. There's no law on this earth to say that every individual in a family has to like each other. But," he added, "that isn't a reason for us not to respect each other. We might not have a right to be respected, but we all have a duty to respect."

She squeezed his arm. There was no need to thank him but at that moment, she was eternally grateful for his support.

"Better slow down a bit," Gerald advised. "I think there's a police car behind us."

Rachel decelerated. She was only doing forty but the hill leading up from the combe was designated a thirty mile an hour stretch.

"It's not far now. About a couple of miles."

"Good. What with one thing and another, this journey seems to have taken for ever."

"I've enjoyed it," she said.

"So have I. But my bum aches.

222

"At the top of the hill, Rachel decelerated even more, almost to a crawl as they passed a woman with a bulldog. She seemed to be struggling. The dog was definitely struggling. She turned her head only slightly as their car drove past.

Gerald turned round.

"Looks like the Queen Mum."

"Except it's not," said Rachel. "She has corgis. That's a bulldog. But you're right. Especially the Paddington Bear hat and the matching accessories."

"Do you think we ought to stop?" Gerald wondered. "She might be in trouble."

"Gerry, believe me. That lady knows exactly where she's going. And that heinous looking dog would see off even the most determined attacker."

"Umm," he said, turning round once again in his seat as the car rounded a bend and the roadside apparition disappeared.

Grace trudged wearily onwards. Her feet were killing her but she was determined. She had got off the bus from Bath at the wrong stop and having asked at the pub by the stop, knew that there would not be another bus until tomorrow. She also knew that Littlecombe was to be a three mile walk.

The light was fading. Cars now had side lights. Grace had never had to judge distances. Her life had been hitherto measured only by known distances along the Holloway Road.

As she walked past the lonicera hedge which was the end of Mr and Mrs Hollingshurst's garden, Beau Boy of Bankside went bananas. The yellow labrador ran up and down the length of the hedge where it met the main road, barking furiously and ferociously. Bullshit stopped, looked up at Grace and, if a dog could shrug, shrugged.

"I know, lovey," said Grace. "I feel exactly the same. But it can't be far."

The Hollingshursts had just returned from choir practice. From the upstairs window, as she removed her hat, Mrs Hollingshurst saw the stately spectacle of Grace

Morgan trudging past. She also saw the police car. Good, she thought, it'll save a telephone call. Mrs Hollingshurst was acutely vigilant and reported anything odd or peculiar which could be even remotely pertinent to the security of the neighbourhood. Quite what threat Grace posed would not have entered Mrs Hollingshurst's head.

Constable Tippett decelerated. Ladies dressed for garden parties carrying holdalls and leading bulldogs were not common occurrences on the roadside verges of the parish of Littlecombe. Grace turned and saw the car. Her heart bumped as the adrenalin from the shock worked its way into her system. She stopped. Bullshit sank to his haunches, grateful for the chance to sit down, oblivious of the peril.

The policeman wound down the window.

"You alright, madam?"

Grace peered at him suspiciously.

"Can I be of any assistance, madam?"

Grace was quickly trying to work out if Constable Tippet in his patrol car was the modern equivalent of the bobby on the bike or whether he was bent on an errand of a more sinister nature.

"Bit late for you to be walking alone, if I might say."

"I missed my bus," Grace replied.

"Where are you making for? Haven't seen you round here, before. Stayin' with friends, are we?"

"Yes," said Grace. "Littlecombe Park, actually."

"Oh. That'll be Mr and Mrs Longingly."

"Yes," said Grace, rather pleased with the instant respect and acknowledgement the name of Kitty's home had prompted. She always knew Kitty had had class.

"I'll give you a lift," offered Constable Tippett. "I'm headed that way m'self. It's another mile, at least. Best get in."

Grace looked down at Bullshit. He seemed to have understood for he got up off his hind legs immediately, waggled his rear end and emitted a rumbling but acquiescent bark. Bullshit was happy. Grace could tell.

"Thank you," she said as he opened the door from the

inside. He pulled the seat forward and Bullshit, with great difficulty and a little shove from Grace, clambered onto the back seat.

"Nice dog," remarked Constable Tippett as he drove off.

"Isn't he?" replied Grace. "So sweet and gentle. Wouldn't snap at a fly, officer."

Not if he could catch your hand first, thought the policeman.

Kitty and Peter were halfway up the drive as le car bounced perkily into the entrance to Littlecombe at about half-past-eight.

They waved as Rachel pulled up. She and Gerald got out and Rachel kissed Peter first and then Kitty.

"You made it, then," said Kitty. "Welcome."

"So you stayed after all, Kitty? I do hope it wasn't on our account. I told dad we'd be perfectly alright. You don't mind, do you?"

"Course not," said Kitty warmly. "I'm glad you came. You too Gerald."

"Hello, Gerald," Peter said, extending his hand.

"Good to see you, Peter."

"Good drive?" Peter asked.

"Wonderful," Rachel replied. "You forget just how lovely England is."

"Well, who's hungry?" Kitty asked.

"We've eaten. In a pub," said Gerald.

"A drink, then," Kitty offered.

"Thanks, Kitty. But after the day we've had, I'd just as soon turn in, if that's alright."

"Rachel told you about Violetta, I suppose," Gerald said to Peter.

"Oh ... yes. She did."

"No news, dad?"

Peter glanced at Kitty.

"Er... yes. Strangely enough, she did get in touch with me. Of course she was mortified about not turning up. So apologetic. She did say most emphatically that when I saw you I was to apologise profusely, didn't she Kitty?"

"Oh. Yes. Absolutely," Kitty agreed.

"And she's going to get in touch with you both here. Tomorrow morning. First thing."

"She *is* alright, I take it?" Gerald asked.

"She sounded ... fine," Peter replied, hoping that his sidestep would be sufficient for the time being.

"Tomorrow it is, then," said Gerald.

"It certainly is," murmured Rachel intently.

"So lets go in, my dears," said Kitty. "I'll show you to your room and then if you want a drink we shall be in the drawing room. I've put a couple of bottles of wine and some glasses in your room so if you'd prefer ... well, do whatever you want to do."

"And park at the back in the yard," said Peter as Gerald and Rachel got into le car. "We'll follow."

The car drove off and Peter and Kitty walked quickly after it.

"Come on, Peter. If we can just get them up to their room, we can do the sorting out tomorrow."

"Kitty. Let them do the sorting out," said Peter as they hurried towards the house. "They're all perfectly grown up."

"But it's my fault, Peter, don't you see? If I hadn't invited them all to our house, none of this would ever have happened."

"Kitty, you might have been the cause, but fault doesn't come into it."

"But it could all go so wrong."

"And it could all go so right."

"If it does, it'll be a miracle," she replied.

Oliver had sat patiently as Julie poured out the truth. He knew it was the truth. He passed her a box of tissues.

"Should 'ave taken me own advice," she sniffed. "Should 'ave come clean in the first place and saved all this carry on. Shouldn't 'ave tried to keep it a secret. I was goin' to tell you, Ollie, I swear. I just thought it would ... would scare you off, y'know?"

She sat on the edge of the bed. He sat beside her.

"Yes," he said. "Perhaps you should." He was quiet for a moment. "But then again, perhaps you were right. Last

226

night, in Zanzibar, I think I would have been wary. Ludo is my friend as well as my client."

"See," she said hopefully, "you'd 'ave backed off on two counts. An' we'd never 'ave known."

"Feeling better?" he enquired.

She nodded.

"An' there's something else too," she said. "Dunno 'ow I could 'ave bin so stupid but I thought it was Kitty that Ludo 'ad gone off with."

"Kitty?"

"Daft, innit?"

"Well, yes. It is. Ludo and Kitty were finished years ago."

"I know. I didn't understand. I thought it was ... y'know, the other kind of love. The bonkin' variety."

He laughed and that made her smile. The carefully applied mascara was now anywhere but on her eyelids.

"Ludo's worried that you're going to make some sort of scene. He'd like to see you. Talk to you."

"Oh, I couldn't! Please, Ollie. That's the last thing I want to do. I'm glad for 'im, honest."

"He's glad for you too. But you must talk to him, you know."

"I will, but not tonight, please? Tomorrow."

Julie looked away and wiped her eyes, running the corner of the tissue accurately along her lids.

"What's she like? This Veeletto," she asked quietly. "She alright?"

"I'm told she's an opera singer and, yes. She seems very nice."

Julie sniffed again."Good. I'm glad. Is she pretty? No. Don't answer. Daft question."

"Not as pretty as you," Oliver replied.

"Get on," she said with the first real smile in half-an-hour. "You would say that, wouldn't you?"

They fell to making up with a will and, this time, with but one interruption. Oliver got up off the bed and scribbled a quick note which he put in a Littlecombe envelope and propped on the floor outside his door.

Oliver had to smile the following morning. The note was still there.

Victor and Nick were still in the drawing room when Kitty and Peter had finished installing Rachel and Gerald in the last vacant bedroom.

"We thought we might go for a walk too," said Nick brightly.

"A short walk," Victor modified.

"Lazybones," said Kitty.

"It's not that. I hurt my leg last night."

"I told you those heels were ludicrously high, Victor." Nick grinned. It was rather sweet, he thought, the way she treated Victor, like a perennially naughty boy. "Dressed like that and pissed as a rat, what did you expect?"

"Not a lot," Victor replied and winked at Nick.

"Was it a marvellous party?"

Peter and Kitty had both taken off their shoes and were curled at either end of the huge Edwardian sofa, their toes meeting in the middle.

"Yes, actually. I won."

"There was a prize?"

"Indeed. I raffled it."

"Very big-hearted of you. What was it in aid of."

"Aids, dear."

"Oh," said Kitty, somewhat humbled. "Sorry. Very commendable of you, dear. Anyone hungry? There's plates of food out in the kitchen. Mrs T will be mortified if no one eats anything."

"I thought she was looking after Wheels," Nick said.

"Wheels?" murmured Peter.

"Yes. Loo's driver. He collapsed as soon as he walked through the door."

"How awful!" exclaimed Kitty, pulling herself to attention. "Where is he?"

"In Mrs T's spare room. She insisted. He's sleeping now."

"So that's why she was in such a sweat," Peter said.

"She loves looking after people," Kitty said. "I don't think she's ever forgiven any of us for growing up."

"So now she has a new baby," Victor remarked.

"If only ...," said Kitty in a mysterious murmur.

"Sorry, mum?"

"Skip it, darling."

"But what *did* you say? You're forever doing that."

Instead of replying, Kitty's attention was drawn to the window. She frowned as she got up.

"Oh, no!" she said. "Who on earth can *this* be?"

She had seen lights at the bottom of the drive, lights which materialised as the headlamps of a car approaching in the dusk.

They all got up. The car, following the curve of the drive, disappeared as it came to the turning area in front of the house. Kitty and Peter went out into the hall and Peter opened the door.

He didn't recognise the view of herself which Grace presented. Grace from behind looked nothing like Grace from the front. Peter wasn't expecting her and had he been, he would certainly not have anticipated her arrival in a police car.

"Who is it?" hissed Kitty from where she was hiding behind the door.

"It's a large lady in chintz getting something out of the back of a police car."

"A police car?"

"Umm," he said and at that moment Grace turned round. Bullshit was immovable.

Her face was a tortured picture of frustration, exhaustion and helplessness.

"Edgar won't come out!" she wailed.

Kitty immediately recognised the voice.

"Grace?" she exclaimed and squeezed forwards between Peter and the oak front door. "Darling!"

"Oh! Kitty, lovey. I'm that glad to see you. I see he's here, then?" Grace pointed to the Mercedes which was still parked where Wheels had left it.

"Yes, but ... Oh, never mind."

"Help me with Edgar, dear. He seems to have quite taken to this nice policeman's car.

229

"Bullshit turned his head slowly. A huge pink tongue lapped out between the fleshy jowls.

Grace handed the end of the leash to Kitty who attempted a tug. No movement whatsoever.

"Got a dog biscuit?" ventured Constable Tippett. "'E might come for that."

"Bullshit!" Kitty said commandingly. "Come!"

"Beg pardon, Mrs Longingly?" said Constable Tippett.

"Oh, sorry, Andrew. Not you. Not anyone. It's the dog's nickname."

"But 'is real name, 'is *proper* name is Edgar," Grace insisted.

"Peter!" Kitty wailed. "*do* something?"

"What would you suggest?"

"Fetch a bit of cold meat from the kitchen."

"Ludo could get 'im to come out," Grace suggested. "Tell me where 'e is an' I'll fetch 'im down."

"No, Grace! Please. Ludo's ... Ludo's having a meeting. With Oliver. We can manage."

Out of the gloom created by the shadow of the back of the house, there came a call.

"'Ere, What's goin' on?"

"Oh, Jenks. Thank goodness," Kitty grunted, hauling with all her might at Bullshit's collar. "Perhaps you can help? Ludo's bulldog won't get out of the car."

"Would that be a dog or a bitch you're talkin' about, miss?"

"Dog," muttered Kitty, tugging with all her strength.

"Oh no you don't, Queenie," growled Jenks.

From behind Jenks, but a little lower to the ground, appeared the mink coloured labrador. Queenie's ears were pricked, her tail was high and she stopped. She raised a paw and cocked her head to one side. It was just enough time for Jenks to slip a noose of baling twine round her neck and take hold.

Neither Grace nor Kitty had ever seen Bullshit move so quickly. Victor had. He appeared in the doorway with Nick just as Bullshit decided that the rampant Queenie was a bait worth taking.

230

"Oh Christ! No!" screamed Victor and, bad leg or no bad leg, fled up the stairs to Nick's room and slammed the door.

"Help!" screamed Kitty as Bullshit began to make off in the direction of Queenie. Peter managed to grab the lead as well and together they were just able to restrain the powerful dog who had begun howling mournfully.

"Take her away, Jenks! Please!" Kitty begged.

Jenks and Queenie made a hasty retreat. Queenie too was in a sudden lather of excitement and was yelping and straining at the makeshift leash.

Nick came out to take over from Kitty and, with Peter, managed to drag Bullshit into the house. Kitty picked up Grace's holdall and ushered her into the house.

"I'll be sayin' goodnight, then, Mrs Longingly," said the policeman as he leant across and closed the door of the police car.

"Oh, yes. Thanks, Andrew. Thank you for bringing her."

"Call it the line of duty, m'um," he said, replaced his peaked hat and started off to resume his patrol.

"Come in and sit down, Grace. You look worn out," said Peter taking her arm. Kitty locked the front door.

"Peter, I can't begin to tell you."

"Sit down, darling," said Kitty, ministering. "Drink?"

"Drop of brandy, lovey if you've got it. My 'eart. Honestly."

Kitty sat down next to her. Nick hovered and Peter poured her a generous noggin of Remy Martin.

"Where's Victor?" Kitty asked suddenly, vaguely recalling somebody hurling themselves up the stairs.

"Upstairs ... he ... he's not awfully fond of dogs."

"Rubbish," said Kitty. "He loves them. He paints them, darling. It's his living."

"Would that be Mr Burke?" Grace asked. "Mr Victor Burke? The painting man?"

"Yes, dear."

"Oh," Grace moaned softly. "Poor man. That was the start of it, see."

"The start of what, Grace?" Peter asked, handing her the

brandy. She took a decent swallow, coughed and then took a deep breath.

"Well ...," she began. The story took some little time and included all sorts of incidents on the train to Bath, the bus from Bath to the point where Constable Tippett had met her, incidents which were very important to Grace although a little confusing to everyone else.

In the telling, Grace settled. Bullshit too seemed to have calmed down by the end of the story, although he roamed the room constantly, snuffling and spluttering, his claws clacking over the oak boards at the edge of the carpet.

"An' I'd do it all over again," she concluded. "I am not 'avin that dog arrested! People think 'e wants to bite them an' all he wants to do is 'ave a little game."

"Don't worry, Grace," Nick reassured her. "We'll get it sorted out."

"We certainly will," added Peter firmly. "In fact, we'll get it sorted out first thing in the morning, won't we Nick?"

Nick nodded, shamefaced.

"I am sorry about this, Kitty, dear. But what else could I do?"

"You were quite right, darling. It really was too bad of Ludo to leave you like that."

"Oh, not really, dear," Grace countered. "I do understand. 'Ave you ... I mean, is she ...?"

Kitty smiled.

"She's lovely, darling. You'll see her tomorrow. I think you'll be pleased."

"Are they ... Is it *serious*?"

"Let Ludo tell her, Kitty," Peter warned. "I think we could all do with a good night's sleep first."

"Oh, crikey!" said Kitty. "Where are we going to put Grace?"

"Mum," Nick said promptly, "put Grace in Victor's room. I can sleep on my couch. Victor can have my bed."

"That's a good idea, darling. Go up and explain to Victor will you? Poor dear. Why didn't anyone *tell* me about his bite. How awful for him to have gone through all that

232

alone."

Peter and Nick exchanged knowing looks and Nick hurried upstairs to tell Victor the good news.

Kitty grabbed the end of Bullshit's lead and with Grace on her other arm, she showed Grace to her room. By the time they had persuaded Bullshit up the two flights of stairs, all the room changes had been made and after Kitty had made Grace a sandwich and brought up a bowl of water for Bullshit, it was finally time for bed.

It was quite some time, though, before anyone in the house or in the coach house finally went to sleep.

Mrs Tarpitt was up for most of the night, sitting by the sleeping Wheels. She'd given him two aspirin and some scrambled egg when he woke at midnight and he was unaware of her presence as she watched over him, her eyes darting in wonder from the birthmark on his chest to his dear, dear face.

Neither did Jenks find sleep easy to achieve. Queenie was not about to let him. She scratched at the bedroom door endlessly.

Bullshit didn't scratch so much as butt. He would whine and get up from the position he'd taken up by the window, wander across the room and collide with the door, looking up in rather cross surprise that it remained closed.

"Peter," murmured Kitty as Peter came back to bed after turning off the bathroom light.

"Umm," he said, snuggling into her as they settled into the cosiness of the duvet, like the perfectly matched teaspoons she had mentioned.

"Why don't we get up very early tomorrow and just vanish?"

"Not on your life," he said, "this is the best weekend I've had in ages."

"You're mad," she said, "absolutely round the bend."

"Goodnight, darling. Sweet dreams."

IN ENGLISH COUNTRY GARDENS

The village of Littlecombe lay just inside the Somerset border. When the county of Avon was created some years before, in a fleeting moment of harmony the inhabitants had collectively breathed a sigh of relief that they were not to be robbed of their county situation by a careless stroke of a bureaucrat's pen. It was to Somerset that they had been born, or had come to, and it was to be in Somerset that they would remain. Avon, indeed! The name had more to do with door-to-door scent sales than with the glamour of a heritage more ancient even than England. To the villagers of Littlecombe, be they ever so humble, Somerset was England; the home of Glastonbury, the county of mystical mounds and magical monuments; yea, even of Camelot, some said.

Constable Tippett was not usually one for such romantic flurries of fancy but on that Saturday morning as he wandered in his dressing-gown round his garden with a mug of milky, sweet tea, checking his marrows, culling a picking of stick beans and checking his roses for aphids, it did occur to him that he felt very much a part of the countryside, its history and traditions. Even at eight o'clock in the morning, the sun promised well for the day ahead and there was nothing in the line of duty which threatened to keep him for long from his garden. Nothing very much had ever happened in Littlecombe while he'd been there to soil the carpet of these pleasant pastures for long.

So, when Inspector Yates telephoned him from Taunton, Constable Tippett was not best pleased. Taunton to Constable Tippett was as far away as London, yea, of Camelot even and its unbidden intrusion into such rural tranquillity was unwelcome.

His wife Sandra handed him the 'phone.

"An' don't forget you promised to run me and the kids into Bath!" she said in a loud whisper without bothering to cover the mouthpiece. "They needs shoes an' you needs pants."

"I know, I know ... 'Ello, Tippett, 'ere?"

"Detective Inspector Yates. That you Tippett?"

"Yes, sir."

They had never met. Yates' tone suggested they had.

"I shall be down your way at midday," he barked. "I'll need you to assist."

"Oh," replied Andrew, "Right. Can I ask what's the matter?"

"Littlecombe Park?" said Yates. "Know it?"

"Yes, sir. Mr and Mrs Longingly's place. Nice people."

"That's as may be. Their guests could be a very different kettle of fish."

"Guests?" murmured Andrew, wondering exactly what a Queen Mother lookalike could have done to engender such attention from the powers on high.

"Yes. Pop singers and the like."

"Oh," Andrew replied. He was still quite a fan. He loved Queen and Elton John but wasn't quite sure about Grace. Could she be one of the Roly Polies, perhaps?

"Noticed any untoward comings and goings, Tippett?"

"No, sir. Not that I can think of. I was there only last night, matter of fact. Took one of their visitors the last mile along the road."

"Tall man? Longish hair, name of Morgan? Probably disguised in sun-glasses."

"No, sir. Short lady. Early sixties. No noticeable disguises."

"That's his mother, Tippett."

"Oh. Whose mother would that be, sir?"

"This pop singer. Ludo. Ludo Morgan."

"Get on!" exclaimed Andrew Tippett. "In Littlecombe? Ludo Morgan. You're pullin' my leg, sir."

"I am not pulling your leg, constable! This could turn out to be a serious matter."

"Oh," said Andrew, by now completely baffled. "Right."

"If the mother's there, the son can't be far. How did she seem to you?"

"Oh, you know. Very nice. Very nice indeed, as a matter of fact."

"She gave no sign as to be under the influence of any substances."

"She weren't drunk, sir, if that's what you be gettin' at."

"I am not, Tippet. I was meaning ..." He lowered his voice. "Illegal substances. Did you have any suspicions on those lines?"

"Oh, you mean drugs, sir?"

"Yes."

"No."

"Oh." Inspector Yates sounded very disappointed.

"I'll meet you at twelve, constable. Your place."

"Right you are, sir."

The call was terminated without further ceremony and Andrew Tippet scratched his head.

"'Ere, Sandra!" he called into the kitchen, "you'll never guess who's stayin' at the Park!"

Grace woke early, as she always did. Light was already streaming into her room at seven o'clock. She had carefully hung up the floral suit the night before and was relieved to be able to put on her usual functional pleated skirt, blouse and housecoat. Finery was only necessary when travelling.

She used the bathroom quickly, leaving no traces and returned to her room. Bullshit was up and raring to go. She slipped on some nylon knee-highs and her gardening shoes and took a tin of Chum from her holdall.

Bullshit, shortsighted as he was, still recognised the familiar sight of breakfast even in unfamiliar surroundings and gave a rumbling woooof of approval.

"Yes, darlin'. Granny's got your breakfast. Come on, boy."

She slipped on his lead and together, they left the room and went downstairs to the kitchen. She found a can opener on the wall, emptied the contents of the tin into the bowl Kitty had given her last night for Bullshit's water and

236

set it down on the floor for the hungry dog.

The breakfast lasted three ravishing mouthsful before it was demolished.

"You greedy boy, Edgar. You're as bad as Wheels. You'll get ulcers wolfin' your food like that." Grace was whispering, unsure as to who might hear, who was up and who she might encounter. Grace was not overfond of staying in other people's houses. In fact, apart from her sister Stella, with whom she had stayed several times in Bristol before the dementia struck, Littlecombe Park was the first house other than either her own or Ludo's in which she had ever spent a night.

Bullshit looked up hopefully. Grace's eyes scanned the kitchen, found the kettle, the teapot, the tea and, in a cupboard, breakfast mugs. She filled the kettle at the sink and as she was doing so, looked out and saw Jenks emerge from his front door and stretch in the early morning sunshine. He turned and caught her eye as she stood watching. He waved.

It must be said that for a man of his sixty one years, Jenks was not a bad looking chap. Many in Littlecombe, not least Kitty, had hoped that he and Mrs Tarpitt might strike up some sort of entente but it was not to be. Jenks had been Mrs Tarpitt's Arthur's cousin and there were some things which to both Jenks and Mrs T were always to be held sacred.

Grace waved and smiled. The blight of instant suspicion or social reticence had never touched Grace. Unshackled by the responsibilities of life in the Hampstead mansion, Grace would talk to anyone and everyone. And did.

Jenks sauntered across the yard and Grace, in response, opened the kitchen window.

"Mornin'," said Jenks. "I'm Jenks."

"Good Morning, Mr Jenks."

"Oh no. I'm not Mister Jenks. That's what they calls me 'ere. Jenkin is my proper name."

"And mine's Morgan," Grace replied. "Grace Morgan."

"Mine's Tom." He turned briefly and looked out eastwards, over the downs. The sun was already high.

237

"Lovely day for it."

"Isn't it?"

He returned his attention to the handsome woman behind the taps.

"Fine lookin' dog you got there."

"Isn't he? 'Is name's Edgar. An' I s'pose that would be your labrador, then?"

"Yes. That's my Queenie. She's on heat at the moment, I'm afraid. Sorry about the ruckus last night."

"No matter. S'only natural, Mr Jenkin. Do you live here?"

"Yes. I'm the gardener."

"Oh, you don't say! It's a lot to keep you busy, then. I've always heard Kitty talk of it but I never imagined it so big."

"Six acres," said Jenks. "Enough to keep me busy as you say. T'was bigger once, of course. But a lot's been sold off."

"Would you like a cup of tea?" Grace asked. "I'm just about to make one."

"I just made me own, thanks all the same. Gives Queenie a bit of breakfast then 'as me tea."

"Oh, well," said Grace, "p'rhaps as I shall see you later. I'd love to see your garden, Mr Jenkin."

"Like gardens, do you?"

"Oh, I do. Now I'm on my own, it's what keeps me going, I think." Grace drew the veil from her widowhood delicately. "I live with my son, now. He's not got a green finger in all ten so the garden's my special responsibility."

"It'd be my pleasure to show you," Jenks replied with what, for a countryman, must pass as alacrity. "After we've 'ad our tea?"

"Oh, that'd be lovely. Then I can take Edgar for 'is doin's."

"I'd take the bitch," said Jenks. But, well ... you know."

Grace tittered; she simpered; she may have even blushed.

"Best not risk things, eh?"

"You come and knock on my door, then," Jenks concluded. "The yellow one. Just across the yard, there."

He pointed with a work-scarred finger of a horny hand and Grace nodded. She closed the window and put the kettle on.

Ludo had gone to sleep quickly and early and had slept like he thought he'd never slept before. Violetta stirred, moving slightly in the bed to be closer to him. Ludo opened an eye and looked at his watch on the bedside.

Half-past-seven.

Instead of groaning, closing his eyes and going back to sleep, he lay awake for a few moments before extricating his arm gently from beneath Violetta's head and getting out of bed. He wrapped a towel round his waist and went over to the bay window. The full length curtains didn't follow the bay, they were drawn across it, like stage drapes. Carefully, to avoid opening them and waking Violetta, he slipped behind them and looked out of the leaded windows and onto the park.

As well as the expanse of lawns, the trees, the dew-covered grass and the remains of a slight mist rapidly clearing in the heat of the sun, all of which he might have expected to see, Ludo saw his mother. And his dog. And a strange man.

Both were unmistakable. The man was bending down at the edge of a long herbaceous border showing Grace a specimen. Bullshit was dancing excitedly straining at his leash in a direction altogether opposite from the one which the humans were taking. The trio appeared not twenty yards from beneath the window as Jenks, sensitive to Grace's predicament, took the lead from her and shortened it, wrapping the excess round his hand.

What the hell was going on, thought Ludo? He leant as far out of the window as he could safely do and called as loudly as he dared.

"Mother!"

A bird flew flapping through the foliage around the window. Ludo had surprised it. It surprised Ludo.

"Christ!" he muttered. "Mother!" he called again.

Grace would not have heard him so deep was she in her admiration of Mr Jenkin's horticulture had Jenks not turned round and pointed towards the house in reply to a question from Grace. She turned to look in the direction he was pointing and saw Ludo, hanging out of the window. She waved immediately and after a brief explanation to Jenks, she hurried across the lawn to stand beneath the window.

"Hello, love. You're up early!" She spoke at her normal volume.

"Ssshh! You'll wake everyone."

"Sorry!" she whispered loudly

"What are you doing here, mum?"

Violetta woke. She pulled herself up onto her elbows, saw Ludo was gone and then heard his hoarsely whispered question from behind the curtains.

"Ludo? What's up, love?"

He withdrew from the window, parted the curtains and stuck his head through.

"Morning, Vee."

"Good Morning," she grinned sleepily. "What's going on?"

"Dunno. I'll tell you in a minute. Stay put."

He vanished, like Eric Morecambe.

"It was Edgar," Grace said after he reappeared at the window. "I'm afraid he got out last night and the police say he bit someone. They said 'e might 'ave to be put down. So I smuggled him away. On the train. He was ever so good." She paused, gaugeing his reaction. "I didn't know what else to do, love."

Violetta slipped out of bed, put on her dressing gown and hid beside the curtains, listening.

"But how on earth did you find out where I was, mum?"

"Mrs Haines."

"Who the hell is Mrs Haines?"

"Kitty's cleaner. Kitty had already left 'cos she couldn't get through to here on the 'phone."

"I know that," hissed Ludo. He sighed as the towel fell down from round his waist.

"Ludo! Cover yourself. You're not decent!" He bent to retrieve the towel.

240

"I'll come down," he said. "Wait there."

"No need, love," Grace replied confidently. "We're in very good hands."

"Whose?" he rasped. "Who *is* that man?"

"Mr Jenkin, dear. The gardener. He's showing me round. You go back to bed for a bit. I'll see you later."

She turned away and was about to return to Jenks and Bullshit when she remembered.

"Everything alright, love?"

"It was," he said pointedly.

"Nothing to tell me, dear? No ... news?"

Grace looked so happy and relaxed that Ludo couldn't help shaking his head and smiling at his redoubtable mama.

"Who told you?"

"No one," she said indignantly. "They said I should wait for you." She hesitated. "Well, are you gettin' married, love?"

"Yes."

"An' she's a nice girl?"

"She's *very* nice. Satisfied?"

Behind the curtains, Violetta grinned and, feeling the conversation beyond the curtain was drawing to a close, hurried back to bed.

"See you later, dear."

"Alright, mum. Take care."

Ludo pulled the window closer and Grace scampered away, excited and delighted to tell her news to Mr Jenkin and to regale him with the course of events which had steered her to Littlecombe Park.

Ludo got back into bed.

Violetta snuggled against him.

"You will never believe who's turned up," he said.

"Oh, I would, love. I would."

"Who?"

"Your mother. She sounds so sweet."

Ludo looked astonished.

"How did you know?" he demanded, tickling her playfully.

241

"I eavesdropped," she said as the tickling took its inevitable toll.

As Mrs Tarpitt finished dressing, wondering what time breakfast would be required over at the house, Queenie whined fervently in Jenks' kitchen through the partition wall.

On a whim, she pulled back the net curtain at her window and saw Jenks disappearing through the yard gate in the direction of the front of the house with a woman and a short, heavy looking dog. Funny, she thought, as Jenks hadn't even mentioned that his sister might be coming or that she had got herself a dog. Very funny, she thought, that Annie Crisp would even think of bringing a dog with Queenie so deep in heat.

Then she heard stirring in her spare room. She scurried across the narrow corridor and peeked round the door.

Wheels was awake, propped against the padded headboard of the single bed.

"'Ello?" he said with a grin as Mrs Tarpitt's face appeared.

"Good mornin'," she beamed. "Sleep alright?"

"Never better," he replied, then yawned magnificently. "I could get used to all this. Those scrambled eggs were great!"

"Oh, that's nothin'. Wait 'til you 'ave one o' my proper breakfasts."

"I got to thank you," said Wheels. "For lookin' after me an all that. Felt a proper charlie, droppin' like that last night. And I don't even know your name."

"Ena," she replied. "Ena Tarpitt." She bit her lip. She wanted to rush in, headlong. She wanted to tell him that she hoped she was more than just plain Ena Tarpitt. But she was a sensible woman and she had waited a long, long time. A bit longer would make no difference and might in the end make all the difference.

"An' I don't know your name, either," she said.

"Oh, that's easy. It's Wheels."

"Wheels? What sort of name is that?" she said disapprovingly.

"Wheels. 'Cos I drive. Not me real name of course. That's Mick. Well, Michael actually."

"Michael ..." she repeated, smiling to herself. "Umm. Michael's a very nice name." She jolted herself from musing further. She wanted to say what a very nice name Arthur was as well, but pulled back. "So you feel better, then?"

"Feel great. See, I told them there was no need for doctors. Doctors make me shiver."

Mrs Tarpitt couldn't stop staring at Wheels' birthmark. She and Nick had put him to bed in his underpants and his chest was bare. He saw her looking at it and covered his chest with the top edge of the sheet.

"I'll just bring you in a cup of tea, then I must do a bit of work. Most unusual, that on your chest," she remarked. She left the room and returned in a moment with tea. "Sugar?"

"No. No thanks. Just milk, please." She handed him the cup and sat on the edge of the bed. The sheet rode down once again, baring his chest.

"It's just like a butterfly, Michael."

"Yeah. Some people don't like it. They think it's cancer or summat."

"Well, even I know it's nothin' so silly. What fools folks are!" she exclaimed indignantly.

"Personally," he said, sipping at his tea, "I believe it's something left over from another life. When I got reborn. But you'd think that was daft, wouldn't you?"

"Not at all," said Mrs Tarpitt earnestly and she meant what she said. Ena Tarpitt had more than flirted with spiritualism. She'd been to meetings. Even gone to see Doris Stokes in Bristol once. Trying to get in touch. "Course," she added, weighing her words, "your mother would be able to tell you."

"Tell me what?"

"If you 'ad it when you were born."

"Oh, I've always 'ad it," said Wheels.

"Did your mother tell you?"

"'Aven't got a mother," he said matter-of-factly. "Was an

243

orphan, me. Got meself adopted somehow then they was killed. Motor accident. On a bike. Then it was Doctor Barnardo's. 'Til I was sixteen then I got a job. Driver's mate. Passed me test and then joined the band."

Mrs Tarpitt felt tears welling in her eyes as every word of Wheel's potted version of his life's history stung more painfully than any horsefly. Her hands went to her mouth, suppressing her instinct to cry out.

"Now, now," Wheels soothed, noticing her distress. "None of that Ena! Don't let me go upsetting you. It's alright. Honest."

"But, it's so cruel," she sniffed.

"No! It's alright. Didn't do me no harm, did it? Got a good job. I know people who'd kill for a job like mine. I get lots of time to myself, to read. I'm gonna write a book one day too."

"But who looks after you? Who takes care of you?"

"Oh, lots. Mrs Morgan's very kind to me. Cooks me things and does a bit of mending, y'know."

"Who's Mrs Morgan?"

"Ludo's mum. My boss."

"Oh, Mr Ludo. Who you came with?" Wheels nodded.

"S'right. I got a room in 'is place and 'is mum's got the granny flat upstairs. Boss won't let 'er fuss over 'im so I get it instead."

"Oh," murmured Mrs Tarpitt, feeling suddenly deeply envious of the maternal Mrs Morgan. And a granny to boot. She was doubly envious. Mrs Tarpitt hadn't heard of a granny flat before.

"An' as far as the old trouble and strife goes, who'd want to take on an old toerag like me?"

"Toerag? Trouble and strife?"

"Bit of rubbish. Dross," he explained in more polite terms than was accurate. "An' trouble an' strife's wife. Get it?"

"But you're not rubbish! You're a good boy. It's obvious you are."

"Thanks," he grinned. "Thanks for the vote of confidence. But enough of all this worrying. I'm fine and

I'm gonna *be* fine." He patted her arm where it lay on the bed. "Something tells me you got kids, Ena. You're just the type to make a smashin' mum."

"Oh," she said, swallowing hard. "Oh, Michael ..." She got up and went out of the room before she succumbed completely. Collecting herself at her front door, she called, "I'll do you some breakfast later."

"No hurry, Ena. I'll be here."

When Nick went downstairs for some coffee, Mrs Tarpitt was singing in the kitchen, a mellow contralto was wrapped around a version of the lyrics of 'Happy Talk' from *South Pacific*.

"Morning Mrs T? How's Wheels?"

"He's very much better and his name's Michael. I'll thank you to use it too, Nick."

"But he's always been called Wheels."

"And who by, may I ask?"

Nick drew back. Perhaps Victor was right. Perhaps Mrs Tarpitt had found a new baby.

"By ... I don't know. Everyone."

"Well, everyone isn't his mother," she replied, not sharply but very definitely. "Some poor soul, God rest it, gave the boy that name in good faith and her wishes should be respected."

"Oh," said Nick. "Right. Any coffee through yet?"

"For you and Mr Burke, is that?"

"Yes. Thanks."

"I'll put it all on the one tray, Nick." Mrs Tarpitt swiftly laid a tray with mugs, milk jug and sugar.

"Is mum up yet?" She shook her head. "Dad?"

"No. Him neither. And I don't know what Jenks is up to, I'm sure. I need salad things and beans and peas an' he's wanderin' round with his sister Annie and some great dog she's got herself."

"Was it a bulldog?"

"Could 'ave been. Why?"

"Ah."

"Ah what?"

"That's not Jenks' sister, Mrs T. That's Grace. She came

245

late last night."

"Lordy!" exclaimed Mrs T. "An' who else arrived when my back was turned, pray? And who ...?"

"And Peter's daughter Rachel and her friend Gerald. No one else."

"Standing room only, then, is it?" Mrs Tarpitt exclaimed again. "Better get some more lamb out of that freezer, I s'pose."

"Yes. Quite like old times, though."

Mrs Tarpitt shook her head negatively.

"I'm afraid not, Nick. Nothin's ever like old times. There's only new times, thank heavens. You must never look back too long to compare in life or you'll come a bad fall."

"Yes," Nick replied. He was still too bleary to begin to ponder such a moot philosophy. "I'll see you later, then."

"Off you go, dear. If you see your mother about, ask her what's happening about breakfasts, will you?"

Nick went upstairs with the tray.

Victor was lying in the double bed, looking out of the window. On the other side of the room, the studio couch had had its covers pulled back and the sheets rumpled just to show willing. Nick handed him a mug and then got back into bed.

"Hello, handsome," Victor said.

"Mrs Tarpitt always told me that handsome is as handsome does."

"Well, tell her for me that this handsome does just fine. And shouldn't you lock the door? Your mother has a habit of wandering everywhere she's not supposed to be."

"Then it would seem very odd if she tried to come in and the door was locked."

"If she got in, dear boy, it would look even odder to see us two lying in bed together."

"She was fine last night about us sharing a room."

"Perhaps. But she wouldn't be so fine about my sharing your body."

Nick laughed.

"I do like you, Victor."

246

"Good. And likewise. What's the time?"

"Eight-thirty."

"At nine sharp I shall ring Hampstead police station and drop those charges.

"Oh, good. That'll be a load off everyone's mind." They finished their coffee. "Then what do we do?"

Victor rolled over and gathered Nick into his arms.

"Then we try and behave for at least twelve hours."

"I hope Grace stays."

"I don't. Hope she goes and takes that vile dog with her."

"Victor, if she goes, you'll have to move back into the other room."

"Oh," said Victor. He shrugged. "Then let her stay."

Half-an-hour later, true to his word, all charges were dropped against both Bullshit and his owner. As Victor was telephoning from the study, Kitty came in. She gave the thumbs up to Victor as she overheard him retracting his complaint and signalled that she would be in the kitchen.

"Morning Mrs T."

"Morning, Miss Kitty. Sleep well?"

"Yes. Like a log. How's Wheels this morning?"

Mrs Tarpitt didn't answer for a moment, pretending preoccupation with the washing of some carrots which Jenks had pulled the day before. Kitty poured herself a mug of coffee and sat down at the kitchen table.

"Darling, did you hear? I asked how Wheels was?"

Mrs Tarpitt stopped washing the carrots but did not turn round. Slowly she withdrew her hands from the muddy water and wiped them slowly on her apron.

"Do you believe in miracles, Miss Kitty?" she asked quietly and still she hadn't turned round.

"Well ..., yes. I suppose I must. What sort of miracle?"

Mrs Tarpitt whipped round and fairly threw herself into the chair opposite Kitty. Kitty was still waking up and, as Nick had been, too fuzzy with sleep to appreciate Mrs Tarpitt's beaming ardour. It was faintly blasphemous of her, she supposed, but she dearly hoped she wasn't going to be told that Mrs Tarpitt had seen the Virgin Mary or one

247

of the more immediate saints anywhere near Littlecombe Park.

"I think it's 'im," she said urgently. "I think he's found 'is way back to me."

"Really? Who exactly, darling?"

"My baby."

"Your ...?" Kitty was dumbstruck. Quickly, she tried to shake off the last skeins of sleep. She had an awful feeling Mrs Tarpitt had finally cracked. "You mean, you think that Ludo is your baby that you gave up all that time ago?"

"No, Miss Kitty! Not Ludo. That dear Michael. His driver!"

Kitty looked at her old friend again. Mrs Tarpitt didn't look mad although Kitty wasn't quite sure what real madness looked like. Yes, her eyes were shining, her cheeks were a little flushed but Ena Tarpitt definitely didn't look mad.

"What makes you think that Wheels is your baby?"

"Because of the birthmark," said Mrs Tarpitt. "When my little lad was born, he had a red birthmark on his chest. Like that Russian chap. Mr Gorbiechiff."

"Gorbachev, darling."

"Well, 'im. Just like that except my lad's was very regular an' on 'is chest. Almost like a little tattoo it was that perfect."

"On his chest?"

"Exactly like a butterfly it was, even with them wavy things butterflies 'ave on their 'eads."

"Antennae," said Kitty

."That's them. Michael out there has got the selfsame mark. Look!"

Mrs Tarpitt pulled out of her apron pocket the eight by ten photograph of her baby son. Sure enough, on his chest, was the birthmark. Kitty took the photograph and wiped the glass, really to make sure it wasn't a dirty smear. She felt awful about doubting the dear woman.

"Gosh. It's certainly very unusual."

"And this lad was adopted too," Mrs Tarpitt went on. "And he's exactly the right age. It *must* be him, Miss Kitty.

248

It has to be. What do I *do*?"

Kitty bit her lip and tried to think what to say for the best. Peter would know something, that was for sure. And if he didn't, he'd know someone who in the law who would.

"I don't know, darling. I honestly don't know. Perhaps you should talk to Peter. And, before you're absolutely sure, check things again. You know. Be a bit clever about it. Don't let on why you're asking." Kitty hesitated for a moment. "And don't forget, that even if you're right, you could be very happy but *he* might not be."

"I know, I know," replied Mrs Tarpitt slowly, "I've thought of that. I shan't rush it, Kitty. Never fear on that score." She held out her hand and Kitty returned the photograph which she dropped back into her pinny pocket. "Would Mr Peter be up?"

"I'll wake him soon," Kitty replied. "I must let him have a little peace this weekend. But you go back over to the flat. I can take care of breakfast."

"You sure, Miss Kitty?"

"Positive. You've got more than enough on your plate for a bit. What're we having for dinner, though?"

"Lamb. It's all ready defrostin'. Lunch is all seen to." Mrs Tarpitt already had her pinafore off and was halfway out of the scullery door. "I'll get Jenks to bring in more vegetables later."

"Alright," Kitty called after her.

Kitty got up and was just going to take advantage of the quiet in the house and walk down to the greenhouse when she heard footsteps in the hall.

Oliver appeared first. Julie had spotted Victor coming out of the study and they exchanged a few pleasantries at the foot of the staircase.

"Hello, Kitty," Oliver said mellifluously.

You, thought Kitty suspiciously, are being deeply sweet. He was dressed in Olympus T-shirt and running shorts, obviously all set to go out and jog.

"Morning, Oliver. Sleep well?"

"Marvellously. Always do down here, though."

"Umm. Coffee?"

"Yes." Oliver took a mug.

"You'll need two mugs, Oliver, unless of course your mystery friend is going to share yours? We do have mugs enough, you know."

"There are always mugs," Oliver muttered wryly. "This isn't exactly easy for me either, Kitty," he said more loudly.

"No. I suppose it isn't. I'm sorry. I was being silly and bitchy. It's crunch time, isn't it? It's finally, finally over."

"Talk later?" he suggested.

"Umm," she replied. "Yes. I'd like that. And I think we need to, Oliver. I'm not sure how many more weekends like this I can take down here."

"Later," he said. "I promise." Oliver laughed. "Thank God, we're English."

"Why do you say that?"

"If we were Americans, can you imagine us being here. Together. Divorced and talking like this?"

"I'm not sure that that isn't jingoism," said Kitty. "I think we should just thank God we're you and me, don't you?"

"Point taken."

Kitty got up from the table and handed her mug to Oliver.

"Pour me another, would you? I'm going to check on the food situation." In her bare feet, Kitty wandered through into the scullery where the freezers lived and where the huge old Kelvinator still whirred and wheezed, outmoded and outdated but somehow still very functional.

Julie came into the kitchen. She looked nervously about. She wore the black Head track suit over her shorts and singlet and her hair was tied back, severely, into a simple pony-tail.

She shrugged, begging the question. Oliver nodded assuringly and pointed in the direction of the scullery

."Coffee?" he asked.

"Yeah. Thanks, Ollie."

Kitty had heard the kitchen door flap. Then she heard the briefly exchanged conversation. Ollie? A new name. Who was Ollie? Ollie was a man she had never known. A new man. Another person in her life. She stood for a moment staring at Mrs Tarpitt's handiwork arranged on the wire shelves. She could make no sense of menus or lunches or teas. She stood with the fridge door open, chilled by the cold within, knowing that she was marking time until she had no alternative but to go back and meet Ollie and also Oliver's girlfriend.

"'Ello, Kitty," said a little voice anxiously behind her. "Can I 'elp? You must 'ave an awful lot to do."

Kitty jumped. Involuntarily, she grabbed the first thing she could from the fridge, a bag of bacon and closed the fridge door quickly. Now, only her feet were cold. She gripped the bacon tight, turned and looked over her shoulder.

"Julie?" she said incredulously.

"Yeah. It's me."

The two women surveyed each other for what to both of them seemed an eternity, both lost for words, both with so much to say.

"I must apologise ..." Julie blurted out whilst at the same time Kitty said, "Don't blame youself for ..."

The ice cracked and bubbles of laughter and tears welled up and escaped from beneath the frost. Kitty laughed. Julie relaxed. Kitty held out her arms and the women hugged each other.

In the kitchen, Oliver listened. He closed his eyes and prayed. There was too much at stake to even contemplate the meeting not working. He didn't know Julie, yet, but he was fairly sure of Kitty. Kitty was Kitty. She had always been Kitty. She hadn't overnight changed into Catherine. To everyone, she was always Kitty. When Oliver heard the laughter, he knew his gamble had paid off. Life could continue in the perspective he had worked for. Oliver was not a selfish man but he was a man and what he had, he wanted to hold.

"I don't believe it!"

"Believe *me*, Kitty, nor did I?"

"But where did you *meet* him?"

"In Zanzibar," Julie bubbled. This Thursday."

251

"You mean after I'd seen you outside The Sanctuary?"

"Yes! Sort of weird, innit?"

Kitty laughed again and whirled round clutching the bag of bacon.

"So, it's alright?" Julie asked.

"What is?"

"Me. Bein' 'ere."

"Of course. Why shouldn't it be? It makes absolute sense if you think about it."

"It does? I dunno, Kitty Llewellyn. It's all bloody Greek to me, love," laughed Julie.

"Oliver!" Kitty called, winking at Julie.

He came immediately into the scullery, too immediately. It was as though he had been waiting and listening. He had been.

"Ah! So you two have ... have ...? Yes."

"Be very careful, Oliver," said Kitty, wagging her finger, parodying the stern school ma'am.

"Of what?" he murmured, looking suddenly worried.

"Of a monstrous regimen, darling."

"A what?"

"Us," Julie said, joining in. "The sisterhood."

"All very well in the pages of a little black book, Oliver but when they emerge, in the flesh, we're an impossible army to beat!"

The women shook hands, closing their deal.

Oliver grinned. It was a joke, wasn't it? Oliver had never been quick with jokes.

Then Kitty remembered Ludo.

"Er ... Julie, I ..." She turned to Oliver. "You have told Julie who's ...?" She pointed upwards.

"Yes, yes. All sorted out."

Julie was quick to cotton on.

"You mean Ludo?" she said to Oliver. "It's alright, Kitty. There isn't a problem. Ludo and I were ... well, it was fun, y'know. It ran on longer than it should have done. Some things do, don't they?"

"Yes, thought, Kitty, for how could she fault Julie's reasoning? She looked from Oliver to Julie and concluded that, as Oliver had said, the spectre of Julie's unquiet spirit had been exorcised.

"Now, be off with you both," said Kitty. "Go for your run or your jog or whatever you do in such excruciating pain for your vanity and leave me to the glories of flab and more coffee."

"We'll see you later, then."

"And," added Julie as Oliver took her arm and led her towards the back door, "thanks."

"By the way," Oliver mentioned, "d'you think Jenks would like a painting of Queenie? I thought as Victor was here, I might commission him?"

"I think that's a lovely idea. Might as well make use of him since you brought him."

"Me?" said Oliver. "I didn't bring him. I thought you did?"

Before Kitty could reply, Oliver and Julie left and the back door closed. Kitty watched them start to run across the yard. She was left, clutching the bacon and feeling strangely maternal towards her ex-husband and her ex-lover's former lover. Yes, she thought, agreeing with Julie, it is all Greek. Maybe, she imagined as they disappeared through the arched gateway in the rear wall, maybe there could be something for them, superficially mismatched though they were and, she reminded herself, Oliver must particularly like Julie to have brought her down. The alternative, how long it might have been before Oliver told anyone had the current mix-up not have occurred, Kitty brushed aside.

She put the bacon back in the fridge and returned to the kitchen. The question of Victor arose in her mind. His presence puzzled her. Not that she minded, of course. Victor was welcome as both hers and Oliver's friend. But if Oliver hadn't brought him, who had? She was just about to go upstairs and find out when Ludo and Violetta came in.

"Good morning!" Kitty beamed. "I don't think I need to ask whether you slept well?"

"It's a lovely house, Kitty," Violetta said. She kissed Kitty warmly. "And, yes. We 'ad a lovely sleep."

Kitty turned to Ludo. Standing there in her kitchen doorway, it seemed that he looked no different from a moment twenty years before on the morning of her wedding to Oliver. The hair a little shorter, the round, dark Lennon glasses had gone along with the beard and moustache and there were perceptibly more laugh lines around the eyes, but essentially Ludo looked the same. Mrs Tarpitt had been putting a final stitch into the hem of Kitty's wedding dress. After surprising them, Ludo had excused himself but Kitty had called him back. 'How do I look?' she had asked. He had seemed very sad and had not replied. Mrs Tarpitt had sensed his unease and hurried off in the pretence of finding her scissors. Kitty climbed off the kitchen chair. 'What's wrong, Loo?' 'You look so happy', he'd said. 'I wish it was me.' She'd kissed him, on the cheek and then he'd hugged her. 'I wish it could have been too,' she replied. 'But I'll always love you.' He'd pulled away from her. Kitty had known it hadn't been easy for him to accept the invitation and she could feel the effort he was making to control his feelings. 'Yeah. I'll remember,' was what he'd said. 'See you in church, then?'

Now, in her dressing-gown instead of her wedding dress, it was twenty years later and the same man was standing in the same place and grinning from ear to ear.

"Seems we've been here before, Kit?"

"Just what I was thinking, darling."

They embraced and it was then that Kitty knew that though it might have been the same man, it was a different person.

"I'm sorry, Violetta," Kitty said as she left his embrace. "Memories."

"Don't be sorry, love. If you 'adn't turned him down, I wouldn't be standing here, now would I?"

"Let's sit down," said Kitty, pulling out two chairs from the table? She set two glasses down in front of them and a jug of orange juice as they took their seats. "Coffee?"

"Thanks, Kit."

"Hot and strong," added Violetta. "Then we thought we'd go for a walk. Would you come?"

"Later, yes," said Kitty as she poured coffee for them. "Toast or something? There are croissants too, if you'd like?"

Neither wanted.

"And what are we going to do about mum?" said Ludo. "What is all *that* about?"

"You've seen her?"

"Yes. She told me all about it. God! That dog of mine causes more problems than a delinquent child. I'd get Wheels to take her home but I don't know what sort of state he's in."

"We'll go and see in a minute," Kitty replied. "Mrs T is doing the necessary." Kitty sat down. "There is one thing I have to talk to you about, though. Actually, there are about twelve, but this is the most urgent."

"Sounds ominous," said Violetta.

"Peter says I should stay out of it, but ...," she shrugged. "You know me, Loo."

"So out with it, Kit. What's up?"

"Well," Kitty began. "Peter's daughter Rachel is here and ..."

"Oh, no!" Violetta exclaimed, interrupting. Her hands flew to her face as she immediately remembered the interview. She felt a flush of embarrassment rouge her cheeks. "How *awful* of me! I can't believe I could do something like that!"

Ludo was immediately worried.

"What? What's happening, Vee?"

Violetta was most upset, as Kitty had gauged she would be.

"Oh, Ludo! I completely forgot yesterday I was being interviewed for the *Daily Standard*. Y'remember, Peter's daughter. At Kitty's?" He nodded. "Well it was her. She was the journalist and ... and ..."

"And what?" he said, putting an arm round her protectively

."And I was supposed to meet her at the bloody Ritz! Oh, God! I stood her up. She must be furious?"

It was Kitty's turn to nod."You can safely say she's

255

pretty cross. And her editor's pretty cross. And she found out from the doorman at the Ritz that you'd stayed there the night before and ..."

"And, don't tell me," said Ludo grimly. "She's here."

"And, Violetta," Kitty added finally, "she's not alone."

"Don't tell me! She's brought a photographer!" exclaimed Ludo.

"No," said Kitty. "At least not yet, although I know she smells a story."

"Bloody inkhounds," Ludo remarked acerbically.

"Oh, no, love. It's not like that. She's a critic."

"Bloody critics then. They're all the same."

"No, darling. She's on my side. You don't understand. This is terrible. If only Gerald had reminded me."

"Gerald was trying to get hold of you, darling," observed Kitty. "But he's been terribly helpful, all the same. It's thanks to him that Rachel's under control. Don't worry he's still on your side too."

"But ... has Gerry 'phoned?" Violetta asked, now bewildered as well as buffeted.

"Is this Gerry? Your ex?"

Violetta sighed and nodded.

"Oh, gosh," said Kitty. "You don't know, do you?"

Ludo and Violetta shared a desperate moment of mutual angst. Ludo beckoned with his hands, implying that Kitty hold back no longer.

"He came with her. They arrived last night. After you'd gone to bed. Of course we made things up. Well ... we pretended you'd been in touch. Neither of them knows you're here. Yet."

The tap dripping into the sink was the only sound that broke the ensuing silence. Ludo made rings on the table with the wet bottom of his glass. Violetta twisted her finger in her hair. Kitty waited, feeling a little de trop. She could hear Nick and Victor talking in the hall and knew that it would not be long before the others surfaced and drifted down for breakfast.

"I must just go and have a word with Nick," she said, getting up from the table. "But for what it's worth and

256

other things apart, I think you should do a bit of gentle grovelling. I don't know how you want to handle your engagement but you could do worse than talk to Rachel" Kitty left them with that thought.

She had missed Nick and Victor who had gone out of the front door and were already walking away from the house. She hurried upstairs to where she knew Peter would be propped up in bed with the papers and the coffee she'd taken up earlier. Umm, she thought as she watched Nick and Victor striding across the lawn, reminding herself that Victor Burke was next on her list.

"So, how d'you feel, Vee?"

Violetta got up and poured more coffee.

"Odd," she said. "More coffee, love?"

He nodded and she refilled his mug.

"I haven't exactly been very honest with him," she said, retaking her seat. "I found it ... awkward."

"I know," he said, remembering Julie but mentioning nothing. "I see where Millie fits in now."

"S'pose its a case of your sins always finding you out," she remarked in conclusion.

"And what about what's-her-name. The journalist?"

"Oh, I'm sure we can work something out. She can have her interview here."

"And us?"

Violetta thought for a moment.

"What d'you think?"

"I don't want a great fuss," he said. "I'd thought of not letting anyone know until we'd done it."

"If we'd been able to, we'd have been very lucky," she pointed out. "People like us ... well, it's the price we pay, love."

Ludo nodded.

"I've got nothing against her," he observed as he delved for a solution. "I thought she was rather nice."

"Even though she's a critic?"

"Yeah. But it's not me I'm thinking of. What she thinks of me and my work isn't important. It's you, love. You and your's."

She reached out and held his hand.

"But I'm going to be an old married lady."

"And you're also a wonderful singer. You're going to be both, Vee. You know it. I know it. Best face the music, I reckon."

She laughed.

"Oh, very good. I like that."

They fell to thinking again.

"Well, if you don't mind, Ludo, I think we should give Rachel a scoop. She's not a hatchet-girl and it's not often that the opera journalist gets a crack at a front page story, is it?"

"Indeed. Better let me call my publicity people, though. Their 'phone'll be ringing off the hook as soon as the *Standard* piece comes out."

"Oh, Ludo. Do you think we're going to be good for each other?"

"Trust me?"

"Trust you."

"That's my girl. Kiss?"

And they did.

Mrs Tarpitt saw them through the window as she came across to the house. Had she not had other matters on her mind, she would have felt embarrassed but she was on an errand and Ludo was the very person she needed to talk to.

They heard her open the back door. When Mrs Tarpitt arrived in the kitchen, they were merely smiling.

"Excuse me Mr Ludo, Miss ... Miss. Would you come across to see young Michael? He's been that anxious that he's letting you down. I know if you just popped in, 'e'd feel that much better."

"Sure. I was just coming. Vee? Will you be alright for a couple of minutes?"

"Absolutely. Give him my love. How is the lad, Mrs Tarpitt?"

"Very much better, Miss" Mrs T replied as Ludo got up from the table to follow her. "I'm sure 'e'll be up and about later, right as rain again."

Ludo turned and blew a kiss to Violetta. She took it on the chin.

She finished her coffee and was thinking about going into the drawing room where she had noticed a baby grand piano. If it was in tune, she would try some scales. Left unexercised for even a day, she knew her voice would not be at it's best next week.

Mrs Tarpitt needed all the information she could get hold of. She felt rather naughty, dragging Ludo out in this way but Wheels was having a bath and she knew she could safely use the time.

Ludo listened to her as he heard Violetta testing the piano. Then the voice, clear and pure, dancing over the arpeggios, up and up in thirds, fifths and down again. He felt immensely proud.

"So can you remember, Mr Ludo? Has 'e ever said where 'e came from?" Mrs Tarpitt concluded hopefully.

"As far as I know, Mrs Tarpitt, he doesn't know himself. And I'm afraid I can't help you. What's brought all this on? Was he talking in his sleep?"

"Oh, no. Nothing like that. It's just that 'e told me a bit about 'is life and ... well, 'e's such a *nice* boy, it made me ... curious?"

Ludo put his arm round her.

"The person who could help you is my mum, Mrs Tarpitt."

Mrs Tarpitt sighed, thinking of that lucky lady in her granny flat.

"P'raps you might ask her when you goes home, sir? An' let Miss Kitty know?"

"You can ask her yourself. If I can find her?"

"She's here?"

"She most certainly is. You haven't seen her, have you? With a big old bulldog?"

"Oh!" said Mrs Tarpitt as the light dawned. As Nick had started to tell her, it had not been Jenks' sister at all, but Mrs Grace Morgan whom she'd seen earlier. "That'd be the lady with Jenks. They've gone for a walk through the park. Try down in the greenhouse maybe. Or in the old tennis house, down by the court."

"Thanks. I will. If I find her, shall I send her along?"

"Please, Mr Ludo. If you would. I'd be very grateful."

They parted, Mrs Tarpitt feeling very positive. Mrs Morgan being a mother herself, would surely help her?

Of course, they heard Violetta before they saw her. Even from their room on the other side of the house, as Rachel and Gerald made their bed, strains of the vocal exercises floated up as though someone had opened a huge musical box downstairs.

Both Rachel and Gerald dropped the counterpane at precisely the same moment.

"That's her!" exclaimed Rachel.

Gerald frowned and listened more intently.

"You're right."

"I *thought* there was something strange," said Rachel, bristling as yet more salt seemed to be sprinkled on her wounded pride. "After all, why would Violetta ring here? She wouldn't have known the number for a start."

"But she did say she was going to Bath," countered Gerald. "In her note. It's not that far away."

"Gerald, darling," said Rachel with a cold determination, "I have a feeling you are finally going to meet Millie."

"I know. But which Millie is it going to be? Stay here." Gerald made to leave the room.

"Why?" said Rachel.

"It'd be best if I saw her alone."

"No, Gerry. This concerns us both. And not only as individuals but as us. And it's only fair to her. OK, she might have some explaining to do but so do we?"

Gerald smiled, rather weakly perhaps, but he smiled. Rachel had said us. In their two nights of lovemaking so far, tenderness had been somewhat obscured by passion.

"You're right," he agreed. "Come on."

They left the bedroom and on the landing met Peter and Kitty, both still in dressing-gowns, who were leaning over the pine balustrade, listening to Violetta practising.

"It *is* her, dad, isn't it?" Rachel accused.

Peter wanted to smile but knew this would infuriate

260

Rachel even further.

"Yes," he said simply."You knew she'd be here, didn't you?"

"Ah," he said defensively. "I believe I *said* she'd told me that she'd contact you tomorrow."

"It wasn't really a lie, Rachel," Kitty interposed.

Rachel glared at her. She grabbed Gerald's shirt sleeve and pulled him away in the direction of the staircase. Gerald resisted. He would have much rather faced Violetta alone, for several reasons, most of all because of Rachel herself. Violetta was used to dealing with awkward customers. At home, in the chippy in Wakefield, the drunken aftermath of a Saturday night in the pub held no terrors for her. The last thing he wanted was a showdown between the past and the present.

He glanced up at Peter and Kitty as he was impelled down the stairs. Peter shrugged and Kitty winced.

"I shall never give a dinner party again," said Kitty as a moment later the singing stopped and a momentary silence took over. They took advantage of it to creep away from the edge of the landing. "In fact I think I'll go straight back to bed and stay there the whole day."

"Nonsense," said Peter propelling her back to their room. "You're going to shower and change into your nurse's uniform."

"Peter!" she exclaimed. He had a thing about nurse's uniforms. "You do choose the strangest moments!"

"Unfortunately, sweetest Kitty, I meant that rather in the sense of first aid. How are we off for sticking plaster?"

Downstairs, in the drawing room, the atmosphere could best be described as vibrating. A tuning fork, placed on the piano, would probably have sounded a high C sharp.

Shock, surprise and suddenness strangely contain elements of their own diffusion. Sails which previously were full of wind and providing seemingly unstoppable momentum, sag unexpectedly in the windless tranquillity of the eye of a hurricane. Deceptive, maybe, but the hiatus provided breathing space.

Violetta initially had her back to the doorway as she

261

stood by the piano, sounding a note and then singing to the open window and the green park beyond. She stopped in mid-note as she heard their footsteps on the oak floorboards at the door.

"Hello, Violetta."

Gerald began grimly but his intentions faltered as she turned round.

"'Ello, Gerry, love."

Rachel, still with her fist clenched around Gerald's cuff, slowly released her grip and his arm fell limply to his side. Violetta crossed the room.

"Rachel, love. I am so sorry! I wouldn't have done that to you for the world. Please understand ... I wasn't m'self yesterday. I'm afraid I haven't been lately ... sorry, Gerry."

Faced with the nub of her problem, Rachel too found her bluster wilting.

"If only you'd 'phoned ..." she began to say.

"If only I'd remembered, love," said Violetta gently.

"But it's so unlike you, Violetta," said Gerald. "What came over you? It was very important you did that. Don't you realise that next week your career could go one of two ways; it could stay on the level it's been for a while or it could take off. It could soar."

"You have to have that kind of good exposure, Violetta," Rachel elaborated, "or your career will only ever be appreciated, it'll never be acknowledged. There's a world of difference, you *must* see that?"

Violetta was plucking up her courage. She had butterflies, worse butterflies that on any first night and these butterflies seemed to have teeth as well as wings.

She indicated the sofa with a timid gesture.

"Sit down, would you. Gerry? Rachel?" As they sat down, she remained standing. She felt better standing.

"Are you sure you're alright, Violetta?" Gerald enquired. He was concerned. Her behaviour and her manner were not those of the Violetta Abizzi he had lived with and worked for, devoted himself to and chivvied and bullied and coaxed for almost twenty years.

Violetta smiled nervously.

262

"Gerry, Rachel, I've said I'm sorry about yesterday and so I hope you both know it's well meant." She paused. "You do, don't you?" she asked anxiously.

Both nodded and Rachel, especially, felt badly that her famous anger, but for this confrontation, could have possibly spawned such a stupid, spiteful and unnecessary reaction as she had contemplated. Revenge writing. Inside, she shuddered.

"Good. And never fear, Rachel. You'll get your interview. We can do it here, love. This afternoon. In the garden maybe? You never know. It'll probably be a better atmosphere for both of us. You'll get the real Violetta Abizzi."

"What d'you mean?" Gerald exclaimed.

"The real me, Gerry. The one you met in the foyer of the town hall. Remember? The one who'd just sung 'Jesu, Joy of Man's Desiring'?"

Gerald looked askance; he looked at the floor. Rachel, on the other hand, came alive.

"The name of that young podgy girl," Violetta continued, "was Violet Hargreaves. Remember her?"

"Of course," he muttered."I'd quite forgotten about her," Violetta went on. "Oh, maybe a few times she's surfaced since that first night we planned and plotted and dreamed, but not often. You see, Gerry, it wasn't only my name you persuaded and finally convinced me to change, it was me. Me, myself, I. And don't get me wrong. I liked Violetta Abizzi. I liked her very much. But I only liked her when she did things that only Violetta Abizzi would do. You and me, our marriage, that was what Violetta would do. Sweeping onto concert stages and into dressing rooms, that was Violetta too. She loved it. Still does. But I made a great mistake in forgetting Violet Hargreaves. Y'see, Gerry, Violetta is nothing without Violet. To you I was only Violetta. I was more part of your life than you were ever part of mine. You *are* Violetta."

Rachel felt now not merely humbled, she felt awed. What Violetta had said was word for word what she had been trying to say to herself for years, except for Gerry, she

263

would have said mother.

"I'm sorry," Gerald said lamely, "I never realised you were so unhappy."

"But I wasn't, Gerry. What I did, what we did, wasn't like some Trilby and Svengali. I wanted it as much as you did. Believe me. But there were other things. Children, for example. Violet Hargreaves wants children. She wants a home. Mebbe a cat or a dog or a tortoise which lives in a garden. She wants to be loved for being Violet. I realised you didn't understand me ages ago. It took me a long time to convince you to get a divorce and then, when we were, it never mattered a jot, did it?"

He shook his head, his negative affirming her positive.

"So who is he?" he asked quietly. Gerald Ward felt very much alone. He was going to be very important. He, whoever he might be, was going to change the direction of Gerald's life.

Rachel's breath was not only bated, she felt her lungs would burst if Violetta held out much longer. Rachel Bailey, both woman and journalist, knew she was party to information that only comes along once in any lifetime.

"He's ... well, I suppose, he's very much like me. Circumstantially at least. He's very kind, very attentive, very courteous. He's ..."

"Oh, for God's sake, Violetta!" cried Gerald. "*Who*?"

"Ludo Morgan," she said quietly.

Gerald's eyes nearly popped.

Rachel exhaled deeply. For an awful moment, she had honestly thought that Violetta had said Ludo Morgan.

"Ludo Morgan?" Gerald echoed.

Christ, thought Rachel with a jolt. She *had* said Ludo Morgan.

"Have you thought about this?" Gerald asked, not from anger, but from deep concern that perhaps a sexual peccadillo had deranged her perspective.

"I've thought about nothing else."

"Not even next week?"

"Not even next week, Gerry. Sorry."

"I don't know what to say," he muttered in abdication

and shock.

"Well, I do," said Rachel after a moment's pause. "And I think it's what you want to hear, Violet." She got up and kissed Violetta on both cheeks. "I'm very, very pleased for you."

"Thanks, chuck," Violetta said, her lips quivering as she felt the sincerity of Rachel's feeling.

"You are ... I mean, has he ...?"

Violetta nodded, not knowing whether to laugh or cry.

"Yes. We're getting married." Suddenly Violetta clutched at Rachel and hugged her. "Is that a scoop for you or what?"

The women were almost dancing with joy.

"Oh, it is! It is!" she laughed. "And you'll make a wonderful Violet Morgan!"

"Oh, don't worry, love," said Violetta, wiping away a tear, "you don't get roles like that written for you every day!"

Their initial effervescence subsided as they both became aware of Gerald, still sitting thoughtfully on the edge of the sofa.

"Gerald?" said Rachel quietly.

He sighed and looked first at Rachel, as if for encouragement. She winked. He got up and faced his client.

"Forgive me?" he asked simply

."There's nothing to forgive, Gerry," she replied. She added something. "Partner?"

"Congratulations, partner." He took her hands in his and, like Rachel, felt very, very full. "I hope you'll both be very happy."

"He's a good man," she replied. "I'd like you to be friends."

It was then that they embraced, the frustrated, misdirected affections of fifteen years finally together, in tandem.

"After all," she said when they broke the hug, "I can't have my manager and my husband not liking each other, can I?"

Gerald hesitated. He pondered the moment. He knew that he had as much to say as Violetta. To postpone was too risky. He felt he could be so easily dissuaded just by·being carried along by her wave of euphoria.

"No, Violetta," he said, shaking his head. "It's not only one change, I'm afraid it's all change. I've been doing some thinking too. You're not the only one who's been in a bit of a spin lately."

"Gerald," said Rachel softly, "not now."

"Yes, now," he replied.

"Rachel, love, it's alright, y'know. I mean, with me. You and Gerry an' all that."

"It's not only that," said Gerald quickly.

"I hope it's part of it," countered Rachel.

Gerald smiled.

"I hope so," he said. "Though we haven't got as far or as rapidly as you have Miss Abizzi ... sorry, Hargreaves!"

"Be patient, lad," grinned Violetta winking in sisterly conspiracy at Rachel.

"There are things that I want to do as well," Gerald explained. "Like you, except not so ... so natural, shall we say. Professional things. Y'see, If I'm not still in love with the artist, I'm still in love with the art. You and I have gone as far as we can go together, Violetta. If we stay together, we'll hold each other back. Separately, we can go on. Am I making any sense?"

"Course you are, Gerry."

She sighed and then laughed a little ironic laugh.

"What?" he asked.

"It's a bit like Frankenstein and his monster, really. The dedicated scientist strives for years and years to make the dream come true and when it does, the reality of it presents no challenges, only problems."

"I suppose."

"But don't rush it," Rachel advised. "After all, Gerry, it's not as though you have a train to catch."

"No," he said somewhat ruefully. "Still, the waiting might be interesting."

"Would you mind?" Violetta said, excusing herself. "I'd like to go and find Ludo. Rachel, we'll do that interview after lunch. Ludo says you can also turn it into a story for

266

him too. You've got an exclusive, love!"

Violetta took both their hands and squeezed them before she went out in search of Ludo.

The course of Rachel and Gerald's conclusions were interrupted as Rachel looked out of the window and saw a police car coming slowly up the drive.

"Good Lord," she said, pointing out to the park. What's that?" As she spoke, Victor and Nick passed the window on the way to the back of the house. Rachel waved to Nick and pointed at the police car. Nick shrugged and shook his head as the car drove slowly round to the front of the house.

They spotted the tall figure of a man coming across the park to the sheep gate which led out of the walled garden and into the meadowland. The figure started to run and as Rachel and Gerald watched, Violetta ran round the side of the house and across the lawn.

"Who's that?" Gerald asked, pointing to the man.

"That," Rachel replied, "is Ludo," as the doorbell rang loudly in the hall. "Now do you suppose we should answer that?"

"Oh, no," Gerald replied firmly, slipping his arm round Rachel and leading her away from the beautifully framed picture of Ludo and Violetta kissing, lost in the perspectives of Jenks' perfectly mown lawn. "I think we should ignore it and just quietly disappear."

Inspector Yates rang the bell again. Impatiently. Constable Tippett shuffled uncomfortably by his side and, deferentially, one pace behind. Andrew Tippett had been feeling awkward and uncomfortable ever since the inspector arrived and told him of the nature of the visit they were paying on the Longinglys of Littlecombe Park. The constable felt doubly awkward since driving past his wife, Sandra and his two children waiting at the bus-stop at the end of Littlecombe Lane for the bus to Bath. Sandra was furious with him, stopping at home after the inspector arrived only to make a desultory mug of coffee for the visitor and to tut very loudly when she overheard the reason for their Saturday being summarily defeated before

267

it had begun.

"For God's sake!" grumbled the impatient inspector. "Why doesn't someone answer the door!"

"For God's sake," called a half dressed Kitty from the landing upstairs, "there's a houseful of people here somewhere! Couldn't *one* of you answer the door?"

She hurried back into the bedroom, half in and half out of a tracksuit. She heard footsteps cross the hall and the scraping metallic sound of the door curtain being pulled back across the brass rail.

Mrs Tarpitt opened the door to the policemen.

"Yes?" she said somewhat stentorianly until she spotted Andrew Tippett behind the inspector. "Oh, 'ello, Andrew?"

"Mrs Longingly?" Inspector Yates enquired.

Does she look like Mrs Longingly, thought Andrew Tippett to himself?

"No," said Mrs Tarpitt. "I'm Ena Tarpitt. Tell 'im, Andrew. You know who I am. You know who Mrs Longingly is too."

"Mrs Tarpitt is the housekeeper, sir," interposed the constable. "This is Inspector Yates, Ena. From Taunton."

"Oh," said Ena, suitably impressed. Taunton was a long ways away. "You better come in then. I'll call Mrs Longingly for you. She's ... she's ... well, she's upstairs," she decided, properly. Inspectors from Taunton might not think it decent that the lady of the house was still not dressed at midday.

Once inside, the inspector didn't wait.

"Is there a Mr Ludo Morgan staying here, may I ask? And," he added opening his notebook and checking the names, "a Mrs Grace Morgan and a large English bulldog?"

You bloody know there is, said Constable Tippett to himself and wishing the floor could open and miraculously swallow him up.

"Er ... I'm ... I'm ," Ena stammered. "I'm not supposed to say, inspector. It's a secret, see."

"Who is it, Mrs Tarpitt?" Kitty called from the landing as she hurried down.

"Oh, thank goodness, Miss Kitty. It's the police."

Kitty appeared at the foot of the stairs, anchoring an earring which refused to go through her ear.

"Hello Andrew," she said, smiling a welcome. "Hello," she said to the inspector. "I'm Kitty Llewellyn. Can I help you."

"Yes. I am Inspector Yates. You are Mrs Oliver Longingly?" the inspector intoned formally.

"No. I was. I'm Ms Kitty Llewellyn now."

Andrew Tippett wanted to laugh.

"Well, your titles are your own affair, miss."

"Ms," Kitty insisted. "Miss makes people my age sound like spinsters, inspector."

"Do you have a Ludo Morgan, a Grace Morgan and a large English bulldog staying with you, madam?"

Kitty decided not to object to the madam.

"May I ask why, inspector? Why do you want to know?"

"My business is with the aforementioned persons, madam."

"Then why don't we go into the drawing room, Inspector. We could be much more comfortable there.

"Kitty didn't wait for an answer and led the policemen across the hall. Mrs Tarpitt scurried back into the kitchen to tell Wheels.

"Now, inspector. Andrew. Will you sit down?"

"No, thank you, Madam. As I said, I only wish to talk to the afore-mentioned persons."

"Well, I think the aforementioned persons are out for a walk," Kitty replied, wondering if the visit had anything to do with Victor's formal complaint.

"Presumably the dog is accompanying them?"

"Oh, yes. Bullshit," said Kitty defiantly. "Except I rather think that they're accompanying him." She had decided that she did not like Inspector Yates one little bit and she was being very grand, as she could do very well when roused.

The inspector's eyes narrowed and his lips moved silently as he echoed Bullshit.

Andrew Tippett explained.

269

"It's the dog's name, sir."

"Ah!"

But Inspector Yates remained unmollified. Kitty waited and as she waited, she observed a strange change overtake Andrew Tippett.

The constable's eyes glazed and his hitherto upright and proper bearing elasticated as he drooped at the sight of Ludo Morgan walking past the drawing room window. Ludo Morgan. He couldn't believe it. From the days when Ludo headed The Force, through the rock 'n' roll years of Andrew Tippett's teenage, the festivals on the Isle of Wight, at Knebworth, the weekend he'd met Sandra on the bus with the youth club going to Wembley to see Ludo Morgan reunited with the surviving members of The Force.

"There he is, inspector," said Kitty, waving to Ludo through the window and beckoning him inside. Ludo pointed to himself and Kitty nodded.

"Yes! You!" she called loudly in a spirit of forced gaiety. Keep it light, she thought to herself.

Constable Tippett was ashen.

"Perhaps you'd take some notes, constable," murmured the inspector, oblivious to the turmoil thrashing in the constable's unsophisticated breast. Andrew remained motionless, himself oblivious to his superior's instruction. As though hypnotised, he had turned mesmerically from the window and his eyes were now fixed on the drawing room door, unable to believe that through it would come the man who had been one of his idols for years. "Did you hear me, constable?" Inspector Yates barked.

As Andrew began to pull himself into some semblance of readiness, the door opened and Ludo came in with Violetta.

"Did you want me, Kit?" he asked. Violetta smiled at the policeman.

"Yes, darling. This is Constable Tippett," she said, indicated Andrew whose jaw had dropped almost to his lapels and whose bug-eyed stare resembled someone well into the first stages of trauma, "and this is Inspector Yates. I think he wants a word."

270

"Shall I go, love?" Violetta asked.

"No. Stay, Vee. Please. You too Kitty. Where's Wheels?"

"In the kitchen, I think. Shall I go and fetch him?"

"Please, Kit."

Ludo was feeling vulnerable. He was used to people around him. He felt naked and exposed without his usual hefty phalanx of entourage.

"Mr Morgan?"

Ludo nodded to the inspector.

"Do you own a British bulldog?"

"I do."

"And are you the animal's registered keeper?"

"I suppose so," replied Ludo, who had no idea what a registered keeper was other than someone who worked in a zoo. "Bullshit's my dog, if that's what you mean."

"So you are responsible for licensing the animal?"

"Sorry?" Ludo queried. This was a reality of a sort he couldn't handle. The only licensing Ludo was aware of had to do with his name being blazoned on mugs and T-shirts sold at his concerts.

"Under the law, Mr Morgan. A dog has to be licensed. Can you produce such a licence?"

Wheels came into the drawing room. He heard the question.

"I ... er, yes. I think?" He turned to Wheels. "Can't we?" Wheels shrugged, his expression betraying his ignorance of the whereabouts of such a document. "D'you think mum's got it?" Again, Wheels shrugged.

"So you can not produce the dog's licence, Mr Morgan?" said Inspector Yates with a great deal of obvious satisfaction.

"We think my mother could," Ludo replied, sharing his hopes with Wheels.

"Would that be Mrs Grace Morgan?"

"Yes."

"Who is also staying here?"

"You know she is, inspector," Kitty interrupted.

"Andrew, I mean Constable Tippett would have told you that. He brought her here in his car for heaven's sake!"

271

The inspector glared at Kitty. Andrew coughed nervously, pencil poised and shaking in his unsteady hand. He hadn't written a word.

"Look, what's all this about, inspector?" Ludo said crossly. Violetta laid a hand on his arm in pacification. "If it's about Bullshit biting Victor Burke, we're way ahead of you. The complaint has been withdrawn."

Kitty heard footsteps in the hall, tiptoed to the door and spotted Nick and Victor skulking past.

"In here, you two!" she called. "Quick march!"

Nick and Victor came in, followed by Peter who had been finishing his newspapers in the study, attempting to be scarce. He'd half heard what was going on but had been as busy inventing excuses for not involving himself as he had been studying the leaders.

"This is Victor Burke, inspector," Kitty announced. "He is the man who mistakenly thought that Mr Morgan's bulldog had bitten him, aren't you Victor?" She nudged him fiercely.

"Oh! Yes," he exclaimed."

Are you Mr Victor Burke?"

"Yes."

"And you are now telling me that the dog didn't bite you?" the inspector asked with suspicious incredulity."

Yes."

"The Royal Free Hospital in ..." The inspector consulted his note book."

Hampstead," Nick piped up.

"Thank you ... in Hampstead, says that you were treated for a dog bite last Thursday evening. Were you or were you not bitten by the bulldog?"

"Inspector," said Peter stepping forward, "I'm Peter Bailey. I'm a solicitor. I think I could be of help."

"Thanks, Peter," murmured Ludo as Peter approached the policeman.

"Indeed, sir," remarked the inspector smugly."Yes," said Peter. "First of all I understand that Mr Burke withdrew any formal complaint he made to the police in Hampstead, is that right, Victor?"

272

Victor nodded and glanced at Ludo guiltily.

"This morning," he confirmed. "Nine o'clock. I spoke to Sergeant Griffiths there."

"Secondly," Peter continued, "there is a witness to the alleged attack which, although thought to have been made by a bulldog, cannot possibly be positively ascribed to Mr Morgan's dog."

"What witness?" Kitty asked.

"Me, mum," said Nick. "Remember? I went out to help Grace and Wheels look for Bullshit? Well, I found Victor, just when the dog bit him."

"Oh," said Kitty. "You never said."

"Victor's stomach churned over as Kitty inclined her head with a questioning look in his direction.

"Good for you, Nick," abetted Ludo to general murmurs of approval."Do we need to go on?" Peter asked.

Andrew Tippet folded over the scribbled page of his notebook wondering how he was going to pluck up enough courage to ask for Ludo's autograph.

"There, inspector," Kitty said brightly but with a puzzled glance at Victor. "All cleared up. Perhaps we'd all like a glass of sherry before lunch?"

The inspector was at a temporary loss for words. He fairly glowered as he surveyed the oddly assorted assemblage of faces all turned in his direction, awaiting his reaction. He felt thwarted, he felt cross, he felt humiliated, he felt ... And the more he felt, the more determined he became not to be outdone.

"Just one moment, madam."

"Ms," Kitty corrected. "In my book, madams run houses of ill repute, inspector."

"I'm sure I can't comment on that," replied the inspector with an insidious undertone. "However, there remains the fact that after being formally warned not to remove the dog from the premises, Mrs Grace Morgan deliberately contravened the instruction, thereby possibly committing an offence in obstructing the course of justice."

"Oh, really, inspector," said Peter as reasonably as he could.

"Now, look here!" exclaimed Ludo angrily.

Violetta and Kitty shook their heads in abject amazement.

The inspector held up his hand for silence as a babble of outrage followed his announcement.

"And," he declaimed, "there also remains the matter of the licence!"

"How ridiculous!" cried Violetta. "Seven-and-bloody-sixpence!"

Kitty slammed the lid of the piano which sent a crashing, atonal reverberation through the room.

"Ludo, I'm really sorry about all this," Victor blurted out. "It was ... well, before I ... I didn't realise."

"Before what?" Kitty asked. Certain pieces of the jigsaw were beginning not to fit so snugly.

"Don't worry, Victor," Ludo said. "We could all have made the same mistake. Look, inspector, my mother is an old lady. That dog is her pride and joy as well as mine. She's told me all about it and surely you must sympathise with her? Some copper ... sorry, one of the Hampstead police told her that if a magistrate decided, the dog might have to be put down. She panicked. Simple."

"Yes," said Violetta and Kitty together.

"Be a little human about it, inspector," Violetta added forcefully.

"I wish to interview Mrs Grace Morgan," replied the Inspector flatly. "And I want sight of that dog! Otherwise, I shall have to institute a search of the premises."

Oh shit, thought Constable Tippett, the bastard's going to bust them for something.

"She's out for a walk, inspector. I told you. She might not be back for hours," Kitty intervened.

"Then I shall return. At the end of the day. By which time, someone will have informed Mrs Morgan she is required to see me. Good day. Constable?" Inspector Yates indicated he was ready to leave. Inwardly, Andrew groaned. He could see the rest of his day falling into ruins. And he was due to play cricket at two.

"I'll show you out," said Kitty, leading the way out to

274

the hall.

At the front door, Oliver and Julie were standing by the police car, breathless after their jog which had taken longer than usual because of an unlisted rest stop in the conifers which had turned into something quite else. Kitty opened the door.

Constable Tippett, already suffering, now experienced a second trauma at the unexpected sight of one of the most famous Page Three girls of all time standing on the gravel not three yards away from him.

"Morning, Andrew," said Oliver. Andrew Tippett merely gaped. "What's up?"

Julie smiled at the inspector and, brushing a wisp of hair off her face, her bosom heaving with breathlessness, beamed at Constable Tippett. He nearly died. Fright, terror, surprise, shock, fear, guilt all conspired in an orgasm of incomprehension. He thought his guts were about to drop out of his backside.

"'Ello!" said Julie brightly, instinctively recognising a fan. He gulped. She walked across to him. "'Ere, you alright, love?" She laid a hand on his arm.

He opened his mouth to try and speak but the only sound which emerged was an incomprehensible gargled burble.

"It's alright, Oliver. I'll explain," said Kitty.

"You, miss, are not Mrs Grace Morgan, by any chance?" Inspector Yates enquired of Julie.

Julie was outraged.

"Well thank you very much!" she exclaimed. "Who the 'ell d'you think you are!"

"It's alright, Julie," said Kitty quickly, "the *inspector* is only doing his duty."

"Oh," said Julie acknowledging Kitty's wink, "'Course."

"Come on, Tippett," hissed the inspector, "don't stand there like some stuffed idiot, get in the car!"

Somehow, Andrew Tippett managed to a) find his car key and b) to insert it into the ignition. Sandra would never believe this. In fact, he thought, perhaps it was better that Sandra never even knew, especially about Julie Burge.

Andrew Tippett had a very private, very special relationship with Julie Burge carried on in the imtimate privacy of his garden shed.

Kitty, Oliver and Julie watched the car drive away before returning to what had become a very spirited and highly indignant public meeting in the drawing room. On the way in, Wheels emerged having been dispatched by Ludo to find Grace.

THE BIRDS AND THE BEES

Wheels dashed into the kitchen, almost crashing into Mrs Tarpitt who was carrying a huge platter of cold meats and the ham she had cooked earlier into the dining room for lunch.

"Slow down, Michael! You'll find yourself back in bed if you don't!"

"Ena," he said breathlessly, "do us a favour, will you?"

"What?"

"Come with me. I gotta find Grace, Mrs Morgan that is. And the dog."

"But the lunch? They'll be wantin' lunch soon, dear."

"I'll help you with that. Please!"

"Alright," she said and put down her load. "Most of it's done. Are they 'avin sherry yet?"

"I think they're needing more than sherry," Wheels replied. "Any idea where Mrs M might be?"

"We'll try the ..." Mrs Tarpitt hesitated. She was about to say the old tennis house but as Wheels took her arm to hurry her along, she thought again. If the young man standing by her was the young man she was convinced he was, the memories which lay in the old tennis house were especially poignant.

"I think I 'ave a fair idea," she said instead.

"As they walked past first Ena's and then Jenks' doors, Wheels heard Queenie whining piteously. She was scratching on the inside of the door madly, desperate to get out.

"Poor Queenie," said Ena."She's been like that all morning," Wheels replied. "Is she alright?"

"Not like Jenks to leave 'er so long," Ena replied. "P'raps best to 'ave a look at her."

Ena tried the handle of the door and it opened. However gingerly she pushed the door back, Queenie in heat was no match for her gentle hand on the knob. The dog's nose and then her forepaws inserted themselves in the gap. The door flew open and the labrador ran barking furiously between Mrs Tarpitt's legs and off across the yard, following the direction that Jenks, Grace and Bullshit had taken earlier in the morning.

"Oh, no!" Ena exclaimed. "Jenks'll kill me!"

"No, he won't, love," said Wheels reassuringly. "She'll find her way to him and no harm'll come to her."

"But she's on heat, Michael! What if she goes off and meets a village dog?"

"Then they'll have village babies, won't they?" Wheels laughed. "Come on, Ena. Nothing you can do. She won't go far."

"Oh, dear," said Ena fearfully, "what a hurly burly this is all turnin' out to be."

Indeed, Jenks, Grace and Bullshit were ensconced in the old tennis house. They'd been there for some half hour ever since Jenks had spoken to the young woman standing at the bus-stop on the other side of the fence which surrounded the entire perimeter of the Park.

"Mornin' Sandra," drawled Jenks, wandering through some scrubby bushes to the roadside. "Where you off on a fine day like this? Thought you was doin' cricket teas today?"

"Don't talk to me about cricket teas!" she replied sharply. She noticed Grace and Bullshit and nodded, smiling. Grace smiled and waved back. What cheery folk they are, she thought, in the country. All very friendly and nice. "That's all you men think about," Sandra concluded. "Cricket and work."

"Summat's got into you today," Jenks remarked.

"You can say that again. Andrew was supposed to be takin' us to Bath. Now some ruddy inspector's arrived from Taunton. They're comin' down to see Mrs Longingly right about now I should think."

And Sandra explained what she had overheard as she had thundered loudly around her kitchen, hoping her ill mood would communicate itself as forcefully as possible through the half closed door into her lounge where the

278

men were talking.

"You means they're goin' to arrest Mrs Morgan there," Jenks said, indicating Grace waiting on the path. "An' all for a bloody dog bite?"

"Daft, innit? Waste of time and trouble," Sandra replied. "'Ere, is it true then, Mr Jenkin?"

"Is what true?"

"That you got Ludo Morgan stayin' with you over there."

"Might be," he said enigmatically. "Then again, might not be."

"Go on," she said more jovially. "I knows it's true."

"Then why'd you ask?" drawled Jenks.

"Any chance of an autograph?" Sandra asked

Further conversation was curtailed by the arrival of the green bus. Sandra's request went unfulfilled as she realised that Shane, their eldest, an unruly boy of seven, had wandered away from the bus-stop.

"Shane!" called Sandra. "You come 'ere or you'll get what for if we misses this bus!"

Jenks hurried away from the fence.

"Cheery sort of girl," Grace remarked.

"Mebbe," Jenks replied. "But what she 'ad to say for 'erself warn't quite so cheery, mind."

"What did she say?"

"'Er hubby's the law round 'ere. The one who brought you last night. With 'im," he said, pointing with the stem of his pipe at the panting Bullshit. "An' 'e's the problem. Seems as the police are comin' after the pair of you. And your lad."

"Oh, no!" Grace said, immediately thrown into great consternation. "That's what I came away for, to escape all that."

"Long arm of the law!" Jenks exclaimed. "It's all them computers and what 'ave you. No one's safe nowhere these days."

"And they're comin' here?" Grace asked. Jenks nodded thoughtfully. he was trying to work out an escape. "What'll we do, Mr Jenkin?"

Poor Grace. Her face was again a field of furrowed frowns. Bullshit looked up at them, disconsolately as though he could sense his number was imminently coming up.

"We hides, my dear," he said slowly.

"But where?" Grace wailed.

He looked down at the woman he had met not three hours ago. He hadn't spent a nicer three hours in a very long time, he reflected to himself and he was damn sure that the rest of the day wasn't going to be spoiled by any flatfoot with nothing better to do than hounding innocent creatures whether they be canine or human. Jenks took Grace's hand and patted it firmly in reassurance.

"Don't you worry your head, my dear", he said encouragingly. "Old Jenks'll see you're alright. Follow me."

He took Bullshit's lead from Grace and with her following in his wake, ploughed through a patch of unmown meadowland in the direction of what seemed to Grace like a wall of ivy and virginia creeper.

The old tennis house was exactly what its name implied. Falling apart and almost rotten, the Victorian Swiss/German chalet had been usurped when the hard tennis court had been put in closer to the house and a new tennis shelter erected. The old tennis house had been many things before being pensioned off. There were many generations of ghosts in and around the three roomed chalet where at least four generations of Llewellyns had sat and imbibed glasses of iced tea, home-made lemonade whilst listening to the clop clop of tennis balls and the huzzahs of victorious players.

For Kitty it had been dolls' hospital, schoolroom and zoo and it was where she had first been kissed on her fourteenth birthday by an American boy whose parents had taken the Priory for the summer.

For Nick and his friends from the village, it had been wild west fort, pirate headquarters, submerged submarine, space station Zero as well as where he had first felt those strange stirrings in his jeans when Freddie Harper, the son of the local market gardener and he had fought with each other in mock battle for possession of the laser sword of Darth Vader. In the film, Luke Skywalker only ever kissed Princess Lea.

To Jenks, it was where, in his youth as the under-gardener, he had sloped off in the heat of summer afternoons for a quiet smoke and to reflect on why only a pair of flat feet made the difference in Arthur Hinton being called to the army and Jenks being a civilian. At the time, he hadn't felt in the least lucky to have his application to join up refused. There was nothing he wanted more than to get out of Littlecombe. He'd walked ten miles one weekend to see Arthur one Saturday night when the regiment was exercising on Salisbury Plain. He went specifically to try and join up again but Arthur had dissuaded him, told him he was better off in Littlecombe and told him to keep an eye on Ena. It was the last Jenks ever saw of Arthur Hinton.

Jenks pulled aside the curtain of trailing creeper which hid the door and went in with Bullshit. He held the curtain back for Grace to follow him.

"In 'ere, my dear. We'll be safe as houses in 'ere. An' I can see when the coppers come and when they go."

Grace entered the chalet slowly and looked about. The roof had holes in it, so did the walls but there were two old cane chairs, still serviceable and a wooden crate on which there was still jumbled the tiny cups and saucers from the last dolls' tea party. Old tennis racquets, their stringing long ruptured, hung on hooks on the wall and an ancient tennis net decayed in a heap in one corner like the rigging in the tomb of a dynastic Egyptian ship.

"Sit down, my dear. No one ever comes 'ere now." Jenks arranged a chair for Grace and then took up a position by the shuttered window. The shutter creaked outwards as he pushed, just enough for him to see the entrance to Littlecombe's drive.

"Oh, Mr Jenkin," she sighed. "What 'ave I come to? Breakin' the law at my age. It's very wrong, all this, you know."

"It's not such a very marvellous law, Mrs Morgan, that

281

chases innocent people and animals. I mean to say! Look at that great old dog. There's not an ounce of harm in 'im." Jenks patted Bullshit's head roughly to make his point. Bullshit panted and looked up adoringly at this man who smelled so strongly and muskily of the current object of his dog's desire.

"I dare say you're right, Mr Jenkin," she replied. "But I tell you one thing, it would never 'ave appened to me in my little flat off the Holloway Road." She looked lovingly at Bullshit. "'E's not even my dog. It's all Ludo. Everything's Ludo's and as soon as I come along, everything goes wrong. If I've told 'im once, I've told him a thousand times. I shouldn't be with him, Mr Jenkin."

"Would you do me a great favour?" Jenks asked.

"Of course."

"Call me Jenks, would you? Mite formal for me all this Mister stuff."

"Then you'll call me Grace. Is that a bargain?"

They shook hands.

When Jenks turned back to the window, the police car appeared between the pillars of the gates and drove down towards the house.

"Well, they're 'ere," he announced. Grace shivered. It was cool in the shaded chalet.

"I feel I'm keepin' you," Grace said after a moment. The smoke from Jenks' pipe wafted through the room taking away some of the smell of damp, rotting wood.

"What from?" he laughed. "Oh, I might 'ave gone down to the cricket, later. But what's a game of cricket when I got such good company?"

Grace took the compliment well. She felt flattered."

That's very nice of you to say so, Jenks. Ladies don't seem to get that sort of talk after we're fifty."

"Ooh, I don't know," he replied. "Look at that Joan Collins. Wonderful for 'er age. Mind you, wouldn't reckon on 'er bein' much good around the house. Only one room she'd be good for, eh?"

Grace giggled.

"Oh, Jenks! What a thing to say! An' I'm a good bit older

than that Joan Collins!"

"Well," he said, "it's true. Life goes on in more than one room of a house, I says and not everyone's blessed with the money to get others to do the dirty work for them."

"Quite right," Grace agreed. "I seen it more than most. With my own son. All the money in the world an' 'e's never been really happy. Mind you, perhaps now. With this new girlfriend." She sighed. "But who knows? There's many a slip twixt cup and lip as they say."

Jenks nodded and knocked his pipe out on the floor, tapping out the embers with the underside of the bowl.

"Your life and your health's the most important things, Grace. Long as you've got those, you're alright."

"And family," Grace added. "Though you might think I'm hard on my boy, I wouldn't be without 'im for the world. Nor Kitty. I think of her as my daughter an' I always will."

"And what about husbands?" Jenks asked, quite matter-of-fact. "Good lookin' woman like you. Should 'ave someone to see for you."

Grace didn't reply. She fidgeted with her hands.

"Oh, sorry," said Jenks. "Please don't think I was pryin'. I hates that when folks does it to me."

"Oh, no, Jenks. Don't mind me. But ..." Grace sighed. "Well, you know what it is. You go for so long with only memories and even they've faded so's you often don't even remember what the memories tell you. Ludo's dad was such a good man. 'E was taken much too soon. Ludo was but ten. Never really 'ad a father, not like boys should. Cancer, it was."

"Oh," said Jenks softly. "I am sorry, Grace."

"Thirty years ago and more," Grace said wistfully. "Daft, really, when you think about it. Nowadays it would be different. Lots of widows remarry and all right and proper that they should. Still difficult mind, specially if you've got even one kiddie but in my day, there was nowhere to go to meet anyone. Nowhere 'cept the pub that is and it wasn't thought proper, you know. The weeks turn into months, then to years and before you know it, you're workin' so

283

'ard to keep what you got, tryin' to make some sort of a life for you and your kiddie that all the rest goes out the window. You get passed by."

"Yep," Jenks agreed. "Times is very different now and that's a fact."

"And what about you, Jenks. 'Andsome chap like you," Grace teased. "Bet you've been a one with the girls in your time, eh?"

Jenks chuckled.

"Aaah! One or two, p'raps. But never the right one. My dogs was my family, I s'pose. Bred 'em, I did. Got lots of cups, even a third at Crufts one year. Only got the one now, though. My Queenie."

"She is lovely," said Grace. "'Spect she's wonderin' where you've got to?"

"Best she stays where she is," Jenks replied. "Seven now, she is. One good litter left in 'er and then that's it. No more. Let her enjoy what's left to 'er."

"Will you keep them?"

"No," he said quickly.

"I could never be without one," said Grace. "It was only after my old Punch died that I went to Ludo's. Couldn't 'ave the old chap upset. Lovely dog. Labrador, like your's. 'Is kidneys went, so the vet said."

"'S'awful that," he remarked. "And you left on your own too."

Grace began to cry at the memory of that awful day. Ludo was having minor surgery in the Princess Grace and so it fell to Wheels. He had called for her in the other Mercedes and they drove through the pouring rain to the Hornsey vet. Afterwards, not having a garden of her own, Wheels took Grace and the dead dog back to Hampstead and they put Punch in the garden. Grace later planted a magnolia, a grandiflora.

"There, there," chided Jenks gently as he left his sentry duty and squatted by the side of Grace's chair. "Can't 'ave this. Think of all the happy times we 'ad with them. That's what I does. Only think of the good, my dear."

Grace nodded. She searched for a hanky or a tissue in

284

her cuff and found none. Jenks pulled out his red spotted kerchief and with it she dried her eyes and blew her nose.

"What a fool," she sniffed. "I am sorry, Jenks. I'll wash this for you later."

The revving of a car engine disturbed the hidden tranquillity of their refuge as Inspector Yates, driven by Constable Tippett, came down the drive. The car waited briefly at the pillars and turned left up Littlecombe Lane back to the village.

"See," Jenks crowed triumphantly. "They've gone."

"But like all bad pennies," Grace remarked, "they'll be back." She was still subdued, but, nevertheless, distinctly relieved. Ludo surely would have been able to sort something out. And that nice Peter. And Nick was there too. Perhaps it would all work out, she reflected.

"P'raps you'd like to walk down to the cricket with me s'afternoon?" Jenks invited.

"Oh," said Grace, brightening, "yes. I would. Mind you, I shall probably be sent packin' before then. Don't think my son's best pleased about me being here."

"Blow 'im," said Jenks with a smile. "It's me askin' you. You can be *my* guest. Seems everyone else round 'ere can 'ave who they like, so why not me too?"

"It's not as easy as that," said Grace sadly.

"'Course it is! You'm a fine woman, Grace. You don't 'ave to answer to no one."

Grace smiled. Jenks was being so kind. She appreciated it. Jenks was her friend, her equal in years and outlook and feelings. He wasn't anyone else's friend, for once, not Ludo's or Kitty's or anyone's but hers. Grace felt suddenly quite giddy with the adventure and the rush of emotions so long dormant.

"You know what I'd like most of all, Jenks?"

"You just name it, m'dear."

"I'd love to have a look round your greenhouses."

"It'd be my pleasure," he grinned.

Bullshit barked. Once, then twice.

"Ssshh!" hissed Grace. He remained silent but got up from where he had been sprawled and began jigging and

285

waggling his rear end.

"What's up with 'im?" said Jenks.

"Someone must be coming," Grace replied urgently.

Jenks looked through the shutter.

"It's Ena!" he whispered loudly.

"Who's Ena?"

"Mrs Tarpitt, the 'ousekeeper. Don't worry, she won't let on. But there's some lad with 'er. 'Aven't seen 'im before.

"Grace joined Jenks at the shutter and, shoulder to shoulder, they looked through. Jenks' shoulder was still hard and firm, toughened by years of manual work and Grace could feel his knotted muscles tighten as they crouched down to see out. Grace's shoulder was warm and round and soft.

"It's Wheels. My son's driver!" she whispered. "It's alright. It's friend, not foe."

He grinned. She blinked her relief at him thankfully and felt very safe.

As Wheels followed Ena through the park, she hurrying ahead through the trees and then, leaving the obvious paths, ploughing through the uncut meadowgrass, he felt distinctly nervous. That familiar twinge began to twist itself into an unravellable knot in his stomach, high up, under his rib cage. He felt in his pocket for his antacid pills but remembered he had left them on the bedside table in Ena's flat.

"Where are you takin' me?" he called to Ena.

"You'll see," she called over her shoulder.

"I can't see anything," he replied. "Certainly not Grace or the dog. Either of 'em."

"You wait," she insisted. "I bet I'm not wrong."

The old tennis house was so overgrown that to an outsider, ignorant of its existence, it looked more like a small hill, so covered was it in creeper and surrounded by high brambles interwoven with wild clematis. Old man's beard they called it in the country.

Wheels pace slowed almost to a standstill as Ena drew further and further away. She seemed to Wheels to be heading in the direction of the mound of vegetation. As he looked ahead, it seemed that the sun went behind a cloud. He looked up. There were no clouds. But there was grey. Like a veil, drawn suddenly across the green park and the trees. Behind the veil, Wheels felt his mind ping, as sharply and loudly as though a switch had been thrown and a jolt of electricity had surged through his brain. Then the grey lifted and it was bright and hot where he had felt suddenly gloomy and cold. He felt breathless too, as though he couldn't gulp down air fast enough.

Ena stopped and turned round. She beckoned him on. Wheels stumbled forwards, the tall grasses with their heavy seed heads scratching against his jeans and boots. He heard her calling him on. It was like a dream, as though his feet wouldn't walk any faster, as though he was being held back.

As he caught up with her, Wheels could sense the atmosphere crackling with energy. As Ena pulled back the curtain of Virginia creeper, Wheels saw that beneath all the greenery, there was a structure, a wooden house. Ena disappeared behind the creeper. Wheels bent and followed her.

Grace and Jenks were standing on the opposite wall. Bullshit pulled hard on his lead, yanked it from Jenks' grasp and bounded towards Wheels joyously, snuffling and slavering, his tongue lolling out in abandon.

As Wheels bent down to pet the dog, Jenks stiffened. It was dark inside the tennis house and the light was behind Wheels. But as the young man turned, Jenks started forward.

"Arthur!" he exclaimed quite involuntarily.

Ena smiled quietly to herself. Yes, Ena Tarpitt, she told herself, you are right. He is."

No, Jenks," she said gently. "It's not Arthur. This is Michael."

"Well, bless me," whistled Jenks in surprise.

Wheels stood up.

"Mrs M?"

"Hello, dear. I suppose Ludo's sent you to find me?"

"Yes. Best come back to the house. And Edgar. You're

287

both wanted."

As Grace looked up at Jenks, he put an arm round her shoulders. Wheels watched. It was strangely still inside the tennis house, as though it had become a holy place. Mrs Tarpitt moved slightly and her face was illuminated by a shaft of sunlight coming through one of the holes in the roof. It was a sharp, bright image, like a golden painting hanging in the darkness on the walls of a church and when Wheels turned suddenly to look at Ena, he was transfixed. It had happened. What, he wasn't sure. But the gathering force he knew had presaged some unforecast imminent event was now spent. The future had come as he knew it would and Wheels had come with it. He didn't understand but as he looked at Ena's faint smile of contentment and looked into the dark pools of her eyes, he felt a sense of total peace. He hardly dared breathe for fear of breaking the spell. There was no pain in his stomach, no bitter taste of bile in his throat. He felt totally at one with his body for the first time in many years.

The feeling lasted only a moment but in that moment, it lasted forever. Wheels know that he would never forget it.

"Best be getting on, my dear," said Jenks.

Grace nodded and smiled at Mrs Tarpitt.

As Jenks bent down to retrieve the end of Bullshit's lead, the dog lurched back and growled.

"Edgar, dear!" Grace remonstrated. "That's no way to behave!"

Bullshit glanced over his shoulder and seemed in two minds whether to obey Grace or to obey his instincts.

Jenks made another attempt to grab the lead and as he did so, Bullshit made his decision. Whether he heard Queenie barking in the meadow as she chased in between the grazing cows or whether some sixth canine sense urged him, he turned on his hind legs with surprising speed and shot out of the tennis house, through the creeper and at top speed away through the park.

"Oh, no!" Wheels yelled as, leading the trio who immediately fell in behind him, he chased after the fleeing dog.

"Michael!" called Mrs Tarpitt. "Don't over do it!"

"He'll be off back up the house," Jenks commented authoritatively. "After the bitch."

"Oh!" wailed Ena, "Jenks! I have the most terrible confession to make!"

A LATE, LIGHT LUNCH

Violetta was more nervous than she had anticipated at the prospect of meeting her future mother-in-law. Kitty had given her a brief run-down into which Ludo threw some deftly aimed spanners. Kitty's view of his mother was essentially one to which distance lent its usual enchantment. The reality, he knew, could be very much more stark. But, like Violetta, he had his fingers crossed.

Grace, on the other hand, was far from nervous. In truth, she was somewhat irritated when Jenks explained to her that she had better go into the main house for lunch. Grace had suggested walking down to the pub or, better, that Wheels take them in the car. Wheels steered her away from that idea and agreed with Jenks. After Jenks had gone back to his flat to collect Queenie's lead, promising that by the time lunch was over he'd be back with the two escapees, Grace left Wheels and Mrs Tarpitt in the kitchen.

"Nothing to stop us, though, Ena," Wheels said. "I'd like to buy you a lunch out."

Ena laughed.

"Better not, Michael. I am supposed to be staff, you know."

"So am I. But so what? Honestly, I'd like to very much. I'll never have a nicer girl on my arm."

"Get on with you!" Ena replied as she helped him to a baked potato and cold ham.

Grace felt that she wasn't quite properly dressed. She'd picked off all the grass seeds and burrs that she could see from her skirt but she didn't feel at all anxious to go into the drawing room.

Of course, she was somewhat surprised to see Julie Burge but everyone was so kind and welcoming, even Julie, she put all questions to the back of her mind.

Everyone, it seemed, had a glass of something."

Darling," said Kitty who had just finished smoothing

down some of the maternal mountains which Ludo had been creating out of the molehills of his mother's life story. "Let me get you a drink? What would you have? Little gin?"

Grace shook her head.

"No, dear. Sherry, please. Sweet. And just a small one."

"Mum," said Ludo, taking Grace's arm and leading to the bay window seat where they had been sitting. "I want you to meet Violetta."

Violetta got up as Grace walked across the room. Her eyes met Grace's and though their first meeting had started no fires, Ludo sensed that Grace's first feelings were warm.

"What a very pretty name, my dear," said Grace as they shook hands.

"Thank you Mrs Morgan."

"Oh, no," said Grace shaking her head. "Lets start off as we mean to go on, lovey 'cos I 'ave a feeling we've got a good long way to go. I'm Grace."

Violetta laughed.

"And that's a pretty name too."

"It is," Grace replied without a hint of modesty. "Ludo tells me you're a singer."

"Yes. I am."

"Hope it's none of that noisy old stuff he gets away with," said Grace. She was teasing but it was what she truthfully felt.

Oh, thought Violetta as Ludo winked at her, you're a tough old bird, Grace Morgan.

"Opera, actually," she said.

"Oh!" Grace said with pleasant surprise. "You mean proper singing?"

"Yes, mum, proper singing."

Nick brought Grace's sherry and then went back to join Victor, Gerald and Rachel who were deep in conversation about the Picasso exhibition at the Tate and who had read all Arianna Stassinopoulos Huffington's book.

"Far too deep," he said and brushed his hand surreptitiously along Victor's bottom. "Much too intellectual for lunchtime."

291

"I thought you were supposed to be an intellectual," said Rachel.

"Only on weekdays," Nick replied as he went over to join Julie who was temporarily on her own. Peter and Oliver were discussing the state of Lloyds.

"You alright?" Nick asked. "'Nother drink or anything?"

Julie shook her head.

"No, thanks. Better behave, I s'pose." She winked. "It's all a bit like probation, innit?"

"You're telling me. I know it's family and all that but sometimes I'd love to take off all my clothes and jump up and down naked on the sofa. Oh, sorry, no disrespect."

She laughed.

"None taken. But as I spend most of my working day with me clothes off, I'll keep mine on if you don't mind."

Nick knew immediately he liked Julie. There wasn't an ounce of side to her.

"I'm pleased about you and dad," he said. "He could do with someone like you. Knock some of the stuffiness out of him."

"He's not stuffy!" Julie exclaimed. "Not a bit. He's alright, your old dad. Even if he is your dad."

"I know," Nick replied. "I wish ..."

"Go on."

"No. Skip it. Forget it."

"No, go on, Nick, What do you wish?"

"I just wish I knew him a bit better. I wish we were closer."

"So, what's stopping you?"

"Oh," he sighed. "I dunno. Usual fences, I s'pose."

"Then lemme tell you somethin'," she said confidentially. "I like you, Nick so here's a bit of advice. Don't sit on 'em."

"On what?"

"Those fences," she said. "You decide which side you want to be on and be on it." She took a sip from her glass of Diet Coke and watched him. He looked at her and from his look, she knew that he knew that she knew. It was enough.

"I think we should continue this conversation later," he

292

said with a broad wink.

Julie nodded.

"An' if you think I can be of any 'elp, Nick, lemme know. I don't know much but what I do know is yours if you need it. You're a nice guy."

"And you're a great girl," he replied as Kitty called them into lunch.

"By the way, mum," said Ludo as he led his ladies, one on either arm, through to the dining room, "is Bullshit alright?"

"Oh," said Grace, "I wish you'd call 'im by his proper name, dear. What will Violetta think of us?"

"It's alright, Grace. I've heard all about the family and very little shocks me. I love dogs. And kids," she added squeezing Ludo's arm. "And I'm lookin' forward to meetin' your Edgar."

"And so you shall," Ludo said, feeling very merry after three of Peter's nifty Martinis. "Won't she, mum?"

"Yes, love," Grace replied, not exactly sure when when would be. She decided not to spoil lunch by confessing that at this moment she hadn't the faintest idea where the bulldog was.

THREE WISE MEN

Julie excused herself after lunch and went upstairs to change. Everyone seemed to drift off. Grace called on Jenks, but only after Ludo had made her promise to be back at the house by four o'clock to see the inspector. Rachel went upstairs to check her tape recorder whilst Gerald made some 'phone calls in the study before joining her.

Violetta and Ludo had a lie-down which surprised no one.

Kitty and Peter went for a walk which they intended to end in a swim at the old mill. They also intended to call in at the post office in an attempt to prise Mr Williams from his garden to issue a dog licence. Kitty had suggested that she would probably be able to persuade him to backdate it, although Peter told her that they were in enough trouble already without falsifying evidence.

Only Victor and Nick were left, contemplating a swim. Victor was rather loathe to go too far from the house due to an understandable apprehension of low flying bulldogs and rather thought he might paint. After Inspector Yates' visit, he had, with Peter, telephoned the Hampstead police once again to ensure that Taunton had been informed that charges were no longer pending against any of the Morgan household.

Inspector Yates and Constable Tippett watched the cricket from Headingly whilst waiting for a warrant to come from Taunton for Inspector Yates to search Littlecombe Park for drugs, given the names and nature of the weekend guests.

Bullshit and Queenie, however, had no plans whatsoever. They were having a marvellous time. Marvellous except for one seemingly insuperable problem. She was rather a tall girl and he, somewhat on the shortish side. But, as in any life, if at first they didn't succeed, at least they spent the afternoon trying, trying again.

After Oliver had set out some chairs and tables on the terrace outside the drawing room window and erected a couple of umbrellas, he saw Nick and Victor in the drawing room.

"Come on, you two," he said, beckoning them outside. "Anyone like a brandy or anything out here? It's a fine afternoon!" He and Julie were playing tennis later and he was dressed in whites. He came into the cool of the drawing room. "Come on!" he urged. "You look far too cosy in here for a summer's afternoon."

"OK," said Victor. "But I'll skip the brandy. It's far too hot, Oliver dear. Even the sight of you in that tennis gear is exhausting."

"Drink, Nick?" Oliver offered.

Nick shook his head.

"No, I'll pass too. Come on Victor, let's sit outside."

They pulled up chairs around one of the white wooden tables and surveyed the park. They didn't speak at first. The warmth and the afterblur of the lunchtime Sauvignon made them mellow. Victor felt more relaxed. Oliver was quietly pleased with the way everyone had taken to Julie. Only Nick was restless with his preoccupation.

"You wouldn't fancy a commission, Victor?" Oliver asked.

"Sure," Victor replied, his eyes closed, face turned to the sun. "As long as the subject has no teeth."

"'Fraid it has. It's Jenks's bitch. The labrador. I think he'd like her immortalised. What d'you think, Nick?"

"Yes," Nick replied thoughtfully. "Nice one, dad. But does Victor want to do it?"

"Umm," said Victor drowsily. "Yes. Why not?"

"Good!" said Oliver. "How much?"

"To you, as my oldest living friend, two hundred."

"Pounds?"

Even Nick laughed.

"Of course," he said, springing to Victor's defence. "It takes him a week to do. Even if he did one a week, that hardly gives him more than the national average wage."

"Thank God for Anderson, Wadley and Baines," said Victor. "And you dear boy, should be my agent."

"Who are Anderson, thingy and whatsit?" Oliver queried.

"My Trustees," Victor replied.

"And do they?" Nick asked.

"Do they what?"

"Trust you?"

"Strangely enough, yes."

Nick chuckled.

"And by the way," Victor added. "If I could ever tempt you to be my agent, my usual fee's five hundred plus. Hardly the average national wage, dear heart."

"But you are an artist," Nick said in justification.

"Thanks, Nick. I'm glad at least you have faith in me."

"I must say," Oliver observed with a hint of reflective pride, "I think it's wonderful that you two should get on so well. It makes me feel ... good.

"Victor opened his eyes.

Nick looked at Victor and Victor looked at Nick. Victor shook his head slightly, as a warning, not, as Nick interpreted, as the signal for what followed.

"How long have you known Victor, dad?"

"Oh, what is it? Best part of forty years, isn't it, old man?"

"Precisely thirty-seven years ten months and, give or take a day, six days."

Oliver groaned.

"Put like that, it sounds like a life sentence, Burke."

"Thank you, Oliver and goodnight."

"So you'd say you knew him pretty well," Nick continued. "I mean, really *know* him."

"Dear boy, in my humble opinion, the longer you know someone the less you know them. Victor is always surprising me."

"But you do trust him, don't you?"

Victor coughed and rearranged himself in the garden chair. He tried to whistle but as he'd never been able to, he couldn't.

296

"Maybe I should just nip upstairs and get my sketch book," he said. Nick put a restraining hand on Victor's arm.

"No. Please stay, Victor. Please?"

Upstairs in Oliver's bedroom, Julie had finished changing for tennis and, hearing voices below had come to the window, out of which she could see the men sitting around the table below. She was just about to call down to Oliver that she was ready when she heard Nick asking Oliver about trust. She listened.

"With my life," Oliver replied, feeling bouyant and oddly fulfilled on a well-spring of sentiment.

"What if someone told you that Victor had committed some terrible crime? Would that make any difference to how you felt?"

"Hey!" exclaimed Victor. "Steady on, darling!"

Oliver was so used to Victor calling everyone darling that he didn't bat an eyelid.

"Of course not," Oliver replied definitely. "That's what true friendship's all about. Through thick and thin and all that."

"And it doesn't worry you that he's gay."

"Well of course not!" exclaimed Oliver dismissively. "Honestly, Nick, there are times when I really think I don't know you at all. You obviously don't understand me one bit and you're the one who's always going on about being tolerant and liberal."

"And you're sure it's *never* worried you?" Nick pressed.

At that moment, Victor wished he was anywhere in the universe but on the terrace at Littlecombe Park.

Julie, upstairs, wondered whether she should not break into the debate, but mindful of her conversation with Nick before lunch, she decided instead to go downstairs and join them. She could sense Nick edging further and further to the brink and she sensed his vulnerability. They didn't know each other very well but she knew they were friends.

"And how about me?" Nick continued. "Would it make any difference to you if I turned out to be a murderer or a bank robber?"

Oliver laughed."As far as I can tell you've even turned out to be a socialist and I still love you."

Victor groaned, as unhappily as any self-respecting skeleton would in the cobwebs of the closet.

"And," Oliver added, rather enjoying the way he thought Nick was goading him, "if I remember correctly, I have actually been told by people that they've seen me collecting you from at least three demonstrations before taking you back to school. Two were about South Africa and what was the third? Gay Pride Week?" He chuckled again. "You're my son, aren't you? What could you *possibly* do that could deny that."Nick took a deep breath and jumped. He remembered only once feeling a similar sensation. Parachute training with the school corps in a cavernous hanger on a disused airfield in Worcestershire.

"I could be gay myself," he said quietly.

Oliver heard but missed the point entirely. Julie could tell; she had tiptoed across the drawing room and stood silently behind the men grouped around the table in the sun.

"You could be," said Oliver. "After joining the Labour Party, nothing would surprise me."

"Oliver," Victor said quietly. "Listen to him."

Victor had realised that there was no way he could distance himself from the inevitable revelation. From the initial panic, as Nick had started talking, he now felt very close to the young man at his side and was proud to be party to the most important moment in Nick's life to date.

"Not being a father, Victor, you can't possibly understand how many of these conversations we've had. They're the what if conversations, very like the why conversations when children get to be two. I *am* listening."

"No you're not," Julie interrupted. She came forward and drew up a chair. "You're not even hearin' 'im right. Go on, Nick."

She held out her hand and Nick gripped it, squeezing it in silent thanks for her support.

"Yes," added Victor, resting a hand on Nick's shoulder, "go on."

Nick looked at his Father across the table. Oliver was beginning to wind up. Those long, Longingly legs were removed from where they'd been stretched out over the table and he sat a little more forward and a little more upright in his chair.

"I am gay, dad."

A breeze blew in from the garden and ruffled the fringe on the edge of the umbrella. Two magpies landed on the lawn and stood, tails waving up and down as they looked dartingly about them.

Good afternoon, sir, thought Victor.

Oliver looked at his son, the beginnings of a frown creasing his forehead. Nick hadn't mumbled his admission. He'd spoken directly to his Father. No words had been lost. Oliver *had* heard. He glanced at both Julie and Victor and their expressions confirmed that his ears had heard.

"You ... are ..." he started to say slowly. He couldn't finish. He couldn't manage to say the word.

"Gay," said Nick, for him.

Victor leant forward and clapped a hand on Oliver's shoulder.

"Like me, Ollie," he said decisively.

"Good boy," said Julie and kissed Nick on his cheek. Nick felt tears. He had imagined this moment so many times in so many places and now it had come, he couldn't believe it was over. Like many things, like parachuting, like taking exams, like meeting people, like dying, it only took the will- power to face it. And like all those things, he'd always imagined having to do it alone. Friends were a luxury he hadn't envisaged. Although he'd rehearsed his part   endlessly, even writing hundreds of alternative scenarios as to how Oliver would react, even he was surprised.

Oliver stood up. His mind had spun, whirling through the last twenty years, re-reeling like a drowning man through the footage of his life. So many unanswered questions, worrying thoughts and misunderstandings found resolution. Of course he'd thought it strange that Nick had no friends - now he understood. Nick must have had dozens of friends but none that he felt he could safely introduce to his mother and father. Of course he wanted his own place, he could hardly have lived with Oliver in deceit, abusing trust, risking recrimination and anger. And Victor? A murderer? Nick, a bankrobber? Oh, how stupid, dense and ridiculous Oliver felt.

"Oh, Nick! I'm so, so sorry."

Nick sniffed and wiped his eyes with his hands as Oliver came across to him and knelt down by his chair.

"Why? You don't have to be sorry, dad. I'm alright, honestly."

"No my dear boy, no. I'm apologising. I should have been there for you. How awful for you to have had to bear all this by yourself. I feel *terrible*. Please forgive me, Nick. I wouldn't have you hurt for the world. You're far too precious to me."

"Oh, dad!"

As Nick burst into tears, he fell forward into Oliver's arms. Victor too was quite overcome, not only with love but with the sadness of knowing what he had missed with his own father. Too many bitter memories flashed back. Julie noticed. She put an arm round Victor and he grabbed at her hand, gripping it tightly.

"Thanks," he whispered.

"Believe me," she whispered back. "It's a pleasure."

Oliver reached back and found Victor's hand which he took in his own. Julie watched as the mens' strong hands entwined. It was such a different kind of love. And she didn't feel excluded, not in the least. As clearly as the picture of that moment would remain in her mind all her life, she understood distinctly how very, very different men and women were and she experienced an urgent need to breed as many of both as she possibly could, preferably and if her instincts could be trusted, with Oliver Longingly.

Some fifty yards away, through the gate at the bottom of the walled garden, came Peter. Oliver slowly relinquished what had been the most rewarding embrace of his life.

"We've got the licence!" Peter called across the lawn. "Kitty had to borrow some money from Adam Ridley.

Good news, hey!" He began to walk towards the terrace.

Nick looked up at his father. His eyes were red but they were shining with happiness.

"Oh, well," he said, "normal service will be resumed as soon as possible, as they say. Sorry about the pun."

"I think you should talk to your mother as soon as possible," Oliver suggested.

"And, Nick, take it easy," Victor reminded his friend. "One thing at a time. Remember? For my sake?"

"'E's right, Nick," said Julie. "One step at a time. She's very bright, your mum. But she *is* your mum. She'll put two and two together 'erself."

Nick fumbled in the pocket of his surfing shorts and pulled out his sun-glasses. He got up from the table.

"Right," he said. "No time like the present."

Oliver clapped him on the back and Nick went off.

He met Peter half way across the lawn.

"Which way is mum coming back, Peter?"

"Through the horse field. I left her talking to Adam and Ernest. She's not far behind me."

"Thanks," said Nick and ran off past the greenhouses and through the walled garden.

Peter reached the terrace and put down the five dog licences on the table.

"There," he puffed, somewhat out of breath, "that should solve one problem. And another little bit of news. Kitty's sworn to Adam Ridley she'll have us all in church tomorrow to swell the choral ranks for 'Jerusalem'. Adam was thrilled when he heard Violetta Abizzi might even be cajoled into a solo verse."

He looked at Oliver, Victor and Julie. Oliver was sitting down again, his mind hovering like a silent helicopter over the path running downhill through the horse field to the village, a path he'd known for so much of his life.

"You alright, Oliver?" Peter asked, calling Oliver back.

Victor put his finger to his lips and nodded to Peter. Julie smiled, a little supportive smile for Oliver's benefit.

"Did you know, Peter?" Oliver asked after a moment's silence.

"Did I know?" Peter repeated. "What?"

"That Nick was homosexual? He's just ... what's the expression ... come down?"

"Come out, lovey," Julie prompted. She got up and went and stood behind Oliver's chair and kissed him on the top of his head before bending over him and putting her arms round his neck.

"Oh," said Peter. "No," he lied. "I didn't." Peter liked Oliver. They had always got on well. It was an enforced friendship but one between two intelligent, rational men which thoughtlessness had never compromised. Peter was a great respecter of friendships. Men like him and Oliver had too few to treat them with anything but respect. "How do you feel?"

"I feel ..." Oliver began. He hesitated for a moment, choosing what he considered only the very best and most accurate words to describe excatly how he did feel. "I feel immensely privileged, old chap. I feel ... no, I know , I've just made the greatest friend any man could have." He paused and looked in turn at each of their faces. "Do I make sense?"

Peter smiled and nodded. He knew very well the sense and wished more than anything that Rachel could open up to him in the same way.

"You're a nice man, Ollie," Julie muttered in Oliver's ear.

"No I'm not. I don't deserve any of you."

"Nonsense," Julie said.

"Look here," said Victor, "Kitty'll be back soon. What d'you think, Peter? Don't you think we should all go for a walk or something? She might want to see Oliver alone."

"Good idea," said Julie.

"Of course," Peter agreed. "Do you play tennis, Miss Burge?"

She nodded.

"Then give me two minutes to change and I'll give you a game 'til Oliver arrives. How are you at umpiring, Victor?"

"Depends what your legs look like in shorts, Mr Bailey!"

IT'S A BOY, MRS LONGINGLY!
A BOY ...

As soon as Nick came over the brow of the hill he saw her. He stood and watched as she walked slowly up the cattle path, leaning forward slightly as she ascended the hill. He saw her stop and bend down, looking down at a tiny flower she thought could have been an orchid. She seemed so small and so far away, so isolated amongst the green of the grazing in her canary yellow track suit.

Then she looked up. She saw the silhouette at the top of the rise and she shielded her eyes from the sun. Nick waved. She waved back. He cupped his hands to his mouth.

"Tea time!" he shouted long and loud, almost singing the two syllables in a falling cadence.

"I'm way ahead of you!" she called back.

"What?" he shouted. "Can't hear?"

"I said I'm way ahead of you! I need a *drink*!"

It was Kitty's turn to wait as Nick ran, once nearly stumbling, down the hill.

The run down only took a few seconds, half a minute at the most but in that time, Kitty re-ran the movie as she watched her only child racing towards her. It was a good movie, she thought, this film of the play of the book of the life. It was her favourite film which she knew she would never tire of. Nicholas Owen Longingly. Funny, she thought, it's so easy to think of a title and yet quite another matter to write The End. Of course, although she hoped she wouldn't be around to see The End she secretly hoped that the last credit might read - Directed by His Mother.

Kitty had been doing quite a lot of thinking since Peter had gone on ahead. She'd asked him to. She wanted five minutes to herself. She didn't need him and there was nothing he would have been able to say to her for she

303

didn't want to talk. She wanted merely to think. She remembered something old Tom Ellman had told her when she went to live with them after leaving Ludo. Before she found herself pregnant and married Oliver. "You can't control other people's lives, Kitty but you can control your own." She'd never forgotten his advice. It was the one piece of practical philosophy she returned to time and time again when she felt sorry for herself.

Ever since Thursday evening, when Peter had been so reticent and monosyllabic in response to her rhetorical queries as to why Nick should have been so quick to help Grace look for the dog, Kitty had been feeling just a little sorry for herself. The cause of the self-pity hadn't become a preoccupation, but she had dwelt on it from time to time, wondering. Wondering. Ultimately she decided that wondering was a pointless exercise.

She held out her arms as he came flying down the hill. He picked her up and hugged her and whirled her round, squeezing the breath out of her.

"Put me down! Put me down, you terrible child!"

They both collapsed on the grass, laughing. Nick took off his sun-glasses and propped them on his head, tucked into his curly hair.

"Hi!"

"Hi."

She took his hand and they sat side by side on the grassy slope, finding their wind, looking over the pleasant land, dotted with cottages and barns, Saturday afternoon bonfire smoke wisping up and above the hedgerows.

"I came to find you, mum." Kitty didn't answer. She merely looked. It was a landscape she usually took for granted. Today, she realised just how beautiful and true and yet how bloody fragile it was.

She sighed.

"I'm glad, darling."

"Why?"

"I sort of hoped you would."

"But why?"

"Oh, I don't know. Call it horse sense. It's something

we're led to believe that mothers have. I don't believe it for a moment, mind you or they'd have called it mother sense."

"I love you, mum."

"I know you do, darling."

"Do you?"

"Oh, yes," she joked "I love me a lot."He nudged her playfully. Horseplay.

"Come on, mum. Be serious. Do you?"

She hesitated. She shielded her eyes again and looked out over the rolling land she loved. Timeless though it sometimes seemed, even Kitty had seen it change, as everything changed.

"It's more than love, darling. I don't think I know what love means anymore. It seems to mean something different to everyone and it's such a silly word for something I couldn't even begin to describe even if I started now and finished on the day I died."

"What do you mean?"

"Nick, if you want me to tell you I love you to make you feel better, then I will. But if you want to feel *really* good, you'll let me finish."

"Course."

She waited for a moment, gathering her thoughts, plucking them like a posy of wildflowers from here, from there, bunching them together until there was a form, a shape. Until she was ready.

"You, darling, are my child. You can never begin to understand what that means and you never will, a) because you're a man and b) because you're not me. So, you just have to accept that when you ask me questions like: Do you love me?. All I can tell you as my answer is that I *am* you and you are me. What pleases you thrills me, what scratches you makes me bleed, what hurts you is torture for me. You are part of me and always will be as much as my leg is part of me or my little finger or the wart on my shoulder. I can't think of myself without thinking of you. But, you see, darling ..."

"But what?"

"But *you* can. You can think of yourself without thinking of me." From looking so terribly serious, she suddenly smiled. "So, baby, when you suddenly decide that you're all grown up and you want to come and talk to me about love, believe me when I tell you that you've come to talk to the expert and believe me when I tell you that I understand you better at this moment than you understand yourself ... And, do you know something else?."

He shook his head.

"That from today onwards, it won't be so easy for me and that makes me sad. Very selfish, sadness but it's a way we female humans have of coming to terms."

Nick frowned. He didn't understand. Suddenly there was another person sitting next to him; a person with a mind and deep feelings, deeper than he had ever had to acknowledge. Gone was the person who had told him not to do this and not to do that, gone was the person who had helped him with French and taken him to pop concerts, gone was the person he'd lectured and patronised and made excuses for as the arrogance of his growing years made him perceive her only as housekeeper, bankroll, policewoman and wife. She smoothed his hair back from his brow and took his face in her hands.

"Coming to terms with what?" he asked.

"With the fact that I'm going to have to share you with someone else; that someone else is going to be doing all the feeling for you, the aching, the hoping. I've seen it, darling. It may have taken me some time but I've seen it. I should have known except I looked in all the least obvious places. But it's there. It's in both your eyes."

"I feel so ashamed," he muttered when she let him go. "I wanted to tell you and you knew all the time."

"I know, darling. But you still had to tell me. If you hadn't tried, I could never have told you what it feels like to be your mother.

"For the second time in less than half an hour, Nick cried. He buried his face in the cotton of her track suit top.

"But I want to tell you I love you," he sobbed."Then tell me," she said, swaying with him in her arms.

306

"Tell me now, now that you know what it means."

"I love you, mum! I love you so ... so much ..."

She let him cry. They sat there in the horse field, watched by four curious cows until she felt he'd done.

"Have you told daddy?"

He nodded.

"I wanted to tell him first. You don't mind, do you?"

"Of course I don't. Is he alright?"

"I think so. I do hope so."

"We were going to have a talk anyway," she said. "Not about you so much. About ... everything."

"Mum, you don't hate Victor, do you?"

"Hate Victor! What on earth makes you think that? Victor is my friend, Nick. The fact that he's your current lover, makes not the slightest jot of difference."

"Current?" he queried quickly. "Why do you say that?"

Kitty looked at him and knew she should have checked herself.

"It was a slip of the tongue, darling. Sort of thing I'd say to Victor, I suppose. Take no notice."

He grinned.

"I do like him, mum. We get on so well together."

"I'm glad, darling. He needs you. Don't hurt him."

"Me? Oh, I'd never hurt him, mum.

"She decided not to say more. He was, after all, now a man. He would find out. Or, strange though it would be, maybe he wouldn't.

"Good. I'm glad to hear it. Now, help me up before I seize up."

He took both her hands and hauled her up off the sward. They walked back up the hill arm in arm.

"And by the way," she said, "and I mean this. You *are* careful, Nick, aren't you? I'm asking you because I don't think I could face having this conversation with Victor. One thing I refuse to be is mother-in-law to one of my oldest friends."

"Oh, of course. I'm always safe. Always." He looked very seriously. "At least," he added, "as safe as we can be. I've known people too, mum."

"Of course," she said soberly. "You didn't mind me asking, darling, did you?"

"I'm glad you did. Now, what were you going to talk to dad about, apart from me, that is?"

"Oh, things. Here. The house. All that sort of stuff."

"You mean money?"

They reached the iron gate in the beech hedge and left the horse field. Nick shut the gate behind them.

"Partly," Kitty said. "You must understand that Peter's not even remotely as wealthy as your father and I'm currently not actually married to anyone, darling. Not that I'm complaining a bit. It's my own choice entirely but, technically, I suppose, I'm one of those single parent families people are so keen on these days. But I can't go on relying on your father forever. Littlecombe is mine and it's my responsibility."

"You're not to even think of it!" Nick cried. "Please, mum. You can't!"

"Can't?" she murmured. "Mustn't, then. But, please, whatever you decide, don't sell it."

"But what am I supposed to do, dear? I'm the world's worst typist and I'm hopeless with machinery and I'd loathe doing directors' lunches which is about all I'm good for. What would you suggest? And I'm far too old to go on the game."

"Ludo! He'd help you."

"Nick, that's ridiculous. The fastest way to kill off friendships is to borrow money. If you don't know that now, you'll find out soon enough the more you lend or borrow. If you have to borrow, do it from banks. It's what they get paid for."

"Then there's my money. I'm twenty-one next year. You've always told me how rich I'm going to be. There must be enough there."

Kitty kissed him as they walked across the lawn back to the terrace. Oliver stood up as he saw them come into the walled garden.

"Darling, that's *your* money."

"But I don't want it. I don't believe in it."

"You can't *not* believe in it!" said Kitty, laughing. "It's there. Well, it's somewhere. Daddy knows where."

"I want you to have it!" Nick insisted. "How much is it?"

"I thought you didn't care?" Kitty scolded.

"I do if it means whether this place stays or goes. There's Jenks to think of and Mrs T. My God! You couldn't throw them out."

"Isn't this conversation just a teensy weensy bit feudal for one whose pennant is reddened in the blood of the martyr dead? You're sounding more like the lord of the manor. Droit de seigneur and all that."

"Oh, mum! You know what I mean. How much does Littlecombe cost?"

"Thousands and thousands, I should think," Kitty replied. "I don't know."

"Ten? Twenty? Take it, mum. It's your's. I mean ours."

Kitty waved back to Oliver as he walked towards them across the lawn.

"I wouldn't hear of it," she replied. "Although since we've had this little talk, darling, there is one thing I'd rather like from you."

"Name it," he said fiercely. "It's yours."

"Oh, good. In that case, I'd like to ask for your indulgence."

"Anything, mum. Anything you want."

"I," she said, "and you may regret this, am going to give up the *Guardian* and go back to the *Telegraph*. Call it wilful but it's my treat to myself." She poked him, playfully, in the ribs. "I think I've earned it today."

ACKNOWLEDGEMENTS

This book could not have been written without the following:

Nigel Quiney, Pat and Mary Evans, Marion Quiney, Elizabeth Evans, Kate Anderson, John and Sarah Standing, Robert and Caroline Lee, Mrs "Percy" Boucher, Bryan and Nanette Forbes, Peter Straker, Freddie Mercury, Edward and Gillian Thorpe, Ann Ortman, Edmund Beldovsky

and many others whom I thank for their friendship and encouragement including

Kris Ellam, Rose Tobias Shaw, John Jesse, Chris Banks, Richard Smith

not forgetting Homewood Park, Hinton Charterhouse
nor, ultimately, Peter Burton
and, for the inspiration,
Armistead Maupin.
Thank you all.

On The Edge

Sebastian Beaumont

In this auspicious debut novel set in the north of England, nineteen year old Peter Ellis is on the edge of discovery - both about the artist father he never knew and whom his mother refuses to discuss and about the directions of his own life. Although he has had heterosexual relations with the teenaged Anna and the somewhat perverse art student Coll, it is with his life-long friend Martin, himself a painter of promise, that Peter seems happiest. *On The Edge* combines elements of a thriller - the mystery surrounding the life and sudden death of Peter's father - and passionate ambisextrous romance and provides an immensely readable narrative about late adolescence, sexuality and creativity.

ISBN 1-873741-00-6

"Mr Beaumont writes with assurance and perception ... The writing is fluent and engaging and gently informative with regard to the complexities of a young man who is about to enter the world of adult men ...

"Tom Wakefield, *Gay Times*

David of King's

E F Benson

Originally published in 1924, E F Benson's *David of King's* has been unavailable for more than fifty years. The sequel to the classic *David Blaize*, this novel is set during the six foot and blond David's three years at Cambridge University. Here the enchanting hero, a seductive combination of aesthete and athlete, continues his intense and clearly homoerotic relationship with the three year older Frank Maddox. Here, too, David mixes with the sporting, artistic and academic fraternities - loved and admired by all. Like *David Blaize*, *David of King's* is strongly autobiographical and includes sharp portraits from life of such notorious characters as Oscar Browning (disguised as 'Alfred Gepp') - an Eton schoolmaster, dismissed because of a scandal, who found safe haven at King's College, Cambridge. *David of King's* has a new introduction by Peter Burton.

ISBN 1-873741-01-4

"A handsomely produced edition of a long out-of-print book with a strong nostalgic appeal for a great many people ..."

The Tilling Society Newsletter